LION TRIO THREE: FEMMES FATALE

SIN PIT
by Paul S. Meskil

DARK THE SUMMER DIES
by Walter Untermeyer, Jr.

THE DEVIL'S DAUGHTER
by Peter Marsh

Stark House Press • Eureka California

SIN PIT / DARK THE SUMMER DIES / THE DEVIL'S DAUGHTER

Published by Stark House Press
1315 H Street
Eureka, CA 95501
griffinskye3@sbcglobal.net
www.starkhousepress.com

SIN PIT
Originally published in paperback by Lion Books, New York, and copyright © 1954 by Paul Meskil.

DARK THE SUMMER DIES
Originally published in paperback by Lion Books, New York, and copyright © 1953 by Walter Untermeyer, Jr.

THE DEVIL'S DAUGHTER
Originally published and copyright © 1942 by Jonathan Swift, Inc. Reprinted in paperback by Lion Books, New York, 1949.

This edition copyright © 2022 by Stark House Press. All rights reserved under International and Pan-American Copyright Conventions.

"A Trio of Lions: An Introduction" copyright © 2022 by Gary Lovisi. All rights reserved.

ISBN: 979-8-88601-006-0

Cover & text design by Jeff Vorzimmer, ¡caliente!design, Austin, Texas

PUBLISHER'S NOTE:
This is a work of fiction. Names, characters, places and incidents are either the products of the author's imagination or used fictionally, and any resemblance to actual persons, living or dead, events or locales, is entirely coincidental.

Without limiting the rights under copyright reserved above, no part of this publication may be reproduced, stored, or introduced into a retrieval system or transmitted in any form or by any means (electronic, mechanical, photocopying, recording or otherwise) without the prior written permission of both the copyright owner and the above publisher of the book.

First Stark House Press Edition: September 2022

7
Introduction
by Gary Lovisi

11
SIN PIT
by Paul S. Meskil

83
DARK THE SUMMER DIES
by Walter Untermeyer. Jr.

173
THE DEVIL'S DAUGHTER
by Peter Marsh

279
Bibliographies

SIN PIT

"She was very young and very pretty and very dead . . . and as naked as a fully clothed person could be." Barney Black is a tough cop in a tough town, but when he goes looking for the dead woman's killer, he isn't ready for Grace Trudo. Grace is married to Willie, a small time gambler, who had taken in the dead blonde when she first came to town. Willie could be the killer, but it's Grace who gets Barney's attention. Grace is pure, raw sex, and Barney wants her the moment he sees her. Is Grace worth the risk, or could she be trying to hide a kill-crazy husband? Barney is going have to bend more than the rules before he can solve this one.

DARK THE SUMMER DIES

Tony Bianchi has a great summer job teaching kids to dive at the local pool. He's got a sweet girlfriend, Betty, and on weekends they go out together; and sometimes they kiss. Life is good for teenage Tony—but he's restless for something more. So when he meets an older woman named Vickie and she invites him out to dinner while her husband is away, he takes her up on the offer. Vickie is ten years older, a sophisticated blonde, and just as restless as Tony. But Vickie's got a different kind of restless. What she doesn't realize is that what to her is just a quick fling might mean a whole lot more to young Tony. And so quickly his dulcet summer turns into a living hell . . .

THE DEVIL'S DAUGHTER

Michel Perry is the owner of a chic nightclub, but he is also a man with a secret. He used to belong to a bootlegging gang. The six men who were his partners have all died, some violently, some mysteriously. Now, as he lies in his upstairs apartment with an alluring woman named Laura, he begins to understand that he might soon be joining them. Because Laura is not whom she seems. She is really Maria Buonarotti, out to avenge her husband's death. She assures Michel that he is safe, that she is in love with him, and merely wants to share her stories, to unburden her soul. Night after night, as the two of them lie in each other's arms, Maria tells her stories of revenge. But what will happen to Michel when Maria has no more stories to tell?

SIN PIT
"It has everything that makes great noir and then some. There are bad cops, worse criminals, juicy sex, graphic violence, and a variety of deliciously brutal killings."
—Ron Zack

"There are a lot of classic pulp motifs present here from the good cop twisted by an irresistible woman, the dreadful power of desire, the poor country girl turning tricks, the innocent man on the run, the frame-ups, the tarnished badge."
—Dave Wilde

"You should definitely seek this one out if you like your noir twisted and perverse . . . highly recommended."
—*Paperback Warrior*

"This had all the back-stabbings, femmes fatales, and sordid tough guys one could want out of a 50s noir."—Jack Tripper

"Hardly a word is wasted ... and it hits all the right noir notes along the way..."
—David Rachels

DARK THE SUMMER DIES
". . . a film noir version of an Andy Hardy movie... keeps you reading to the grisly end."
—Jeff Vorzimmer

THE DEVIL'S DAUGHTER
"Story of modern Scheherazade who night after night in the arms of the man she both loved and feared, told him how she had killed six of the seven men who had helped to murder her husband."
—Florence Stonebreaker, *Writer's Digest*

A TRIO OF LIONS:
An Introduction
by
Gary Lovisi

There was a time many years ago when a publisher of what were considered lower-end magazines, pulps and comics books named Martin Goodman, also wanted to expand his line by producing a series of paperback books. Goodman's overall publishing line was called Magazine Management, and one of the iconic lines he published through them was Marvel Comics. His paperback book line was called Lion Books, which began in 1949, a smaller publishing outfit that only lasted 9 years, from 1949 to 1957, and therein we begin our story of the three novels that make up this book.

Goodman's first editor for Lion Books was Arnold Hano who was hired as editor-in-chief in 1950. Hano was a hard-boiled guy, a World War II vet — as were many of the readers of these early paperbacks — most of whom were male. He knew the kind of violent action and passion readers wanted in their books and he gave it to them. Hano had previously been an editor at Bantam Books for two years and came to Lion with a large 'backlog' of manuscripts Bantam had declined to publish — but he liked them. Goodman gave Hano the green light to published what he wanted to publish. So Hano did just that, published books that he liked and that today are recognized as some of the greatest crime noir novels ever written. Thus the Lion Books line was born.

The Lion Books series today is remembered fondly by those in the know, for publishing many genuine masterpieces of hard crime noir. Works by such masters as Jim Thompson (who they showcased in 11 original novels!); but also criminous noirs by Richard Matheson, David Goodis, Robert Bloch, Day Keene and many others.

Those 'many others' are what we are concerned with here. That is because the Lion Books list of 233 paperbacks, offers a deep mine of treasure — at least two-thirds of which are hard crime noir novels. And most have been out of print for decades — in some cases the Lion Books paperback is the *only* edition of some of these very collectable and desirable books!

This new book from Stark House Press (the 3rd in their *A Trio of Lions* series*), presents three of the best, rarest, and much sought after novels from the vintage era heyday of noir paperbacks.

SIN PIT by Paul S. Meskil; THE DEVIL'S DAUGHTER by Peter Marsh, and DARK THE SUMMER DIES by Walter Utermeyer Jr., offer up a delightful feast of crime, murder, betrayal, shock, depravity and twisted hungers that lead men and women into their own worst versions of noir Hell. The original editions of these charming small size vintage paperbacks would be hard to track down today, some can be quite expensive in nice condition, but Stark House has done all the work for you, and now all you need do is sit back and enjoy reading this omnibus containing three of the best Lion noirs you may never have known about.

SIN PIT by Paul S. Meskil (July 2, 1923 - Oct.11, 2005), was originally published as Lion Book #198 in 1954. In it, you are going to read a long-lost classic written by a master craftsman. SIN PIT was Meskil's only novel — but what a novel! Meskil had a four decades long career as a newspaperman on such papers as the *St. Louis Dispatch*, and the New York *Daily News*. He had been an investigative journalist for many years, writing books on organized crime, the Mob, Nazi war criminals, and other subjects. Some of these books have become classic reference works, but it is with SIN PIT where Meskil gives us characters and a story that plunge the reader into the low world of crime, crooked cops and dread femme fatales in a poisonous brew. All that, and a surprise ending you will surely savor.

You know you just gotta read this one when from the back cover of the Lion edition, the blurb loudly proclaims a statement by the book's hero, Sergeant Detective Barney Black:

"SHE WAS DIRT…and hungry and cheap and demanding. But it didn't matter. She was all those things, and I knew it, but she was much more, too. She was fire and ice and fury, and when she came up to me — that first time — her mouth making little squirming noises, I knew she was all I ever wanted.

"I was a cop. An honest one. Tough, but honest. And she was the wife of another man. Maybe she was a killer. Maybe she was a — a kind of person even tough cops don't talk about except in dirty whispers.

"But I didn't care. I had to have her."

I met and got to know Paul Meskil in 2004 when he saw an article I had written praising this book. Paul and I, with his son, Brian, became fast friends. They were even guests at my annual book show in New York City. Back then, I published a short-run 100-copy edition of SIN PIT for my show (using the original Lion Books cover art), in an effort to get it back into print after 50 years. By then, that original Lion paperback had become prohibitively expensive and there were no other printings. Today, my 2004 Gryphon Books, Crime Classic #1 edition is out of print and rare. The Lion edition is rare too. In fact, it is almost impossible to find any copy of this book — so thank you, Stark House!

SIN PIT is one of my favorite crime novels. Knowing it was Paul Meskil's one and only foray into crime fiction, one wonders what might have been had he continued writing fiction in the genre. For surely he had it all down right and true — he could sure tell an interesting and brutal crime story. No doubt, had he written more fiction this novel would have already taken its proper place in the ivy halls of great crime novels.

Or as Paul himself wrote in his afterward to that 2004 Gryphon edition, "I was sitting at my desk in the city room of the New York *Telegraph* one day in 1953 when I received a phone call from literary agent, Berthina Klausman. She had seen some of my crime articles in the newspaper and wanted to know if I could write a crime novel in a hurry. I said yes, and she sent me to the paperback publisher, Lion Books. An editor there gave me a contract and told me I could write anything I wanted as long as the locale was other than New York City, Chicago, or Los Angeles — which were then the sites chosen for most crime novels.

"That was fine with me because I had come to New York from St. Louis, where I worked as a crime reporter/writer for eight years. I knew St. Louis and East St. Louis very well and used this area as a scene for my first and only novel, though I wrote several factual crime books and about one thousand magazine articles on organized...and disorganized...crime.

"SIN PIT got little publicity except for a plug in Walter Winchell's column and a review in the magazine of the Missouri Bartenders Association. My original title was "Blood Lust" and they changed that title without my knowledge. I also originally wrote the book in the first person.

"After the book came out an anonymous reader sent me a key to the hotel room where the last chapter took place. I'm proud to have this book appear in print again after 50 years and I hope you have enjoyed it."

Paul would have been pleased to see this newest edition of his hard-hitting crime classic. He was a fine writer, and class act; a real gentleman, with a good sense of humor.

Of the other two novels in this volume, each is something truly special and offers stark and brutal truths in twisted noir settings. I love these books and know that you will too.

THE DEVIL'S DAUGHTER by Peter Marsh (Lion Book #16, 1949), is an author who usually wrote as Alan Williams. This is one of three books he wrote as Peter Marsh. In it, Marsh gives us one of the earliest Lion noir reprints, of the pricey and collectable 1942 hardcover first edition. As a Lion Book, it has all the trappings of the femme fatale noir, the cover blurb boldly proclaiming, "She destroyed six men — would he be the seventh?"

It is the story of a woman who *chose* to go by the name of Laura, who was on a hell-bent revenge mission to kill the men who had murdered her husband. She had already killed six of them! Now the seventh man came into her web, Mike Peruzzi, and the two fell into a turbulent doomed love. Was he a devil, a demon? She had mixed emotions about him. She knew she should plunge the knife into him as he slept, but she only kissed him very gently. But he awoke and felt her looming presence, even as she felt his demonic power over her. They don't write nasty noir better than this, but don't let that stop you from diving hip-deep into the muck then swim for your life!

DARK THE SUMMER DIES by Walter Untermeyer, Jr. (Sept. 19, 1924 - Feb. 15, 2009), Lion Book #138 from 1953. This is a classic dark noir, by a talented author, and he wrote a book that many crime aficionados rate highly. Untermeyer, Jr. is a rather elusive Lion author and not much is known about him, although we do have a photograph of him on the back cover of the Lion edition. According to Hubin, he wrote only two crime novels — the other is EVIL ROOTS — and both were paperback originals for Lion Books.

This is a dark twisty tale of a young man and a manipulating older woman named Vicky, who has a scheme and a shame. As the back cover blurb warns us, Vicky:

> "…had time on her hands…so she picked on the boy. She turned him and twisted him and made him do her bidding. She didn't think it was dirty; she didn't guess she was ruining the boy, making him hate himself. To her, it was just a game.
>
> "But she didn't know what was going on inside the boy, the torment in the secret pits of his soul, the dark urges storming to the surface, the hate and love and lust and madness. She didn't know what she was doing. And that was the greatest shame of all."

One wonders about the authors of these three noir masterpieces. How they could write so convincingly of these dark subjects. What they must have seen, or experienced in their lives? We know Paul Meskil saw crime in real life, as it was evilly committed, and he wrote about it. So I wonder what each of these authors must have seen or gone through to reserve their own ring-side seat at the arena in the depths of human Hell. No one can know for sure, but they left us these books, and for that we thank them.

With the three novels that make up A TRIO OF LIONS: BOOK 2, you will fall into the SIN PIT, find yourself overwhelmed by dark desires, view deep depravity, brutal betrayal and vile corruption that you cannot imagine. Prepare to be shocked, awed, and overjoyed as a noir crime fiction aficionado. These are wonderful reads. Oh, how I envy you first timers! Enjoy!

—*Brooklyn, New York*
June 30, 2022

---

* The first Stark House Press book collection of A TRIO OF LIONS appeared in 2016. It contained *Hero's Lust* by Kermit Jaediker; *The Man I Killed* by Shel Walker; and *House of Evil* by Clayre & Michel Lipman; with introductions by Gary Lovisi and Dan Roberts. The second volume from 2019 contains *Tall, Dark & Dead* by Kermit Jaediker; *The Savage Chase* by Frederick Lorenz (Lorenz Heller); and *Run the Wild River* by D. L. Champion.

SIN PIT
by Paul S. Meskil

CHAPTER ONE

She was very young and very pretty and very dead. Her hair had been soft and blonde, but now it was dark and sticky with drying blood. When the night breeze off the river stroked it, you could see the small round hole where a bullet had slammed into her skull.

One little chunk of lead and she wasn't young or desirable anymore. One singing slug, humming the lullaby of death. The song that rocked her to sleep forever but snuffed out all her dreams, whatever they had been.

"Flip her over," I said.

Gomez, the big beat cop, placed one of his platter-size feet under her body and rolled her over onto her back. He didn't want to get any of the blood on his uniform. I didn't blame him. No use wasting a cleaning bill on a corpse.

Gomez swung his flash so the beam shone directly into her wide, dark, sightless eyes. In the harsh light, her face had the color and appearance of modeling clay, molded into a grotesque mask of horror.

"Jesus," Gomez breathed as the flashlight beam swept slowly over her firm, lithe body.

Her naked breasts and thighs were criss-crossed with livid lines as if she had been lashed with a whip.

She was as naked as a fully clothed person could be. Her blouse was ripped down the front and across the side. Torn away from her breasts, her bra hung by a single shoulder strap. Her skirt was in tattered strips, bunched up about her narrow waist.

The man who had found her licked his lips nervously and shuffled his feet. He was staring so hard it seemed his eyes would pop right out of his face.

I took the flashlight from Gomez and knelt down for a closer look at the lash marks. They were a devil's sign, unhealthy as murder itself. Some of the welts were fresh ones. Others were faint discolorations that must have occurred several days before.

Looking at them, I felt a strange stirring in the pit of my stomach. Not nausea.

Excitement.

"No sane man could do a thing like this," Gomez said.

Overhead, traffic sounds drifted down to us from the new bridge across the Mississippi to St. Louis.

Traffic was light and the auto horns sounded lost and lonely. Most of the motorists would be tired St. Louisans going home to sleep off their after-hour drinking, gambling or whoring—three major industries on our East Side.

When a car came the other way, to our side of the river, the headlights washed a sign at the bridge exit. "Welcome to East St. Louis, Ill."

Welcome to Sin City, sucker. Bring a bankroll and enjoy our hospitality.

Gomez and I had been enjoying a little hospitality ourselves while the girl was being killed. I went off duty at three A.M., locked my reports in the desk drawer at Police Headquarters and joined Gomez in a ginmill on his waterfront beat.

Gomez and I had been rookie cops, then partners together in the old days, but I went upstairs and he went down. Now I was Detective Sergeant Barney Black while he was back pounding the levee because he had made the prize mistake of arresting a politician's son. Of course, the son was drunk and the little boy beneath his auto was crippled for life, but you don't arrest a politician's son in these parts.

Anyway, Gomez and I were on our third round when the man burst into the bar, looking for us. He was a local character named Fairmount Sims who made a living peddling policy numbers and information.

"Sahgent Black," he hollered as he galloped to our table. "Come quick. Dead white gal in the Valley."

So we leaped up and ran with him because the Valley wasn't a place you'd expect to find a white girl at four A.M., dead or alive. Not any more.

It used to be that everyone who felt the need for female companionship came to the Valley. There were girls of just about every age, color, nationality, price and technique. Anything the roving male could desire, from a two-bit bottle dance in the street to the plush houses where demure maids answered the door and jeweled dowagers introduced customers to lovelies in evening gowns.

Traffic rolled through the Valley every night in a steady stream that seemed as slow and endless as the Mississippi. Deep holes in the hard-packed unpaved streets kept the speed limit below five miles an hour.

When the weather was warm, girls wearing no more than panties and bra would cling to the sides of the crawling cars while others hung from windows and in doorways, all loudly advertising their wares.

But the bombs which fell on Pearl Harbor killed the Valley. The Army and Air Force took a dim view of the flesh markets there, closed the shops and scattered the girls. Most of the buildings later were torn down.

A few of the madams tried to open up things again after the war, but the Valley's days as the nation's most sinful spot were over. Even the holes in the streets disappeared as the Valley's main drag was paved for a new bridge approach. Only a few Negro shanties were left standing on the old tenderloin.

The nearest of these shacks was about half a block from the junk-filled lot where the girl's body lay. The windows were dark but I could sense movement behind them. I could feel the eyes which are always watching from dark, unseen places when police come into the Valley.

Leaving me his light, Gomez ran back to the bar to call Headquarters and to summon a meat wagon from Jansen's Funeral Home.

I shed my topcoat and draped it over the corpse. There'd be a cleaning bill after all, but I couldn't leave the kid lying there nearly naked the way she was, even though her body had been stared at plenty of times before. She couldn't have been more than seventeen or eighteen but there was something about her which told me she had piled up a lot of mileage for her years. If she had ever reached twenty, it would have begun to show. She wouldn't have to worry about that now.

Her lipstick and nail polish were a couple of shades too bright. The mouth paint was a crimson splash which ruined the shape of her lips. One gold loop dangled from her ear lobe. The other earring was missing.

I flashed the light about but didn't find it. I didn't find the gun either. All I found was one of her spike-heeled shoes, lying about a foot from the body.

A siren screamed. Gomez had completed his call. The radio cars and detective cruisers were shooting away from the curb in front of Police Headquarters, a few short blocks away. The ambulance-hearse would be along any minute now.

"What you doing prowling around down here this time of day?" I asked Fairmount Sims. I had to repeat it before he took his eyes off my coat and the still form beneath it.

"Roamin'," he said. "Just roamin', Sahgent Black. I wasn't up to nothin'. Just tryin' to see can I find a drink, maybe, or a woman. I see somethin' lyin' over here and I think maybe it's a drunk that I can help out."

"Help out, hell. Roll, you mean."

"No sir," he protested. "I just roam around nights here and there. I don't roll nobody. I don't do a thing like that."

"What did you do with her purse?"

"You got this all wrong, Sahgent Black. Soon as I see what happened to this lady, I come runnin' after you. I don't see any purse or anything else."

I didn't press it. There would be time enough for that later. The siren screamed like a hopped-up banshee, then trailed off to a growl as the radio car pulled up at the lot. A Chevrolet sedan, carrying two detectives, was right behind. One of them was my boss, Inspector Flynn.

"Hello, Barney," he said when he reached my side. "Out late, aren't you? What have you got here?"

"Murder," I told him. "Looks like a sex case. Shot once in the back of the head. Probably raped. Maybe beaten with a whip. No identification on her."

The wind was blowing harder from the river, carrying the stink of oil and muck and garbage and dead things floating by in the night. Above the stench I could smell the girl's cheap, sweet perfume like rotting flowers. Flowers for the dead.

"Tough break," Inspector Flynn was muttering. "The son of a bitch that did this ought to have his guts cut out, piece by piece. She's no older than my kid."

He had a daughter. Blonde, too. She was in a convent where things like this didn't happen. But he was probably thinking of his daughter as he stood holding the topcoat aside, muttering curses and staring hard at the naked flesh as if he hoped to find the killer's name tattooed there.

"Maybe she got a lucky break," I said. "These young chippies might just as well be dead as working their asses off to keep some pimp in coke."

The Inspector fastened his stare on me, but he didn't say anything. He let the topcoat drop back over her.

CHAPTER TWO

The ambulance-hearse from Jansen's Funeral Home arrived. Gomez helped the driver load her into it and he rode with the one-way wagon to St. Mary's Hospital where an interne, for the record, pronounced her dead.

Inspector Flynn and his driver took Fairmount Sims to Headquarters for questioning. He was in for a long night.

When they were gone, I left the radio car boys at the lot and walked to the nearest shack and banged on the door with my fist. The door shook but nobody answered. I tried it. It was locked and bolted. I banged on it some more. Louder, this time.

"Police officers," I shouted. "Open up."

I thought I heard something move inside, a rustling sound so faint it was almost no sound at all. The taste of death was still bitter in my mouth and I thought there could be a killer on the other side of the door, waiting.

The radio car boys hurried over when I whistled for help. One of them went around back. The other came up on the porch with me, service revolver heavy in his hand. He stayed behind me, to the left of the doorway, so as not to be caught in any crossfire.

While he covered me with his gun, I threw my two-hundred and ten pounds at the rickety wooden door. Lock, bolt and door gave way with a splintering crash and I plunged head-first into a room that was blacker than a loan shark's heart.

I landed on my hands and knees, rolled to the side and stayed down for a few seconds to see what would happen. Nothing did.

I got up cautiously, .38 ready, as the patrolman allowed me inside and flicked his light around. A broken-down double bed stood against the far wall. In it was a girl.

Both of us knew her. She was a mulatto named Star. An old knife wound made a jagged white line down her left cheek. Otherwise, she was still fairly attractive. If you went for that type. Personally, I didn't. Some of the other boys from the station did, I had heard, because her favors were cheap and her shack was within easy walking distance from Police Headquarters.

I switched on the lamp that stood on a table beside the bed. She raised her hand to shade her eyes from the light. She wore a flimsy cotton night gown that was too small for her and clung to heavy, pendulous breasts.

"Why didn't you let us in when I knocked?" I asked. She opened her mouth but no words came out. She was breathing heavily, through her nose, and the fear poured from her in tiny droplets of sweat.

"A girl was killed out there," I said, pointing out the door. "In that lot down the street. You could see it from your window. You must have heard the shot. What do you know about it?"

She kept shaking her head back and forth without saying anything.

Rage bubbled inside me. Rage because a young girl was dead and a killer was loose and there was nothing I could do about it. Later, maybe. But not now. Rage because a potential witness sat before me without telling me anything, without doing anything at all to help. It was always that way—the sight-less eyes, the deaf ears, the dumb tongues of the witnesses who could cry out against murder and send a killer to the Hell he deserved.

She wore the mask of terror that they all hid behind. I wanted to knock it off and see what lay behind it. I wanted to tear the truth from its cloak of fear. The dead girl couldn't talk, but this one would.

I knocked her hand away from her face with my left, brought up my right, slapped her hard with the open palm, then backhanded her.

"Answer me, goddam it," I growled. "What happened out there tonight?"

I raised my right again, in a fist this time, and suddenly she was more afraid of me than of a killer outside somewhere in the dark.

She started to talk and whimper at the same time. The words came out in a choked, jumbled rush.

"Don't hit me," she wailed. "Don't hit me. I didn't see nothing. All I know is, I was lying in bed here, trying to go to sleep, when I heard a noise outside like a backfire or maybe a shot. Then I heard a car going away fast.

"When I got to the window, I didn't see nothing out there. I don't want any trouble, so I went back to bed. That's all I know. Swear to Jesus."

"Why didn't you open the door when I knocked?" I asked her.

"I was afraid," she whimpered. "I don't want trouble. Ain't you ever been scared?"

Yes, I had been scared. Many times. The rage inside me cooled as I looked down at her and somehow I was almost sorry for her. Not so much for her as for all frightened people, everywhere.

"Okay, Star," I said. "Sorry I had to get rough. Next time a cop asks questions, tell the truth right away and you won't get hurt."

I motioned the patrolmen outside and flicked off the lamp. Star turned over in the dark and buried her face in the pillow. She was still whimpering as we left.

Outside, the air smelled clean and refreshing after the shanty, One of the cops climbed into the radio car for a nap. The other stood guard alongside it and the glow of his cigaret was the only light in the Valley.

No use waking any of the neighbors in the shacks farther along the line. They would be there in the morning. They had no place else to go.

I said goodnight to the sentry cop and walked back to the bar where I had parked my Ford. The tavern was closed and the customers had stumbled on their way. Through the glass, I could see the owner counting his receipts behind the bar. I tapped on the glass door.

He grabbed for the pistol he kept handy in a drawer under the register. When he saw who it was, he relaxed and let me in. I had two straight shots to wash the taste of death out of my mouth. Dawn was smearing the sky with pink and grey when I finally started home. Across the silent river to the west, St. Louis still lay bundled in night's black blankets. A tugboat honked offshore and a drunk lying in a doorway scratched himself in his sleep.

CHAPTER THREE

In my dream there was a giant arm, big as a telephone pole. It held a black, ugly whip as it rose up and down and the crack of the whip was like thunder.

The girl's eyes were wide and her mouth was open and she tried to scream her terror as the whip rose and fell, rose and fell. She looked at me and tried to tell me her name, because she was someone I knew, someone I had seen before, but the slashing roar of the whip drowned out her anguished cries.

I tried to help her. I longed to ease her pain. But there was nothing I could do because the whip arm was mine and I was powerless to stop it.

Her face was still there as I struggled back to consciousness. Then, suddenly, she was gone. My head ached and my throat was dry. My pajamas and pillow were moist with sweat.

I tried to bring her face back for I knew the dream was not entirely unreal. I hadn't realized it last night in the Valley, but I knew the murdered girl. Or had seen her, talked to her maybe. Where?

The alarm clock on my dresser told me it was noon. I showered, shaved, and took my time about dressing. I put a fresh pot of coffee on the stove and thought about last night while waiting for it to boil. Questions about the murder kept tumbling through my mind like a troupe of acrobats.

Who was she?

Why was she killed?

Was the killer a sex fiend who dragged her into the lot to ravish her and who killed when she resisted?

Or was there another reason?

What about the lash marks?

We hadn't found any purse or billfold, but robbery didn't seem a likely motive. She didn't look as if she ever had much money.

Maybe there was a love angle. With her looks, there must have been plenty of boy friends. I poured some coffee, lit a breakfast cigar and thought about this last theory. I wondered what it was like to be in love with a pretty young blonde. So much in love it might lead to murder.

"Love is a form of insanity," I liked to say when the subject came up. And yet . . .

I wondered about it often because love was something I had never known in all my thirty-two years.

Women, yes. Plenty of them. They were something to take when the need arose, like a cup of coffee, a cigar, a shot of whiskey. They were there to satisfy a need.

When they got to be something more, a man was ruined. It was harder to cure than the dope habit or chronic alcoholism. That's how I felt and that's why I had no use for love. Or so I tried to keep telling myself.

Maybe I didn't really feel that way. Maybe I had had it rubbed in by my old man so often and so hard I had no way of feeling otherwise. Maybe I learned about women wrong, out of the gutters and off dirty unwhitewashed fences in four-letter words and in cat-houses. To hell with the maybes, though. Love wasn't anything you had to learn. You knew about it or you didn't. So far, I didn't. Maybe later, when I was old and gray and past the age where women meant a toss in bed, maybe then I'd figure them different, and give love a tumble.

In any case, I wasn't going to go about it the way my old man did.

My father found it out the hard way. He married a tramp—my mother. When I was a baby, she ran off with a salesman. My father tried to raise me the best he could after that, but he kept thinking about the way things had turned out. He was a cop, too, but it got so he wasn't much good to the Force. He thought too much and tried to wash the thoughts away with rotgut. One night he discovered that the rotgut didn't help any more so he put the muzzle of his revolver in his mouth and blew out his brains.

After that, I grew up in an orphanage. They treated us well there. When I finished high school, I joined the Marines and stayed there until a sniper won me a Purple Heart. I recovered in a Stateside hospital, picked up my discharge and came home to East St. Louis where my father's old friends made a place for me in the Department.

As a patrolman, I wore his badge. They let me keep it when I became sergeant and pinned on a new shield.

All this came back to me while I sipped coffee and thought about the dead girl. I wanted to find her killer, because that was my job, but I couldn't feel sorry for her. There were too many tramps in the world. One less didn't make any difference to me. There would always be another, and another cup of coffee, when the need arose. There would always be killers, too. And cops who got paid to catch them.

I washed out the coffee cup and put it away. Then I sat down at the table again, took the shells out of my revolver, cleaned it and reloaded it. I wiped the inside of the holster with an oily cloth.

I was very careful with that gun. It was my life insurance policy and I treated it like a mother does her firstborn baby.

When I was sure it was in perfect condition, it went back in the holster and onto my hip. It was ready for a hard day's work now. So was I.

I put on my hat and jacket, locked my apartment and stepped into the sunshine. Fortunately, the day was warm enough so I wouldn't need a topcoat. It was as fine a day as we ever get in East St. Louis. The river smells were overcome by the odors of chemicals, railroad smoke and the sprawling National City Stockyards. A light smoke haze floated lazily in the air.

I dropped my blood-spattered topcoat off at a cleaning shop, then drove on to Main Street, which isn't the main street at all, and parked in a vacant space across the street from City Hall, which is next door to Police Headquarters. I locked the car, walked to the corner of Main and Missouri Avenue, picked up the East St. Louis *Journal* and the St. Louis *Post-Dispatch* and went on down the block to a hashery known as Nick's.

Nick Pappas was back of the counter. He was chewing on the end of a twisted black cigar.

We nodded and I ordered coffee, ham and eggs, sunny-side up. Then I turned to the papers so I wouldn't have to watch him massacre my order. There we were on the front page of both sheets. Sex slaying, the papers called it.

The East St. Louis *Journal* had all the details and it spelled my name right, which made me happy. The *Post-Dispatch* account was a trifle more conservative and there was no mention of Gomez and me. Inspector Flynn had grabbed all the free advertising space. The bastard.

I was half way down the column when Nick shoved a plate in front of me with a sliver of ham and two mangled eggs. The coffee could have been ink or black turpentine, maybe a mixture of both.

"How come you're working the counter by yourself?" I asked, to make conversation.

"Mary got drunk last night," he grunted. "Busted a bunch of dishes. I fired her."

That was the first improvement he had made in the place. Mary was a sloppy, sullen brunette with a beer barrel physique and all the charm and personality of a meat-axe.

"She was a doll all right," Nick said, as if peering in to my thoughts.

He laughed harshly, ran a hairy paw over the beard stubble on his chin, and spat cigar juice on the floor.

"I wish I could find that little broad who worked here before Mary," he said. "She wasn't much of a waitress, either, but she brought in lots of customers."

Then I remembered. It hit me like a blackjack.

I hadn't recognized her last night, the way her face was contorted and her makeup smeared. It had been several months since I had seen her in Nick's and then only once or twice. I had noticed she was pretty but I hadn't tried to make her, like most of the other customers did. I hadn't paid much attention to her at all. She had worked there a week or so and then she was gone and Mary was behind the counter. Outside of thinking that the new girl was a mess, I hadn't given the change any thought until Nick mentioned it. But now I was reasonably certain the murdered girl was Nick's former hash slinger.

"Why did the blonde leave?" I asked.

"Who knows?" Nick shrugged. "One day she just didn't show up. She never came back. She had half a week's pay coming, too. Found something better, I guess."

"Who was she?"

"She went by the name of Randy. Randy Harding, I think it was. I got it someplace in the file.

"When she saw the sign in the window for a waitress, she came in and I hired her. She said she just hit town from Little Rock, or some place down there, and to call her Randy. I didn't ask too many questions because I figured with her looks the customers wouldn't worry too much about how their meals tasted. They were too busy drooling over her."

"I sure would like to see that broad again," he said.

"Then put your coat on," I told him. "I'll take you to her right now."

"I can't leave the place. I got no one to take over."

"To hell with the place," I said. "Lock it up and come along with me. This is official. I think Randy was the girl we found murdered last night and you're going to identify her if it was."

He came along without any more argument, but he didn't like the idea.

A detective cruiser and the coroner's Cadillac were parked in front of Jansen's Funeral Home when we got there. Dr. Silas Ethridge, the county coroner, had just finished his autopsy. He was standing in the front hallway, talking to Inspector Flynn.

I was surprised to see the Inspector up and about so early in the day. He usually didn't start stirring until after dark. Most of the cases he worked on involved night clubs, gambling joints and other places that paid well for special protection.

Things had been dull in his line recently, however. County grand juries and the Senate Crime Committee investigation, plus a cleanup at top state level, had closed the biggest gambling houses some time ago. Those that didn't stay shut had reopened as night spots and restaurants.

The smaller handbooks and the card and dice games in neighborhood taverns were going full swing again, as they did after every anti-gambling drive. But there was little trouble there.

I figured Inspector Flynn was tired of the inactivity. He didn't even have to protect the local racket boys from out-of-town mobsters any more. The Chicago syndicate had taken the locals in or put them out of business for good. It was all one big, happy family. There hadn't been a single gang killing in more than a year.

So this case was something to break the monotony. Besides, it was good publicity for the Inspector. He had been in the newspapers several times before, but most of the publicity wasn't good.

"Hello, Barney," he said when we came in. "Did you bring Nick around for some stew meat?"

"The blonde used to work for him," I said. "At least I think it was her. What did the autopsy show?"

Coroner Ethridge flashed a set of dazzling mouth china at me and fluttered his delicate hands.

"She wasn't raped," he said. "Death was almost instantaneous, from a single bullet that entered the skull slightly behind the left ear. It was fired at close range, although it didn't pass completely through the skull.

"As I say," Ethridge continued, "she hadn't been raped, but she was far from virginal. I'd fix time of death somewhere between two-thirty and four A.M. She had been beaten with a belt or strap, or possibly a whip, within the last three days and on occasions prior to that. There are no other scars, tattoos, or identifying marks on the body. An interesting case, I would say. Have you uncovered her background yet?"

"Not yet," I told him.

Inspector Flynn said the slug from her head had been sent to the State Police lab at Springfield for a ballistics run. I took Nick back to Jansen's workshop. The body lay on a metal table with rubber-tired wheels. A rubber sheet covered it. We walked to the table and I pulled back the sheet.

The lipstick had been washed off her face. So had the horror. She looked even younger than she had last night. A wax doll waiting for someone to play with.

"That's her," Nick said. He looked sick. "That's her."

He turned away and walked swiftly from the room and down the hallway and out into the air. I covered her up and followed.

We drove back to Nick's ptomaine palace and started going through his records. They would have given an accountant nightmares. Everything was scrawled in pencil in a large, finger-marked, grease-spattered notebook.

It took a lot of hunting, even with Nick's help. Finally we found it. The name Randy Harding and the date she started work and the date when Nick decided she wasn't coming back. Beside her name was an address on Mildred Avenue, just outside of town.

She had quit the first week in June—four months ago. Right after Memorial Day. That probably didn't mean anything, but it was a start.

Memorial Day was a big occasion in this town because it marked the opening of the Spring racing season at Fairmount Park, between East St. Louis and Collinsville. Maybe she hit a daily double and decided to retire. Maybe a lot of things. Collinsville Road, where U.S. Route 40 flows past the track, is a lively place during the racing season. A pretty blonde could make good there.

I jotted down all the information that Nick's meager records could give me about the girl.

"You got some bookkeeping system," I said. "What do you do when someone comes snooping around about taxes or wages or unemployment compensation?"

Nick shrugged and moved the cigar stub around in his mouth.

"Same thing as I do with you guys. Give them a few bills to let me alone. Nobody worries about a hole in the wall like this. If it wasn't for the punchboards and the numbers, I couldn't afford to stay in business." I punched out a couple of numbers on his two-bit board before leaving. As usual, my luck was bad.

I went back to Police Headquarters. There were still hours of daylight left before I was due to begin work, but I was eager today. Eager to catch me a killer.

My partner, Cliff Radnik, wasn't around yet and Inspector Flynn was out riding the town. He had passed out pictures of the dead girl to the boys and they were making the rounds, seeing what they could find out about her. Flynn had left two of the pictures on my desk.

The detective rooms were deserted, so I stuck one of the photos in my pocket and went downstairs again. I left a message for Radnik with the desk sergeant. He told me the murder lot had been combed clean. An empty purse was found in a pile of rubbish. Could have been hers or anyone else's. The missing earring was still missing. And the gun. All of the Valley's residents had been questioned. Nobody knew a thing, of course.

The black detective squad car was gassed up and ready to roll, so I drove it out to Mildred Avenue, south of the city near Parks Airport, and found the address I was looking for.

It was a white frame bungalow, set back about fifty yards from the street. There was a white picket fence around the yard. The house was neat, but the white paint was already turning grey as everything white does around here. I could see a garage behind the house. It was empty.

The door opened almost as soon as I rang the bell and I felt the breath catch in my throat with surprise. She was wearing navy slacks and a pink sweater. Her breasts were full and high, straining against the soft wool. Her hair and eyes were the darkest I had ever seen and her mouth was a scarlet gash in her pale face.

She wasn't beautiful. Her mouth was too wide and her nose seemed a trifle flat and the cheekbones made her face somewhat hollow and thin. Her shape was good, but a trifle on the too-slim side.

She wasn't beautiful, like the movie dolls are beautiful, but she had more of what it takes to be a woman than anyone I had ever seen before. She was pure, raw sex. And I wanted her, just like that.

"We don't need any," she said. I thought she had been reading my mind, then realized she must think I was a salesman. She started to close the door. I leaned my shoulder against it, blocking the doorway.

She stepped back and an angry light flickered in her eyes as if someone had struck a match beneath the surface of an inky pool.

"Go away from here," she said. "I'll call my husband."

I got my wallet out and flashed the gold badge at her. "Do that," I said. "I'd like to talk to both of you."

Then I introduced myself and she opened the door wide and invited me in. She pointed to a chair and moved away from me, walking with the soundless fluidity of a cat. Cat-wise, she curled up on a pale green divan and tucked her legs under her.

She plucked a cigaret from a Chinese box on the blond mahogany table in front of the divan, lit it and blew smoke through her nostrils. The flame was gone from her eyes now and they were narrow slits, curious and watchful.

"What can I do for you, sergeant?" she asked.

"I'd like to talk to your husband, too."

"He's not here now. I just said that—to make you go away. You frightened me when you shoved the door like that. I didn't know who you were."

Her voice was husky, almost a whisper. Although her eyes still waited for me to answer their questions, she didn't seem excited as people usually are when a cop shows up at their home. It was almost as though she had been expecting me, or some other badge, to call.

I brought the photograph from my pocket and handed it to her.

"Do you know this girl?"

"Yes. She used to live here. Why?"

"She was murdered last night. I want you to tell me all you know about her."

She hesitated a moment, trying to get the proper look of shock and frightened surprise into her expression. The result was good, but not good enough.

"How horrible," she said.

"But you're not surprised."

"No," she admitted. "I heard about it on the radio. Somehow, from the description, I thought it might be Randy."

She said Randy's real name was Harriet Randolph Harding and that they both came from a small town in Arkansas, outside Little Rock. When

Randy's parents died, she worked for a while as a waitress in Little Rock, then came to East St. Louis.

"She had no place to stay; so we took her in," the husky voice continued. "She stayed here about a month, until she got a job. Then she moved out. She said she wanted to get her own room so as not to put us to any more trouble.

"She didn't say where she was going. I think it was someplace near the racetrack. After that she would drop by about once a week, on her night off, and we would go to a movie or shopping together. Then she stopped coming around. I didn't know where to get in touch with her."

I asked her a few more questions and learned she was Grace Trudo, Mrs. Willie Trudo, and that was another surprise. Her husband was a small-time tout and gambler who made a living off suckers and drunks, a leading profession in our town.

I couldn't imagine how Willie ever got a woman like this.

"Where was Willie last night?" I asked her.

"Who knows? Cheating some damn fool in a card game, probably."

"Where were you?"

"Here. Asleep. By myself."

"That's a shame," I told her.

Her eyes met mine and held them there for a long moment. "Yes," she said, "isn't it?"

She uncurled from the divan, picked up another cigaret and walked slowly over to my chair, holding the Pall Mall in front of her.

"Light me," she said.

I stood up, fumbled in my pockets, found a folder of matches and set one on fire. She dragged in smoke and lazily blew out the match.

Then she was in my arms. I could feel her hard breasts pressing against my chest hungrily and her fingernails were clawing into my back. Her lips were hot and wet against mine, tongue flicking, teeth snapping. She caught my lower lip and bit it. I tasted the warm salt of blood.

"For Christ's sake!"

I pushed her away from me, holding her arms until my fingers bruised the flesh. Still holding her with my left hand, I got out my handkerchief and dabbed at my lip.

"What got into you?" I asked. "Willie wouldn't like that."

"Willie isn't here. To hell with Willie. That sawed-off little punk makes me sick. I want a real man for a change."

And I wanted her, but not here, not now.

She looked at my face, read all that was there and laughed, a harsh, dry laugh.

"You're not so goddam tough," she said.

No, I wasn't so tough. Not anymore. Not after that fierce, demanding kiss. But she would never know it. I pulled her to me, clamped my arms about her waist and squeezed until her breath was a strangled gasp. Then I returned her savage bite, leaving her mouth smeared with her blood and mine.

She was limp when I let her go. The flames were back in her eyes, only now they burned with desire instead of anger. Her nails scratched the lapels of my coat, clutching at my shirt buttons, unfastening my tie.

I shoved her away from me so hard that she bounced backwards a few feet, hit the coffee table and fell across it with a crash.

Then I slammed on my hat and made for the door.

"No," she screamed at me as I stepped outside. It was the first time she had raised her voice and it was a screech straight out of Hell.

"You lousy cop bastard!"

CHAPTER FOUR

I kept my foot down on the speedometer pedal all the way back to Headquarters, but my heart was going faster than the car.

This was it, part of my mind kept shouting. This is the woman you've spent your life looking for.

The other half of my mind cried even louder that it wasn't so. She was a tramp, it said. A no-good bitch who would never be anything but trouble to the men who wanted her.

Be realistic, this part of my mind told me. She's trying to trap you. She knows more about the murder than she told you. A woman like that could do anything, even kill.

I was furious at myself for the things she had made me feel and do. If there had been anything at all to go on, I would have driven back and arrested her. I didn't have enough yet, but I promised myself I would find it if there was anything to find.

She was everything I had hated all my life. A scheming slut who would cheat on her husband with any man who came along when she was in heat. I told myself a woman like that could never mean anything to me. I told myself and knew I was a liar.

I pulled up to the curb in front of the police station, went inside and up the stairs to our detective bureau. It was still deserted.

On my desk was a copy of a teletyped report just in from the state crime lab at Springfield. It said the murder gun was a .32-caliber weapon.

A pin-prick of memory stuck the back of my mind. I hurried down to the records room and rummaged through a sheaf of old reports until I pulled out the one I was searching for.

It was a stolen gun report. On a .32 snub-nose revolver issued to one William J. Trudo. And it was dated only three weeks ago.

It said someone had broken into his car and grabbed the gun from the glove compartment. A routine report, but interesting.

I didn't think Trudo would be dumb enough to report it stolen if he planned on using it soon. But his wife knew where he kept it. She might have taken it and made it look like an outside job.

Of course, there were a lot of .32's floating around and the murder gun might be any one of them. This is mainly .38 and .45 country, but those that like to be dainty or inconspicuous go in for the smaller stuff.

So far, I had nothing to indicate Trudo's gun was the one that killed the blonde. But I thought I would have soon. Unless the gun was at the bottom of the Mississippi.

My stomach sent up hunger signals. I went out the back way and through the alley to Third Street and Smitty's, where they serve the best sandwiches in town if they know you.

The tavern lights weren't on yet, although it was growing dark outside. I almost sat on a pop-eyed pekinese who was napping on a bar stool. Its twin snoozed on top of the bar, at the far end.

Two love birds were in a cage at the rear of the tavern—not loving, just sitting. Must be an old married couple, I thought.

Smitty turned on the lights, uncapped a bottle of Stag beer and built me a meal-sized ham and Swiss on rye, painted with mustard.

Gomez dropped in on his way to report for duty and we talked shop and politics. Everybody talks politics around Smitty's, but it doesn't prove anything. The City Hall machine stays the same, no matter how the talk goes.

Two East Side reporters for the St. Louis *Post-Dispatch* and *Globe-Democrat* were shaking the dice cup for drinks down the bar.

They came over while I was finishing my second bottle of Stag and asked about the murder. Nothing new, I reported. I told them who the girl was and where she used to work, but they already had that. Inspector Flynn had grabbed the publicity bag again.

I didn't say anything about Grace or Willie Trudo. That could keep for a while.

They asked if they could write that a roundup of sex degenerates was in progress. Sure, I said. Say anything you want.

The news boys bought a drink and I sent a round back at them. Then it was time to start work again. Radnik, my partner, was waiting in the office. He was lolling in the battered swivel chair with his feet holding down the desk top.

Radnik wasn't the smartest cop in the world, but he was handy. Although he was a half foot shorter than my six-feet-two, he could spot me a few pounds. And he was solid as he was wide. He was built on the lines of a hundred-record juke box, only bigger and not quite so musical.

I got out the pictures of the dead girl and handed one to Radnik. He studied it thoughtfully for several seconds.

"Nice," he said. "Very,"

We took the pictures with us, piled into our squad car and started making the rounds again.

We headed east on Collinsville Avenue to St. Clair Avenue, then north under the railroad overpass. Then we were in "Whiskey Chute," a block-long assortment of cheap gin-mills and lunchrooms across the road from the stockyards.

It was early yet for the Chute. Business didn't start picking up until after midnight, when the cattle farmers rolled in and unloaded their livestock. Half a dozen cars and two empty cattle trucks were parked at right angles to the curb.

The smell of thousands of hogs, steers, sheep and other animals was almost overbearing. We braced ourselves against it as we found a place at the curb and got out.

One of the bars had no name. Just a blue neon sign advertising BEER-WHISKEY-EATS. It was run by an ex-pug named Frog Gaffney and its main attraction for the cattlemen was a poker game which ran nightly from midnight until dawn. Willie Trudo occupied the dealer's slot.

There was talk that the game wasn't as honest as it might have been but we had received few complaints and the Frog made regular contributions to our welfare. We seldom bothered him.

The corner juke was blaring when we came in.

"Don't roll them bloodshot eyes at me . . ."

Only two customers were in the place, a weather-worn cattleman in a slouch hat, leather jacket and overalls, and a husky youngster who looked like a livestock handler from the yards and smelled the same way.

The farmer was drinking boilermakers while the kid was sipping a Stag and trying to figure out a lucky number on one of the punchboards which littered the bar.

Frog Gaffney sat in a chair behind the bar, squinting at a newspaper. He was short, squat and bulge-eyed, like the creature which gave him his nickname. He got up when he saw who we were and shuffled around the far end of the bar to greet us.

"Willie around?" I asked.

"Out to supper," he grunted. "Should be back after a bit. Anything I can do for you boys?"

"Where was Willie last night?"

"Here. He came in about nine or ten and stayed till we closed-about five A.M., I reckon."

"He never left? Not even for a few minutes?" Frog's eyes got shrewd and hard, the blank look the wise boys wear when a cop starts asking things.

"No, sir. He was here all night. Why? He in some kind of trouble?"

"Not if he was here, he isn't. What kind of car does he drive?"

"Green Buick, '52 Roadmaster sedan. I don't think he had it last night, though."

"Where was it?"

"I think his wife had it. I drove him home after we locked up."

I asked a few other questions, to make it look good, but I didn't get anywheres. Besides, I had another piece for the jig-saw now. I still wanted to talk to Willie, but it wasn't too important. I thought of his wife and the fire in her eyes, the hot, hungry flame that I would put out when I threw her into a cell.

We had a drink with the Frog before we left. The cheap whiskey burned my swollen, tender lip almost as much as her mouth had. I could taste her again as I gulped it down.

"You told me you loved me; you told me a lie," wailed the nasal-voiced juke box.

We took a fistful of cigars from a box which the Frog shoved at us. The farmer at the bar uncrossed his lean legs, crossed them the other way and ordered another boilermaker. The kid from the yards cursed as he lost another dime to the punchboard. We walked out into the cool, clear, stockyard-stinking night.

CHAPTER FIVE

Almost without realizing where I was going, I turned east off St. Clair into Collinsville Road and took U.S. 40 out of town towards the racetrack.

Subconsciously, I had been thinking about the Road all day. Ever since I learned that Randy quit her waitress job about the time the racing season began. Then Grace mentioned the blonde had moved out near the track. In this town, that could mean only one thing.

Collinsville Avenue and Collinsville Road are both busy thoroughfares. Collinsville Avenue is the downtown main drag, lined with small shops, department stores, restaurants and a few night spots.

Collinsville Road is all night spots—of a slightly different nature. Even the track operates at night. And, when the last race has been run, there are other forms of entertainment along the Road.

During racing season, the girls come in by plane, train, bus, car and truck. Many of them bring their own trailers, and trailer communities spring up behind little roadside shacks with red, green and blue neon tubes above their doors. Most of the neon lights don't form any advertising words, but everyone who knows the Road knows what is sold there. For Collinsville Road is what the Valley used to be.

The Road runs wide open during the racing season. Then business falls off and only three or four places stay open through the Fall and Winter.

Mona's was one of these. Mona had been around so long and knew so many people that she was a local legend. No one, not even the governor, was big enough to keep her place closed for long.

Her neon sign said simply "MONA'S" and there was another sign, a hand-painted one, on one of the porch pillars which added: "Truckers Welcome."

While most of the houses near the track were frame shacks of three or four rooms—one for a bar, the rest for beds—Mona's was an impressive green-and-white, two-story structure.

From its windows, you could look out over the race-track, closed and empty now until the next racing meet in the Spring.

The gravel drive made crunching, complaining sounds as our car disturbed its rest. No other cars were out front, although the neon sign still shone invitingly.

I braked to a stop directly in front of Mona's porch steps and climbed up them. Radnik stayed in the car. Before I had a chance to knuckle the door, it swung open and there was Mona, wide as the doorway, her owl eyes peering out into the dark.

If she was surprised at the visit, she didn't show it.

"C'mon in, Barney," she rumbled. Her voice was harsh with years and whiskey, sounding as if it came from the bottom of a deep, dry well.

Business must be slow, I thought. She hadn't been expecting many customers. Mona was a gal who had made a fortune on her back, then spent a fortune on her back in expensive clothes. But now she wore a simple, flowered house-dress and bedroom slippers.

I followed her into the perfume-sweet sitting room and dropped into a comfortable chair while she switched on a dim table lamp and poured a drink. Double shot. Single ice cube.

She pulled a straight-backed chair close to mine and parked in it, flowing over the seat on either side.

"Business or pleasure?"

"Business," I replied.

"Hell," she said. "That can wait. Business is so bad the girls are trying to give it away to keep in practice."

She swung around in her chair until she was facing a drape-covered doorway at the rear of the sitting room. Opening her mouth, she cupped a fat hand around it and roared: "Louella! C'mon out here!"

Tiny sounds of movement came from behind the drapes. Squeaking sounds like bedsprings. Rustling sounds. Sounds of high heels on bare floor boards.

The curtains parted and Louella came in. She was yawning and her eyes were half-shut. She ground her fists into them, then opened them wide when she saw me. She gave me a pearly, professional smile.

Her half-open black negligee covered and didn't cover a lot of woman, but I wasn't interested. I turned back to Mona and finished my drink.

"You must be getting deaf," I told her. "I said this is a business call."

"Well, we're here for the business, sugar," Louella said with a nasal drawl.

Mona chuckled from deep down in her throat and told the girl to go back to bed. She shrugged and returned to her room.

When she had passed through the curtains again, Mona settled as comfortably as she could in her chair and folded white, diamond-ringed hands over her huge stomach.

She smiled at me through half-closed eyes. The smile of the Sphinx. It was my play now and she was waiting to see the cards.

I didn't disappoint her. I pulled the photograph of Randy Harding out of my pocket and handed it to her.

She took her time studying it. First she looked at it in the dim light, holding it in front of her as if she were reading a book.

Then she hauled herself up off the chair with a grunt and waddled over to the lamp on the table. She placed the picture directly under the lamp shade and studied it some more without saying anything.

After a long, silent moment she handed the photo back to me and mixed another drink.

"What do you want from me?" she asked, the cheerfulness drained from her voice.

"Information."

"She was the one who was murdered," she said. It was a simple, flat statement, not a question. Yet she wasn't trying to tell me anything. She just said it.

"Yes."

"A pretty girl," she said. "So young, too. When I first saw her, I said to myself 'That kid is heading for trouble.' And now she's dead."

She emptied her glass at a single gulp.

"That's the way the ball bounces," she said, trying without success to bring some of the old animation back.

"You can do yourself a favor by telling me about it, Mona. Tell me everything you can about her. Who she was, who she knew. All of it."

"She never worked here."

"I didn't say that. What do you know about her?"

"Not much. She was new on the Road. I just saw her a couple times. She worked at Club 40. Nice looking kid. It's too bad."

"Yeh," I agreed. "Too bad."

"Go over to Club 40," she said, a dry, bitter note in her voice now. "Ask Big Red about her. If he did it, throw the book at the bastard."

This was more like it. The pieces were falling into line, one at a time.

She threw another ice cube and a splash of bourbon into my glass and I tossed it down. Then she walked me to the door.

Her deep, well-bottom voice followed me out to the car. "Take it easy," she rumbled.

Radnik sat up with a sleepy grunt as I slid into the seat beside him. I flicked on the ignition switch and headlights and wheeled the car around.

Club 40 was a short distance down the road, on the opposite side of the highway from the racetrack. It was more wooden shack than night club. Its liquor license had been taken away some time ago and the only booze on hand was that kept for the comfort of the host, Big Red Shelton.

Big Red was a mean man, with connections that made him all the meaner. He was a three-time loser who learned that pimping is a safer, more lucrative profession than armed robbery.

The right people gave him the okay to open up his meat market and he thanked them with a cut of his profits. He took care of all the top politicos and cops in his county. And they saw that he wasn't bothered, so long as there weren't too many complaints about his place.

Technically, his stand was out of our territory, as it was in the next county. But I decided that this wasn't the time to fall back on technicalities.

I had never met Big Red, but I had heard enough about him. His friends hated him. His enemies were mostly deceased. A nice guy in a nice business.

The neon sign in front of Club 40 was dark when we pulled up. The heavily-curtained windows didn't show any light either.

I went around the side of the building to the back. A grey Cadillac was parked there, glinting richly in the moonglow. Big Red must be home.

Going back to the front, I climbed the three rickety steps to the door. Radnik followed. I banged on the wood. There was silence inside for a second, then a tinkle of glass. As I raised my fist to knock again, the bolt slammed back and the door swung part way open.

"Sorry, boys," Big Red growled at us. "No girls tonight. Come back next week maybe."

I shoved my foot into the narrow opening, rammed my shoulder into the door and knocked him off balance. Before he knew what was happening, Radnik and I were inside.

"Police," I said, palming my shield as he got set to rush us. "Don't get cute."

Big Red pulled himself together and thought things over. His little eyes glittered at us from under thick red brows.

He wore a loud, silk sport shirt covered with pictures of dancing girls. His arms and chest were matted with long red hair. Beneath the arm grass were blue tattoos of girls, hearts, the usual needle-parlor gallery.

Still glowering at us, he backed up to the tiny bar which faced the entranceway. Behind the bar was another door which would lead to the pleasure rooms. A single bottle of rye, three-quarters gone, stood on the bar. And a single empty glass.

"What you guys want?" the big ape asked.

"We came to talk—about Randy," I told him.

"Who's Randy?"

"Cut out the crap," Radnik said. "You know goddam well who's Randy."

"Let's have a drink first," Big Red said. He moved around the bar and one of us should have had better sense, but we just stood there and watched him. He bent down and came up with a fresh bottle. Then he bent down again and came up with a .45 automatic that looked as big as a howitzer.

"Now you guys get the hell out of here," he said. "You jerk-town bulls got no business out here. This ain't your county. I don't have to tell you a damn thing. You want to know something, ask the cops that run things over here. I talk to them, nobody else.

"You walk out that door and get in your car and go back where you came from or I'll blow your friggin' brains out and say you were out of your territory, trying to shake me down."

Radnik was fast, but not fast enough. He whipped his revolver out of its shoulder holster but the automatic boomed before he could find the trigger.

Radnik spun around and toppled over backwards, his gun going off in the air and slamming a slug into the ceiling. Big Red watched him drop, then tried to level on me. I was over the bar and on top of him before he could start blasting again.

He was as tough as he was big but I was just as big and handy. He cracked the gun barrel alongside my head. It felt like an axe splitting my skull. A wave of black nausea swept over me. I shook it off, rammed the flat of my hand across his Adam's apple, smashed my right knee into his groin.

The little bar splintered and collapsed on its side when we piled into it. We slugged and kicked, grappled and gouged. He was fighting to get his gun free and I put everything I had into tearing it away from him. A second knee in the groin softened him up so I could jerk his arm behind him and snap his wrist.

He yowled like a turpentined cat when the wrist bones cracked. The .45 fell out of his fist and went skidding across the floor.

I let go of his wrist and he bent over double, cold sweat drops standing out on his forehead. Moaning and cursing, he held the limp wrist out in front of him.

I stepped back about three feet, took aim and teed off with a right to the jaw that lifted him off the floor and dumped him across the shattered bar. The building shook from the crash he made coming down.

He lay perfectly still for a long moment, face down alongside his broken rye bottle. I thought I had killed him. Then a long, low moan squeezed through his swelling lips. He was alive and I didn't care very much one way or another except for the fact that corpses can't talk. I wanted to hear what he had to say before he was ready for the boneyard.

I picked up his automatic and dropped it into my pocket. The weight of it dragged my suit coat down. It flapped against my side, making me realize I was bruised there, too. I was one big bruise from socks to skull.

Turning my back on Big Red, I crossed the room to my partner. He was sitting slouched against the wall, holding his right shoulder with his left hand.

Radnik started to get to his feet. I helped him up and steadied him. Blood dripped from his oozing red sleeve and formed a tiny puddle on the floor. I tried to ease him out of his coat but it was glued to his injured arm by drying blood.

With one quick wrench, I ripped off the coat arm and the shirt sleeve underneath.

"For Christ's sake," he complained, "this suit cost me eighty clams."

There was a nasty hole in his upper arm, but it didn't look too serious. Soon it would heal good as new. I tied a handkerchief around the arm to stop the flow of blood.

We were a gory sight, we three. Luckily for me, I showed the least damage.

Still moaning, Big Red picked himself out of the bar wreckage and stood tottering on rubber legs, glowering at us from hate-filled eyes. I went around him to a pay phone on the far wall, dropped in a coin and dialed St. Mary's Hospital. I told them who I was and where to send the ambulance.

When I hung up, I started tossing questions at Big Red. About Randy. He nailed his stare to the floorboards and kept it there. He was hurt and all the fight was knocked out of him. Yet he wouldn't say a word. From far off down the highway, we heard the ambulance shrieking.

Radnik grunted with the effort of picking his service revolver off the floor.

"Get out of the way, Barney," he said. I stepped aside and he aimed it at Big Red's stomach. The hammer came back with a click that seemed as loud as a thunderclap.

Big Red's eyes jumped from the floor to the gun muzzle and hung there, hypnotized.

"Now talk, you bastard, or you're a dead man," Radnik said in a low, tense voice, holding the gun steady in his left hand.

"He means it," I added. Big Red looked at the gun muzzle and knew Radnik meant it without my telling him. Death was so close he could see it and smell it and taste it. He didn't want it to come any closer.

"I'll talk," he moaned. "Anything you want to know."

"Who was Randy?" I repeated: "Why did you kill her?"

"No," he said, "I never touched her. She just worked here. Two, three months ago was the last time. Then she went away."

"Who with?"

"Trudo, the dealer. The guy who brought her here."

Before I could ask him anything more, the ambulance came roaring up. But I had heard what I wanted to know.

I didn't want to leave Radnik alone in the back of the ambulance with Big Red, so I rode to town with them. After the pimp was patched up, I took him over to the station and booked him for assault with intent to kill. The fear had run out of him by this time and he stopped answering questions.

That was all right with me. I didn't think he could add much more to our conversation, anyway. Just to be on the safe side, I also ordered him held as a material witness in the murder case. The double booking should keep him under wraps as long as we needed him, I thought.

After tossing him into a cell, I called for a radio car and had a patrolman drive me over to Radnik's house. Waking his wife and explaining what had happened was the toughest part of the evening.

It took all my powers of persuasion to convince her he hadn't been killed. Then she wanted to rush right over to the hospital. I told her he had been given sedatives and was asleep and that she should wait until morning.

Finally, she calmed down and promised me there wouldn't be any more whooping and hollering. She agreed to take a stiff shot, if there was one in the house, and go to bed.

The patrolman drove me back to Club 40, where I had left the department's car. I dismissed him there and went through the place carefully, finding nothing of interest except a blackjack and a black notebook containing the first names of several girls, followed by columns of figures. The bookkeeping department for mattress mileage, I presumed. I stuck the book in my pocket. Randy was one of the names.

When I left, I didn't bother to lock the door or turn out the lights. If any burglars wanted the place, they could have it.

The sky overhead was crammed with shimmering stars and the moon turned a cold spotlight on the lonely racetrack across the highway. I could see the grandstand and the clubhouse almost as clearly as if it were day.

And I could see Mona's white house, down the highway. The neon sign was out now. A big tractor-trailer swished past on U.S. 40, heading east towards Indianapolis and New York. I watched it go until the tail-light was a tiny pin-prick of red in the distance. Then I got into my car and headed home.

CHAPTER SIX

The telephone yanked me out of a beautiful, bottomless sleep. It rang and rang until I struggled awake, sat up and lifted the receiver off its cradle.

I mumbled something into the mouthpiece and the other end almost bit my ear off.

"Black?" Inspector Flynn barked. "Come on in. We need you right away."

He signed off with a loud click and I remained sitting there for a few minutes more, holding the receiver an inch away from my ear and waiting for the barking to begin again. Suddenly, I was wide awake.

I went into the bathroom and turned the shower on cold. While icy darts pricked my skin, I tried to figure out what Flynn wanted. Something to do with the murder, I knew. But that was as far as I got.

On days like this I wondered why I ever wanted to be a cop. Work all day, work all night. No overtime, not even any thanks.

My thoughts shifted gears and Grace Trudo moved into them. There was something about her that excited me, even under a cold shower. I tried to get her out of my mind. For the moment, at least. She was one luxury I couldn't afford even to think about. Not yet.

Showered and shaved, I dressed as quickly as possible. White shirt, red-and-black striped tie, grey flannel suit, black leather shoes, brown leather holster, blue steel revolver.

Inspector Flynn was at his desk when I walked in. He was leaning back in his swivel chair and the afternoon papers were spread out on the desk top, only he wasn't reading because his neatly-creased hat was on top of the papers.

A cigaret hung in the corner of his mouth and a thin line of smoke zig-zagged towards the ceiling. He plucked the cigaret from his face and squashed it in a glass ashtray.

"What's the idea, grabbing Shelton?" he asked.

He wasn't barking this time. His voice was low and calm, though I sensed it might reach the roaring stage any moment.

"I wanted to talk to him."

"You know you got no jurisdiction over in Madison County."

"And I also know I'm working on a murder case," I told him. "Or ain't I?"

"Yeah," he said. "You're still on it. Only next time you feel like charging into another county for a prisoner, talk to me first. Shelton's been raising hell. Wants to see his lawyer. Claims he was trying to protect himself when you guys started bouncing him around."

"I didn't lay a finger on him until he shot Radnik."

"That's another thing," Flynn said. "If you hadn't gone over there, Radnik wouldn't have been hurt. I got nobody to replace him. Think you can handle this thing by yourself?"

I nodded.

"All right," the Inspector concluded. "But I hope you're right about Shelton. He's got some powerful people behind him."

It was not quite 1 P.M. when the interview was over.

That left the afternoon to kill.

I put down a sandwich and a bottle of Stag at Smitty's, dropped by the hospital to see how Radnik was coming along, then drove out to the grey-white house on Mildred Avenue.

A green Buick sedan stood in the driveway alongside the house. It was freshly washed and waxed, which might or might not mean anything.

No one answered the doorbell. That was luck. After waiting two or three minutes to make sure no one was home, I went around the side of the bungalow to the car.

The front doors were unlocked. The glove compartment wasn't, but I forced it open with my jackknife. In it were a small flashlight, a road map of Arkansas, a deck of cards and an empty aspirin box. Nothing to indicate a killer might have used the car.

The seats and floor were clean, so I yanked out the front seat to look underneath it and saw something sparkling there. It was the missing gold earring. The mate to the one the dead girl wore.

"What do you think you're doing?" an angry voice behind me said.

Folding my fist over the earring, I straightened and turned to face her. She was carrying a bag of groceries and her eyes shot at me like white-hot rivets.

"Just looking," I told her. "Do you mind?"

"You might have waited until somebody was home. You could have asked first."

"Why? You got something to hide?"

She hesitated for a moment, still watching me. Then, without answering, she stalked towards the house with the grocery bag pressed tight against her breasts. This time she wore a blue sweater that might have been painted on.

I stood in the driveway for a second more, watching the catlike motion of her hips, the toss of her black hair as the wind ruffled it. Then I followed her. When I came through the back door, she was emptying the grocery bag onto the kitchen table. I reached her side and took the last two cans from the paper sack. Vegetable soup and corned beef hash.

"Do come in," she said sarcastically. "Make yourself at home."

"Where's Willie?" I asked.

She shrugged her shoulders. "He got up early and went out. He didn't say where he was going."

"But he left the car here?"

"I didn't see him go. Maybe somebody picked him up. He doesn't always take the car."

"How about the night Randy was killed? Who had the car then?"

"I don't remember."

"It doesn't really matter," I assured her, hoping to throw her off guard. "You don't go in for jewelry much, do you?"

I had noticed she wore only a plain wedding band on her left hand. Otherwise, no jewelry. No earrings, bracelets, pins or other knickknacks. Even around the house, I would have expected something. She was the type who wore a lot of it—or none at all.

"Not much," she replied. "I'm not the jewelry type. I settle for the simple things. Like money."

"How about this?" I asked, fishing the earring out of my pocket and holding it in front of her.

She recognized it, all right. Her face had been pale before. Now it was dead-white.

"Give me that," she demanded, moving a step towards me. I put it back in my pocket.

"Give me that," she repeated. "It's mine. I lost it the other day."

"Have you got the mate?"

"Certainly. It must be around here someplace. I'll go get it."

She hurried out of the kitchen and went into a bedroom off the hall. I followed her quietly and stood in the doorway, watching her rummage through dresser drawers.

Obviously, she slept alone. Through the open closet drawer I could see dresses, blouses, lingerie. On top of the dresser were a perfume bottle, a cold cream jar and other feminine accessories. It was a woman's bedroom from the frilly curtains on the window to the ruffled satin bedspread.

I stayed in the corner of the doorway, just in far enough to watch her and out far enough so she couldn't see me in the dresser mirror. She was so busy yanking things about that she didn't bother to look over her shoulder.

She uncovered something in the bottom drawer that she hadn't intended to touch. Quickly, she piled scarves, gloves and handkerchiefs on it and pushed it to the rear of the drawer. But she wasn't quick enough.

"Gimme," I said, coming up behind her.

She tried to smile disarmingly, but there was fear in her eyes. Fear that I would find what she was trying to conceal.

"The earring isn't here," she said. "I have a jewel box in the other room. It must be there."

"Let me look," I said, reaching for the middle drawer.

"No," she snapped. "You stay out of there. Those are my personal belongings. I won't have you running your dirty paws through my things."

I pushed her out of the way and yanked open the drawer. Then she was on me like a bagful of bobcats. Her long nails clawed my face, almost gouging my eyes. When I tried to grab her, she bit my hand.

The sudden pain made me react instinctively. My fist swung up and slammed her alongside the jaw. She toppled over backwards, landing on the floor. Her head lolled to one side and the black hair fanned out around it like a nest of angry serpents.

Except for the rise and fall of her breasts, she didn't move. Her scarlet lipstick and the angry mark of my fist were the only color spots on her face.

I knelt down beside her, to see if she was badly hurt. Then I picked her up and placed her gently on the bed, propping two pillows beneath her head. Her forehead was cool to the touch as I stroked it.

She moaned and stirred slightly and her eyes came open, looking up at me with a strange, childish emptiness.

"You hit me," she whispered.

"I'm sorry, darling," I heard myself saying. Me, the tough, steel-hearted, woman-hating cop. "I didn't mean to hurt you. I must have gone out of my mind when you lit into me like that." She was silent.

"It doesn't take much guts to slug a woman," I added remorsefully, wondering why I had never thought about that before.

"I hurt you, too," she smiled. "So we're even now."

She raised her right arm slowly and the scarlet-tipped fingers caressed the wounds they had left on my cheek. Her touch made the claw-bites fade away.

Then her hands were behind my neck, pressing my face down to hers. Hard. Her mouth caught mine with hungry urgency and hung on. Her hands moved down my back, pulling me over on top of her.

I ran my fingers over her heaving breasts, straining to burst loose from the sweater, over her cool thighs, quivering beneath her skirt. My fingers found the snap and zipper and she moved her body underneath me as I yanked the skirt down over her legs.

I tried to remove the sweater, too, but she pushed my hands away and bit my lips as she had done the first time I met her. Only now the fury was on us and I didn't care. She loved as wildly as she fought.

Afterwards, the tension went out of her and she lay limply in my arms. The cat was a kitten now.

"You look just like an Indian with war paint on," she teased. "You better go into the bathroom and wash up. People will think I was trying to murder you." Murder. The word brought it all back. Our moment was gone. I was a cop and she was a suspect again. Nothing had changed, I tried to tell myself, knowing that everything had changed and nothing would ever be the same again.

I got out of bed and went into the bathroom, closing the door behind me. I took a washcloth off the towel rack and dabbed at my face. The nail marks were angry red lines down my cheeks.

There was a nauseous feeling in the pit of my stomach. I wondered what I would say to her. How I could phrase it. What else was there to say? Simply: "You're under arrest. For murder."

I felt in my hip pocket for the handcuffs, in case she got violent again.

The face looking back at me from the mirror showed something I didn't like. It revealed weakness—something I had never seen there before.

"Barney, the lover," it seemed to sneer. "Love 'em and lock 'em up."

I turned the water on full and splashed it over my face and hair, spilling some of it on my shirt front. The water got into my nose and eyes and ears but it couldn't wash away the bitter thoughts.

Suddenly, above the rush of the water, I heard a car motor roar. I charged out of the bathroom and shot a fast glance through the bedroom door. She was gone.

Without pausing, I sprinted through the quiet house and got outside in time to see the Buick skid from the driveway into the street and flash away in a cloud of dust.

I grabbed for my revolver and fired a shot in the air. She didn't stop, so I aimed at the speeding car and tried to squeeze the trigger. I couldn't do it. My hand seemed paralyzed, incapable of movement.

Chances were I would miss the car anyway, and almost certainly would miss her. I told myself I wanted to hit her, wanted to empty my gun at her until the car went into a spin and crashed and they dragged her body from the tangled wreckage. But I couldn't pull that trigger.

Next best thing was pursuit. I ran to my car, jerked open the front door and lunged behind the wheel. But I could have saved the energy, for she was a thoughtful girl. She had taken my keys from the ignition switch.

How stupid can you get?

I sprinted into the house and picked up the telephone. I called Headquarters and put out an alarm for Grace and the Buick.

At least I had sense enough to get the license number. I didn't think she would go very far.

I found a cigar in my shirt pocket, unwrapped it and bit off the end. Fumbling in my coat for matches, I felt the smooth coldness of the earring. It seemed somehow as if Randy was calling me from the grave for revenge. And I had let her down.

I found a book of matches and lit the cigar. The smoke tasted stale. It wasn't what I needed.

Back in the bedroom, I could smell the faint, tantalizing scent of the perfume she wore. The pillow was indented where her head had been. The bedspread trailed on the floor.

I opened the bottom drawer, pulled it out all the way and dumped the contents onto the rug. Nylons, blouses, silky feminine things came fluttering down. And, from the back of the drawer, a small black purse landed with a thud.

I picked it up. Even for a woman's purse, it was heavy. Peering inside it, I found what I had expected to find. A chrome-plated, snub-nosed .32.

A patrol car drove up after a few minutes more. The driver handed me a duplicate set of keys for my car. He didn't ask why I had called for them. He didn't ask anything. He didn't have to.

He gaped at the scratches on my face and tried to hide what he was thinking. He might as well have said it, though. And he was right.

I started up the cruiser and followed his black-and-white radio car back to town. My radio crackled to life and the dispatcher's voice repeated the alarm.

"Proceed with caution," the flat, monotonous voice said for perhaps the tenth time since my telephone call.

"This woman is wanted for murder."

CHAPTER SEVEN

It was the murder gun, all right.

We didn't wait to send it to Springfield for a ballistics run. We rushed it across the river to St. Louis Police Headquarters, where the lab boys fired it into some cotton wadding and checked the markings on the fresh bullet and the death slug. They matched.

That wrapped it up, so far as we were concerned. Grace had the gun when her husband reported it stolen. She had learned he was playing around with Randy.

While he was working, she picked Randy up and took her for a drive. The blonde lost an earring in the car. Grace didn't figure on the earring. When they got into the old Valley, she forced Randy out of the car and shot her. Then she tore the kid's clothes to make it look like a sex job.

After that, she didn't take time to get rid of the gun. She went straight home, planning to dispose of it later.

It was a perfect case. Motive, weapon, evidence. And a suspect who would soon be back in custody.

We found the Buick on Chouteau Avenue in St. Louis, just across the MacArthur Bridge. That brought the Missouri law in on our team. And the Federals, if we needed them, now that she had fled across a state line.

The only trouble was, it was a little too perfect.

It was so perfect that it worried me. Going over it again, step by step, I couldn't find a single flaw in our case. Of course, the marks on Randy's body remained a mystery but they might not have anything to do with the murder.

The whole jig-saw puzzle seemed complete, yet I knew some pieces still were missing. I had to find them. Somehow. Somewhere. The badge I wore made me a professional puzzle player and the stakes in this game were life and death.

Before leaving St. Louis, I dropped by the homicide bureau and left a report with the lieutenant there. He said he would assign two men to the case, on top of the city-wide alarm that was out for Grace.

This would teach her to make a sucker out of a cop, I thought. But I didn't get as much satisfaction out of it as I should have.

First thing I saw when I got back to Headquarters was the Commissioner's big Caddy parked at the curb in the official zone. That meant trouble. Police and Fire Commissioner Seibel never dropped around unless there was trouble or an election at hand. The Chief's official wagon was there, too, and he was almost always gone this time of day. His arthritis had been bothering him so that he didn't stay around any longer than he had to. Usually, that wasn't very long.

I started to go upstairs to the detective rooms but the desk sergeant spotted me from his first-floor cage and whistled for me to come in.

"Big pow wow in there," he said when I walked up to the desk. He jerked his head at the closed door which carried the words CHIEF OF POLICE on the frosted glass.

He put his newspaper down, unscrewed a soggy cigar stub from the corner of his mouth, dropped it into a wastebasket reluctantly and came out from behind the crime counter. He tapped respectfully on the Chief's door, poked in his head and announced: "Sergeant Black just came in."

Then he turned to me and told me to go right in. The look he gave me held curiosity mixed with sympathy. The sergeant had been around a long time. He was pounding a beat when I was a baby. He had worked with my father and he knew me all my life. The look he gave me said "Good luck, kid."

As soon as I stepped into the Chief's office, I knew I would need it.

Chief Bergen, a worn, tired man, slumped behind his big, paper-littered desk, but the one in charge was Commissioner Seibel.

He was standing alongside the desk, five-feet-two-inches of flabby politician, and thumping on it with a tiny pink fist. His face was red and his jowls shook like cherry Jello.

Inspector Flynn sat in a leather chair in front of the window, looking bored. He nodded at me as I came in. Not a friendly nod; not unfriendly, either. Just a nod.

"So here you are," Commissioner Seibel yipped. "What have you got to say for yourself, Barney?"

"About what?" I asked, playing innocent.

"You know goddam well about what. About how your prisoner got away. That's what. Can't you even arrest a woman? First she claws you up, then she steals your car keys and gets away clean. I'm surprised she didn't put your handcuffs on you and shoot you with your own gun."

"It was unavoidable," I said. What else was there to say?

The Commissioner whinnied like a horse in heat.

"And another thing," he continued. "What business did you have going over in Madison County and grabbing a prisoner without asking anyone in authority over there?"

"There was no time to ask anyone," I said. "With what I had to go on, they wouldn't have helped anyway."

He went on as if he hadn't heard me, hardly pausing for breath.

"We've had repercussions," he said. "A county judge called me. What could I tell him? I couldn't even apologize, with one of our own officers shot. Puts me in one hell of a spot, politically. What do you think will happen next time I need a favor over there?"

He went on like that for a few minutes more until he ran low on steam. Then Inspector Flynn surprised me. "Barney did a fine job of police work," he said quietly. The Commissioner spun around as if he had been slapped.

"How's that?" he croaked.

"All of us here know we sometimes have to use some means that aren't exactly legal," Inspector Flynn said. "Maybe we hold somebody forty-eight or sixty hours without booking him, when twenty-four hours is the legal limit. Or maybe we get a prisoner that St. Louis wants and we don't bother about extradition procedure—we just turn him over to them in the middle of the bridge, at the state line.

"Maybe we use a little persuasion, sometimes, when a suspect won't tell us what we have to know. Maybe we even look the other way when it comes to enforcing some laws which we don't think should be enforced."

The Commissioner turned a few shades redder. I expected to see smoke come out of his ears. I couldn't tell if his lobster complexion was due to anger, or if Flynn's words were hitting too close to home.

"I don't see what that has to do with this case," he said.

"Just this," the Inspector added. "Barney was wrong in going out of his territory to make a pinch. But only because he hauled in a lousy ex-con punk with big contacts. If it was somebody who couldn't squawk upstairs, nobody would care.

"Going over the line to make an arrest helped crack a murder case. That makes it right, in my books."

"How about the girl who escaped?" Seibel inquired. "I suppose that was a brilliant piece of work, too."

"Cops are like fishermen," Flynn replied. "Every once in a while, a big one gets away. Somebody else will catch it, though. Besides, you'll always catch plenty more if you stay with it long enough."

Commissioner Seibel didn't look convinced.

"The important thing is that Barney solved the case," Chief Bergen growled suddenly. His sudden jump into the conversation startled us all.

"I'm not going to suspend a man for doing a good piece of work. I'd turn in my own badge first. We wouldn't know who we were looking for in this thing if Barney hadn't found out. Of course, we would have found out eventually but he got there first. All we have to do now is pick her up."

Reluctantly, Seibel agreed to let the matter drop. The Chief was old and weak, tired and sick, but trying to persuade him to change his mind could be like arguing with a Sphinx.

I wondered why Flynn had made the speech for me. Perhaps because, despite the thousands he had taken from gamblers, gangsters and flesh peddlers, he was still a cop in his heart.

Perhaps he merely disliked Commissioner Seibel.

Or perhaps he remembered the dead blonde who had reminded him somehow of his own daughter. And, remembering, hated all those who break the law for a living. Even those who had lined his pockets. Even himself.

Or perhaps it was simply the loyalty of one cop for another when a civilian—even a police commissioner—intervenes.

Leaving the Chief's office, I went upstairs and sat at my desk, trying to figure out the next move. It was growing dark outside and the detective rooms were crowded with shadows.

The swivel chair groaned as I parked in it. Back in the detention cells, a throaty voice was singing the lonely words of "St. James Infirmary."

The shadows in the room grew larger and darker by the second but I didn't switch on the desk lamp.

Someone came up the stairs and paused in the door way. He was silhouetted in the light from the narrow hall. His features were wrapped in the shadows but I could see from his outline that it was Inspector Flynn.

"Barney?" he asked, trying to peer through the gloom.

"Yes. Over here at the desk."

I pressed the lamp button and the brilliant white glare struck me in the face, blinding me. I knew how my prisoners felt when they sat in this chair for questioning, the harsh light searching them relentlessly.

Standing over me now, a black shape against the grey-black shadows, Inspector Flynn stayed just outside the light circle. As I had done so many times.

"How did she get away?" said his voice from the shadows.

"She started to bite and scratch me. I belted her one and she dropped. I thought she was out. I went to the bathroom for water. While I was there, she ran outside, grabbed the keys from my car and drove off in the Buick."

"That all?"

"That's all."

"Seibel was worried about the publicity, what the papers would say." He paused to light a cigaret, made it two. His hand came out of the dark with one of the glowing cigarets and offered it to me. He exhaled and a thin blue veil flowed across the light circle.

"As if they ever say anything good about us," he added, thinking of the newspapers.

"Seibel would have busted you to a beat, or worse, if it hadn't been for the Chief," he said.

"And you," I said. "Thanks."

"Don't thank me. It's only that I like to see a man finish what he starts. Now go out and find that dame. I don't care how you do it—that's unofficial—but get her unless somebody else grabs her first. If you need help, you'll have it."

"I'd rather handle it alone, until Radnik comes back."

"What do you plan to do first?"

"Pick up Trudo."

"That's what I figured. We've had his house and the Frog's place staked out all afternoon. He hasn't showed yet. You know what to do when he does. The boys have orders not to nab him until you get there, unless it looks like he's going somewheres."

"Thanks again," I said.

"It's the last favor you'll get on this case," the even, mechanical voice went on. "One more foul-up, and back to pounding pavements. Or worse."

CHAPTER EIGHT

The evening traffic was light and in a few minutes I was on the outskirts of town, running through Whiskey Chute past the stockyards. The cows and pigs didn't smell any better since my last visit.

One of the Department cars was parked a few doors from Frog Gaffney's, where the occupants could watch who went in and came out. I pulled up alongside it.

Tom McGlynn and Jerry Earle were the detectives inside the car. They sat there with their headlights off and their hat brims pulled down as if they were just a couple of stews, loafing. But they couldn't even fool the farmers. The word POLICE might as well have been written all over the sedan in red-and-white letters three feet high.

I wondered if I had that look about me that spells "Cop." I probably did, by this time. Almost every cop did, sooner or later, no matter how hard he tried to look like something else. It was a mark of the business like a lawyer's briefcase or the grease paint on a clown.

"Trudo went in a few minutes ago," McGlynn advised me. "He was driving Gaffney's heap—that Olds over there with the banged-up fender."

"Let's go," I told him.

They eased out of the car without hurry or excitement. They were experienced man-hunters, both of them. Sturdy, sure of themselves. That was another part of the cop's look.

We entered the tavern in single file. I went first, then McGlynn, then Earle. An old farmer sat at the bar, buying doubles for a washed-out blonde with tattooed hearts on her fat left arm. Two men from the yards were playing a pinball machine near the jukebox.

Frog Gaffney was behind the bar, polishing glasses. That was a sure sign he had spotted us. Those glasses usually didn't look as if they were polished more than three times a year.

"Evening, boys," he said.

McGlynn planted himself on a stool at the center of the bar. Earle stood at the end of the bar nearest the door. I went straight back to the tiny room where four men were seated around a table in the glare of a light suspended from the ceiling on a chain.

Three of the men looked like cattle farmers. They were wiry, sunburned, serious. They held their cards close to their chests, concentrating so hard that they didn't hear me come in. The fourth man was the dealer, Willie Trudo.

He heard me and looked up at me with shining marble eyes that saw everything and said nothing at all. The trace of a smile flickered in the corners of his bloodless mouth, then was gone. He put the deck down silently and placed his hand over it, never taking his eyes off me.

"Game's over, gentlemen," I said. "Your dealer just quit for the night."

Only then did the players look up, their mouths gaping open in astonishment. The only sound in the room was the scrape of Willie's chair as he got up. He took his suit coat from a wall peg, slipped into it and preceded me into the barroom. He wore no hat. He was too proud of his wavy, oil-slicked hair.

When he saw McGlynn and Earle, he stopped. He hadn't expected so much law.

"Am I under arrest?" he asked me.

"That depends. So far, I just want to talk to you."

"Then we can all have a drink first."

"Sure," I agreed. "We can all have a drink."

Frog bustled over and poured him a jolt of bourbon with a dash of water on the side. I had a bottle of Stag. McGlynn and Earle had already been taken care of.

The faded blonde down the bar looked at us through a haze of stale booze and muttered: "Cops. Sonsabitches." The old geezer put an arm around her suet waist and clucked at her. He raised his fingers to signal another round but Frog didn't pay any attention to him.

The three card players came out of the back room, chatting quietly. They went on past us and drifted out the door, trying to appear as inconspicuous as possible. They didn't want any part of us.

"Willie here isn't in any trouble, is he?" Frog asked me, straining to make his voice sound genial.

"Maybe. Maybe not. His girl friend is dead. His wife is wanted for murder. Do you call that trouble?"

"Well, well," Frog exclaimed, trying to sound surprised. "Who would have thought a thing like that could happen?"

He rubbed a hand over his bald spot and refilled Willie's shot glass.

"That's enough," I told the dealer. "Finish it and let's get out of here."

We traveled back to Headquarters in silence. Earle rode in the back seat with Trudo while I drove. McGlynn followed in the other car.

When we got him in the detective rooms, we started throwing questions. They were easy, gentle questions at first, then tougher ones.

We worked on him, the three of us, for two hours without learning anything new, except that his wife had an uncle in St. Louis. The uncle's name was Sam and he was a counterman in a hamburger joint on Broadway. That was a big help. There wouldn't be more than a hundred hamburger stands on Broadway, the run-down street which stretches across St. Louis from north to south along the river.

He said he met Randy through his wife and she came to live with them. Then Randy made a play for him. Grace got jealous and kicked her out. He didn't see Randy after that. That's what he said.

We hammered on that point for maybe an hour more until he admitted he had continued seeing her. He said he had been worried about her and wanted to make sure she was all right.

"So you got her a nice safe job out on Collinsville Road," I said.

Willie made believe he didn't know what I was talking about. I sent Earle back to the detention cells to get Shelton. One of them was lying and I wanted to find out who.

Earle came back in about five minutes. By himself.

"Somebody sprung him," he said. "A lawyer came around while we was bringing in this greaseball."

"Can I go now?" Willie said with the trace of a sneer.

"Sure," I said. "Any time."

He stood up and stretched. Then he straightened his necktie, buttoned his collar button and ran a comb through his glistening hair.

"It's been fun, boys," he said on his way towards the door. "If you want anything more, call me."

I followed him to the door. As he reached it, I tapped him lightly on the shoulder. My fist buried itself in his stomach as he turned around. The seat of his pants hit the floor and he stayed there, choking for breath, doubled over and wishing he could die.

"Get him out of here," I said.

Earle and McGlynn each grabbed an arm. They dragged him down the stairs to a car, dumped him in and took him home. When they were gone, I walked down the block to Bowman's long, noisy bar and had a long, quiet drink.

CHAPTER NINE

It was three A.M. when I got home and the shrill ringing of the telephone was unnaturally loud in the pre-dawn quiet. Trying to hurry, I fumbled the key in the lock. I finally got the door open and ran to the bedroom where the phone stood on a night stand beside the bed.

I expected it to go dead as soon as I picked up the receiver. That's the way those things usually happen. But it kept ringing until I grabbed it and then her voice floated over the wire.

"Barney?" she said when I answered. "I've been trying to get you for hours."

She didn't say who it was, but I recognized Grace Trudo's husky contralto.

"Where are you?" I asked.

"Never mind," she said. "I just wanted to tell you you've got it all wrong. I'm not the one you want."

"Then why did you run away?"

"Because you were going to arrest me. You wouldn't have listened to me. I had to get away until I can prove I'm innocent."

"Where are you?" I repeated.

"I'm going to hang up now," she replied. "But I'll never forget the way it was this afternoon. Someday maybe it will be that way again, if you want me."

"Grace," I shouted. "Wait!"

No use. The line was dead. Reluctantly, I dropped the receiver back in place, stripped and called it a night. Lying in bed, I tried to relax enough to lure some sleep. I closed my eyes but I couldn't keep out the things I wanted to forget. Dawn was scrubbing the night away before I dropped into a troubled sleep.

I dreamed she was standing on a long, lonely street, calling my name. She raised a hand and the sharp, bright fingernails beckoned. Her moist, red lips parted slowly and the pink tongue darted out in invitation.

She took a step backward, then another, as I moved forward to crush her in my arms. She moved away from me slowly, motioning to me, and no matter how I hurried I could not catch her. Overhead, the sky trembled and Inspector Flynn's voice thundered: "Find that dame!"

So that was what I set out to do when the dream was ended.

I piled into my car and crossed the muddy Mississippi to St. Louis. I had even less right being over there than I had in Madison County when we grabbed Shelton. That was simply another Illinois county; this was a different state. I felt easier about it, though, because the Missouri cops were clean and cooperative. They had no political axes to grind in our state.

First thing I did was have a cup of coffee. I took it in a diner on Broadway, near the Greyhound Bus Terminal.

The counterman was busy squashing hamburger patties so flat they only had one side. On forty bucks a week, he was trying to make the owner a millionaire.

"Your name Sam?" I asked.

"Yep," he replied, making my heart do a broad jump. "Sam Willoughby. How'd you know?"

"Guessed it," I told him. "I like to look at people and see can I guess their names. You look like you might be called Sam."

"Bull shit," he said, flipping the mashed meat. "Whatever you're selling, I don't need!"

He wasn't as dumb as I thought he was. I kept on talking, though.

"I was kidding, Sam," I said. "I got your name from your niece, Grace."

"Now I know you're lying, mister," he said. "I got only one niece and her name is Rosemarie and she's not old enough to tell anybody anything."

That was that. I apologized, said I must have the wrong party and got out of there as quick as I could without making him more suspicious.

From there, I worked my way south along Broadway. This would be a better bet than north, I figured. Grace had abandoned her car on the south side. The first few places, I ordered coffee, cokes or sandwiches before asking any questions, but the human stomach will stand only so much punishment.

Soon I was merely asking questions. I never knew so many Sams were tossing 'burgers for a living. I must have uncovered half a dozen of them in the first few hours. None was the right one, though.

Most of them answered my questions quickly enough, probably spotting me for a cop. A few were suspicious until I flashed my badge. The badge wasn't any good this side of the river, of course, but I hoped no one would look that closely. As far as most people are concerned, a badge is a badge. Show them a Junior G-Man button or a dog catcher's shield and they'll believe you if you say you're chief of police.

Then there are a few who use their eyes.

One of these was behind the counter of a greasy-spoon on South Broadway near Marion Street. His name, of course, had to be Sam. He wouldn't tell me more than that, so I palmed the buzzer in his face. I didn't give him time to stare at it, but he didn't need more than a glance.

He shoved a cup of coffee at me, excused himself and ducked into the kitchen. When he came out, he was carrying a stack of hamburger rolls. That fooled me for a few minutes, until the two burly dicks walked in.

One of them stood directly behind me while the other, an elderly, grey-haired man, planted himself at my left side.

"Stand up slow and put your hands on the counter, palms down," the older man said.

Spotting the gun bulge beneath my coat, the other cop unholstered his revolver and prodded me in the back with the muzzle.

"Easy," he said. "Real easy till we see who you are."

The older detective hauled out my gun, then my billfold. He peered at my badge, flipped through my other credentials and handed everything back.

"Sorry, sergeant," he said. "I'm Sgt. Morrison and this is Detective Pizzo. We didn't know you were working over here. Sam, here, saw your badge wasn't from our department and put in the trouble call."

He nodded towards the interested counterman.

"He's okay, Sam," he said. "East St. Louis police."

"My brother's a cop," Sam told me. "That's how come I noticed your badge was different. I thought you were trying to pull something."

I told the St. Louis dicks what I was after and they told me to go ahead and nose around all I wanted. They didn't mind that I was out of my territory, so long as I promised to bring them in on any pinch I might make. And I would have to do that anyway. Any arrest would have to be made by the local law, to make it stick.

But, after that, I kept my badge in my pocket. All the St. Louis cops might not be as gracious as Morrison and Pizzo. I kept on along South Broadway, passing all the honkytonks where the hell-raising "hoosiers" hung out. In most other places, hoosier means a resident of Indiana. In St.

Louis, it means a hillbilly or a lowlander who has drifted into town from the mountains and swamps of southern Missouri, Arkansas, Kentucky and Tennessee. Hundreds of them settled along South Broadway.

The bars there smell of unwashed bodies, beer and cheap whiskey. They echo to the sounds of guitar music and the twang of country curses. Fist fights are a nightly occurrence, with knives and broken beer bottles on the later floor shows.

The cops walk in pairs along South Broadway and the stranger who travels there alone should have his insurance paid up in advance.

Two hip-swinging young girls in high heels and too-tight dresses ogled me as I went by. Music floated from open doors and windows. Most of the songs were tear-jerking ballads of the hills and plains, blaring out of jukeboxes. Mixed with them was the chorus of a country hymn, coming from a narrow building bearing the sign "First Gospel Tabernacle."

Worn out from the miles of walking between lunchrooms and my car, I turned into still another hamburger stand and slid onto one of the stools.

"Your name Sam?" I asked the dark-skinned kid behind the counter. I was getting sick of the question. "Sam went off about twenty minutes ago," the counterman said, scarcely looking up from a comic book he was reading. "You'll find him down the block at the Red Door."

"How do I know him?" I asked.

"That's easy. Pick out the drunkest guy in the place and that's Sam. I don't know how he lasted until I came on to relieve him, with the load he's got. Must have spilled some of it, too. The meat smells like whiskey. That ought to drum up some business around here."

I thanked him, left a quarter on the counter and headed for the Red Door. The sign out front said simply "Budweiser," in neat red letters. Other beer ads in the windows read "Falstaff" and "Griesedieck."

The red door which gave the place its name was open and the discordant notes of guitar, fiddle and piano came tumbling out, along with alcoholic fumes.

Three sailors stood at the bar buying drinks for a fat, dirty barmaid with swollen breasts. A tough looking hoosier in dungarees was nursing a bottle of beer. Three or four other nondescript characters lounged at the bar, waiting to see what would happen.

A small, dark, neat man in a grey silk sportshirt was behind the stick. I pegged him for the owner. We had never seen each other before but he nodded at me when I came in as if we were old friends. Evidently he recognized my line, too.

A white-haired boozer with grease spots on his shirt and an empty shot glass in front of him seemed to be the drunkest customer. So I squeezed up to the bar alongside him and bought a drink.

"You serve a fine hamburger, Sam," I said.

He glanced sideways at me with a bleary look that had a trace of shop-worn cunning behind it.

"Sure," he mumbled. "Serve nothing but thoroughbreds. All the also-rans come to us. And the glue factory rejects."

He had a sense of humor, this one.

"Give Sam a drink," I told the man behind the bar. He refilled the shot glass without giving Sam a chaser and he made me a fresh highball.

"Thanks, stranger," Sam said. He wrapped thumb and forefinger around the tiny glass and tossed the contents neatly down his throat.

"Thanks, friend," he said.

The barmaid and one of the sailors grabbed each other and began doing the old fashioned belly-rub in the middle of the floor. A trio in cowboy boots and hats kept sawing away at the music from the bandstand.

Sam and I had a few more and started telling each other the story of our lives. As he had lived considerably longer than me, it looked like a big evening.

"What you got in the sack?" I asked after a while, pointing to the brown paper bag that stood on the bar between us.

"Sandwiches," he said proudly. "Made them myself."

"You planning on having a picnic?"

"Nope," he said. "Gonna take them home."

"For your wife?"

"Not married. For my dog."

"Who ever heard of a dog eating sandwiches," I said, trying to play him along.

"My dog eats sandwiches," he chuckled. "She's a bitch."

He went into drunken giggles at this private joke and it took another shot to bring him back. I decided to hang around and learn more about that sandwich-craving dog.

After a few more drinks, I was convinced he was the Sam I was looking for. And, if he wasn't, it didn't matter much. I was beginning to like it there. The nerve-jangling music sounded like Guy Lombardo if you listened to it long enough and if you didn't go deaf first and had enough in you to tide you over the rough spots.

When Sam teetered back to the men's room, I peeked into his bag. They were sandwiches, all right. And a container of coffee. I doubted if even a dog could stand Sam's coffee when it was a few hours cold.

I bought another round and the owner bought a round and every once in a while Sam managed to buy a round. Next thing we knew, the cowboys and the sailors and the barmaid had gone. The clock said it was closing time. East St. Louis was still going strong, but on this side of the Mississippi the story was: "You don't have to go home but you can't stay here."

Then we were out on the sidewalk, saying goodnight. We shook hands a few times and I tried to remember what I was doing over there in the Times Square of hoosierdom. It had something to do with the murder, but

I wasn't sure exactly what. It seemed I had known Sam a long time and we were bosom chums.

We shook hands again and parted company. We each went a few steps in opposite directions before the owner suddenly unlocked the red door and hollered: "Hey, Sam. You forgot your sandwiches."

That brought it all back, to me and to Sam. He returned to the door, took the battered bag and thanked the man. Surveying the sack sadly, he hiccupped. I walked back to say goodnight again.

"Sanwishes," he said mournfully. "She muss be hungry's hell."

"Who?" I inquired.

He thought that over, trying to remember what he had told me before. "My dog," he said.

So we shook hands again and went our separate ways. I knew I had a car parked in the vicinity, but I couldn't recall where. I walked north on Broadway for a few yards, ducked into the darkened doorway of a second-hand clothing store and peered out to see where Sam had gone.

He was nowhere in sight.

For an anxious moment, I thought I had lost him. I hurried back to the corner, looked around it and saw him lurching off down the side street. I waited until he reached the next corner, then started after him.

He didn't look back but I kept close to the building fronts, in the shadows, in case he should. He was weaving all over the sidewalk. Once he dropped the bag, stooped to pick it up and came within an inch or two of falling on his face. I couldn't figure out why he didn't.

Having retrieved the sandwich sack, he stumbled on his way. My feet were giving me difficulty, too. I caught myself zig-zagging towards the curb a few times and forced myself to walk as straight as possible back towards the buildings.

Three blocks more and he crossed the street and staggered into an areaway alongside a four-story tenement. Light from a street lamp in front of the building flickered into the narrow passage.

As swiftly and quietly as I could without rousing the entire neighborhood, I galloped after him and got through the areaway to the rear of the tenement in time to see him climb the rickety wooden outside stairs to the top floor. He stood there fumbling the key in the lock for several minutes.

When he finally got the door open, he stumbled inside and slammed it shut after him. I wasn't sure at that distance, but I didn't think he locked it again.

I waited there for a while, staring blankly at the space where he had been. That didn't accomplish anything, so I went around front again.

Leaning against the lamp post, I unwrapped a cigar and set a match to it. I looked up at the old brick building, but the view I wanted wasn't so good from there so I crossed the street and tried again.

Something that could have been a face was at one of the top windows. There was a white blur and then it was gone. I shook my head to clear some of the alcoholic cobwebs away and looked again, but there was only the hollow eye of the window in the crumbling brick.

If it was a face, I was spotted. No use wasting any more time there. Trying to keep my steps steady, I walked slowly to the corner and turned north. I decided to circle the block and come up through the areaway.

On the second corner, I came to a police call box. I opened it and was about to pick up the receiver and call the nearest precinct for reinforcements.

Then I realized that I didn't know Grace was hiding out there, that I was out of my territory again, that I was not quite sober, that if there was anything to be done I would have to do it alone.

I finished circling the block and stationed myself about three doors down the street from the tenement, out of sight of the window. From there I would be able to see anyone who might leave by the front way. I didn't think I had to worry about the back. I had seen a high fence around the small, cramped, rubbish-littered yard.

My cigar burned down to a tiny stub before I threw it into the street and started moving again. Almost an hour had gone by since Sam stumbled up the back stairs. I decided to try it myself.

Cautiously, I headed along the areaway, vaguely lit by the street light behind my back. I reached the rear of the tenement and then the stairs. Each one seemed to creak louder than the one before as my big feet hit the ancient boards. The railing shuddered under my hand.

One of these days, I thought, old Sam won't make this mountain-climb. One of these nights he will tumble down the steps or through the railing and break his whiskey-drenched neck.

It probably took no more than ten or fifteen minutes to reach the top deck, but it seemed like a dozen years. Finally, I made it and I pressed myself against the wall alongside the back door to listen for movement inside. If there was any, I didn't hear it.

So I tried the door and hoped it didn't have an automatic lock. It didn't, and Sam had neglected to lock it with his key or draw the bolt. With a slight squeak, it opened.

I went in and stood perfectly still for several seconds, wondering what to do next. My brain machine had too much of the wrong kind of oil.

Then his snoring rushed at me like the roar of a famished lion, It rose and fell in wild, drunken waves of raucous sound. I jumped and grabbed for my gun without thinking. Then I realized what it was and relaxed. The snores rolled through the room and bounced off the walls, shattering the night stillness. I wondered why I hadn't heard them a block away.

I found a book of matches and lit one, shading the glow with my palm. Sam was stretched out on a cot in a corner of the room, which turned out to be a kitchen. There was a sink, complete with dripping faucet, a lopsided table, three crippled chairs, and a cabinet which probably contained the kitchenware.

Behind the kitchen was another room, a bedroom or living room with windows facing the street.

I told myself that if I had been marked for shooting, I would have been drilled when I fired the match. I had been a shining target then. I told myself I had pulled so many boners this night that one more wouldn't make much difference.

So I did what I never would have done had I been sober. I whipped out my trusty .38 and went blundering through the black into that other room.

The clinging breath of her perfume was the first thing I noticed. And the last. Before I could make any more foolish moves, a bolt of lightning cracked me on the back of my brainless skull.

CHAPTER TEN

I awoke with the great-granddaddy of all headaches and unglued my eyes. I was lying on my back in a strange bed. Daylight sneaked in under unwashed blinds. The light sent spears of white-hot pain probing through my skull.

When I tried to move, I found that my hands were locked behind my back. The cold rings of metal on my wrists would be my own handcuffs. My hat, coat, shoes, necktie and gun had been taken off. Otherwise, I seemed to be intact. Except for my clanging head.

I tried to sit up, but the effort was too painful. I closed my eyes and lay there, listening to myself breathe, until high heels tapped into the room. It was Grace and she was smiling down at me.

"You slept a long time," she said.

"No wonder," I snarled. "That was some sleeping pill you gave me. Damn near broke my skull."

A shadow crossed her white face. Concern, perhaps, or pity. Without her makeup, she looked like a school girl, almost, and her unpainted lips were the pale pink of rose petals. Her hair flowed across her shoulders in a wild, dark stream.

"I'm sorry," she said. "I thought you were—somebody else."

"Is that why you handcuffed me?"

"No. After I hit you, I didn't know what you would do when you came to. I was afraid. I thought you wouldn't give me time to talk to you, but if I could talk first everything would be all right."

"Oh, sure," I said. "Everything will be just fine. Now get these things off of me. The key's in my coat pocket."

"Will you let me explain things if I do?"

"Yes."

She went out of the room and came back with the handcuff key. I sat up, my feet on the floor, while she unlocked the cuffs. They were tight and I massaged my wrists for several seconds to get the circulation back in high gear.

Then I grabbed her. My left hand shot out and wrapped itself around the front of her pale blue bathrobe. I yanked her close to me and raised my right to pay her back for the duck egg on my scalp. But my arm froze in mid-air as if it were carved from stone.

The way she looked at me stopped me. She should have been terrified, yet she made no move to fight back or break away. Her mouth opened slightly and her tongue slid between white, even teeth.

"Go ahead and hit me," said the husky, unfrightened voice. "I'm used to it."

She wriggled her shoulders and the robe dropped from them, exposing a livid welt across the pale flesh. I jerked open the robe and pulled it off. Now I was the one sick with horror.

From waist to throat, her lovely body was a network of criss-crossing lash marks.

"Holy Christ!" I gasped, the words strangling in my throat.

"Now you know," she said. "I never showed anyone before. That's why I kept my sweater on before when we . . ."

"Who did it?"

"My husband. I was afraid to tell anyone. He would have killed me, like he killed Randy."

"Are you sure?"

"Yes. I knew when I found the gun, hidden in my dresser. He told me it had been stolen. He had it all the time. When I found it, I got panicky and ran. I was afraid you would try to blame me for Randy."

"But you're not any more?"

"No. It doesn't matter any more, one way or the other. If you arrest me, maybe I'll go to jail or get the electric chair for something I didn't do. But if he finds me, now that I've run away, he'll kill me. I'd rather take my chances with you."

I placed my hands on her bare shoulders and ran the fingertips lightly over her body, feeling her tremble under the gentlest touch.

"Tell me about it," I urged, trying to keep the hatred of him out of my voice and hearing it ooze out in a snarl. "Why did he do this; when did it begin . . ."

"He couldn't be like other men," she said. "There was an accident, I think, years ago. I didn't know it until after we were married.

"The first night, when I was ready for bed, he asked me to walk around the room with nothing on and then he hit me with the bath towel. It didn't hurt very much at first. It just stung. Later on, it was his belt, and then the whip he had made of thin rawhide thongs.

"I stayed with him because there was no place else to go, no one to tell about this thing because I was too frightened and ashamed.

"If I tried to stop him, he would threaten to cut my throat with that big knife he carries all the time."

"What knife?"

She laughed, without mirth. "Look up his record," she said. "He cut a man's ear off once in a card game. Got thirty days.

"The knife was why I had to stay with him so long.

"Then Randy came to our house and it was the same thing all over. I came in late one night from a movie and heard her crying before I opened the door. Not loud, a kind of whimpering, like a dog when it's hurt bad.

"She was sprawled on the living room floor, holding onto a table for support and he was standing over her with that horrible leer on his face and the whip in his hand.

"I took her into my bedroom and bathed the wounds. Next day I gave her some money and told her to get away while she could still go. She begged me to go with her, but I didn't seem to have the strength."

"Did you know she went on seeing him?" I asked.

"No. Not until I heard about the murder. He came home early that night. Early for him. It was about three or a little later. Not more than three-thirty. I could tell something was wrong as soon as I heard the car. He never pulled into the drive fast like that unless something was wrong."

"Whose car did he have?" I interrupted.

"Ours," she said, with no change in expression. "He always took ours when he went out nights. When I went out, I took a cab."

"How about that earring? She was wearing one just like it."

"They were mine. He must have given them to her."

"Didn't you miss them?"

"No. I don't go in much for jewelry. I never thought about them until you found that one in the car."

I wondered how it would feel to know your husband had just killed one of your best friends. And that, in a strange way, they had been lovers. Before I could stop myself, the question came out.

"I guess I should have been horrified," she said. "But I wasn't. I didn't feel too much of anything, really. The years I spent with him were like a nightmare and that was just another part of it.

"When you live with fear so long, it becomes a part of you and you don't realize it's there. Then, when you get away from it, the feeling of it comes back again and you know what it is to be afraid."

She tried to smile. It was a poor effort. Her lower lip trembled and I thought she was going to cry. She didn't, though. I wondered if there were any tears left. She must have cried herself dry a long time ago, I told myself.

"I don't talk much sense, do I?" she asked.

I took her by the arms and pulled her to me. She was trembling. I kissed her forehead, feeling the ivory coolness of her beneath my lips. I kissed her eyelids and her mouth. Then I kissed her mouth, hard.

Her lips were moist and warm, but passive. Desire began to mount in me and I tried to push her gently towards the bed. Suddenly she wriggled out of my arms and stepped away from me.

"Not now," she said. "Please, not now. I want to get away from here, away from the things we were talking about. Right now I wouldn't be any good to you, darling. Later, when I feel better, we'll make love."

She was right. It was no time for it. And I had done without for so long that a few more hours wouldn't hurt me. Yet this was the woman I wanted. Would always want.

She was mine, now. All mine. Her husband didn't matter, for soon he would belong to the undertaker. If I didn't send him there, the state executioner would.

A tiny warning bell sounded somewhere in my mind—the bell that had always meant danger. This time, I ignored it and told myself nothing mattered but this strange, catlike girl with the midnight eyes.

I told her we would go to a hotel, where she would be safe, and register as man and wife. Then I would have to go back to the East Side for a few hours. To check her husband's story bit by bit.

I was sure I could prove he was the killer. If I couldn't, I would take her away with me just the same. This girl I loved could never be a murderess, I told myself. Trudo was the one. I thought of his sadistic cruelty and swore that he would die.

And I vowed I would make her forget him. That I would teach her a gentle, normal love. But was that what I wanted? Could I?

She interrupted my thoughts to tell me Sam had gone to work early, with his usual hangover. He never knew I had followed him home and was handcuffed in the next room.

"Leave him a note," I told her. "Does he know why you were hiding out here?"

"No. I said I was in trouble. He didn't ask what kind. He hasn't the slightest idea. I'll call him later, at the diner, and tell him everything is all right now."

We had coffee in the cluttered kitchen, then went down the sagging back stairs and hunted around the neighborhood for a while until I found where I had left my car on Broadway.

All the clothing she had was what she had worn in her flight from the East Side. I took her downtown and we visited a few shops. When she had about everything she would need, we went to a downtown hotel and registered as Mr. and Mrs. Ed Blackburn from Peoria.

That was close enough so it might explain our lack of luggage. Especially with the packages we were carrying. The desk clerk gave us an impersonal, incurious grin and a monkey-faced bellhop showed us to the room.

The hotel was a fourteen story affair and we were at the top. From the window, we could see the traffic crawling along Washington Avenue like a parade of multicolored bugs. The tiniest bugs were pedestrians scurrying in and out between the lines of larger bugs, racing frantically so as not to be overtaken and devoured.

Grace went into the bathroom and changed into a low-cut white blouse, black skirt and black suede pumps I had bought for her. She was more alluring than ever, and I wanted to stay with her more than I wanted anything else in life. But this time I let common sense throw desire in two out of three falls.

"Have room service send you anything you want," I told her. "Only don't leave the room. Try and get some rest while I'm gone. Or turn on the television set. I'll be back as soon as I can."

She wrapped her arms around my waist and nuzzled her head against my shoulder.

"Don't let him get me," she said in a tiny, mechanical voice. The words sounded as if she were repeating them from memory, without any real meaning behind them any more. A nightmare discussed in the sunshine.

"He won't," I promised her, stroking her rippling black hair. "He won't ever bother you again."

The taste of her lips went with me as I left the room. And the picture of her standing in the doorway, watching me through smoky, midnight eyes.

I left the hotel, crossed Washington Avenue and headed into the chrome-and-leather dimness of Elliott's Cocktail Lounge, a good place to drink where no stranger stayed lonesome very long. But all I wanted was a beer and a telephone.

A redhead down the bar smiled and sized me up as I slid onto a stool and ordered some suds. She stood up and strolled past me to the rainbow jukebox with a rustle of taffeta skirts.

"Play something noisy," the bartender said. "Wake the joint up. None of them hoosier numbers."

The redhead slammed a quarter into the slot and started pressing buttons. The first one out of the box was an Arkansas lullaby, sung by a coyote.

"I knew it," the bartender groaned.

My throat was tight from all the nervous tension. The beer slid smoothly down it, untying the knots. My head still throbbed but the cool beer seemed to wash away the aching.

I signaled the barkeep, gulped another beer and headed for the phone booth at the rear of the bar. The redhead by the jukebox glanced at me, punched another number, followed me as far as her stool.

"Police Department" the tired voice said from across the river. Then the tiredness went away as the desk sergeant recognized my voice.

"Where the hell you been, boy?" he demanded, We been trying to get you all morning.

"Your pal, Big Red Shelton, got himself murdered."

CHAPTER ELEVEN

This time, the Madison County cops had come calling. Two constables had been patrolling the Road while I was making the rounds in St. Louis. They saw Shelton's Cadillac alongside his establishment.

They stopped for a handout. Or to ask how we treated him in East St. Louis. Or to offer their sympathy.

They said they had stopped to make a routine check for law violations.

Anyway, the front door was open so they strolled right in and there was Big Red waiting to greet them.

What was left of him was lying on the floor in front of what was left of the bar.

His throat was cut. So neatly that his head was almost lopped off.

The gash started under one ear and ran all the way around to the other side. It looked like the wide, grotesque, scarlet grin of a circus clown.

He lay in a pool of dried, still sticky blood. The fountain from his jugular vein had poured over just about all of him except the neat white cast on his shattered wrist.

Because the place was a shambles, the Madison County boys concluded there had been a furious fight. I didn't bother telling them I had wrecked the place in the earlier battle with Shelton. Nothing had been added to the wreckage since I left, except another whiskey bottle and a broken glass.

This one was their baby, not ours. But I was sure the two killings had a common denominator. Only the victims and the weapons were different. The killer was the same. And I was looking for a man equally at ease with a knife or gun.

I knew I wouldn't find him at Gaffney's joint, but I went there just the same.

When Frog Gaffney didn't recall the information I wanted, I took him to headquarters and shoved him into the swivel chair in front of my desk.

From the top drawer, I took a two-foot length of rubber hose. It vibrated against my palm like a nervous snake, poised to strike.

"You've seen this before, Frog," I told him, to start a pleasant conversation. "This is one thing I don't like to use, unless I have to. It's up to you." He stared, his eyes sticking out.

"Now, you told me before that Willie Trudo didn't have his car the night that blonde got killed. That true?"

Drops of sweat oozed out on his forehead and his bulging eyes rolled from side to side. His mouth flapped open but no words came out.

There was no sound in the room except his heavy, jerky breathing until I whacked him alongside the skull with the hose. He yelped and raised his arms in front of his face, burying his head in them. I knocked his arms down and batted him again.

"You lied to me, Frog. He had his car. Didn't he?"

"I don't remember," he whined. "Leave me alone."

I yanked his fat arms down again, pinned them there and slammed him across the face from side to side until he sagged limply, barely conscious.

"What about that car?" I asked again.

"He had it," Frog gasped finally. "I would have told you before only I didn't know how bad a jam he was in."

"What time did he leave your joint?"

"About midnight. It was a lousy night. No money customers. Around midnight he said he didn't feel good and he was going home and take some sleeping pills. I told him okay and he drove off. Next morning he called me at home and said if anybody came around asking, tell them he was at the joint until closing time. That's all I know."

"You lie to me and I'll make it so hot for you you'll need asbestos pants," I promised him.

"It's straight stuff," he said, and I could see I had pumped the well dry. He had nothing more to tell me.

The hose went back in its drawer to rest between rounds. I kicked Gaffney out and sent two detectives after him. I told them to stay on his tail, no matter what, and to try and stay out of sight. Maybe he would try to contact Trudo, I told myself.

I wasn't sorry Shelton was dead. But, in a way, I blamed myself. I had told Trudo we had been talking to Shelton. And he knew we had more questions to ask. He must have been afraid of what the answers would be.

Trudo would have gone out to Shelton's place as soon as we let him go, I theorized. If we had held onto him, there would have been no murder. That's why I felt guilty, although I didn't intend to lose any sleep over it.

Now the thing to do was find Trudo. On the long-shot chance that he would pick the least logical place in which to hide, I drove out to the bungalow on Mildred Avenue again.

I parked half a block from the house and walked back cautiously. The windows were dark. No signs of life, but that could be misleading.

The front door was open and I went in with my gun in my fist, half expecting a knife or a lead slug. Nothing happened. I turned on the lights and went through the place as quickly as I could without overlooking anything.

Her room was exactly as I had left it. The faint fragrance of her hung in the air like a caress. As my nostrils caught it, I felt the hunger for her start gnawing at my stomach.

The dresser drawers were full of soft, clinging things, some of which I had seen before I turned them inside out, rumpled through them until something else was under my fingertips. I dug through the clothing and pulled it out.

Coiled in my hand was the whip.

Grasping it by the handle, I shook it and the raw-hide lash danced and quivered as if it were alive. It was a small whip with a hideous daintiness about it. When I snapped it, it made the childish "pop" of exploding bubblegum.

The whip hadn't been in the drawer last time I was there. Or if it had, I had overlooked it. Trudo must have come back and planted it as he did the gun. But Shelton's murder was one thing he couldn't try to pin on his wife.

The house was so quiet I could hear myself breathing. Outside, someplace, a neighbor turned on a television set and the sound blared forth until it was adjusted.

I crossed the hall to the cubbyhole that was Willie's room. He had been there, all right. There were the signs of hurried packing. His bureau drawers were open and empty. So was the closet. He had left nothing to indicate where he might have gone.

His shaving gear was gone from the bathroom. The washcloth hanging on the towel rack had dried and the dark spots that were my blood clung to it. I wondered if he had noticed that before he left.

Off the kitchen was the hallway leading to the rear door and the basement stairs. I switched on the light and went down to the cellar. At first glance, it was exactly the same as other small basements. There was a furnace and a coal bin and the odor of cool dampness.

Beyond the furnace was a partition which cut the basement into two rooms. Revolver ready, I went into the inner room and felt as if I had stepped over the threshold of a world which was insane and horrible.

The room was completely lined with thick padding to cut down any noise. Like screaming. Over the padding was a dull red imitation leather, covering the walls and ceiling. The floor was covered from wall to wall with a rug the same color. It had a springy touch, like walking on tumbling mats.

At the rear of the room was a raised platform, a stage about six feet square. And in the center of it was a hospital bed, the kind that elevates with a hand crank. The kind that can move the human body into any desired position.

It even had leather straps to hold down the arms and legs.

Facing the stage was a modernistic chair, wrought iron and black leather. A squat baby spotlight stood on an ebony stand beside it. I turned it on and it washed the white bed with a hard, bright glare.

Some rumpus room. A room with a view. A modern torture chamber with a lounge chair for watching the floor show. Fingers of nausea stroked my guts as I imagined what had happened in this whipping den. Yet the feeling I had wasn't all nausea.

As I stared about the shining red room, I felt a hot excitement flushing through me. I could almost see her lying there, black hair tumbling wildly, white body writhing against white sheet as the stinging lash rose and fell. I could almost hear the screams which must have split her lips until they were deadened to pain.

I turned off the spot and got out of there. The living room upstairs was back in the normal world. Beneath my coat, I felt the sweat drops crawling down my back, darkening my shirt.

I mopped my forehead with a handkerchief before I picked up the phone. Then I called the office and asked for a man to watch the house after I left.

The Department's black Ford pulled up a few minutes later and Tom McGlynn eased his big bulk from behind the wheel. I walked out to meet him and briefed him on what was happening. He would park down the street and keep the empty house under surveillance, in case Trudo decided to come back.

"Me and Earle just had ourselves a little excitement," he said when I was through with the instructions.

"We was cruising past the Dixie Bar-B-Q when we seen this guy running out. Ernie Todd, the cashier, comes tearing after him, hollering 'Stickup!'

"Well, we get out and each fire a warning shot and then we blast him. I think it was Earle that got him, though. Right through his head. He must have been dead before he hit the sidewalk.

"Ernie said this guy had come in and asked for a dish-washing job, then pulled out this pig-sticker and heisted him. Took about $200 from the cash register.

"Beats me all to hell why they leave that much money laying around loose." McGlynn concluded, an expression of puzzled concern shadowing his granite face.

We chatted a few minutes more, then I returned to Headquarters. Inspector Flynn was waiting for me. He was seated at his desk with the St. Louis *Globe-Democrat* in front of him, beneath a green-shaded desk lamp.

He still wore his wide-brimmed grey hat, tilted now to the back of his head, and a dead cigar jutted from his jaw.

I couldn't read the look he shot me as I came into his office.

He reached into his pocket and took out a dull metal object and tossed it on the desk top on top of the paper. It was a switch-blade knife with a long, deadly, razor-sharp working edge. The handle was silver, engraved with the Gothic initial T.

"McGlynn and Earle just killed a heister," the Inspector said, without looking up again.

"I know. McGlynn told me. I left him at Trudo's as a plant."

"The heister was using this knife," the smooth, unruffled voice continued as if it hadn't been interrupted.

"This dark smear on the blade is blood, probably human. Under the blade is dirt and grass. The T on the handle could stand for a lot of things, but it probably stands for Trudo. My guess is this is what killed Shelton."

I pulled up a chair then and told him all I knew. Or almost all. I showed him the whip, which I'd brought back with me. I told him about the red room and the hospital bed and about the link between Trudo, Shelton and the murdered blonde.

We had gone over most of it before, but I threw in all the latest developments. Except Grace. I didn't tell him I had found her and had hidden her away.

"Shelton was too rough to let some peanut hooligan grab him in his own joint," I said. "It would have to be someone he knew and had reason to trust. Besides, he still had his wallet and diamond ring, so robbery wasn't a motive. He was a personal kill.

"Trudo must have chilled him and tossed the shiv away. The heister probably found it along the road and decided it was too pretty to waste on whittling. That's how I figure it. We should put a nation-wide alarm out for Trudo."

"No," Inspector Flynn said. His tone was like the crack of the whip. "So far as we are concerned, Trudo had nothing to do with this."

CHAPTER TWELVE

I must have shown my surprise, but Inspector Flynn kept on without pause.

"Officially, Trudo is clean.

"And the two murders are separate, distinct cases. Trudo's wife is wanted for the first. The second killer was shot dead in a holdup an hour ago. In case anybody asks you, his name is Emmett Jackson. The papers will be told that Shelton surprised Jackson robbing his place. They fought, but Shelton was no match because of his busted wrist. We won't say how it got busted, of course.

"Jackson beat up Shelton and slashed his throat. He heard a car pull up outside about then and ran out the back way without stopping to get the dead man's billfold. He confessed before he died and we found the murder weapon on him, stained with Shelton's blood. That's how we're going to play it. Is that clear?"

I heard him. I heard every word. Yet I couldn't believe what I was hearing. I could feel the dull burning anger start bursting into flame. There were a hundred things I wanted to tell him, a hundred questions I wanted to ask. Only one of them would come out.

"Why?" I asked. "For God's sake, why?"

"We can't afford to do anything else," Flynn replied.

He unscrewed the dead cigar butt from his jaw, regarded the moist end for a second with studied disgust, then threw it on the floor beneath his desk. He dug into his pockets until he found a fresh one. A cloud of blue smoke billowed from it as he held up a match and puffed.

"The papers would murder us," he continued. "Figure it out for yourself. First the girl gets away from you and we send out an alarm. Then you bring in Trudo and he gets away, too.

"Think what the news boys could do with that. We've had enough lousy publicity without getting any more for turning killers loose. Hanging the Shelton job on that dead heister will clean up the case and make us look good. Quick solution, hero cops, all that crap. It's a perfect out.

"The other case will be forgotten in a few days. Nobody remembers a dead girl very long."

He was lying. I peered through the heavy blue smoke at his tight, strained face and knew he was lying.

"You remember," I said.

"That doesn't make any difference. The public won't. Sooner or later, we'll pick up the Trudo woman and if she's right for it, she'll burn."

I thought of Grace with her long hair chopped off and leather straps holding her lean, hungry body in the electric chair. The mind-picture came and went in a split second, leaving me trembling and cold.

"You can't do it," I said, struggling to keep my voice below a shout. "It was Trudo. Both times it was Trudo."

"Yes," he agreed. "It was Trudo. But not so far as this department is concerned. I got a job to protect. Speaking of jobs," he added suddenly, as if in after-thought, "you're suspended indefinitely."

He dropped his bomb without any change in his inflection or expression. It hit me like a block-buster. The shock was so great that I couldn't do anything but sit there stupidly. I couldn't even find the words to ask why. But I didn't have to, for he told me.

"The Commissioner has been sniffing around," he explained. "He knows Trudo was dragged in for questioning. If he learns the rest of it, we both could get canned.

"If I suspend you, that takes me off the hook. Then I can prove I took disciplinary action in case he comes screaming for your scalp again.

"It also means that you have no further connection with either case, officially. You are free to do whatever you please, even look for Trudo if you want. If you catch him, then we can afford to tell the Commissioner and the newspapers where to go. Until then . . ."

He spread his hands, palms up, in a gesture that said everything and nothing. The fresh cigar was as dead as the old one and the smoke fog was clearing away.

I took the badge out of my billfold, rubbed it against my sleeve from habit, tossed it on his desk. The service revolver and shoulder holster followed. I felt as if I had wrenched out part of my insides and set them there.

"Thanks again," I said. And I meant it. By suspending me now, he was probably saving my job and giving me another chance.

"Barney," he barked as I started to leave the office.

I looked over my shoulder but I couldn't tell what he was thinking. His eyes were riveted to the desk again. On the newspaper there, perhaps, or possibly on the badge and the gun that were part of me. I couldn't tell.

"Take care," he said. That was all. His mouth twitched as he pulled on the cigar without realizing it had gone out.

So that was that. Suspension. No Police Department authority now. No men with clubs and guns to back me up. From here on in, I would have to play it alone. And that's how I wanted it between Trudo and me.

One of us would die.

For the other, there would be Grace. I didn't know what she meant to him but, to me, she was worth all the risk.

I went from Headquarters to my apartment. I shaved, showered, put my blue suit in the closet and took out a tan gabardine one. With it, I selected a white shirt with a spread collar and a dark green tie.

While I was knotting the tie I had to remind myself over and over that I was a civilian now. But the face looking back at me from my mirror belonged to a cop.

It took me maybe twenty minutes to dress. Then I picked up the phone and dialed the hotel. There was an endless wait while the operator dialed the room.

"I'm sorry, sir," the crisp, impersonal voice said at last, "but 1407 does not answer."

Slamming the receiver down, I ran out of the apartment and jumped into my car. Ten minutes later, I was at the hotel. An auburn-haired girl in a neat grey uniform looked me over approvingly as I got on the elevator. Ordinarily, I would have approved of her, too. Her uniform jacket was tight across the breasts and hips, snug in all the right places. But I had no time for such thoughts now.

The elevator ride seemed to take forever. It stopped at four, to let an elderly couple off. A man who looked like a salesman ogled the elevator girl's behind to the tenth floor, where he got off. My stop was next.

"Fourteen," the girl said. She glanced over her shoulder and grinned at me as she opened the door. Then the grin faded as she looked at my face.

My teeth were clenched so tight my jaw muscles ached. Until I knew that Grace was all right, there would be no relaxing. Fear was a chunk of ice inside me as I hurried down the long, quiet, carpeted hall.

My key unlocked the door to 1407 and I shoved it open, expecting the worst. Then the tension let go with an explosive sigh of relief. She was lying on the bed, wrapped in a black negligee. Her eyes were closed and a magazine was beside her.

She opened her eyes and sat up as I came in. The magazine slid off the bedspread and fell onto the floor. The negligee fell open as she bent to pick it up, revealing the full loveliness of her.

Without hurrying, she pulled it together again and stood up, arms spread, lips parted to receive my kiss. "I missed you," she said after a long pause. "What took you so long?"

"Why didn't you answer the phone?" I asked. "I tried to call you and when there was no answer I thought something had happened."

"I was afraid," she answered. "I hoped it was you but I couldn't get up enough courage to answer it in case it was—anyone else. When I finally did pick up the receiver, the line was dead."

Then I told her all that had happened. About Shelton's murder and my suspension. All the things I had done and heard and felt since I was with her a few hours before.

"You're tired," she said when I was through. "Lie down for a while."

She took my hand and pulled me to the bed. She sat on the edge of it, looking up at me, waiting.

In a second more, I would have yielded. Instead, I pulled my hand away. Turning my head, so as not to see her hungry eyes, I told her what I would have to do first.

"I've got to find your husband," I told her. "As long as he's loose, you're in danger. He won't look for you here yet, but he may find you later if I don't catch him."

"Where will you look?" she asked.

"Any place that he might show up. You could help me there. Where did he hang out when he wasn't working?"

"I don't know. The track, during racing season. There were other places, I guess, but he never talked about them. I wouldn't know a single place to tell you."

"How about your uncle?"

"Sam?" She looked startled, almost terrified. "They hardly knew each other. I don't think Willie even knew where he lived. He may have been there once or twice with me, but that's all."

"He might go there to ask about you," I said. "At least, it's some place to start. It's where I went when I was looking for you. Willie might figure it the same way."

She got up off the bed and walked over to me with that flowing catlike stride. She threw her arms around me and pressed her body against me until I could feel the swell of her breasts, the hardness and warmth of her.

"Don't leave me, darling," she whispered. "I'm so afraid when you're not here. Don't ever leave me."

Her sharp nails dug through the cloth of my coat and her lips clutched at mine, demanding that I stay. I felt desire for her grow in me, but I pushed her away, for the night was calling me and a killer was waiting outside somewhere in the dark. The smell of blood to a hunter is stronger than desire.

The light shimmered in the inky pools of her eyes as I left her—a strange, flickering gleam that blinded me until I could not read the thoughts behind it.

"Don't worry about me," I told her. "I'll stop by and see your uncle. Then I'll try a few more places. Then I'll come back. Nothing could keep me away from you very long."

Like a little girl sulking, she turned her back on me and picked up the magazine as I went out and gently pulled the door shut behind me.

The night stretched and yawned like a hungry beast as I walked from the hotel lobby. Cabs and busses honked and jockeyed for position along the busy street. Bar-hoppers and theater-goers were busy making the rounds.

Cutting through the downtown traffic, I turned south into Sixth Street; past the dime stores, the clothing shops, the novelty shops, the giant hulk of Famous-Barr department store, into the honky-tonk midway of Skid Row. Past the shouting, singing cabarets with their sleazy floor shows and painted dancing girls. Past the city's sole surviving burlesque house, the cockroach-littered eateries, the two-bit movie houses, the Broadway factory district and the dismal corner saloons.

Then I was caught in the whirlpool of hoosier honky-tonks again. The sound of brawling, nasal-voiced ballads, fiddles and steel guitars rippled on the night tide. I found a parking space near the diner and went inside, but Sam was gone.

"Got a phone call a couple hours ago and hurried right out," the counterman said.

He wasn't at the Red Door either. The little maxi behind the bar remembered me and wanted to buy a drink.

"Some other time," I told him.

Sam's street was deserted but the blare of radios came from a dozen windows. A dog barked. A baby bawled. Someone tossed a bottle into an alley and it crashed on the cobblestones.

The rickety stairs hadn't grown any sturdier. They squawked and groaned like an old bedspring beneath my weight.

The light was on in Sam's flat and I told myself he must be home. I toiled up the complaining steps to his porch, then shoved open the door and stepped inside.

"Sam?" I said.

He was home all right. I could smell him. The sickly sweet odor of hamburgers and whiskey hit my nose. The smell of old grease, frying onions, sweat and cheap rotgut. The tired smell of aging flesh that has spent too many years without sunshine.

He didn't answer. But he was home all right. He was lying on the pile of rags that was his cot and his eyes stared upward to the naked light bulb and perhaps to something else that he alone could see.

He might have been in a drunken stupor, for his mouth gaped open and a thin trickle of saliva had run down the corner of it, over his whiskey chin. The odor of alcohol surrounded him.

But he wasn't dead drunk this time. He was only dead.

The small black handle of a paring knife protruded from his throat. He hadn't bled much. The blood was a tiny trickle, like the saliva, running down his neck into the wrinkled, grease-and-dirt spotted collar of his shirt.

I bent over him for a closer look at the wound. Even his blood smelled like whiskey.

I couldn't tell if there had been a struggle. But I didn't think so. The room was a mess. But the room had been a mess before, last time I was there. The room probably had been a mess since Sam first moved in with the roaches, the flies and those river rats energetic enough to climb that high for food.

I knew he was dead but, for confirmation, I picked up his wrist with my thumb and index finger and checked his pulse. There was none, as I expected. The flesh was still warm. I figured he couldn't have been gone more than two hours.

He must have come straight home from the diner to meet the killer here. A phone call brought him home. From whom? I looked at the knife handle sticking up out of his gnarled throat. It was all the answer I needed.

I decided it wouldn't do to get caught there. I glanced around the room once more, trying to fit everything into my mind like a photograph, and got set to leave. Then the squeak of the stairs and the clomp of heavy feet told me I was too late.

Quickly, I turned off the light and ducked behind the door. The man on the stairs might have seen the light go off but I had to take that chance. It was safer than being a perfect target.

The footsteps came nearer and the door rattled as a meaty fist pounded it.

"This is the police," a gruff voice boomed. "Open up in there."

The door swung inward, almost banging me in the face. There was a long pause while the cop waited, listened, tried to figure it out. He decided to make his play.

The bulky blue uniform surged through the doorway and I cracked him across the back of the neck with the edge of my palm. That was a trick I hadn't used since the South Pacific days with the Marines.

It was old and rusty, but it worked. Without a single outcry, he pitched forward to the floor. From the way he hit, I was surprised he didn't fall through to the basement. His gun fell out of his hand and clattered on the wooden floorboards.

Once he hit, he didn't stir. I kicked the door shut, flicked on my pencil flash and examined him. He was a middle-aged patrolman, work-worn and tough. He would be all right again in a little while, except for a headache. And that would go away tomorrow. Or the day after.

I moved the flash about until I found his service revolver. Though I had planned to go all the way unarmed, or until I got my own gun back again, I suddenly changed my mind. I picked up the .38 Police Special and stuck it in my belt.

Seeing the unconscious patrolman and knowing I was the cause gave me a strange, frightened feeling. Like a kid who is lost and has no hope of finding home again.

I had ridden all my life with the hunters. Now I knew how the hunted could feel as well.

Yet there had been only one thing to do. I couldn't let him catch me there. I had no excuse, except a weak one. My own Department wouldn't back me up now.

The fact that I was found in a murdered man's room might throw suspicion on me. As a suspended cop, I had no authority, no business sticking my nose in such things. And I had no alibi. If I dragged Grace in, she could be used against me by any smart prosecutor. Triangle, all that sort of thing. My only hope was to get out of there.

I picked up the patrolman's flash and nightstick. The door was still open a crack and I could see there was no one else on the stairs. There was another cop in the yard, though.

"What's going on up there?" he called as I came out onto the porch.

"Sick case," I replied, trying to make my voice sound like the other cop. It wasn't a good imitation, but it was good enough.

The cop started coming up the stairs as I began climbing down. I held the flash in front of me and stayed out of its beam so all he could see was a tall, shadowy form behind the light.

We were both at the second-floor landing when he bellowed: "Get that goddam light out of my eyes. You trying to blind me?"

I threw the light-beam full in his face, then tossed the nightstick. The club hit him in the stomach, catching him off balance, sending him crashing through the flimsy wooden rail. He fell with an angry scream and I prayed that he wasn't badly hurt as I raced down the steps and dashed through the areaway towards my car.

Hurt or not, he was up in a second and after me. His first shot whistled past my ear as I ran. A second slug slammed into the brick wall behind me and bounced off. The third one was on target.

Shafts of pain speared into my left leg, tripping me. Cobblestones banged at my face like brass knuckles but I rolled over, got to my feet again and kept going somehow, until the car seat was under me and I was speeding down the street and the gun was only a cork popping in the night.

The pain spread up my leg into my bowels and stomach and chest, into my throat and my eyes and head. It was a famished demon ripping my guts, shredding my insides and devouring them.

Each time I moved my leg, a fresh wave of pain and nausea grabbed me. At first, I thought of going back to the hotel. Then I realized the blood was flowing down my leg in a crimson stream.

Pausing only for one red light and to pay my bridge toll, I crossed the Mississippi to Illinois and drove straight to my apartment.

There was a first aid kit in the bathroom. I took off my trousers, stopped the flow of blood, washed the wound with antiseptic. No bones were broken, so far as I could see. I was lucky.

The bullet went in the fleshy part of the thigh and passed right on through. There were tiny holes where it came in and where it went out. That meant there need be no probing for a slug.

I wrapped the wound in bandages, limped into the kitchen and poured myself a stiff jolt of bourbon—best medicine in the world. It made me feel like a man again.

Downing it all, I refilled the glass, added a thimbleful of water and an ice cube this time and brought it with me into the bedroom. I took off my shirt, tossed it onto a chair. I fished in the night table drawer until I found my address book, thumbed through it, found the number I wanted and dialed.

A sleepy voice answered after the phone rang for a minute or more.

"Wake up, Doc," I said. "This is Barney."

The voice mumbled several words, none of them clean.

"I know," I told him. "But this is sort of an emergency. Somebody shot me."

The murmuring got louder, hammering my ear drums.

"No," I said. "In the thigh. Bullet passed right through. I'd feel better if you had a look at it, though."

The voice was a mumble again, then the receiver clicked. He would be on his way here in a few minutes. Good man, Doc Kopec. Not the best, or the gentlest, but a good man for things like bullet wounds.

Doc Kopec would come if I called him.

Not because I was a cop. He wouldn't do it for any cop. Just for me.

It was a matter of luck that he did it for me, I guess. I was passing his place one day when a dame stepped out onto the street, and took one look at me, pleading sort of, and then folded to the pavement. I picked her up and rushed her into Doc Kopec's. He gave me a funny look when he saw me and started to say something, something like, "How did you know—" and then he shut up and we put the girl on his table and ripped her clothes off.

She was bleeding, bleeding fast and going even faster. She died ninety seconds after we saw what was wrong. Only *he* didn't have to look.

He had done the abortion and kicked her out of his office too fast, I guess.

He turned to me, his face whiter even than hers, and he said, "Okay, Barney, take me in."

But I didn't.

The girl was Doc Kopec's sister. It was the only abortion he ever did in his life. He had butchered it. It knocked the heart out of him. I knew damn well he'd never do a crooked thing again in his life.

Except—and maybe I was thinking ahead all the time—except if I ever needed him.

We buried his sister in the river weighed down with bricks.

That's Doc Kopec. A good man for things like bullet wounds. In me.

I picked up the phone again and called the hotel. This time, she answered. Her voice was sleepy, too, but she became wide awake as soon as I spoke her name.

"Where are you, darling?" she asked. "Has anything happened?"

"Quite a bit. I don't know where to start. Maybe I should wait until I see you."

"No," she said. "Tell me now. It's about Sam, isn't it? Something has happened to Sam."

"Sam's dead," I told her. "Your husband got him . . . with a knife, like he got Shelton. While I was there the cops came. I had to get away so I slugged one of them. The other one shot me."

I could hear her, and almost see her, gasp at the other end of the wire.

"Darling, you're hurt! Where are you? I'll come to you right away."

"Take it easy," I said. "It's only a flesh wound. It's good as new already. Besides, a doctor friend of mine will be here in a few minutes to take a look at it."

"Are you home now?"

"Yes. No more boy scout hikes tonight."

"I'll come over."

"You better stay where you are," I told her. "There's still an alarm out for you. If a cop spots you, he'll haul you in. And if that happened, I couldn't help you. Not right now I couldn't."

"I'll come over," she said. "You're a cop, too. Remember?"

And she hung up.

Doc Kopec came charging in a few minutes later. He was a wiry little man with a dark, intent face and a frizzled mop of iron grey hair. His face was as wrinkled as his clothes. His black bag was battered and worn but it carried the difference between life and death for many who saw it as I did.

Clucking like a mother hen, he tore off my bandages, probed and patted my thigh, stung me with liquid fire from a small bottle, then wrapped up my leg in clean gauze.

"I should report this," he said when he had me in shape again.

"I know."

"It's the law," he said, trying to rationalize for what he wasn't going to do.

"I'm a cop. I was shot in the line of duty."

"You're a suspended cop. There's a difference."

"How did you hear about that?"

He raised his shoulders in a wide, expansive shrug.

"I been tending your partner, Radnik, too. Dropped by his house tonight to look at his shoulder. He heard about it from somebody at Headquarters. Feels lousy about it. Blames it all on himself."

"He had nothing to do with it."

"I know, I know. But he feels the blame. He says this wouldn't have happened if he didn't get himself hurt."

"You can't duck a bullet," I said wryly. "At least, I couldn't."

The little doctor smiled and put his equipment away. He took a long hypodermic from the bag, filled it, fiddled with it, squinted at it under the light.

"This time, no report," he said. "I hope it was like you say, in line of duty. I'd hate to think you got caught with another man's wife."

That made me wince more than the bullet hole.

"Hold out your arm," he said. He jabbed me with the needle, pulled it out, took it apart and dropped the parts into their case in the bag.

"Now you'll sleep," he said, "I'll drop around in the morning. Then we'll decide what to do with you. Don't move any more than you have to and you'll be okay."

The sedative began working almost as soon as he left. I felt that I had been swimming for miles and the weight of the water was dragging me down. From a long ways off, I heard the door open and close again.

She came in and stood at the foot of the bed, looking down at me. She pulled back the blanket and studied the bandages and the swollen slab of meat that was my leg.

"Did it hurt much, darling?" she asked and her voice seemed muffled in silk as it floated to me through the drug-haze. It seemed to me she kept asking about the pain.

The words floated around me and I tried to answer, without realizing what I was saying or what was being said. She went away from the bedside for a second, to take off her coat, and when she returned she was holding the revolver I had taken from the unconscious cop.

She looked at me steadily, without blinking, the expressionless, calculating gaze of the prowling cat. She stared down at me for what seemed like a long time, the heavy revolver held in both hands, pointing towards me.

Instinct told me to do something, but the doctor's injection had taken full effect. I couldn't move. Then I drifted off into a strange, troubled sleep.

It was the same horrible dream. About the whip. Only I was the victim now. And the pounding in my leg was the whiplash, rising and falling, as steadily as a heartbeat or the everlasting tides.

CHAPTER THIRTEEN

I awoke to the smell of coffee. My leg still throbbed beneath the blanket and bandages, but it was better than it had been a few hours before. My face felt slightly flushed. Otherwise, I was fine.

Grace brought in a tray with scrambled eggs, bacon and a pot of steaming coffee. She placed it on the night table while she propped up the pillows behind my back. Then she put the tray on my lap, so I could eat.

"What time is it?"

"Four o'clock. You slept like a bear. The doctor came by this morning, but I told him you were still asleep. He said he'd come back later."

"Suppose he recognized you?" Not that Kopec would report it.

"I don't think he did."

She sat on the side of the bed and watched me gulp down my breakfast. She lit me a cigaret with my second cup of coffee, and lit one for herself.

She didn't say anything until the cup was empty and the cigaret was almost gone.

"Barney," she said then, "what are we going to do?"

It was a good question. I tried to think of the right answer. It had never occurred to me before, but I didn't have one.

"Don't worry," I said, trying to sound cheerful and assuring. "Things will work out."

"No," she said. The word was final, without hope. "It would be better if I went away. I've been nothing but trouble for you and everybody else. First Randy, then Sam. If I stay here, he'll kill me next, or he'll kill you. With your leg, he could come right in here and murder you and you wouldn't be able to do anything about it."

I managed a grin.

"I'm not exactly a cripple," I told her. "The old man can still handle himself. Besides, I've got that gun you were toying with last night."

"I put it in your dresser," she said. She got up suddenly and took the tray back to the kitchen. When she came back, she went to the window and stood there with her back to me, looking out through the venetian blinds.

"Let me go, Barney," she said. "I'll get a job someplace where he can't find me. Denver, maybe, or the West Coast."

Now it was my turn to say no.

"But I can't stay here," she said.

"If anybody goes, we'll go together. Now don't talk about it any more."

The conversation grew more cheerful after that. She brought me hot water and my shaving gear and she held a mirror for me while I hacked the whiskers off. After that, I decided to try my leg. I swung it over the side of the bed, planted my other foot down and stood up with her holding my arm.

The pain almost turned me inside out with the first step. After that, it was easier. The leg was stiff and sore as hell, but I could get around a little. Things might have been much worse.

While I was limping around the bedroom, the telephone rang. It was Radnik.

"I hear you got it, too," he said. "I'm coming over."

I tried to stall him, to give him some excuse that would keep him away. No use.

"Cut the crap, Barney," he said. "You're in trouble. I'll be there in fifteen minutes."

He hung up abruptly, leaving me holding the dead receiver. I dumped it back in its cradle and told Grace what he had said. It wouldn't do for Radnik to find her here.

She decided to go back to the hotel. I didn't want her to take the risk, but there was nothing else to do.

"Don't worry," she said. "Nobody will recognize me. I'll go straight to our room and wait there. Call me when you decide what we should do."

Her lips were the light brush of butterfly wings on mine. Then she was gone. I didn't think she would have much trouble crossing the river. There was a bus stop two blocks from my house and the buses would be crowded enough for her to get lost on one.

Ten minutes after she left, Radnik walked in. His face was as calm and cheerful as the North Atlantic in a winter gale. He still wore his arm in a sling. Otherwise, he seemed as healthy as ever.

He pulled a rolled-up newspaper from his pocket and waved it in my face.

"Look at that!" he shouted. "It's got everything but your name and address."

Sam's murder was the lead story in the St. Louis *Post-Dispatch*.

"Tipped off through an anonymous phone call, Patrolmen Leonard Frey and John Murphy rushed to the tenement in a radio car," the story continued, after details of the murder and the hunt for a mysterious killer.

"They got there while the killer was still searching the trash-cluttered flat. As Patrolman Murphy entered the building, he was slugged from behind and knocked unconscious.

"The killer then grabbed his nightstick and knocked Patrolman Frey down as he followed his partner up the rear stairs. Frey plunged through the wooden railing, sustaining cuts, bruises and other minor injuries.

"Leaping to his feet, he fired several shots at the fleeing murderer, at least one of which is believed to have taken effect. The killer fell down, as if hit, got up again and escaped in a dark-colored Ford coupe with an Illinois license plate."

The rest of the story was a partially-accurate description of me and what little the paper had been able to dig up about Sam. So far, he hadn't been tied in with Grace or the other murders.

I didn't think the St. Louis cop got a good look at my license number. If he had, I would have had official visitors before now.

"What kind of a mess have you got yourself into?" Radnik said.

"I don't know," I answered, truthfully. "How did you find out about it?"

"Doc told me you were hurt. Said not to mention it down at the office. Then I heard over the radio about this St. Louis trouble and I figured you were the one who got shot over there. Black Ford and all. With Illinois plates, yet. For a smart cop, you sure can pull some stupid stunts. I'm supposed to be the dumb one. Remember?"

We shared a grin on that, but the fun was gone when he asked abruptly: "Why did you kill that old guy?"

"I didn't. He was dead when I got there. Willie Trudo must have killed him. He was Grace Trudo's uncle."

Radnik let out his breath in a long, low whistle. Then we sat down and I explained the whole thing, start to finish, leaving out nothing but my love for Grace and our bedroom scenes. That part of it was not even for Radnik.

"Does Inspector Flynn know where I was last night?" I inquired after giving him the details.

"I don't think so," Radnik said. "But it won't take him long to find out."

"Then what?"

"You know what. Better than me, you know what."

He was right. I knew all too well. Now that I had no badge to hide behind, I couldn't count on the Department to protect me. Inspector Flynn had given me all the breaks I deserved. Now it would be up to him, or someone else like him, to bring me in.

I considered giving myself up, telling the story to Flynn, to the Commissioner, to the St. Louis cops, to a jury if necessary.

But Trudo was still loose and Grace would have no one to save her from him if I were gone.

"How much money have you got?" I asked Radnik. He hauled out his wallet, extracted a wad of bills and handed them to me. There were about two hundred dollars there, I estimated. I transferred them to my own billfold.

"Thanks. You may never get this back, you know." Radnik grunted. Supporting as much weight as possible on my good leg, I limped to the closet and dragged out a traveling bag. Two suits went into it, then shirts, socks, shorts, handkerchiefs, even an extra pair of shoes. I stuck the Police Special in an extra hip holster and fastened it to my belt. It felt like an old friend.

"You crazy?" Radnik asked.

"I can't stay around here, waiting for a frame. I got to go someplace and stay low until you or somebody else gets hold of Trudo. I can't go after him myself for a while with this leg. So the only thing to do is leave town until things cool off."

"This will wash you up," Radnik said. He started to say something more but a look from me shut him up.

When I was through packing, he picked up the heavy bag as if it were a sack of popcorn. He held it in his left hand and helped steer me outside with his injured arm.

"Watch your arm." I told him.

"It's okay," he said and slipped it out of the sling as if to prove it. "Just a little stiff."

He looked towards the garage at the side of the house, where my Ford was parked.

"Better use my heap," he advised, "unless you figure on getting tagged right away."

I slid onto the front seat beside him. He steered with his left hand, but his right rested gently on the steering wheel, ready to take over.

"Stop at Cohen's," I told him.

He shot me a surprised look out of the corner of his eye, but obediently turned into Collinsville Avenue and parked near Sol Cohen's pawnshop, in the heart of the shopping district.

Among other things, people went shopping at Cohen's for guns. In Illinois, you can buy a gun and enough ammunition to stock a fort without a license. Blackjacks, saps, brass knucks are something else again. You have to be a cop to get such luxuries. But anybody can buy a gun. Or almost anybody.

Before we went in, Radnik slipped his arm back into the sling. With my leg and his arm, we were a sad looking pair.

Sol was behind the counter, peering at the works of a wristwatch, his jeweler's glass stuck in his eye socket. He took out the glass and put the watch down and came around the corner to greet us, glancing from Radnik's face to mine inquisitively.

"Hello, boys," he said. "You look like the Spirit of Seventy-Six."

My business didn't take long. I told him I wanted a small gun to carry in addition to my Police Special. I said I couldn't get the Special out fast enough in cold weather, when my topcoat was buttoned. I wanted one to carry in a topcoat pocket.

"Got just the thing for you, Barney. A beauty. You'll love it."

He produced a neat little Banker's Special, a doll-sized weapon that would fit in the palm of a hand. I checked the firing mechanism, squeezed the trigger a few times. Then I peeled some bills from Radnik's roll and paid for it—getting the usual discount reserved for badge boys. Sol evidently hadn't heard about my suspension yet. He threw in three boxes of shells at no extra charge.

Sol was a good friend to policemen, for they were his only friends. And if they stopped being friendly, Sol would probably be lending money to the warden at Menard for twenty years or so.

Pocketing the tiny gun, I went back to the car with Radnik and we started over the nearest bridge to St. Louis. When we were halfway across, I rolled down the window, leaned out and threw the borrowed police revolver as far as I could, over the bridge rail. I didn't intend to get caught with that on me. The little gun would have to do.

Across the Mississippi, the sun was going down. It turned the sky to fire and the muddy stream to molten gold. It held us with its golden eye as we rolled across the bridge. "I hate to see that evening sun go down . . ."

I wondered where I would be when the sun rose again.

A traffic cop was handling the evening rush a few yards away as we pulled up in front of the hotel. He glanced at us casually, then turned his attention back to the endless line of moving vehicles.

Radnik offered me the car, but I refused. He stuck his hairy hand out of the window, with the sling dangling down beneath it, and we shook as people do when they may never meet again.

"Good luck," he growled. "Let us hear from you. And watch the papers so you'll know when we get Trudo."

All the bellhops seemed to be busy elsewhere, so I carried the bag through the lobby to the elevator. The auburn-haired operator was on duty and she seemed concerned as I limped into the car.

"You hurt your leg," she said as if making a great discovery.

"Fell out of bed," I told her.

She gave me a smile reserved for special guests and jockeyed the car up the shaft to the top floor.

"Take care, now," she said when we were there. She stood in the elevator door for a moment as I started down the hall towards the room. Then the door shut with a muffled clang and I heard the car descending.

I put my bag down outside the room and hunted in my pockets for the key. Except for that slight delay, I would have gone barging right in.

CHAPTER FOURTEEN

In the few seconds it took to find the key, I heard the muffled sound of voices on the other side of the door. I pressed my ear to the wood, trying to find out what was going on.

One of the speakers was Grace. The other was a man. The voices didn't sound loud, or excited. It seemed like a normal conversation, although I couldn't tell what was being said.

I took the little gun off safety and dropped it back in my coat pocket with my right hand over it. I didn't want to go in with a drawn gun in case the police were waiting for me. If they had found us, I didn't want any shooting. I would surrender quietly, then try to explain my side of things.

I eased the knob around and pushed gently with my left hand. I was inside the room, door swinging shut behind me, before either of them noticed me.

The man was seated in a chair, facing the bed, his back to the door. His coat hung neatly over the back of the chair and his hat lay on top of the dresser. He was smoking a cigaret. A smoke ring made a halo over his head—the only one he would ever wear.

Grace sat on the bed, facing me, her nakedness partially concealed by the black negligee. Her eyes widened in surprise and she jumped up before I could signal her to be quiet.

"Look out!" she screamed, running towards me.

For a second, I thought the warning was for me. I started to pull out the gun but she threw herself against me, almost knocking me over, before it could clear my pocket.

"Barney," she sobbed hysterically, "he'll kill us."

Willie Trudo swung around in the chair, leaped to his feet, face contorted with fear. A knife blade gleamed in his hand.

"Kill him," Grace screamed. "Don't just stand there, you fool."

Then, for the first time, I began to wonder. Did she mean Trudo or me? I had no time to think about it, though. I got the gun clear but Grace's arms were around me, holding me so I couldn't raise it to fire. Trudo sprang as I shoved her to one side.

The glittering blade drove straight for my face. I got my arm up just in time. The blade struck my wrist, slashing deeply. My hand jerked open and the gun flew out of it.

Before he could come in again, I grabbed his knife arm and hung on. I tried to break his wrist, as I had Shelton's but he fought with the desperation of a fear-crazed animal.

We battled to the center of the room, crashing into walls and furniture. Over his shoulder, I caught a glimpse of Grace's tense, strained face and the look in her eyes was the one I had seen as she stood by my bedside the night before.

She was taking it all in, every blow, with an almost hypnotic fascination.

He was smaller, lighter than I. My extra pounds gave me an advantage until he caught me in the bum leg with his foot. I fell to one knee, doubled over with pain.

Trudo lunged for the kill. I caught his wrist in both hands as it came down and threw him over my back. We rolled across the floor, pounding at each other, gouging for eyes, tearing hair, biting, kicking, slugging, clawing. With my last ounce of strength I brought his knife hand down and twisted it.

Then it was all over. The air went out of him like a punctured tire and he was suddenly limp beneath me, the knife handle sticking out of his stomach. His arms and legs jerked a few times. A wheezing gasp came from his lungs. And then he was dead.

I wound my handkerchief tight around my wrist and tied it with my teeth to stop the fountain of blood. Then, for a long moment, I remained sitting on the floor beside the corpse, fighting to get my breath back.

Grace stood across the room, against the wall, watching us. I thought the shock of what she had seen would be too much for her. Then she began to laugh.

It was a low, soft chuckle at first, bubbling up from her throat. The laughter rose in volume with each new peal. Hysteria, I thought. I struggled to my feet to calm her. And the laughter stopped as suddenly as it began.

"I'm all yours now," she said. "Do you want me?"

Walking slowly, deliberately past the dead thing that had been her husband, she moved to the bed, slipped off her negligee and dropped it carelessly on the floor. She lay on the bed, propped up on her elbows, waiting for me.

And then I knew.

The horror of the thing she was doing, the brutal callousness of it, the way she drank in the sight of blood like a vampire. No sane person could react this way.

Unable to meet her demanding glance, I tore my eyes away. They wandered aimlessly over the room while I tried to revive my stunned senses.

She hadn't been afraid of Trudo. The calm way in which they were chatting was proof of that, now that I had time to realize it. He had removed his hat and coat, lit a cigaret. He had found her and they were talking. But she hadn't been afraid.

Yet when I came in, she was afraid. And she had shouted a warning. But not to me.

"Barney," she whispered. "What are you waiting for?"

I faced her again and the woman I had loved was nowhere in sight. She had been beautiful to me before. Now my stomach crawled when I looked at her.

The pieces all fell together now. The jig-saw was complete. I stared at it and saw the damned thing that she was, waiting for fulfillment now that the smell of blood had stirred her appetite.

"You liked that, didn't you?" I asked, thinking of the way she watched us as we fought our death struggle. "You like to see people maim and kill each other. It made you feel good, thinking we would murder each other over you."

Her pink tongue darted out, licked her lips.

"You got more thrill out of that than you could get from a whip any more. Trudo whipped you, all right, but you loved it. Didn't you?"

"You can do it too, Barney," she whispered. "You want to, don't you?"

Yes, I wanted to. But not for thrills. I wanted to smash her with my fists for the way I had felt about her, for the thing which I knew she was.

I picked up Trudo's coat and drew his billfold from the inside breast pocket. As I opened the wallet, a number of snapshots fell out.

I was bending over to retrieve them when Grace sat up and saw what I was doing.

"Give me those," she said. Her voice had the tautness of near-hysteria. Without answering her, I held the snapshots to the light for a good view. And then I saw what insane evil the human soul can spawn.

The pictures were of Grace and Randy. They were taken in the red-lined basement room of the Trudo home. They showed all the uses of the hospital bed and the whip. They were pictures of the damned, as lovers and as demons.

"Give me those," she demanded again. Shuddering with disgust, I turned towards her and stared into the muzzle of the Banker's Special.

"So that's how it was," I said. I ripped the snapshots in half and threw the pieces at her. "It was you and Randy, not Trudo."

"He used to watch us," she said, sneering at the corpse on the floor. "That was the way he got his thrills. He was a crawling worm, too weak to take what he wanted. All his life, he was afraid.

"That's why I married him, to make him squirm. He wanted me, but he knew he could never have me because he was afraid to do what I wanted. Randy wasn't afraid. She knew what I needed—what we both needed.

"I loved Randy" she said. "Then I caught her out with Willie, in a cheap tourist camp. She said she couldn't go through with what we were doing any more.

"I couldn't stand the thought of them together. One night, after he came home and took sleeping pills, I took the car and went to get her. She thought it was Willie when she saw the car. She got in. Then she saw it was me. She begged and pleaded with me not to kill her. She said she would do anything I wanted if I let her live. She was wearing the earrings I gave her. When she got out of the car in the Valley, she was crying and I shot her.

"After that, I couldn't stop killing. Shelton knew about Randy. Or he guessed it. He would have told I called him that night, after you released him, and he came over to St. Louis and drove me back to his place. He wanted to go to bed with me. After I killed him, I walked back to town and caught a cab from there to St. Louis.

"My uncle suspected I was mixed up in something serious. He wanted me to go to the police. I was afraid he would talk to some of the cops he knew, while he was drunk. I was sorry about him, but it couldn't be helped. I was on my way back to the hotel while you were trying to call me. You were the only one who didn't know."

She started to laugh again, a harsh, mirthless laugh. She threw her head back and let the sound out. Slowly, watching her carefully, I inched forward, towards the bed.

"Why didn't you kill me last night when I was asleep?" I asked.

"You were my alibi," she said. "You would have sworn you knew where I was when Shelton and Sam died."

The crazy laughter brought tears to her eyes. "You would have done anything—for love," she shrieked.

And then she stopped laughing. Her eyes went soft and her mouth loose. Only her fingers stayed the way they were, tight on the gun.

"You would have done anything for love," she said again. "You poor, poor fool." Her eyes filled with something alien. Tears. "Love. Darling, darling, if only we—" And then she stopped. She began to laugh again, harsh, painful, racking laughter.

And that was the greatest joke of all. I wanted to laugh with her, but there was no laughter left in me.

"What about Willie?" I asked, moving another step forward. If I could keep on talking, perhaps I could keep her distracted until I was close enough to try for the gun. "How did he find you?"

"I knew where he was staying," she said. "I called him. He was hiding out because he was afraid of me and he didn't want to come over here. Then he agreed to talk things over.

"He was so scared he couldn't keep from shaking. He could hardly light a cigaret. I told him to take off his coat and relax. That's where you came in. Willie must have known one of us was going to kill him. And you took care of that."

I was almost there now. The foot of the bed was a few short steps away.

"Give me the gun," I said quietly. I held out my hand.

Our eyes met and the light in hers flickered and danced. Their black depths beckoned me, as they had done since the first.

"Give me the gun," I whispered.

"Yes, darling," she whispered back. And then she fired.

There was the choking smell of gunsmoke and the sledgehammer blow of the bullet slamming into my chest and the cop's instinct that made me throw myself to one side as the second slug whistled by. And there were the black depths rushing up to drown me.

Then there were shouts and screams and pounding on the door. I dragged myself back to consciousness and saw through the swirling brain mists that she had climbed through the window.

Naked, she stood hesitant on the ledge, staring down at the bugs that were people and automobiles.

"Open up in there!" a cop's voice bellowed as his burly bulk battered the door. I crawled across the floor to the window. It seemed to take a year. I was afraid she would look over her shoulder and see me coming, but she kept staring at the street scene below, her wild hair blowing in the wind, arms spread like wings of a bird poised for flight.

Trying to keep from passing out again, I clamped my teeth together and forced myself up to my knees by the window ledge. As I grabbed for her, she turned and saw me.

She screamed and stepped out into space. I caught her by the hair as she leaped. She almost pulled me through the window after her but I braced myself against the sill and tried to haul her in. She dangled there for several seconds while I strained desperately to pull her back.

The effort was too great. Strands of hair tore loose in my sweating hands. Her pale body plunged towards the concrete, while her scream, for an endless moment, remained suspended in the twilight-soft air.

I felt people rushing into the room, tearing me from the window, shouting questions that I did not understand. The blackness swelled towards me again but before it reached me, I clenched my fingers over the long, silk-smooth threads of hair and held them tight.

And then the blackness, embracing me, forever. And it was good.

THE END

DARK THE SUMMER DIES
by Walter Untermeyer, Jr.

1

Working at the pool wasn't too bad a job for a guy during the summer. I was supposed to be the assistant swimming instructor, but I was really just Tony Bianchi, general flunky. Sometimes I even helped out at the soda fountain. When the weather was okay, the kids turned out in droves for lessons, so I was in and out of the water all day. Diving was my sport at school. I won the interscholastic championship, and the coach thought I was pretty terrific. In fact, I might get a scholarship this fall to a swanky prep school in Pennsylvania and the following year to a certain college.

Jim Clark, my boss, had a swimming scholarship out West. He was a sensational back stroker. Jeez, he plowed up the pool like an outboard motor, but when it came to diving he wasn't much. That was where I fitted in. Jim was a good guy but conceited as all hell. Big and blonde with a crew cut, he looked a little like Van Johnson. I guess he was good-looking all right, but maybe he wasn't as hot as he thought. He kept telling me I was the slender emaciated type, but not to worry because a lot of girls went for skinny guys too.

Jim was majoring in psychology and always had the answer to everything. He was constantly puffing on a pipe. It gave him a tweedy air. The babes flocked around him. Jim said their tongues were hanging for him to ask them out, but he didn't want to mess around with any of the club members. He thought it was poor policy, but maybe that was just sour grapes because a lot of those society babes wouldn't want to date a guy who worked at the club even though he was a college man—not so much the girls themselves, but their stuffed-shirt mothers. There was always an excess of girls, and maybe some of them wouldn't have minded going to a movie or for a ride some evening, but I wouldn't have had the nerve to ask, and it didn't matter so much because I sort of had a girl. That still didn't stop me from looking over the field.

There sure were a lot of luscious-looking babes hanging around the pool week-ends. Jeez, sometimes it drove me crazy to see them lying around in those suits which showed everything they got. You know how girls take down the straps of their bathing suits so that they get an even burn. Sometimes when they sat that way around the edge of the pool with their feet dangling in the water, you could walk around and see most of their breasts without even trying. It was a funny thing about girls. If they suspected you were looking, they would pull up their suits or put their hand there so you couldn't see, but if they were so modest why did they expose themselves in the first place witha lot of guys around. Another thing, they lay around in the sun on their backs with their knees up, in wide, loose shorts so you could see almost everything they had below the waist. Some of the babes spent the entire day hitching their suits up on top and pulling them down around the thighs. It was really hard for a guy to keep his mind on his job. Sometimes I got to thinking about it so much I had to go down to the locker room and cool off.

The pool at the Highridge Country Club closed at six o'clock. A few members came later after golf or tennis to take a dip, but they weren't supposed to swim after Jim and I went off duty. I started taking in the umbrellas, pads and cushions around five so that by closing time all the gear was stowed away. If anyone showed up later, that was their own business. Sometimes after the dances, the members even swam at night, but nobody really cared. After closing, Jim and I went over to the main club house where we got fed. We had the same chow for which the members paid anywhere up to five bucks a dinner. I ate like a horse. For a thin guy, I sure could pack it away. Jim always told me I was the biggest liability the club ever took on. Usually we ate alone. The golf and tennis pros were married and went home. Jim and I got along pretty good.

Jim had a car, and he was usually willing to let me use it for three bucks a throw provided I put in some gas. It was worth it because what can a fellow do on a date without a car, and I didn't always like to ask my old man. Jim's car wasn't exactly new. It was a 1941 Ford, but it was a convertible job, and any car with the top down looks pretty classy. Girls seem to go for convertibles. They'd rather ride in an old convertible than in a shiny, new sedan. Of course, if you had a new convertible that'd be even better. I guessed there was something romantic about riding with the top down and the breeze mussing up your hair and being able to look up at the stars. Jim's car had a radio too. When I used his car for the evening, I didn't bother to go home first.

2

It was the Fourth of July. Jim and I had polished off a couple of lobsters for dinner, and then I went down to the locker room to shave and shower. Nobody was around. The attendants had gone. It made me feel like a big shot using the same shower, the same can, the same razor all the tycoons around the club used. The showers poured from triple heads. The size of the droplets were adjustable from a large, heavy downpour to fine, stinging needles. There was a low white stool in the corner of each shower stall. I pulled the stool up under the spray and just sat as cascades of warm water poured over me. Then I adjusted the thermostat cooler and cooler until I couldn't stand it. I never used less than a couple of towels to dry myself. Then I powdered from head to foot. It was sort of a ritual with me. At the wash basin there were always clean razors and fresh blades. There was fancy after shave lotion and a selection of hair tonics. When I was all through, you'd think I had had the full treatment at a swanky barber shop. My black hair was slicked down as much as possible to keep out the wave. I surveyed my face in the mirror, a gaunt face with high cheek bones and thin slightly aquiline nose. Not what I would have picked out for a puss if

I had had a choice. Couldn't worry about that now. It was mine, and I was stuck with it. I started to get dressed—dark grey slacks, a white button-down shirt and a red and green bow tie, plaid socks, moccasins and a brown checked sports jacket. Betty always told me I looked like I had stepped right off the Princeton campus. She was my girl. I went upstairs to Jim's room to get the keys for his car. He was lying in his shorts on his stomach on his bed, reading. I took three bucks out of my wallet and handed it to him.

"Leave it on the bureau," he said. "Keys are in the upper right hand drawer." I opened the drawer and slipped the keys in my pocket. "Push in my regards," he said as I was leaving.

"Cut it out."

"What else are you wasting all your time and dough for?"

"Betty's not that kind of a girl."

"Don't be so naive. They're all that kind of a girl."

"What do you know about it? Listen to who's talking." Sometimes Jim just burned me up.

"I'm telling you."

"Shut up, willya," I said walking towards the door.

"What do you do all night? Hold hands?"

"None of your damn business." I slammed the door and went outside.

All the fellows at school talked the same way, and it always made me feel like a dope. Maybe I was slow or something, but with Betty, Jeez. What would have happened if she had gone out with an operator like Jim? Nothing. He was a lot of hot air.

Outside it was just starting to get dark. Ominous clouds were gathering overhead. I found Jim's car. The hinges on the door were sprung, and I had to slam the door several times to close it. I turned the key and threw the ignition switch. I pushed the button on the dashboard to start the engine. It roared through the half shot muffler.

I stayed off the main drags. Some of the roads weren't really short cuts, but I liked going all sorts of different ways. Spasmodic noises of firecrackers punctured the dusk. Even though fireworks were against the law, some of the townships and a few of the private clubs had displays by special permit. Betty and I were going where you could see the exhibit put on by one of the yacht clubs every Fourth. I was a few minutes early when I finally found a parking space around the corner from Sully's Drug Store.

3

Sully's Drug Store was where Betty worked as a cashier. The store was open evenings, but her uncle owned the joint. She could get off pretty much when she pleased. Betty was really just a kid. She was only a junior last year, but she was real sweet and acted much older. She had green eyes and gorgeous, silky reddish-blonde hair which was straight and fell forward over her forehead in bangs. I always kidded her by saying she looked like an English sheep dog, but her hair was really sensational. People always turned around to look at her. She was kind of thin and sort of flat chested, but maybe that's because she was still young. Anyway, she was a swell kid. Everybody at school thought there was a thing between us. I guess I was pretty crazy about Betty at that.

Butterflies flapped around in my stomach like they always did just before I would do anything, like go in a swimming meet or take an exam or call for a girl. I looked at myself once more in the darkened reflection of the store window and pulled at my tie. Then I pushed open the door. The store was fairly crowded. There were only a few vacant seats at the counter. A half a dozen other prospective customers were milling around looking at the toys, book racks, haberdashery and the other stuff you generally found in a drug store. Mr. Sullivan was at the cash register ringing up a sale for a couple of packs of cigarettes. The customer left the matches which Mr. Sullivan tossed back in the box. I waited until the customer walked away.

"How's the business, Mr. Sullivan? Looks pretty good."

"Lot of lookers. Nobody spending any money." His bald head glistened under the overhead light "Betty'll be out in a minute. Excuse me." He drifted across the store to the drug counter to take care of a man with two kids in tow. I watched him as he turned around to mount his rolling step ladder. Then Betty appeared.

She entered the store from the back door which led to the upstairs apartment where the Sullivans lived. I took all of her in at a glance as she strode across the store, and so did a couple of guys sitting at the soda fountain. She was dressed in a light blue affair over which she wore a white sweater, buttoned down the front. Blue and white shoes completed the outfit. She looked strictly from *Mademoiselle* or *Vogue* or one of those fashion magazines she was always reading. Her soft reddish-blonde hair turned up at the ends just above her shoulders.

"Hi, Tony," she said, giving me a peck on the cheek.

"That's a swell outfit," I said, noticing the dress was cut low in front and held together by a small gold bar pin.

"You look awful nice yourself." She linked her arm in mine as we started to leave. Mr. Sullivan was still up on the ladder searching on the top shelf. We didn't bother to say goodnight.

I opened the car door, and Betty slid in. She always sat in the middle of the seat close to me. The movie house was across the street. Fred Astaire's name was blinking in colored lights. Betty had seen the picture. It was lousy, but Fred Astaire was just adorable. He's wonderful in anything, Betty was saying.

"He sure can dance," I said.

"I love the way he sings. He's so cute."

We had almost reached the Yacht Club by the time we had disposed of Fred Astaire. We drove by the main entrance which was flanked by wooden pillars with red and green ship's lights on top. You could get a full view of the entire show from a neighboring semiprivate beach. It was dark now. The fireworks had already started. I found Betty a place to sit on the stone wall abutting the sand. I stood up behind. They set off the display from a barge anchored just off shore. We watched the balls of fire arch into the sky and burst into sprays of colored stars which showered down and then extinguished. There were ohs and ahs from the crowd to greet the more spectacular displays. It ended with a firing of rows of pinwheels. Hand-in-hand we ambled through the crowd back to the car.

Afterwards we drove to Mack's Cabin, a sort of night club on an island off-shore. It was a small, dingy sort of place with checked table cloths, but they had a piano player. There was no cover or minimum, and since Betty only took a Coke or lemonade, it wasn't too expensive. Besides, a fellow from school worked there as a busboy and sometimes he brought us a sandwich without putting it on the check. The piano player knew a lot of the Yacht Club set. He was popular with the married crowd because he played a lot of the old favorites. He also recited off-color poems or stories to a musical accompaniment. It was fast becoming the spot for the final nightcap. You used to be able just to drive up and park, but lately an attendant came to take the car for you and hand you a check. He stopped you at the entrance with a flashlight. Inside, the place was badly lit, smoky, jammed. The stocky ex-bartender who owned the joint showed us to a small square table against the wall in the back. I didn't see my friend. Betty ordered a Coke, and I took a bottle of Bud.

There was a big party at a long table next to us. They were dressed to the teeth, the women in evening clothes with fur jackets thrown over the backs of their chairs, the men in white tuxedo coats. They were all leaning toward a man at the end of the table who was telling a story with violent gestures. They were laughing uproariously. The pianist across the room was idly striking a few chords as he chatted with several couples who were leaning on the back of the small upright piano. The waiter brought our drinks and another round of some fancy fruit concoction for the people at the next table. The story teller must have reached the climax as everyone swept back in gales of laughter. The blonde knocked over her drink violently and some of it splashed on the sleeve of my jacket.

"Darling, I'm so sorry," she said to me. She took a handkerchief from the breast pocket of her escort, leaned toward me and dabbed at my sleeve. She was an attractive woman, in her late twenties or early thirties. She bulged voluptuously over the top of her strapless white evening gown. The man next to her made a futile gesture in my direction and smiled indulgently.

"That's okay, Ma'm," I said. I finished the mopping with my own handkerchief.

"I hope it won't stain," she said, still poking at the spot. I noticed the sparklers on her wrist and the big rock on her finger. As she leaned further toward me, she nearly lost her balance. I grabbed her arm to help her right herself. She smiled at me. "I'm all right," she said.

The waiter came with a towel to wipe up their table. The man beckoned to him. He said something to the waiter and slipped him a bill. The waiter soon returned with three drinks, another for the lady and one for Betty and myself.

The man was slender, dark complected, his scalp sparsely covered by a few strands of hair. I tried to catch his attention, but he was engrossed in conversation with a man on the other side of him. I nudged the blonde. "Is that your husband?" I asked, indicating her escort who had evidently bought us The drinks.

"This one?" she said, kissing him on the cheek and leaving a red mark. He wiped his hand over the spot and looked around.

I caught his eye. "Thanks, mister," I said holding up the drink.

He waved his hand in a casual salute and then returned his attention to his friend. The blonde was sipping her fresh drink. She was looking at us over the top of her glass. She said in a stage whisper. "Your date's adorable. You're a cute couple."

I didn't know what to say, but fortunately the lights dimmed and several spots focused on the piano player. He started with "Stormy Weather." The blonde next to me was beating out the rhythm with a swizzle stick. I looked at Betty and shrugged my shoulders. I set my beer aside and sampled the drink. It was heavily flavored with rum and it was sweet. I sipped it through the straw. Betty tasted hers and pushed it over in my direction. One of the gals who had been hanging over the piano took the hand mike. "Just one of those things . . . Just one of those things . . ." She had a low throaty voice, and she gave the song her all. She wasn't part of the act, probably just a friend of the pianist, but she liked cuddling the mike. She sat down to polite applause. The pianist continued. After each piece he would stop to listen for the names of songs people were hollering at him. There was a growing insistence for "Vera, the Venereal Virgin." He sang about a dozen different verses, drowning out the obviously dirty words on the piano. The house rocked with applause, whistles and shouts of encore. I had finished my drink and part of Betty's.

When the lights went on again, the big party got up to leave.

"Goodbye, cutie," the blonde said to me, clucking me under the chin.

"Goodbye, honey," I said easily, feeling a little high. Betty looked on disapprovingly. "What's her trouble?" Betty said.

"No troubles. She said you were adorable."

"That's not much of a compliment in her condition," she said.

"I agree with her."

"You're drunk too." She was embarrassed, but I could tell she was pleased.

Another party came in to occupy the big table. They were middle-aged, the men in loud sport jackets, the women bulging out of bare back dresses. I asked for the check. "It's been taken care of," the waiter said.

"No kidding?"

"The gentleman who was sitting at the next table," the waiter explained. I left him a buck tip.

On the way out, I saw my friend Joe Tino clearing off a table. We said Hi and Where you been and How you doing and So Long.

Betty and I sauntered toward the car. The man with the flashlight approached. I fumbled through all my pockets for the car check, without success. I pointed out the car and he brought it over. He opened the door for Betty and then ran around to extend the same treatment to me. I was feeling like a big shot. I handed him a buck, too.

As we moved off, I snapped on the radio. I reached for Betty's hand and she slid over next to me. Just a few hundred yards further, I found a side road leading to the water. It was starting to rain. We came to a section of the narrow road which ran across the beach. There were several other darkened cars, spaced for privacy.

I found a spot in full view of the water and turned out the lights. It was raining harder. The drops pattered on the canvas. It was dark except for the distant lights across the sound. The waves lapped the sand. I slipped my arm around Betty, and she cuddled up. I kissed her forehead and her cheek before finding her lips. Her arms slid around my neck. We held each other tight. My left hand wandered over her arm, her shoulder and furtively down to her breast. She shifted her position. Her mouth was moist and yielding. I fumbled with the pin at the top of her dress. I removed it and then slid my hand down her dress. She tightened a little and then relaxed.

My initial success encouraged me. What would Jim think if he could see me now? Our mouths were hungry. Her flesh was soft and warm. She placed her hand on top of mine to halt its progress. I remembered Jim's words. They have to make a show of resistance to salve their conscience. Suddenly Betty sat up, and her hand slapped hard against my cheek. She pushed my hand away violently and jumped to the other side of the car.

"What's the matter?" I said, rubbing my cheek. Any bravado which the couple of drinks might have given me had vanished.

"You don't have to ask," she said. "Take me home."

It was a frustrating climax. "It won't happen again, Betty," I said, moving after her and holding out my arms.

She pushed me away. "Please, Tony, take me home," she said. She didn't look at me. I moved back to my side of the car. We sat for a while listening to the rain rattle on the roof.

"Betty," I started in after a while.

"Let's go, Tony," she said. "It's getting late."

I pulled on the lights. The falling rain glistened in the yellow beams. The back wheels spun in the mud before grabbing. The window wipers bobbed back and forth.

There was no conversation, just the rain and the swishing of the tires as they splashed along the wet pavement. I looked over at Betty. She was gazing out her window.

When we pulled up in front of her house, she opened the door immediately. I started to get out. "You don't have to take me in. Good night, Tony." Then she beat it up the walk to her house. I watched until the front door closed, perhaps with finality. My feelings were a combination of indignation and regret. My pride came to the force. The hell with Betty. As Jim says, a million fish in the sea. At home, I tiptoed upstairs without turning on a light. My kid brother, Mike, was asleep in the adjoining bed. He stirred as I closed the door behind. I found my pajamas in the dark and got undressed. Bed felt good. The rain must have stopped. I finally dropped off to sleep.

4

I woke just as it was beginning to get light outside. The top sheet was all bunched up. I was hot and uncomfortable. It was only five o'clock. I straightened out the bedding and tried to go back to sleep. I kept reviewing last night's scene, my mind full of recriminations. I could still see the outraged look on Betty's face. She trusted me, maybe she loved me, and I had taken advantage of her decency. I spoiled everything with my crudeness. That Jim was a big bag of wind. I had been offensive, and if she never spoke to me again I could only hold myself to blame. I had wanted to be an operator, but Jeez how stupid could I be. If I had played my cards smoothly, if I hadn't been such a pig, everything might have come in time. And what would it have proved anyway? I tossed from side to side. Soon the sun would be inching through the window. I got up and pulled down the shade. I would phone Betty and beg her forgiveness the first thing. If she'd ever see me again, I'd never lay a finger on her. I must have dozed off again because when I looked at the clock again it was eight-fifteen. I examined the clock. The alarm was set and the knob pulled out, but I had forgotten to wind the spring. I jumped out of bed. My brother was still dead to the world. I never understood how he could manage to spend so much time in bed. I pulled out a sports shirt, trousers, moccasins, and dressed rapidly. My father was at the table, eating breakfast.

"Hi, Pop," I called, not going in to see him.

"Good morning, Tony. No breakfast?" he said, turning around.

"Not today. Too late."

"Tony," my mother called from the kitchen. "You've got to eat breakfast."

I didn't feel like talking to my parents. Not this morning. "I'll grab a bite somewhere," I said, banging out the front screen door. My old lady was muttering she didn't know what was the matter with that boy lately. Poor mother—always fussing about my physical well being, when that was the least of my problems. I jumped in the car and unfastened the three hooks which moored the top. You could feel the heat already. It was going to be a hell of a day. I pulled the knob which controlled the top. It strained without lifting. A shove set the mechanism in motion. The top rolled back the rest of the way on its own power. The sun slanted through the trees, casting curious shapes of light and shadow on the road. You had to feel good on a morning like this.

I took a shower before changing to my trunks. Jim was out at the pool sitting under a red and yellow striped umbrella which sprouted from the center of a metal table. He was reading the sports page of the New York *Times*. The members never arrived before ten o'clock.

"Some ball game yesterday. Musial tripled in the eleventh," Jim said. Then he looked up at me. "Hiya, Casanova," he said in a loud kidding voice. "How's my car?"

"No complaints," I handed him the keys.

"You didn't mess up the seats, did you?" he said.

"Get your mind out of the gutter."

"How about those footprints on the dashboard, upside down?"

I didn't answer.

"You must have done all right," he continued. "I know that significant silence." I could have popped him one.

"Shut up," I said. I busied myself with the beach chairs.

Jim was booked for lessons almost all day. More kids wanted to learn to swim than dive. Diving was something they sort of picked up for themselves once they learned to feel at home in the water. I had the Nelson kids from eleven to eleven-thirty, and that was it. A couple of kids, one five and one seven, showed up at quarter of ten for their first swimming lesson. Jim usually taught from the edge of the pool with me in the water demonstrating as he explained. I could already feel the heat of the sun on my shoulders.

Some of the golf bugs might play a full round today, but most of the real golfers would quit after nine holes. The tennis courts were practically deserted. Those who played came to the pool after a set, their faces red and their clothes dripping with perspiration. By late morning the crowds started to arrive. The older people sat in the shade most of the time playing cards or backgammon. The younger ones spent their time showing off. The girls strutted around in their bathing suits like pushcart peddlers showing their wares. The fellows were tossing a football or fooling around in the water. I stopped a bunch of guys playing tag. The old fogies who set up the rules didn't want anyone chasing around the pool. I suppose I did a little showing off myself with a few dives. Of course, you could have called it advertising or keeping in practice, but I could have practiced earlier when nobody was around. I did a swan dive which is a cinch, but it looked pretty, and a front and back jackknife. I realized everyone sitting around the pool was watching. I didn't want to overdo it—just enough.

That's why I didn't try any of my fancy stuff like gainers. It's silly, but girls seemed to go for a fellow who was good at sports.

I got to thinking about Betty. She had most of the girls around here licked a mile. If her old man had a bank roll, the guys would have hung around like flies. Nobody'd look twice at some of the girls around here if they didn't have flashy convertibles and give big parties all the time. I wanted to phone Betty, but thought I'd better wait till later in the day. It would seem more casual. I kept thinking of what I was going to say. I caught myself talking out loud. I'd tell her I lost my head and blame it on the alcohol. Didn't she make me take her drink? Didn't she give me plenty of encouragement? How could I know where I was supposed to draw the line?

The Nelson kids arrived for their lesson. Mrs. Nelson came over for a few minutes to watch and asked how they were doing. I told her they were making real progress. Dick Nelson was nine and his sister thirteen. No matter what I told the boy, he landed flat on his belly with his knees buckled. He never practiced except when his parents were watching. Most of the time he jumped into the water, holding his nose and trying to see how big a splash he could make. His sister was plump and big for her age, but she was quiet and serious. I had her putting her hands over her head and hitting the water fairly straight. I used to hold her feet and give them sort of a flip at the last moment, but now she was beginning to get the hang of it. She wanted to learn fancy diving so if I could do anything with her, I could look forward to a customer for the summer. Her breasts were just budding, and her bathing suit was always loose on top. When she bent over, I could see the swelling flesh, almost like a fat man's chest. I tried not to look because if she ever caught me she'd probably have told her old lady, and that'd have been the end.

It was just about noon when I walked to the pay phone in the caddy house. I could have used the club phone free, but the extension was located at the food bar. I wanted a closed booth in case I had to say things which were nobody else's business. There was that fluttering in my gut as I dropped my dime in the slot and asked the operator for the number. Mr. Sullivan answered the phone. I asked for Betty. There was an interminable wait. Maybe she wouldn't even talk to me.

"Hi, Betty," I said, forcing casualness. My heart was pounding away.

"Hello, Tony," she answered.

"I'm sorry about last night."

"That's all right," she said.

You could have knocked me over with the proverbial feather. "You're not sore," I blurted. I guess that was a pretty dumb thing to have said because why should I remind her.

"I was but I'm not any more. I guess you think I'm an awful prude."

"Hell, no, Betty. I think you're swell." There was a moment of silence. "How about a movie tonight? That new picture is starting." I really didn't mean to make a date because I was sort of broke, but it slipped out.

"Sure, pick me up at eight."

"Okay, swell." I put down the receiver ready to bust out. I leaped over the wall behind the caddy house and trotted back to the pool. I turned a couple of cartwheels along the way. Who was worried anyway?

Back at the pool Jim had gone to lunch. The food bar was jammed. Weekends there was an extra fellow helping Pete behind the counter, so I didn't bother. Pete said I'd only get in his way. He was a character, that Pete. I was walking around waiting for Jim to get back when an old gent listening to the ball game on a portable radio asked me to get him a hamburger and some ice tea. I suppose I could have told him in a nice way that I wasn't a waiter, but maybe he'd have thought I was fresh. It really wouldn't kill me to bring the old gent what he wanted. The crowd was three deep at the food bar. While I waited to put in the order, I took a look at the menu. Seventy cents for a hamburger, forty-five cents for a milk shake. A guy had to be nuts to pay those prices and stand in line, besides. I caught Pete's eye and placed the order. Then I noticed the blonde that knocked the drink over in the restaurant. She was standing next to me. She was wearing a gold two piece bathing suit which matched the frames of her sunglasses. I was hoping she wouldn't notice or recognize me, but some jerk had to crowd out with three ice cream cones, jostling us against each other.

"Excuse me," I murmured.

"Say," she said, "don't I know you?" I wasn't going to help her out. "Where have I seen you before?" She put one hand to her chin in a contemplative pose. I couldn't help but notice her voluptuous figure. "Hmmm . . . last night maybe?" She inclined her head and tapped her forehead with her long, manicured fingers reflectively.

I knew she had me. "At Mack's Cabin."

"Oh, of course. You're the one I spilled the drink on." Pete's assistant, wearing a white chef's cap too and sweating like a horse, was holding up two plates calling out toasted ham and cheese. A fellow from the back reached between the blonde and me. "I didn't know you belonged here," she said. "At least I don't remember seeing you."

"You don't get down to the pool often. I'm here every day. I'm one of the swimming instructors."

"Oh." I couldn't figure whether it was said condescendingly.

"I've been here since June. Swimming's my sport. It's a good way to pick up a few bucks during the summer," I said.

"Sounds wonderful," she said pleasantly.

"Where's your husband?" I asked.

"Either on the golf course or down in the locker room playing bridge," she said.

"It was nice of him to pay our check."

"Nothing to it." Her order arrived, a mixed green salad and ice coffee. She took the tray, and I made way for her. "So long. I'll be seeing you," she said, winking and flashing me a bright smile. Her buttocks rotated invitingly as she walked away. She was pretty sensational all right, particularly considering she was no kid. Then the hamburger for the old gent came. I took the check, the sandwich and the ice tea and carried it over to him on a tray. The radio was roaring. The old fellow was slapping his forehead with the palm of his hand. "Thomson just parked one in the stands with the bases loaded," he said.

"No kidding!" I said.

"Who're you for?" he asked.

I could tell he was a Giant fan so I said the Giants.

"Attaboy," he said, flipping me a half buck.

The day got hotter as it wore on. Fortunately I was in the water most of the afternoon showing the arm movements or demonstrating the kick at the edge of the pool. I didn't envy Jim standing around with his white sun hat and whistle around his neck, saying the same thing over and over. Even though I had a good coat of tan, my shoulders were beginning to burn. The pool was a mass of faces. I caught an occasional glimpse of the blonde sitting by herself on a canvas beach chair, her face pointed upwards toward the sun, her legs extended out straight and crossing at the ankles.

That night I didn't ask Jim for his car. I figured I'd be better off without it. No opportunity to be alone, no temptation. I didn't wear a jacket either, just an open-necked shirt. I didn't expect we'd be going any place special. I got a lift most of the way to Sully's Drug Store from one of the members. Betty was sitting on one of the counter stools. She was wearing a blouse and skirt and sandals. She looked best in casual clothes and low heeled shoes. Freshness was a part of her charm.

We had to stand for a while at the movie and then took separate seats, but after the break just before the main feature we got together by asking a few people to move over. I didn't know if I ought to take Betty's hand, but in the excitement of the jail break, we sort of reached for each other. Afterwards we went back to Sully's for a soda and then walked home. Everything was just like it always was between us.

Betty's family was sitting downstairs in the living room watching the roller derby. I was glad they were there so I didn't have to try and kiss Betty goodnight and maybe get turned down. Her folks invited me to come in and join them, but that seemed dull so I said I was tired. Betty took me to the door and we shook hands. She looked at me a little funny. When I asked her about next week, she said, "I don't know. Call me." Maybe she was still a little sore about last night and maybe our saying goodnight reminded her of it. But why did she go out with me tonight, then?

5

Monday was Jim's day off. It was always a slow day at the club, and especially after the Fourth of July when most of the kids were at camp and a lot of the older members were away. I don't know what it was about

Mondays. Maybe everyone was recuperating from the weekend. A couple of mothers showed up with their kids, but they took them over to the wading pool around the corner out of sight of the main pool. Three girls appeared, but soon left. I was reading a magazine in Jim's special chair under the umbrella when the blonde turned up. She was wearing a two piece black bathing suit with a white towel-like beach coat thrown over her shoulders. She came right over.

"Gosh, where's everybody?" she said.

"Kind of lonesome here today." I put aside my magazine.

"I like it this way." She took off her robe and perched on the diving board, her knees drawn up to her chin and her arms wrapped around her legs. Her toe nails and finger nails were a matching pink. She rested her head on her knees and looked over toward me. "What are you reading?" It was *Male,* one of the magazines that belonged to Jim. I held it up so she could see the cover. She squinted into the sun.

"It's a man's magazine," I said.

"So I would assume," she said. "Do you like to read?"

"Pretty much."

"I read a lot," she said. "I'm alone a good deal during the week."

"Where's your husband?" I brushed a huge fly from my knee.

"He's down in Washington most of the time," she said matter of factly. She told me she didn't come to the club often because they had a pool right on their own place. "That was an awfully pretty little girl you had with you Saturday night." I sort of nodded. "Is that your girl?" she asked.

"Yeah, I guess so," I admitted.

"You probably have lots of girls," she smiled. I couldn't be sure if she was being friendly or just trying to string me along.

"How do you like the piano player at Mack's Cabin?" I asked, just to keep the ball rolling.

"He's clever. Typical fairy."

I didn't know how she figured that out, but I agreed. She moved around on the diving board and lay on her stomach, her hands under her chin propping her head. I could see the cleavage between her bulging white breasts. She looked down to make sure everything was proper. "We go out a lot. Steven hates to stay home for dinner. We went to Bronxville Saturday night for a steak, and it was just terrible. We ordered it rare, but it came in so overdone I couldn't eat it." I guessed she was glad to have someone to talk to. I was beginning to feel at ease. She didn't seem so high-hat as most of the dames around this joint.

"Sometimes," I told her, "a bunch of us get together and buy steaks and cook them down at the beach. That's the only way a steak really tastes good."

"You're so right," she said. "Burned on the outside and red in the middle."

"We take potatoes and corn and throw them in the hot coals too."

"M-m-m," she closed her eyes dreamily. "Count me in next time."

"Sure," I said kiddingly, because now I knew she was stringing me along.

There was a creaking noise from behind as Pete lifted up the lid of the food bar and hooked it open. I turned around. It was just noon. "Hiya, kid," he called to me. He sat down on a stool behind the counter and took out a newspaper. Then the blonde said to me, "Say, you know I've got a thick porterhouse I bought for the weekend. How about coming over this evening and cooking it for me on our outdoor grill?" It sounded like it was just an idea which came over her on the spur of the moment, and it certainly took me by surprise. I didn't say anything. Just then someone's two year old came tearing up from the kiddies' pool, his wobbly legs going a mile a minute, headed towards the edge of the big pool, his mother in hot pursuit. I jumped up and grabbed him and then handed him over. She gave him a potch on the behind and led him back. The blonde looked on with an amused expression.

"Well, how about it?" she said when I had resettled myself.

"I don't know," I said hesitatingly.

"I'll tell you what I'll do," she said. "I'll pick you up just outside the entrance of the club around six. Look for me in a blue De Soto convertible."

"Isn't that a lot of trouble for you?" I was still looking for an out. I think I was scared. But, Jeez—

"God, no," she said. "I live five minutes away."

Her head was turned the other way as she lay on the diving board sopping up the sun. Her skin was a deep brown. She had spent a lot of time working on her burn. The sun glistened on her hair. A party of women arrived with a canasta board. After they were seated around a card table, the wind picked up some of the cards and scattered them. The women gave off little cries of dismay as three of them chased the cards around the lawn while the fourth remained at the table to protect the rest of the pack. Pretty soon the blonde picked herself up. She walked by me and said softly, "I'll see you later."

The rest of the afternoon seemed to drag. The butterflies fluttered inside me. I wished I had never accepted. I wanted to call her, but I didn't even know her name. What had I let myself in for, going over to have dinner with a married woman while her husband was away? Even though it would be harmless, how would it look? Supposing her husband came home unexpectedly. I must have been nuts. I thought about ducking out.

At six I was waiting outside the entrance. I felt guilty hanging around. Several people stopped and asked me if I wanted a lift. I was hoping nobody would be around when she stopped to pick me up. Six-fifteen and no blonde. I was getting more nervous. If she'd only forget to come. Another five minutes and I'd be justified in taking off. But then a long light-blue convertible with the top down rolled into sight. The blonde was at the wheel, a red bandana tied around her head.

"I'm sorry I'm late," she said. I stood there sort of paralyzed. She leaned across the car to open the other door. "C'mon. Hop in." She drove with assurance through the plush residential section. Finally we turned off the road at an entrance between two huge stone posts. Iron gates hinged to each post were swung open inward. There was a sign just inside the property. "Private property. All trespassers will be prosecuted. Steven L. Powers." We wound through the long, twisting, sloping driveway, an evenly spaced row of trees on either side. We pulled up around a circular driveway. The house was a handsome two story colonial. "Here we are," she said.

She guided me through the house and out to a stone patio overlooking a spacious, well manicured lawn which dipped down into woods. There were numerous wicker lounging chairs and a two shelf brass bar on wheels at one side, the bottom tier loaded with bottles of all description, an ice bucket and glasses on the top shelf.

"Sit down, Tony," she said. I didn't realize she knew my name.

"Thanks, Mrs. Powers," I said, sitting on the edge of one of the chairs.

"You don't have to be so formal. Vicky will do." She removed the bandana and fluffed out her blonde hair with her hands. Her hair was different from Betty's. It was shorter and wavy, but it was sensationally golden. She was dressed in a white silk shirt, so sheer you could see the brassiere underneath as clearly as if she had worn nothing over it. The shirt was tucked into a pair of knee length blue denim shorts. "For God's sake, make yourself comfortable," she said, looking at me. She took me by the hand and led me to one of the lounging chairs. "There," she said, as I settled into the chair. "Isn't that better? How about a drink?"

"I don't think so, thanks."

"You must. I don't like to drink alone." She walked over to the bar. "What'll it be?"

"Oh, okay. Anything."

"Martini?"

"Swell." I had never had one before, but that sounded as good as anything else. She uncorked a bottle of gin and measured off five cocktail glasses and poured them in a shaker. Then she added a glass full of vermouth. She mixed it with the finesse of a bartender. "You like them real dry?" she asked.

"Sure." She tossed a handful of chipped ice from the bucket into the glasses.

"Olive or onion?"

"Olive," I said, feeling I oughtn't to take an onion.

She placed the shaker and glasses on a tray along with a platter of little sandwiches, the small fancy kind, little round and diamond shaped caviar and pate sandwiches, rolled ham, deviled eggs. Then she took another of those lounging chairs and started to wheel it over. I started to get up to help. She put a restraining hand on my shoulder. "Just relax." She parked the chair parallel to mine and placed a serving table between us. Then she brought over the tray. She poured us each a drink before settling in the adjoining chair. I picked up my glass by the stem. She took hers, leaned over and touched it to mine. "Here's to a pleasant evening."

"You said it," I answered. I took a sip. The drink burned and tasted like medicine. As I swallowed, I almost threw up.

"How is it?" she asked.

"Fine." My eyes were watering.

I felt I had to down the drink. I took another swallow and ate a sandwich to take the taste away. It was a warm night. The crickets sounded in unison, punctuated by an occasional, throaty bull frog in the distance. The sun was just lowering itself behind the tops of the trees.

"Beautiful spot," I said.

"Just mad about it," she answered. "This is just where we sat the first night I met Steven. No wonder I fell for him. You could fall for anybody in a setting like this. His family was in Europe that summer. It was their place originally. We moved in here a couple of years ago when Steven's mother died."

I managed to finish the first drink. It was beginning to taste a little better. Before I could protest, she had filled my glass again. My body was tingling. My head was becoming lighter. There was a sense of excitement sitting here in this glamorous setting. It was like a movie.

"What did you think when I invited you here? You didn't want to come, did you?"

"I did," I answered. "I just didn't think I should, your being a club member."

"Was that all you thought about?" She drew a package of Parliaments out of her pocket and offered me one. I declined. She lit her cigarette with a gold lighter and blew out the smoke. "Well?" she said, looking at me quizzically with a raised eyebrow.

"I thought you were. . ."

She read my mind. "Attractive for someone so old?"

"I guess that's it."

She took another puff on her cigarette. Then she flipped it on the terrace. Sparks bounced as it rolled off into the grass. "I'm only twenty-eight. That's not so old. You wait another ten years and see if you think twenty-eight is old. I don't feel any different than I did ten years ago. I look even better. I was too thin when I was younger. Some people get more attractive. You'll be a knockout when you're older. You've got that lean, hungry look that ages well. After you fill out and maybe get a little gray around the temples, you'll be terrific. In fact, you're cute right now."

"You're okay yourself." I felt the color mount into my face. I gulped at the second martini.

"I'll tell you what," she said bouncing up. "Let's start the fire while it's still light. We'll take the martinis with us." With cocktail shaker in one hand, she led me down a graded cinder path off to the right. We walked several hundred yards before coming on a beautiful natural pool rimmed with flat stones. A circular float was anchored in the middle. On the near side was a small beach of soft, clean sand and a low building consisting of two large bath houses with a half open patio in between. The patio had a stone floor, and in one corner a huge built-in fireplace served as a grill. An assortment of shiny, bronze cooking utensils hung from hooks by the fireplace. A tremendous refrigerator stood adjacent. Vicky opened the door and we looked inside. Cold soup, a mixed salad, ice tea, a frozen dessert—everything was already prepared. A magnificent porterhouse steak was lying on a piece of waxpaper.

"Looks wonderful," I said. The fire in the grill was already constructed. I took a match from my pocket and touched it to the newspaper underneath the pile of kindling and charcoal. It flared up. "We'll have to wait now for the hot coals," I said.

We sat down by the pool on canvas chairs. Vicky poured more drinks. I knew I had had enough, but I found myself sipping on it. It was starting to get dark. The crickets blared away in ever mounting crescendo. The air was still, warm, oppressive. My head was going around. A feeling of remoteness crept along my legs.

"What do you say we take a dip before dinner?" she suggested.

"It might be a good idea, but I haven't a suit." My voice sounded peculiar. I was having difficulty talking.

"Don't wear one. I won't either. That'll make it even."

I kept thinking of the cooling water. If only the trees would stop moving up and down. Behind us the fire was subsiding, but occasional sparks were drawn off through the chimney as though they were a soda being sipped through a giant straw. They flew out the top mingled with thin wisps of smoke.

Vicky had slipped off her shirt and shorts and was standing beside me.

"C'mon, sissy," she said. I was gaping at her but with little inclination to move. The fireflies were darting against the dark background of the trees across the pond like sparklers on the Fourth of July. Vicky bent down to remove my shirt. I raised my arms. I could feel the warmth of her body as she brushed against me. It was the striking of the match. Her hot lips bruised my mouth. I drifted with the storm of passion.

6

I awoke with a start. I was in a soft, comfortable bed. I tried to raise myself. My head was pounding. I reached out and switched on a lamp resting on a table beside the bed. It was a good-sized room with red and white wall paper. I was wearing a pair of blue silk pajamas. I struggled to a sitting position and threw back the white sheet which was covering me. Outside it was still dark. My clothes were folded over a chair in one corner. The bed was almost irresistible, but I felt the room was a prison—a magnificent, luxurious prison which was confining me. I felt sick. Jeez!

Whatever I had had to eat and drink was in my throat. I staggered over to the chair and dressed slowly. My head hurt worse when I bent over. It seemed to take an age to get on my shoes and socks. Then I turned off the lamp and walked to the door. There was a light outside. I tiptoed through the heavily carpeted hall and down a wide circular stairway which led me right to the front door. It creaked as I opened it and I didn't close it for fear someone might hear me. I started down the long driveway to the main road. I could no longer contain what was inside me. I ran to the side of the road and let go. I retched until I thought my very insides were coming out. My throat was stinging. I covered up the mess with some loose dirt and continued on my way. It was quiet on the main road. I didn't know which way to go. I didn't want to go home anyway. A little way down the road there was a field. I clambered over the stone wall and laid down and fell asleep.

The sun saw to it that I didn't oversleep. My head was still throbbing. My throat was sore and parched My whole mouth felt like it was full of bits of cotton. What's more, I was tired and stiff and worried. What had happened last night, what had I done? What about Vicky, Mrs. Powers, that is. She would tell her husband and he'd kill me. Maybe he wouldn't do it himself. Maybe he'd send around some strong armed guys to beat me to a pulp. How did I get into that bed last night? Who carried me? Why didn't they take care of me then, or were they letting me rest up for the slaughter? They might be looking for me right now. I couldn't go back to the club, of course. A milk truck came along and gave me a ride into the nearest village. I decided I'd better go home.

As I walked into the house my father called me. He always rose early to read the paper and putter around in the garden. "Is that you, Tony?"

"Yes, sir," I answered meekly.

He was sitting on the side porch. "What are you doing home at this hour?" It wasn't a question of my sleeping home because occasionally I stayed over at the club. I didn't know what to answer.

"Come here, Tony," he said. I appeared hesitantly at the screen door. He was reading the paper and looked over the top. "For God's sake," he said. "Where have you been? You look like walking death."

"Please," I said, "don't ask me any questions. It's a very personal matter."

He didn't press me. "C'mon, let's have a cup of coffee."

We walked into the kitchen. I sliced some bread as he filled the coffee pot with water and spooned the coffee into the top of the percolater. We sat there in silence as the water bubbled against the glass stopper. "If you're in any trouble, son, you can tell me," he said.

"Everything's okay," I said. We drank our coffee and ate buttered toast. My eyelids were drooping. Finally, much to my relief, father glanced at the kitchen clock and announced he'd better go. He was a setter at a jewelry manufacturing plant and had to be at the bench at 8:30. "If you want my advice," he flung at me over his shoulder, "get some sleep before your mother sees you, and wipe the lipstick off your face." I automatically wiped my hand across my lips.

After breakfast I went upstairs and took off my clothes. There was my brother again, sleeping peacefully. He never thought much about girls or himself the way I did at his age. Sometimes I thought he was a little dopey, but now I envied the simplicity of his existence. I took a shower and stayed under the water for about fifteen minutes, scrubbing myself thoroughly as though I could erase all memories of the night before. There was still a dull pain across my forehead. I lay down on my bed but couldn't sleep. The picture of Vicky hovering over me in her underwear kept running through my mind.

I tried to piece the rest together. It was hot, and as the morning wore on I became sticky with perspiration as I lay in bed just in my shorts. Around 9:30 my brother got up and dressed. I pretended to be asleep. Soon, a knock on the door. I didn't answer. Then the door opened slightly and my mother stuck her head in. "Phone for you, Tony. What's the matter with you today, anyway? Don't you feel well?"

"I'm ah right."

"Then get up and answer the phone."

"Who is it?" I said.

"Some man. I didn't ask."

"Do me a big favor," I said. "Find out who it is."

"I will not," she said. "This is the second time they called. They called earlier and I said you were asleep."

I pulled myself together. My heart was crashing against my ribs. I went downstairs to the phone inside the closet and closed the door behind me. "Hello," I said, dropping my voice half a dozen notes for disguise.

"Hello, hello, Tony. This is Jim. What's the matter? You sound so funny."

"Hi, Jim," I said, back on key. "What's up?"

"What's up! That little Snyder girl is waiting for you. She had a lesson at ten."

"Oh," I said.

"You sound like you had a rough night."

"I don't feel so good."

"Can you be here tomorrow? The Snyders are going up to Maine next week. That girl wants to learn how to dive decently before she goes. That's your department."

"Okay," I said. Jim hung up.

My old lady was waiting in the hall to know what it was all about. "Well," she said. She was dressed in a house dress with a white cloth tied around her head. I started upstairs. "You're white as a ghost. Do you want me to call the doctor?" I did not. "How about taking a physic," she continued. "There's some milk of magnesia in my bathroom." Mother felt that a physic was the cure for all ills.

"I'm all right, I tell you. Just taking a day off."

I got dressed. My mother was in the kitchen cleaning up. "I'll be back this evening," I called to her.

"Where are you going?" she said. It troubled my conscience to be so rude, but why did she have to be such a nuisance? Why couldn't she leave a fellow alone?

"I'm going down to the village to take care of something," I said. I got my bike out of the garage and peddled downtown. I stopped at a drug store for a sandwich and a black and white soda. It was insufferably hot walking along the cement sidewalks. As I passed a movie, a wave of cool air pushed out. I didn't bother to see what was playing. A couple of young kids were hanging around the box office. They each held out a quarter. "Will you take us in, mister?"

My initial reaction was annoyance. "Oh, please, mister," they said.

Well, why not. I bought two children's tickets and one adult. I shook them as soon as we got inside. The theatre was almost empty. It was 1:15. I had come in almost at the beginning of a Western, but before it ended my head started to nod. When I looked up again, it was quarter to six. I was hungry. I walked to the back of the theatre and bought myself some candy and a coke. I sat through the show again. The last movie was a gangster affair in which a newspaper reporter ran down a ring of counterfeiters. The reporter fell in love with the gangster's girl. The gangster caught them together in a roadhouse and took the reporter outside. They beat him mercilessly and left him to die by the side of a lonely road. The girl eventually found him and drove him to a hospital.

The parallel kept impressing itself upon me. Whose side would Vicky be on? I watched until I could take it no more and went outside. It was almost nine o'clock. I had left my bicycle in a side street. I had to pass a bar along the way. Several men were standing outside. I wanted to cross the street, but that would have been giving in to my imagination. Otherwise the street was empty. I walked close to the curb. As I came abreast of the group, one of the men approached me. I dodged into the street and started to run. I picked up my bike standing in a vacant lot. Nobody was following me. I fumbled with the key in the lock which chained the back wheel. Then I shoved the lock in my pocket and leaped on my bike. I peddled away as fast as I could. Along the main street, a car was creeping behind me. I turned off into a side street, but the car didn't follow.

When I got home, I was out of breath. Perspiration oozed out of my forehead. The back of my shirt was wet. My parents were in the living room watching television. My mother called to me. "Do you feel better now, Tony?"

"Fine," I said. I went into the living room and sat there a few minutes before excusing myself and going up to my room.

The thought of going to work the next day terrified me. Maybe Jim's call was bait. Maybe there was no lesson at all. They just wanted to get me to the club. I thought about leaving town. I had almost dropped off to sleep when my brother burst in and turned on the lights.

"Are you asleep, Tony?" He always wore those awful school T-shirts, blue jeans and sneakers.

"I was."

"You want to hear some hot poop?" He sat down on the side of my bed, making a valley in the mattress.

"You know that guy Katie was going with?" Katie was the older sister of my brother's pal. "He's taken a powder and enlisted in the Navy. Katie was bawling all over the place, and is her old man sore! Says he'll kill the bastard when he gets his hands on him."

"Don't use that kind of language."

"I don't." His voice broke into a whine. "That's just what her old man said. They sent me home."

I rolled over facing the other way. "Do you mind turning off the lights?"

"I just thought you'd be interested." His shoes thumped to the floor one by one. His bed groaned and creaked as he thrashed around, getting settled. On my back with my hands clasped I prayed quietly... "And please, God, help me out of this mess. Amen."

7

I got to the club early the next morning. Jim was in the locker room. He didn't act like a man conspiring against me. There was nothing subtle about Jim. It would have been obvious. "Say, Tony, there was a lovely blonde around asking for you yesterday." He smiled knowingly as he unbuttoned his shirt and hung it in his locker.

"What do you mean, asking for me?"

"All right, all right," he said. "What's to get on your ear about? I'm just telling you." The muscles in his back rippled as he bent over to take off his shorts. He pulled on his jock. "Lovely, voluptuous," he cupped his hands. "Just my type too, if I didn't have all I can take care of."

"Was she alone?" I asked, unlocking my locker.

"What do you mean, alone?" He eyed me curiously.

I didn't want to ask but felt compelled. "Were there any men with her, one or two?"

"What's the matter?" he said. "Do you want an exclusive?"

I knew I'd get that kind of an answer. "You don't understand," I continued. "I'm not interested that way. It's something else. It's important."

Jim pulled on his swimming trunks. "Say, you've got it bad." He stared into my face. "She was alone." He adjusted his belt. "C'mon," he said, "I'll see you out at the pool."

I approached the pool warily. No one was there but Jim, sitting under his umbrella, feet up on another chair, reading the morning paper. I joined him. "Want part of the paper?" he said, handing me the first section.

I looked at it but couldn't concentrate. Promptly at ten the Snyder girl and her brother showed up for their lessons. They brought over a couple of friends for instruction. That would occupy the morning. Only a handful of others appeared, mothers with their kids. By noon everyone had gone again. Jim went to lunch.

I was no sooner alone than the blonde appeared. I saw her first leaning over the balcony at the other end of the pool. She spotted me and waved and then swung down the stairs. It was as if she had been lurking, to catch me alone. She had a different bathing suit again—a white, polka dot sort of romper affair. Her hair was tied back with a blue ribbon, and she looked like she could have been Betty's older sister as she sidled down the side of the pool. I couldn't duck out so I just sat and waited. She flashed a big smile as she approached. "What happened to you the other night?"

All my imaginings of the past thirty-six hours seemed crazy in the broad sunlight. "I went home."

"How did you go? You didn't walk, did you?"

"I got a ride most of the way."

She laughed easily. "I once walked home from a date, but this is the first time anyone walked home on me."

"I didn't feel well."

"I can imagine," she said pleasantly. "Why didn't you call someone?"

I shrugged my shoulders.

"If you had wanted to go, you should have taken my car. The keys were in it." She walked toward the counter. "How about a Coke?" I shook my head. She brought a Coke to my table and sat down. "Sip?" she asked.

"No, thanks."

"Did you have a good time?" she said, her face down sucking on the straws, but looking up at me out of large, blue eyes.

"I guess so. I don't remember much except that I felt awful after I woke up."

"No wonder," she said. "All those martinis and no dinner. We never did get around to the steaks, did we?"

"I guess not."

"They're still sitting in the icebox waiting for you. How about coming over tonight, and this time we'll make sure we get around to the steaks." She finished up the Coke and set it aside.

She looked disarming enough, but my suspicions returned. "I can't," I said.

"Do you have a date with that sweet little girl of yours. Bring her along."

"No, I haven't got a date. I just can't do it though." But maybe it didn't sound too convincing.

"Are you angry at me?" she said, looking kind of hurt.

Maybe I should get it over with. If anyone had it in for me, I might as well go and take whatever was in store. I couldn't keep running all summer. "All right," I said softly. "I'll come."

"Wonderful," she said. "I'll pick you up outside, same time as before. And don't worry about getting home. You can take my car and leave it in the parking lot here. I'll pick it up sometime. I can always use the station wagon." She flashed her teeth charmingly. Then she walked to the diving board and dove in. She cut the water cleanly. Jeez, if I could only get that Snyder girl to do that. Then she moved with an easy stroke to the shallow end of the pool: Jim was returning to relieve me for lunch. When he saw the blonde, he said, "That was the one asking for you yesterday."

"I know," I answered.

"Not bad for you," he said. "Or maybe too bad for you." Sometimes Jim gave me a royal pain. Always a wise guy. I headed for the locker room without looking around.

8

Once Vicky had picked me up, the butterflies in my stomach lay down. The nightmare I had been living through was just the result of my morbid, wild imagination. I must have been nuts. I was really just a boor who got drunk and passed out. Vicky had slid over to let me drive. I got a kick sitting behind the wheel of the huge convertible, feeling it respond to the slightest pressure on the accelerator. It was sensational not to shift gears. We chatted easily about cars. She had had a Buick before. She liked the De Soto better. Maybe it wasn't as popular, but it was really a finer automobile. It had that new finger tip steering. It handled like a kiddy car.

A manservant met us as we drew up in front of the door. He must have been the one who had carried me to the bed. If so, he gave no sign of recognition. "Good evening, Ma'm," he said, bowing slightly from the waist. He was outfitted in striped trousers and a black sort of house coat.

"Good evening, Herman."

"Shall I put the car away, Ma'm?" he said, holding the front door.

"No, Mr. Bianchi is going to use it later. Is everything ready?"

"Yes, Ma'm." He closed the door and padded off.

We went directly down to the pool. The fire had been started. The charcoal had already reduced itself to glowing red embers. There were martinis in the ice box. Although I had promised myself not to indulge, I consented to just one. It made me glow. Vicky sat sprawled in a chair watching me, one leg thrown over the arm so that her skirt rode over her knee. It was a wide skirt, flared at the bottom. She smoothed it down against the cushion. She wore flat red shoes with yellowish crepe soles. She sipped her drink and watched as I prepared the steak, salting it and lightly coating it with mustard. The steak was short and about two and a half inches thick. We both liked it rare. I decided to give it fifteen minutes to a side.

Vicky finished her second drink, hoisted herself out of the chair and came over for a look. She put her hand on my shoulder and stood close. I could feel her warmth. A chill ran down my back, and I shook involuntarily.

"What's the matter?" she said.

"Nothing. Don't you ever shiver? My grandmother always said that meant ghosts walking across your grave."

She laughed pleasantly. "You're a funny boy," she said.

The grease fell on the hot coals and the flame reached up at the steak. "I hope you don't mind the black," I said.

Vicky bent over and took a long whiff like she was smelling some flower. "M-m-m, looks beautiful. How long will it take?"

"About another fifteen minutes," I said, spearing the meat with a long fork and flipping it over.

Vicky transferred the rest of the dinner from refrigerator to table. Out of the corner of my eye I watched her plying back and forth with shrimp cocktails, salad, bread and butter, ice tea. Her dress was entirely bare in back. I could see the outline of her spine as she bent over the table. There were no shoulder straps either. I wondered what held the dress up. She seemed so out of character with even such minor domesticity. I went over to help. She fingered a shrimp, dipped it in the sauce and put it in my mouth. Then she headed me back to the fire. "You watch the steak," she said. "This is my job."

There was the wonderful stillness of a summer's evening. An occasional frog croaked to his mate out beyond the pool, and she answered. The crickets brought back faint recollections of the night before, and it set my blood racing. Betty crossed my mind. What would she think if she could see me here? It didn't really matter. Nothing mattered. Forgotten too were the entire foolish fears of a previous night and day. Vicky was waiting at the table, looking away, fondling her glass. Her profile was sensational with its straight, turned up nose. Jeez, she was really beautiful. Too good to be true, too good to approach. Guys I knew only tackled the ugly girls. They were supposed to be easier. Maybe because they were more grateful. The others were sort of hands off. You took them places and spent money on them, but that was all. That's why Betty had been my girl. None of the real operators ever asked her out. She wasn't considered the type. I couldn't even imagine why Vicky had asked me over again, except maybe she felt she had to after she had told me about the steak, and I had told her what an expert I was at cooking them outdoors. She could have asked practically any guy. Even Jim would have been drooling for an invitation. Jeez, any dope could cook a steak. That stuffed shirt butler could have done it. Vicky was pouring herself another drink. She didn't offer me one. I guess she didn't want me to conk out on her again.

"Tony," she was almost yelling.

"Huh?" I looked up.

"I've been trying to get your attention. How's the steak coming?"

I rotated my wrist to see my watch. Jeez, eighteen minutes on this side. I jabbed the meat with the fork and dumped it on a wooden platter. I was afraid it might be overdone. I put a wad of butter on top. The butter melted and cascaded over the sides in several streams. I cut into the steak with the long, thin carving knife. It was still a little pink inside, but another few minutes would have ruined it. I carved six slices and brought the platter over to the table.

"How about a little music?" Vicky said, turning on the little portable radio which was sitting on the floor next to her. She tried several stations before tuning in on a good band. "How's that?" I nodded my approval.

I waited for her to start. Then I picked up the tiny fork and stabbed a shrimp. When I looked over at her, I felt all choked up like there was a weight on my chest.

"Don't you like shrimp or is the sauce too hot?" she said, looking over at me. "Sometimes Herman overdoes the horseradish."

"It's fine," I said. It was funny how I wasn't hungry. There was a lull in the conversation. I wanted to keep talking, but I couldn't think of anything to say. Other guys she knew wouldn't just be sitting here like a clam. She could only think of me as a dumb kid.

"Don't finish it if you don't want to," she said, taking the shrimp away. The music stopped and a news broadcast came on. "Do you want to hear the news?" she asked.

"Sure. Anything." There was one thing about a radio. Nobody had to talk. We made steak sandwiches and ate our salad as the newscaster droned on about the European situation. Vicky kept raving about the steak. Out of this world, she said several times. Half cantaloupes filled with ice cream topped the meal. I could only toy with the dessert.

"I'm worried about your not eating," Vicky said.

"I had plenty. What'll we do about the dishes?"

"Just leave them." She got up, took the radio in one hand and led me to a swinging couch. "Let's just relax a while." The couch retreated as we sat down, then swung forward and back again on its base until finally it came to rest at a comfortable angle. Vicky leaned back, her eyes half closed. Maybe that was a hint for me to go.

"I can't stay too late," I said, looking at my watch.

"I know," she said. "I'm tired too, but I don't want you to go."

We listened to a comedy team and jazz orchestra on the radio. It was starting to get dark. Water splashed into the pool, and there were the crickets again and the hoarse frogs.

Vicky swung her feet up and laid her head on my lap. The couch agitated and squeaked before resettling itself. "You don't mind, do you?" Vicky said. I couldn't answer. She made herself comfortable. Her hip jutted up at me like a mountain peak, her legs were curled, knees in, her feet locked together. I wanted to push her head away, but I didn't dare, and maybe I didn't really want to.

She looked up and said, "You're sweet, do you know?"

"So are you," I managed to get out, swallowing hard.

She put her left arm around my neck and lifted herself up. Our mouths sort of fused. I could feel the warmth of her as she pressed against my chest, rubbing gently.

Gone were any inhibitions. She pulled up my shirt and kissed my bare chest. Then she was all over me like a woman half-crazed. We rolled off the couch, tugging at each other's clothes until we felt free. . . .

I felt my shoulder and looked at my hand. It was bleeding from where she had sunk her teeth, but there was no pain. My mind was a blank. Nothing registered. After a while, desire mounted again. I lay there, bending to her will, not taking any initiative, but happily led. Then the flood of emotion, painful, torturous, and the tension was over. We were perspiring. My flesh stuck to the floor. "Come on," she said. "Let's cool off."

Vicky sat on the edge of the pool near the shallow end and lowered herself in. I went to the deep end, dove in and raced two laps. I pulled up at the same end I had started, breathing heavily, but with a new sense of liberation. I hung on to the edge with one hand, water up to my chin. The moon had risen, half full and brilliant, stealing the stage from her supporting cast of stars. Vicky climbed out of the water. There was something natural and unashamed about her white nakedness radiant in the subdued light of the moon and the flood from the pavilion. All the dirty mystery of the human female form was exposed as an open secret. It was just another body.

Vicky gathered up her clothes and went into the ladies' bathhouse. I floated around lazily in the pool, letting my body drift in the weak current. I heard the shower running. Finally I emerged and entered the men's side. I dried myself off and dressed. I combed my hair forward over my eyes, shaking the water out at the end of each stroke. Then I parted it and slicked it back, smoothing it down with the palm of my hand. Outside I eased myself into a chair and waited. Finally Vicky appeared, neat and fresh. Hand in hand, we wandered around to the front of the house.

"I can't see you any more this week, honey," she said.

This remark was the first practical note. I had forgotten that there'd ever be a tomorrow. I hadn't thought about seeing her or not seeing her again. It was like talking about dinner when you felt bloated from a tremendous lunch. "I'll leave the keys under the sun visor," I said, opening the door at the driver's side. She put her arms around me and offered up her lips. I didn't feel like kissing now, but I couldn't avoid it. Her lips were hot and wet. I stood it as long as I could, then I took her arms from my neck and slipped behind the wheel.

"I had a lovely time," she said.

I knew I should say something, but only managed a "Me, too." I turned on the lights and searched around for the starter. "It's on the ignition key," she said. "Turn it all the way to the right."

She was standing watching as I rolled around the driveway. I waved goodbye. The headlights pierced the semi-darkness. On the wide concrete road, I stepped hard on the throttle. The breeze ruffled the canvas top. The tires squealed on the curves. I pulled alongside of a Chevy at a stoplight. When it turned green, I raced out front leaving the Chevy as if it were standing still. I was too big and strong for anything on the road. I parked the car several blocks away so it wouldn't lead to any questions in the morning. I let myself into the house quietly. I fell asleep as soon as my head touched the pillow.

9

It was something new for me to be awake before the alarm clock went off. The grackles were lined up on the telephone wires screaming like they were being goosed with a hot poker. Stupid birds. As I lay in bed, I started to think about the girl in my chemistry class who had to leave in the middle of the term. Jeez, supposing Vicky had a baby? Sometimes I had listened in on bull sessions by the big operators. You were really taking a chance only a few days during the month. It was ten days before or after or something like that. No one was too sure. It would be just my luck to hit the jackpot. There was a sex book in the library once which my mother had hidden after she caught me reading it. Maybe she had put it back. I went downstairs. Carefully I examined all the titles. Then it occurred to me it might have been stuck behind the other books. I pulled a few books out from each shelf, and there it was on the bottom row—*Fertility in Marriage*. I thumbed through the chapter headings and scanned some of the more intriguing paragraphs. It was all about how to make babies— nothing about how not to have one. Jeez, it would have been wonderful to have had an older brother that you could ask about certain things. Maybe Jim, but you never could tell about that guy. He might just kid the hell out of me. What about my old man? I wondered if he'd know. He must know, but then I tried to picture him and mother—my old man with his fat stomach and his eyeglasses, mother in her apron. Jeez, no.

As I got dressed, I noticed in the mirror the scabs on my shoulder and the neat red marks. Anyone, it seemed to me, would recognize them immediately for what they were. I tried to cover them with a band-aid, but it wouldn't stick. Downstairs my old man was just finishing his breakfast. My orange juice was waiting on the table. Pop put down his paper to say good morning. I was thinking we might have a talk sometime when Mom came in with the coffee pot. She poured a cup for me and one for herself. There was a pause while she and my old man looked at each other. Then they put me on the firing line. Where had I been keeping myself recently, what had I been doing, I looked tired, big rings under my eyes, why didn't I ever spend an evening home—particularly from my old lady. I remembered when I was a kid reading about the curious catibus, a feline animal that had to ask 100 questions a day or curl up in its rocking chair to die. She must have come from a long line of curious catibuses. I was just so mad I clammed up. If I had ever thought of speaking to my old man seriously, this was out. He wanted to drive me to the bus line, so I had to stall around in the bathroom until it got so late I knew he'd have to go ahead without me. As soon as he left, I also beat it. I wanted to get to work early so I could leave Vicky's car without anyone noticing.

The Weather Bureau had said partly cloudy with occasional showers in the afternoon, but the clouds kept thickening and then it started to come down. The rain dotted the pool. Jim and I raced around to get everything inside, and then we sat down in the men's bathhouse waiting for the weather to break. The T-shirt which I had been wearing to conceal the marks on my shoulder was soaking.

"Why don't you take that wet shirt off before you catch cold?" Jim said.

I guessed that might not be a bad idea. It would be a good way to open the conversation. Jim was the only guy I might be able to talk to about that kind of stuff. I stripped the shirt and wrung the water out on the floor, facing Jim all the while so he'd get a good look, and he bit.

"What happened to you?" he said, grinning broadly.

"I bumped it." I could afford to be cute because I knew he wouldn't leave it at that.

"You're getting bumped regularly." He laughed uproariously at his own joke. I looked at him uncomfortably. "You get it?" he said.

"I get it," I answered solemnly.

"How dumb do you think I am?" he asked. He took a pipe and pouch from the pocket of the blue blazer with the college insignia over the breast pocket which he always wore back and forth to the pool He filled the pipe, packing the tobacco carefully. "Well," he said. "Go ahead. You want to tell me all about it." That psychology stuff again. He always was figuring out what you were thinking. "Some dame bit you. It might have been that little girl you hold hands with, but I doubt it because even if you worked up enough nerve to go after her, it would have been an unsatisfactory business, and she never would let herself go enough to really enjoy it. So it probably was that blonde who was asking for you the other day. She looks like you'd have to beat her off with a broom if she ever got you alone."

I was getting a little red. "What makes you think it, was either of them?"

"Listen," he continued, "you can't kid your Uncle Jim. It was that blonde dame, and it was the first time." Jim was lighting his pipe, looking at me over the match. "How was it? D'ja have any trouble?"

I was blushing all over, but I told Jim all about it. I was afraid he might give me the needle, but Jim could be a swell fellow when he wanted to be.

"Don't worry about it," he said. "That babe knows more about taking care of herself than you'll ever know. You're not the first and you won't be the last." The pipe was drooping out of the corner of his mouth. "Supposing she was pregnant. What does she want from you? Dough? She's got more than she can use. Does she want you to marry her? She's got a husband, and even if she didn't she sure as hell wouldn't want you. She's playing around, having a time for herself, and if anything happened she'd know just what to do about it. Just don't take it seriously, that's all." Jim lit his pipe again.

"You won't say anything, will you?"

"For Chris' sake, who the hell'd be interested except maybe her husband and a few people like that."

Jim could never be on the level for very long. There was no point in saying any more. Jim wouldn't mention it. He was just trying to give me a bad time. I felt reassured. What he had said made good sense. How did he know so much about people? If that's what he learned in psychology, I wanted to study it too, if I ever got that far. I walked to the door and looked outside. It was thin, steady rain—the kind that lasted.

Then I went to the John to take a leak. The guy who invented the Athletic Supporter never gave much thought to some of the practical details. Or maybe he expected you to urinate in the water. Most people did. I flushed the toilet and pulled up my trunks. Jim was standing in the doorway holding his hand out to catch the raindrops as though he really had to feel them to believe what he saw.

"I'm going back to my room," he said. "Stick around for a while. If it doesn't clear by noon, you can knock off for the day." He bent over to pull on a pair of sneakers. "Keep away from that blonde though. Give her a rest." He gave me the usual smirk. Then he took off for the clubhouse like someone was chasing him. He lost his footing on the slippery tile, and I thought he was going on his can, but he kept his balance and then disappeared.

There was nothing drearier than an outdoor swimming pool on a rainy day. The dressing room was small and nobody used it much except for the toilet and to stow gear at night. I found an old magazine around and tried to read a story, but I started to think about Vicky and couldn't concentrate.

10

"Is that you, Tony?" my brother called as I opened the door after clomping up the outside steps.

"Yeah, where's ma?" I took off my wet shoes and left them outside.

Mike was upstairs. "She went out to her sewing group," he hollered down. "How about a game of soldiers?"

"Okay. Soon as I get something to eat." I went into the kitchen and pulled on the light. A sensational smell came from the stove. I opened the oven and there was a partially browned rolled beef sitting in the roasting pan. The oven heat was turned way down. I stuck my finger in the drippings and licked it. I looked in the ice box. There was nothing much but a pie which I guessed was for tonight too. I took some bread and peanut butter and washed it down with a glass of milk.

My brother had all the soldiers out and was practicing. I hadn't played in a long time. It was sort of our own game. You stood up soldiers in a certain formation, and you'd alternate shots with a marble to see who could knock down the other's army first. It was a question of being a good shot and of arranging your men so they would be least apt to be hit or, at worst, see that no more than one would be felled with the same shot. I invariably won. "I'm getting pretty good," he said, aiming at a soldier about three feet away. He missed by several inches. "What color do you want?"

I had always chosen the reds because that was the color of Betty's hair, but this time I decided to take the blues because Vicky's eyes were blue. We used the empty space between the bed and the window as the battlefield. I spread my men along the floor, occasionally standing a concentration behind a cannon or a tank which was heavy enough to ward off a marble unless it were coming hard. Mike took a while because he kept knocking some of his soldiers over with his feet as he crawled around setting others up. It was like the old problem of the frog in the well. How long would it take Mike to set up a hundred soldiers if he set them up at the rate of ten a minute, but knocked one down for every two he stood up? Tall, gangling, ungainly Mike. Long nosed, thin-lipped, homely Mike. Not dumb, just sort of simple. "The bottoms are bent," he said in apology.

"I know," I replied. I couldn't watch. I looked out the window. The rain had filled in some of the squares of the screen so it looked like a crossword puzzle. What was a five letter word for what I was thinking about? No, I would have to get her off my mind.

"Hey," Mike poked me.

"Huh?"

"I'm all ready."

"Oh, okay."

Mike held out two hands. I chose the left because it bulged with the supposedly hidden marble. This won me first shot. I placed the marble between the tip of my second finger and the top of my thumb. Then, knuckles to the floor, I took aim and let go. I picked off a couple of Mike's men. He could have done almost as well blindfolded. He kept watching his men go down. He seemed to feel for them as if they were alive. Then we changed colors and tactics, but the results were the same.

I heard the front door and the familiar tap of my mother's footsteps on the wooden stairs. She was delighted to find us amusing ourselves so quietly. She still thought of us as boys, either good or bad depending on whether we behaved. She would never comprehend our growing up. She entered the room and bent over for us to kiss her hello in turn. Her skin was lined and loose. I wondered if ten years ago she had been really young like Vicky.

"Dinner's at half past six sharp," she said.

"Oh, boy!" Mike said, his face lighting up.

"And look at your hands, boys." Both Mike and I automatically glanced at our hands, filthy from the floor. "Be sure and wash up before dinner." Then she walked out.

Pop carved the roast. Although he really must have known after all these years that my mother and I liked it rare and Mike wanted his well done, he invariably asked as he poised the knife over the beef. The plates were then passed over to mother who applied the potatoes and vegetables. There was no use in saying easy on the string beans. Everyone had to eat everything. Mother asked Pop what was new at the plant. Pop said nothing was new. Mother told my old man the neighborhood gossip. Someone's child was sick, somebody else had won a new deep freeze at a church raffle. Mostly I kept my eyes on my plate and ate. After dinner, Mike and I dried the dishes while mother washed. I wondered where Vicky was and what she was doing and if she ever had dried a dish. I couldn't imagine it. When everything was put away, mother dismissed us and we joined my old man in the living room. He was watching the TV. I excused myself early and lay in bed in the dark, just thinking.

11

Saturday was a terrific day. Cooler, dry air had driven away the heat and the stickiness. There wasn't a cloud in the sky. As I passed the first tee on my way to the pool there were several foursomes waiting their turn, swinging their clubs to limber up after a five day stretch at the office. The pool would be crowded, too, because the sun would be hot. Jim's first lesson was booked for ten thirty, so we just sat around waiting for the crowd to appear. I did a few bending exercises and bounced up and down on the springboard.

"Let's see a front somersault," Jim said. I didn't need any more encouragement. The water was invigorating. "Not bad for a beginner," Jim said as I climbed up the ladder.

"Not bad, hell. Pretty damn good." I had confidence on the springboard. It sort of changed my whole personality. I sat in the sun to dry off. The warm sun beating through the crisp air felt sensational, like standing in front of a fire on a winter's day. As people started to show up I began to look for Vicky. Her husband might be around, too. I wished I had something to do tonight. I thought about calling Betty. She'd think it was funny that I hadn't asked her. Once I picked up the phone, but then I changed my mind. Betty was sweet all right, but she was really only a baby. Give her time to grow up. San Quentin quail, as Jim would put it. Betty probably had other plans anyway. She didn't have to wait around for me.

The club truck swung around behind the pool with Pete riding in the front seat. He unloaded trays of frankfurters, hamburgers, rolls and other supplies. "Hey, kid," he called to me, a container of ice cream under each arm, "better get some clothes on. My helper ain't showed up, and you're it."

"The hell you say."

"I ain't woofin' you," Pete said. "And act lively." Pete had been in the army and never got over it.

"Take it easy," I said. "The war's over." I started slowly for the locker room. On the way I passed the tennis courts, I heard applause. I looked in through a flap in the green canvas backing which lined the fencing. There was a doubles match on the first court. It looked so easy. Lucky bastards who had nothing to do but play tennis on a day like this. I was sure I could play the darn game, too, if I had money to spend on lessons and time to practice every day. Jeez, why didn't my old man have a lot of dough so I could belong to a swanky club and have a big convertible and a house with a pool. The dumb bastard. But then as I turned to walk towards the locker room I started to feel pretty ashamed of myself for thinking like that because my old man did work pretty hard, and he was proud of his skill. His old man before him had been a jeweler, too, and Pop never had a chance to do anything else. I was going to do something better. That's the way he wanted it. Then I thought about Joe Tino who worked nights as a busboy at Mack's Cabin—and all the other guys at school who had it much worse. So what was I bitching about?

I hoisted myself up on the counter and swung my legs over and dropped on my feet behind the counter. Pete just looked at me. "For Chris' sake," he said finally, "ain't there no doors where you live?" He lifted an apron from a hook on the wall and tossed it to me. Then he took one of those white chef's cap and made as though he were going to place it on my head. I grabbed it from his hand and threw it back on the shelf. "Uh, uh," I said, waving my hand in protest. "That's where I draw the line."

"If you're going to be a chef, you oughter at least look like one." Pete went over to the shelf, picked up the hat and fluffed it back into shape before standing it up gently.

"I don't have any intention of being a chef," I said, smoothing back my hair with a comb.

"You young punks is all alike. Being a chef ain't good enough for you. I suppose you'd rather peddle dope or something." Pete looked at me and shook his head in disgust. "Well," he said, "I guess you can take care of the soda fountain if that ain't beneath your dignity."

I watched Pete get everything ready. The trays of hamburgers, all the same size and height, were stacked handy to the grill. Boxes of rolls, both for hamburgers and franks, were placed within easy reach. Then he spread the frankfurters on the grill and deftly rolled them around until he had jockeyed them into even straight lines. Pete was short and stocky with a swarthy complexion and the kind of a black beard that always looked like he needed a shave. But he really knew how to manipulate a spatula. That was just as much of a talent as anything else except nobody stood around and applauded.

It was almost noon. There were lots of women sitting around, sopping up the sun, but gradually the men drifted down, attired in shorts or slacks and sports shirts and wearing cleats. Each one bowed and helloed to everyone he passed along the way, seeking out his respective wife. Then he would lean over and give his wife a casual peck on the cheek. It was funny how the chatter and laughter would start up as soon as a man joined the group, like a bunch of hens cackling for a rooster.

Then the rush came, and I was too busy to pay much attention as to who was ordering what. Pete kept shoving checks at me between doling out hot dogs and hamburgers and making up other sandwiches. He seemed everywhere at once. It didn't matter how many people hollered at him. He was calm, deliberate, masterful. A milk shake was without ice cream, but some people expected it to have ice cream, and some people expected two scoops, and some wanted the ice cream mixed up and some wanted it floating around, and then there was a question whether to use vanilla or chocolate, and it all was pretty complicated with everybody in a hurry. I brushed a couple of sodas off with my elbow and they crashed to the floor splattering over my clean slacks. I mopped up the floor and then started on my trousers.

"Forget it," said Pete looking over. "Send the club the cleaner's bill."

When I looked up, Vicky was standing in the background. Her husband was milling in the crowd to get the order. I recognized him immediately. Two other men were standing with Vicky. She was wearing that same gold two piece bathing suit she had on the first time I saw her at the pool. Her hair was pulled back straight and fastened behind in a horse's tail. She was talking to the two men. One of them was short and squat and bald, built like a wrestler, covered with hair like an Alaskan brown bear. The other was blonde and handsome in a paunchy way. He looked like an ex-athlete, now confined to leaning on bars. The butterflies had started up in my stomach. I couldn't imagine what she could see in either of these lugs, but she was giving them her attention like they really were something. I was hoping she wouldn't see me, but when she looked right through me without a flicker of recognition, I felt like hell. Her husband rejoined the group with four hamburgers and four milk shakes on a tray. They found Vicky a chair, and the three men sat around at her feet. So that's why she had said she couldn't see me. I found myself wondering if they were staying with her in that room with the red and white wall paper. Maybe both of them or, still worse, only one. Somehow I didn't feel any jealousy towards her husband. He was just her husband, and I had to accept him as such. But what about the others? The blondish guy I decided was sort of insipid looking, and flabby like you could drive a fist in him, and it would sink all the way. The hairy guy should have been kind of revolting, but maybe after a few martinis it would have been with him like it had been with me.

As the crowd thinned out in front of the counter, I could see them plainly. Vicky looked around several times but never seemed to notice me. After a while when the lunch hour was mainly over and there were just a few occasional stragglers, Pete tapped me on the shoulder. "Okay, kid, you're fired now." I went out the back and made a roundabout trip to the locker room. I hated the damn job. The locker room was alive with men laughing and talking and ribbing each other. I dawdled around in the corner by my locker, changing to my swimming trunks. When I came back to the pool, Vicky had gone. I was glad.

The afternoon dragged. A steady din of voices rose from the groups around the pool, punctuated by occasional shrieks of laughter, amplified as they carried across the pool. There was a constant splashing of water as people bobbed around in the pool. There was a periodic sucking and gurgling as excess water emptied down the drains located in the gutters along the edge. There was an air of quiet, despite the buzz of voices. Jim and I sat on chairs overlooking the pool.

"Say, wasn't that your girl I saw here before—that blonde?"

"She's not my girl," I said.

"So I see. That's what I told you before. You don't have to worry about that babe."

"Forget it," I said. "Forget all about it. Forget I ever mentioned it."

He was twisting the pipe stem to take it apart. Black goo dripped from the metal drain. "Okay," he said. "You don't have to get sore. You were the guy that brought it up originally. I thought maybe you were still worried." Jim got up. He walked over to the trash barrel, reached inside and picked up a slightly used napkin. After wiping the gonk off his pipe carefully, he bunched the napkin and dropped it back in the basket. He returned to his seat. "But, boy," he said, "Marilyn Monroe's got nothing on that babe." He started to elaborate.

I got up and walked away. I made a trip around the pool straightening out chairs and ash trays and picking up any debris lying around and putting it in the trash barrel. I sat down at the other end of the pool where the water splashed into the pool in streams from two separate nozzles. There were a few puffy white clouds overhead. The sun was beginning to lower itself. Occasionally it would duck behind a cloud for a few minutes and, without its warming presence, the afternoon was quite cool. I started to think about evening again. I couldn't stand another evening at home. I wondered what Vicky would be doing—probably making the rounds of clubs and bars. Maybe she was wondering about me. Fat chance. Maybe I could try Betty, but jeez, it was so late now. She'd say she was busy whether she was or not. Maybe Jim would go to a movie or something. I'd ask him later.

12

A hazy mist hung over the shower room despite the effort of the creaky exhaust fan to suck it away. Jim was standing up, drying himself.

"Whatcha doing tonight?" I asked him.

"I've got a hot date, son."

"Jeez, I wish I had something to do."

"What! The young romeo has nothing on the fire? You're slipping, boy," Jim said, sawing away at his back with the towel. I was adjusting the hot and cold water of the shower. I held the palm of my hand under the flow to make sure it was the right temperature.

"Well, don't look like you lost your last friend. Do you want me to see if I can get you a date?"

"Jeez, I don't want to horn in on your fun." I had to say that much, but he wouldn't have to ask me a second time.

"You won't bother me," he said. "I'll call my girl and see if she's got a friend." He had one hand on the door leading from the shower room. "Do you want me to?"

"Sure, that'll be swell." I only spent a few minutes under the shower and was still half wet as I knotted the towel around my waist. I stopped at the door to take a pair of brown paper slippers from the rack.

Jim was talking on the phone. "Okay, sweetie, I'll see you later." He hung up. "You're all set kid," he said, rubbing his hands. "She's getting her sister."

"What's she like?" The knot loosened around my waist and the towel fell off. I bent down to pick it up.

Jim playfully snapped his towel at me, not hard, but accurately. I straightened up and rubbed my behind. He sang, "I know a girl upon the hill, she won't do it but her sister will." I had never seen Jim in such good spirits.

We ate at the club and left right after dinner. The girls lived in Croton, about a half hour's trip. On the way I took my wallet out of my pocket and looked inside. Seven dollars mightn't go too far if the girls wanted to go any place special.

"Don't worry," said Jim. "This is going to be a cheap evening." He pulled up in front of a drug store and got out. "Do you want me to get you a package?" he asked, leaning through the window on my side.

"No," I said. The prospect of the evening was beginning to make me a little nervous. It was all too coarse, too planned.

"Have you got any with you?"

I shook my head.

"Well, hell, I'd better get you some then."

"I may not need any."

"A gentleman is always prepared," Jim said. He turned around and strode into the store.

I was sorry now I'd come along. I could duck out while Jim was in the store, but if I did I could never face Jim again. I thought about the first time I had gone to a house with a couple of my friends. There were only two girls. We had drawn lots. I had lost. I waited around downstairs in the dimly lit, shabbily furnished room. When my turn came, the girl led me upstairs. We had sat down on the side of the bed. The girl was wearing nothing but a stained yellow silk kimono. She looked tired and dirty. There was a smell about her, about the whole room. It made me sick. Or maybe it was my imagination. That's the way I am, I guess. I just sat there, looking down at the floor. It needed a good scrubbing. I wondered what my mother would have thought of the place. Suddenly I felt sick. The girl took my hand and squeezed it and smiled up at me. I pulled my hand away.

"For Christ's sake, sonny," she had said to me, "don't be wasting my time. I'm busy." She tried to fondle me, but I couldn't stand it.

"I guess I'm not in the mood," I had said, and offered to pay her. She wouldn't take the money. She had seemed insulted. "I'm sorry," I said.

"Grow up and come back." She was still sitting on the bed nude as I closed the door behind me.

It made me sick to think about it. Jim returned, and we were off. He took a little package and pressed it in my hand. "Slip this in your wallet," he said.

I took it and put it away. We stopped at a light in the center of a fair-sized town. There was a bus station across the street. "If you think I might be in your way, I can still go home."

"What's the matter?" Jim said. "Getting chicken? A big operator like you."

"Hell, no," I said. Those butterflies were bobbing around. "I just don't want to cramp your style."

"You won't. Don't give it a moment's thought." Jim was driving with one eye on the mirror, and I noticed he was slowing down. Then a motorcycle shot by us, and he picked up his speed. "There ought to be a law against those guys. They're enough to give you heart failure. I thought for a minute it was a cop." He flipped on the radio, and we listened to a disk jockey. Jim wound around through Croton, and finally we were on Chestnut Street. It was beginning to get dark. We drove along until we pulled up in front of an old brown, shingle house with an open porch in front.

We walked up the cement walk and up the drab steps which sagged in the center from wear. The railing was a dirty yellow, and the paint was peeling. Jim pushed the bell. Then a light flashed on inside through the frosted glass top of the front door, and the door swung open.

"Tony Bianchi, meet Alice Sickles," Jim said. We shook hands. She led us into the living room. The house had a musty smell. The furniture was as old as the exterior. There was a couch and striped wing back chairs, and they had lace affairs on the back and on the arms. The tables were mahogany with heavy, carved legs. Faded scatter rugs spread over the floor.

"Sit down," she said. "My sister'll be down in a minute."

"Didn't I tell you Alice was cute?" Jim said. "Tell me," he said to her, "how do you get so cute?"

She smiled. She was shy a couple of teeth on one side. She had coarse, brown hair, chopped short. Her eyes were small and close set.

"How've you been, beautiful?" Jim said. "Did you miss me?"

"Of course not, silly." She took his hand and brought it over on her lap and put her other hand on top of it. They were seated on the couch, and I sat on the chair opposite. I stared around the room. The black fireplace was piled up with artificial coal in a grate. There were somber-looking prints on the wall, depicting Christ on a cross and other religious subjects. I got up and walked around, stopping to examine a calendar that had almost every day marked as some sort of holiday or occasion. It showed a picture of angels on top.

"I wonder what's keeping Madge," Alice said. "I'd better go see."

"How do you like her?" Jim said, after she had left the room. "Some figure, huh?" She had large breasts, particularly noticeable because she was so thin. Her legs were spindly.

"She seems very nice," I said.

Alice returned soon, followed by her sister who was similarly dressed in a skirt and sweater. Her sister had the same full bosom, but she was built different. She was dumpy, and her legs were heavy. She wore flat rubber soled saddle shoes. Her chin was covered with pimples, and she had gold-rimmed glasses. Alice performed the introductions. Then she returned to the couch and sat with Jim. Her sister took one of the large chairs opposite the couch, and neither of us said anything.

"How about a dance," Jim said. In the corner there was an old standing radio, an Atwater Kent. Jim sat on his haunches fiddling with the dials while Alice stood over him, her hand on his shoulder. Then they tuned in on some slow music and started in. I asked Madge if she wanted to dance.

"Swell," she said. We picked up a couple of the rugs and folded them back to make more room. Madge was a terrible dancer. The top of her head came up to my chin. I looked over at Jim and Alice. Her left hand was up around his neck, stroking the back of his head. Both of his hands were around her waist. They were hardly dancing, just necking to the music.

Madge was socking her fat body against mine. I wanted to push her away. I could see Jim and Alice had stopped dancing. Her arms were around his neck, and they were kissing. Their profiles were silhouetted in front of a lamp. You couldn't see any light between them.

Then Jim danced Alice toward the door, and they disappeared.

As soon as were alone, Madge moved in, pressing her head into my chest. I was trying to think of a way of dislodging her without hurting her feelings. A glass of water, that was it. "Say, could I have a glass of water?"

"Water? Why sure." She took me by the hand.

"Are you sure we won't be disturbing your. . .?"

"No," she said, "they probably went upstairs."

Madge led me out to the kitchen. "Would you like a coke instead?" she said, pulling on the light by a drawstring.

"I think I would at that." The kitchen was in keeping with the rest of the house, an ancient stove with the oven on top, an old sink permanently stained with rust, and an old-fashioned refrigerator with the outside coils. Madge opened two Cokes, and we sat down at the table in the center covered with cracked linoleum.

"What do you do?" I asked.

"I work," she said, fumbling with a pearl necklace that hung down over her sweater. One particular pimple on her chin glowed red and nastily in the bright light.

"Where do you work?" I asked. You seemed to have to pull things out of her.

"At Kresge's in town. I work at the hardware counter."

I eyed my glass. It was chipped around the rim. "Where are your parents?" I asked.

"They went to the movies. They'll be back." She took the glasses, rinsed them and left them in the sink.

We went back to the living room. I eyed the stairs as we walked past. There was a lone light on top. There were no sounds. The radio was still playing in the living room. I purposely avoided the couch, sitting down on one of the stuffed chairs. It was one of those chairs in which you had to sit up straight. Madge stood in front of me and swayed to the music. "How about a dance?" she said, leaning over to help me up.

"No, thanks," I said. I noticed that her skirt had a couple of big spots in front. Her sweater was discolored under the armpits. I thought about Vicky, how fresh and immaculate she always looked, her skin so clear and well scrubbed. Betty, too. It was like the difference between eating off a table with a clean white cloth and lapping your food off the floor.

"Don't you like to dance?"

"Not much."

She turned around and lowered herself on my lap. She arched her neck so she could get her face close to mine. I couldn't stand it. I struggled forward and slipped out of the chair, leaving her in possession.

"Say, what's the big idea?" she said.

"I dunno." I couldn't think of a better answer. I walked over and gazed out of the window. A street lamp glowed across the way.

"Don't you like me?" she said.

"That's not it. I guess I sort of don't feel well."

"That's too bad." She came over to me and took my hand as if to lead me back to the couch. "Maybe I can make you feel better."

I pulled my hand away. "Please, just leave me be."

"The hell with you." She turned around and stalked off. I heard her climb the stairs.

I felt like a mean bastard. Madge couldn't help her face. She had only been trying to be like her sister. It was me who was peculiar. I thought about following her upstairs and apologizing somehow, but I didn't know which room was hers, and if I went around knocking on doors, I might be interrupting Jim right in the middle of something. I sat down to wait for them. There were a bunch of magazines under one of the tables, an American Legion magazine, *Kiwanis,* a few copies of *Life,* all six months to a couple of years old. I picked up *Screenland* and looked through the pictures. There were the vital statistics of a young starlet, 36 bust, 24 waist, 34 hips. If I held my hand over the face, it could have been Vicky. I thought about that big paunchy blond guy I saw her with that afternoon. By this time, they might be sitting some place in the dark. Maybe she was wearing that white evening dress I first saw her in, cut low in front. They could be sitting in her car. He might have his arms around her and his hand sliding down ... Jeez. I felt hot. I stood up and walked out of the living room and opened the front door. I went outside and sat on the steps.

Pretty soon Jim and Alice came down the stairs making a lot of noise—probably to give Madge and me warning of their return. I got up and came back into the house.

"Where's Madge?" Alice said. Maybe she thought I had disposed of her and stuffed her remains in the incinerator.

"She went upstairs," I said.

"What did you do to her, lover boy?" Jim said in his usual dry way.

"Nothing," I said meekly, kind of shrugging my shoulders.

"My sister's funny sometimes," Alice said apologetically.

I noticed she had on fresh make-up. The lipstick was more purplish than what she had had on originally. "Can I make you some coffee?" she said.

"Why bother," Jim said. "Let's go out and get a bite."

Jim drove us to a near-by diner. They sat next to each other and held hands. We ordered cheeseburgers and coffee. There was a juke box control in the booth where we were sitting. Jim put in a quarter letting Alice press the buttons for the selections.

"Isn't she just as cute as a bug's ear?" Jim said, looking at her soulfully.

"Oh, go on!" Alice said, lapping it up. "Doesn't he tell that to all his girls?" she said to me.

"I wouldn't know."

"Didn't I tell you she was something special?" Jim said.

The counterman slid the three cheeseburgers down the counter in our general vicinity. He ran three coffees into thick white mugs and set them steaming beside the sandwiches. I squeezed out of the booth and went over to pick them up. Now Frankie Laine was bleating over the juke box. "I just love that recording, don't you?" Alice said. She took Jim's hand to her lips. I guess she really went for him, but she wasn't much of a prize. After we drove her back, I waited in the car while they kissed goodbye lingeringly in the doorway.

"How did you like her?" Jim said on the way home.

"She seemed very nice," I said.

"She's a good kid," he said, "and boy, does she know how! What happened with you and Madge? You should have done all right. She's a real pushover."

"I guess I'm not her type," I said.

"The hell with her. Better luck next time."

Jim drove himself back to the club, and I took the car from there. I could still see Alice's gaunt ugliness and her sister's greasy broken-out complexion.

And something else, I saw, too. They looked desperate. Not Alice so much; she had Jim. But her sister. She had nothing. That's why she tried so hard. I felt sorry for her. She was ugly, and it gave me the shudders just to think of kissing her. Poor kid; I wondered if she'd ever get married.

Then picture of the Sickles girls faded in my mind to be replaced by one of Vicky, lying full length on the diving board, the divided white of her sensational breasts pressing against the top of her black bra, her wavy, golden hair framing her face. Jeez.

13

It was reasonably early when I arrived home. Downstairs all the lights were on. I recognized the car parked out in front. It was a maroon Frazier. I was hoping I could sneak upstairs and avoid them, but my mother called out.

I went in the kitchen where the Miller's and my family were sitting around drinking coffee. Undoubtedly they had been spending the evening playing rummy. I made the rounds kissing my parents and shaking hands with the Miller's. Both Miller's were round and short. Mr. Miller had a bristly fringe of reddish hair framing his bald dome. He ran a butcher shop in town and had made a lot of money during the war.

"How's about a cup of coffee, son?" he said, fingering the white enamel coffee pot. My mother gave him a dirty look. "Can't he have one, mother?"

"Good lands, not at night just before bedtime."

"Oh nonsense," Mr. Miller said. "Make him sleep like a top so long as he's got a clean conscience. Get yourself a cup, boy."

"No, thanks." There was no point in saying I already had some coffee. "I really don't care for one."

Mr. Miller poured a second cup. He added a couple of lumps of sugar and then cream so full some of the coffee overflowed into the saucer. As he lifted the cup, drippings from the bottom splashed on the table. He solved the problem by leaning forward and meeting the cup halfway. My mother watched nervously, waiting for him to finish, then leaned towards him and wiped the table with a paper napkin.

Mrs. Miller was engrossed in a piece of cake. My old man was sipping quietly on his black coffee, blowing gently on the top of the cup to cool the liquid before each sip. Mother was waiting on everybody and not eating. "Pull up a chair and sit down, dear," she said. I brought over a white stool.

Mr. Miller picked up his dead cigar butt which was resting in an ash tray and started chewing on it. "How's swimming, boy?" he said. "When're you heading for the Olympics?"

"Diving," I corrected him.

"Swimming, diving, all the same to me, boy."

"You should see our Bobby play golf," said Mrs. Miller. "He plays only two years now and shoots already below 80." Then she turned to my father and pointed to the cake. "Just another sliver, please. It's just delicious."

"You don't say about Bobby," my mother said in just the right tone of admiration and amazement.

Outside the crickets chirped faintly, but in the woods beyond her pool they would be booming away. I wondered if they were finishing off the evening with a swim. Not her husband and the dark stocky guy. Just Vicky and the blondish fellow. I could see her dropping the straps over her shoulders and slipping out of that white evening gown.

"Tony, Mrs. Miller's talking to you."

"Excuse me," I said.

"She asked you if you knew her Ellen. She goes to Larchmont High," my mother said. My old man was stifling a yawn.

"Yes." I tried to recall a quiet, skinny, mousy girl. "Sure I do."

Mrs. Miller folded her hands over her ample expanse. "Each night there's another fellow. She's so popular, but never home before midnight. What do you young people do that you never can get home at a decent hour?" It didn't require an answer. It hardly was a complaint. Mrs. Miller was just boasting. I tried to imagine why anyone might want to take Ellen out. But then why not? Even a guy like Jim might be interested. If Ellen was that kind of a girl, it wouldn't take long for the word to get around.

"Ellen's so pretty," my mother said. Mother always tried to say the right thing.

"We must get you and Ellen together sometime," Mrs. Miller said.

"That'd be fine," I said, thinking *fat chance*. Mr. Miller's eyes were beginning to close.

"Your mother tells me you're going away to school this fall. We must do it soon. September will be around before you know it." Her voice rose and fell sweetly. I would have hated to take Ellen out even if she'd been a queen, and have Mrs. Miller spread the news all over the neighborhood. And supposing something happened like with Vicky? Supposing my mother knew Vicky's mother if she weren't married and had a mother? Mr. Miller's head was starting to sag to one side. All of a sudden he opened his eyes with a start as his wife started to say something. "For God's sake, mama, are you still talking. C'mon. I take you home." Mr. Miller struggled to his feet and pulled his wife's chair back so she could get up. Mrs. Miller gathered up her knitting bag. We saw them to the door.

After they left, father snapped off the outside light and yawned out loud. "I never thought they'd go home," he said.

"I was so embarrassed," my mother said. "You were so rude, yawning in their faces." She bustled around emptying ash trays into a large bowl. My father paused with one hand on the railing at the bottom of the stairs. "I was rude! Miller was half asleep."

"That's no excuse."

"Yackety, yackety, I never thought she'd stop." My old man plodded up the stairs wearily. I followed him and we said good-night in a whisper on top of the landing. I wondered if my folks were still in love. Their lives together seemed a mutual tolerance. They were constantly bickering over matters of no importance. So did all their friends. Was this the way all marriages were? Was Vicky's marriage like this, or hadn't they reached that stage yet? When did being in love leave off and this business of living together take up? If Vicky had other guys all the time, did all married women if they could get them? Not my mother. She never had another guy. What would my father do if she had? That's the way it was in the movies sometime, but then they married the other man. Maybe that's the way it would be with Vicky and this blond guy. He was more her age and more in her league. All these thoughts funneled through my head as I lay in bed, but there was one picture which kept recurring. Vicky and the blond guy were down at the pool, and the crickets were chirping madly. She slipped out of her white evening dress, and this soft, paunchy jaded-looking bastard with the rings under his eyes slipped his hands around her from behind. She mightn't want to, but that feeling would take hold of her, and Jeez.

14

When I got home the next night from the club, I knew something was up. It was before dinner, and my old man and old lady were sitting out on the porch. I could tell from the exchange of glances between them. It seemed to be that sort of shall-we-discuss-it-now-or-wait-till-after-supper look. My old lady excused herself, saying she had to go and turn the chicken. My father's shirt was opened at the collar, sleeves rolled up. The evening paper was folded on his lap. He rubbed his hand across the grain of his beard. I could see he was embarrassed and didn't know how to begin.

"How's the job coming, Tony?" he said.

I sat down on another of the cane-backed rocking chairs. "Pretty good."

"How's Jim?"

"He's fine."

"Making any new friends?"

"No, I don't get to know anyone really." This was all just preliminary. I wanted to get to the point. "What's on your mind, Pop?"

"Your mother's worried about you," he started in.

"Worried about me?"

He looked down and noticed the zipper on his trousers had slid down a little way from the top. He pulled it up and secured it. "She thinks you've been acting peculiar lately."

"Peculiar, what do you mean?" Poor Pop. He hated to have to discuss anything. His talents lay in his hands, not in his tongue. When it came to his hands, there was nothing Pop couldn't do.

"Well," he said, "you've been getting in at odd hours, and we never know where you've been, and you seem strange. Is anything bothering you?" He drummed on the arm of the chair with his fingers.

"Nothing special." Women in a man's life weren't anything special. Nothing that you took up with your parents.

He thought for a minute. "I hope you're not getting in with the wrong crowd at that club."

"I'm not getting in with any crowd. I told you."

My brother came racing up the front of the house on his bicycle. He braked hard and swung to the ground. He stood his bike up against the front of the porch, clumped up the wooden stairs and walked around to where we were sitting. "Hi, Pop, Tony," he said. "What's cooking?"

"Hello, Mike," Pop said.

"How'd the Yankees make out? Through with the sports section, Pop?" he said, taking the paper from my old man's lap.

"Take the paper and leave us alone for a few minutes, Mike."

Mike spread the paper and looked at the box score on the front page. "Oh boy!" he said, folding the paper and stuffing it in the back pocket of his jeans. The screen door slammed as he went in the house. It startled a bird, perching on a bush next to the house.

My old man reached in his breast pocket and drew out the tin package which Jim had bought for me and which I had left in my wallet on the bureau. He handed it to me. "Your mother found this in your room."

I tucked it away in my trousers. "So what?"

"Your mother's afraid you're getting in bad company."

It was really none of their damn business. I was old enough to do what I pleased. But it wasn't my old man's fault. He probably didn't want to talk about it any more than I did. "I know how to take care of myself," I said.

My old man tugged at his chin. "That part's all right," he said. "There's cures for those things. It was a helluva thing to get one of those diseases when I was a kid, but it's not so bad today. I was talking to one of the fellows at the plant. He says they can cure it easier'n they can cure a cold." My mother walked across the living room which adjoined the porch. She paused for a second as if to listen. "We'll be in in a little bit," he called to her. Pop rolled his sleeves up another turn. "Your mother doesn't know much about that sort of thing. I guess it was different in our day, but the main thing, Tony, don't get yourself involved. I've known lots of fellows who had an opportunity of getting somewhere, but they got themselves mixed up with a woman, and before they knew it they were married with a few kids to take care of. Then you can't do anything but keep the job you've got because you can't afford to quit."

Although he didn't say so, I was sure he was speaking about himself. Everybody indirectly speaks about himself unless he's a minister or doctor or professor and knows something about everybody else. Suddenly the lines in his face melted, and I could see him as a young guy. I felt sad about him.

"I want something better for you, Tony. Go to school. Learn to do something with your mind instead of your hands." He opened his right hand and looked at the hard callous on top of his enlarged thumb. Then he tapped his temple with his first finger. "That's what pays off. Woman can only get in your way. They bring a man down to their own level. I don't mean your mother, of course. She's a wonderful woman in a way, but they never did a man any real good. I'll help you out all I can, but make something of yourself, Tony, and don't spoil your chances right at the start by getting tied up with some dame." He seemed to be speaking easily, but the perspiration stood out on his forehead. He was looking right at me, and I looked down to avert his gaze. Tears welled up in my eyes, but I held them back. He was a great guy sometimes.

I stood up and put my hand on his shoulder. "I understand, Pop," I said, "but don't worry. It's not the way you think." I couldn't explain myself any better. I left the porch and rushed upstairs. In my room I broke down and cried, except I really didn't know why I was crying.

15

I was sitting along the ledge of the pool being the fall guy for a couple of card tricks. When a member's son said, "Take a card," I figured I'd better do it, especially since this kid's old man was on the Board of Governors. All this nasty little twelve-year-old jerk had to do was tell his old man I was surly, and it might have been the axe. He had a reputation for that. He'd got a couple of waiters around the club fired. The kid wore glasses. He had the malicious screwed up face of a real con man, and the line to go along with it. If he had gone to our high school, this little bastard would have been slapped around plenty, but when your old man was a big shot, I guess things were different. I looked at my card, the six of spades.

"Now you know your card," he said professionally. I nodded my head. He extended the pack. "Slip it in," he said, riffling the pack. "Now shuffle the deck good." I shuffled it carefully four times, because if there was any way of lousing up the trick I wanted to do it. "Now," he said, smiling and exposing a mouth full of gold bands, "you're sure you remember your card. Look over into the bottom of the pool and see if that's not your card." I looked over the side, and the little brat gave me a push. I couldn't right myself and tumbled into the water, scraping myself on the side of the pool as I went in. When I came up, the little monster was laughing himself sick. I could have poked him one. I climbed out of the pool. The flesh was scraped, but nothing serious. "Did I do that?" he said.

"How do you think it happened?" I said.

"I didn't mean to do that," he said. It was the best he could muster by way of apology. He didn't say he was sorry. I suppose he really wasn't.

"Listen," I said, "don't pull that on anyone else around here. You're liable to hurt someone."

"Don't be such a sourpuss. I said I didn't mean it." Then he trotted off.

I walked into the bathhouse to get a towel. "Why didn't you swat the little stinker?" Jim said.

"You know who that is."

"Sure. You don't have to take that kind of stuff."

"You know he'd just run to his old man."

"Ah, his old man'd be glad if someone knocked the hell out of him."

That might be all right for Jim. Maybe he'd get away with it, but not me. I sat down with Jim at his favorite table. Except for week-ends, the club really didn't need two of us. There was just the usual crowd of females developing their sunburn. They had nothing better to do. A few of them had reflectors under their chins to intensify the radiation. I was staring at them when the phone rang. Pete answered. "Hey, kid, it's for you," he called to me.

I picked up the receiver, and when I heard the voice on the other end the butterflies started their flapping. "What have you been doing?" Vicky said.

"Nothing much."

"I missed you over the week-end." Her voice was huskier than usual.

"Bull."

"Why would I kid you?"

"I don't know." I leaned forward and talked with my lips almost touching the mouthpiece. "You seemed to have plenty of company."

"You sound jealous." She laughed with that musical lilt. "One was my cousin and the other was a client of my husband, if that makes you feel any better."

"It really didn't matter," I lied.

"Listen," she said. "I'm lonesome. How about taking me to dinner tonight."

"Fine," I said, my ego swelling up like a balloon.

"There's a wonderful restaurant in Connecticut, *Le Canard*. I haven't been there in a long time, and I just feel like some of their duck. They serve it with an orange sauce and wild rice. You never tasted anything so delicious."

I was going crazy inside. "Sounds sensational," I said, remembering I didn't have much money and didn't have a shirt or tie either. I'd have to go home first. I couldn't have her pick me up there, so I arranged to meet her in the center of town in front of the bank. By the time I hung up, I was beaming all over. "What happened, kid?" Pete asked. "Somebody die and leave you a million bucks?"

"Nothing like it," I said. Jim was filling his pipe. I watched him as he drew a big wooden match from his blazer which was draped over the back of his chair. Then he scraped it along the underside of the table and waited for the sulphur flame to subside. The flame licked down into the bowl as he sucked in. "Say, Jim, can you loan me some dough till Friday?"

"How much?"

"About five bucks." That would make a total of eleven bucks, and that was enough to eat anywhere.

"Sure," he said. "Blondes are expensive, huh?"

I grinned proudly.

Jim sucked on his pipe. There was a gurgling noise from the stem. I guess he knew what I had in mind. "Didn't you like my women the other night?"

"They were okay."

"But you'd rather have your blonde? So would I, if I were casting for Miss America. But you just can't fool around with a girl like that and not get yourself all screwed up. You might even get stuck on her, and then it preys on your mind. Maybe someone gets hurt. It never works out quite right with a girl that's too pretty. I've got my own life to lead."

It sounded like my old man talking. "I can take up with a girl like Alice," Jim continued. "No strain, no complications. When I'm ready to move on, I'm free to go." I'd never seen Jim so serious. He was a hard guy to figure out. This was the first time he'd ever opened up about himself.

"What about from Alice's point of view?" I asked.

"She knows where she stands," he said. "I've never given her any wrong impressions."

I guessed Jim was right, but maybe I was more romantic. I couldn't kiss a girl and tell her I liked her if I really didn't give a damn. I couldn't even hold her hand, because it meant more to hold a girl's hand that you felt that way about than do everything with some babe you didn't. Maybe that was dumb, but that was the way I felt.

16

"You look so nice, Tony," my mother said. She was sitting out on the porch waiting for my father to get through watering the lawn in back.

"I'll bet you say that to all the boys," I said, bending over to kiss her on the cheek.

"Where are you going?" she said. I suppose it was natural enough for mothers to want to know where their kids were going, but I hated it all the same. I would never ask my kids.

"I got a date, Ma," I said, one foot on the stairs leading from the porch. I remembered my old man saying that my mother was worried because she didn't know what I was up to. I wondered what she would have said if I told her I was going out to get laid.

Mother was working away with a crochet needle. "With Betty?"

"No, Ma, with another girl. You don't know her." The grackles were out again in full force, screaming at the top of their lungs from their perch on the connecting wires of the telegraph poles. "What are you making, Ma?" I said, changing the subject.

"A shawl, Tony." She held it up for me to see.

Poor mother. She never relaxed or wasted a minute. "It's pretty," I said. "It's going to be beautiful."

She folded the loose end back into the knitting bag and resumed. Her hand moved swiftly and tirelessly, like an automatic bobbin. "Don't you ever see Betty any more?"

I didn't mind spending a little while talking. I had some time to kill. "Sure, not recently though."

"She's a lovely girl, Betty," mother said.

"She is," I agreed. I could never think of much to say to my family. Why couldn't you really sit down and talk to them. They must have gone through it all themselves. Did they forget, or was it just because they were your family? Mother's needle flew.

"Hand me those directions, please," she said, pointing to an open booklet on an adjacent table. I handed it to her and she studied the open page. I stood there for a little while leaning against the railing. Honeysuckle vines grew up the outside of the porch. The smell was sensational. I plucked a blossom, pulled out the long slender tongue and sucked it. "Well, I guess I'd better get going. Good night, Ma."

"Good night, dear. Get home early." She said it mechanically. They were just words.

It was only a short walk downtown. If I had taken a bus, I'd have been early and have had to hang around. It would have been better to be a few minutes late, although maybe if Vicky came by and didn't see anyone, she wouldn't wait. I ambled along the sidewalks I knew so well. I recognized the squares we used for hop scotch and the places where the cement was cracked or parted which meant a bump to a fellow on roller skates or on a bike. I passed the house where the Adamses lived. Mr. Adams was sitting on his front stoop in his undershirt and suspenders. He waved to me.

The Casale house was closed, and then I remembered my mother saying that the Casales were visiting relatives in North Carolina or some place. The Levins were eating. I could see the tops of their heads sitting in what I knew was the dining room. The Levins were the first Jewish family that moved into the neighborhood. Everybody talked about it for a while, but they seemed like everybody else except that they used to hire a girl to come in and do the housework. My mother always said that was such a foolish way to spend money.

As I started down the hill where we went bellywhopping during the winter, I found a round stone and kicked it along until it rolled off into a sewer at the end of the block. Then I decided not to step on any lines in the walk. If I did, something would happen. Vicky wouldn't show up. I stepped on a line unthinkingly, but that didn't count—only if I did it again. Broadway was a wide street with lots of tremendous red brick mansions and gorgeous lawns. One of those foreign two-seater sports models was parked in front of a house. It was so low to the ground, and the gear stuck up from the floor between the two seats. I would have rather had a convertible like Vicky's, and the funny part was it didn't cost any more.

Soon I was passing stores—Brown's Electrical Appliances run by the twins, Mrs. Schultz's bakery, The Jewel Shoppe where my father always stopped to look in the window at the diamond rings and tell us how overpriced they were. Then I got to the corner and waited in front of the bank. It was a new building with round bronze doors. A man came by with a package, took his key, opened the night deposit box and dropped his bundle inside. I watched him and he eyed me suspiciously.

Finally the big, blue De Soto convertible came along, creeping slowly I walked toward the curb and held up my hand. Vicky greeted me with a warm smile. She was dressed in a dark linen suit with a white scarf around her neck. She leaned across the front seat to open the door.

"Hello, cutie," she said. "Do you want to drive?"

"Sure." I walked around to the other side, and she slid over. Her blonde hair contrasted sensationally against the dark material of her jacket. "How do we go?" I said.

"Up the Hutchinson River Parkway, and then I'll tell you where to turn off."

We zoomed off. The radio was playing softly. "It seems like ages since I saw you. Did you miss me?" she said.

"I guess so," I said, playing it cozy.

"What did you do over the week-end?"

"I had a date Saturday night," I said mysteriously.

"I couldn't imagine you sitting home," she said, giving me that wonderful smile. A teacher once told me a smile was the greatest asset you could have, and I used to practice in the mirror. I never could manage anything like Vicky's. It was like turning on a light in a darkened room.

I stopped at the toll booth on the parkway, and, as I fumbled in my pocket, Vicky touched my arm. "My treat this evening," she said. I wondered whether she meant dinner, too, but I didn't say anything. Now we were in Connecticut. Signs advertised the speed limit as 55. We were moving along effortlessly at 60. It was a magnificent parkway divided by a wide center strip and beautifully landscaped. Before we seemed to have gone any distance, Vicky was saying, "Take it easy. It's the next turn off." I slowed as we cut off the parkway, along a black tar road.

Le Canard was a smallish restaurant in a converted private home. The parking lot in front was filled mostly with Cadillacs, Buicks and station wagons of one sort or another. As we walked from the car, Vicky took my arm. She carried herself straight and seemed taller in her high-heeled shoes. She looked older, too, or at least more sophisticated, more like the first night I had seen her. The scarf was knotted high at the neck and held together by a small, round diamond pin. Only the bulges in her jacket revealed the fullness of her figure.

The head man dressed in black with a bow tie greeted us at the door. *"Bon soir, Madame,"* he said.

"Good evening, Paul," Vicky answered.

"Have a drink at the bar, Mrs. Powers. We'll have a table for you and *votre ami* in a little while." He seemed to grasp our relationship immediately, but it was all very matter of fact.

We sat at the high stools. Bottles of every description capped with silver spigots lined the shelves opposite. Antique beer steins were spaced between the bottles. Vicky ordered a scotch on the rocks, and I said make it two. The bartender showed us a bottle. "Give us Grant's twelve year old," Vicky said. There was a crock of cheese and some crackers at my elbow. I made myself a sandwich and then remembered I should have offered one to Vicky first. When the drinks were set before us, we clinked glasses together. "Here's to us," Vicky said. The scotch didn't taste as bad as the martinis, but it burned more as it went down, and then left me with a warm glow. Vicky threw hers down almost in one gulp and ordered another immediately.

The bar was small and poorly lit. Two other couples and a party of four sat at the tables. Everyone knew the bartender by his first name. He was more like a host. The other pairs were seated shortly, and then Paul came over to us. "I have your table now, Mrs. Powers." He smiled obsequiously and indicated with a sweeping gesture of his left hand. Vicky ordered a drink to be brought to the table. The head waiter or whatever he was held Vicky's chair for her. He unfolded two large menus and presented one to each of us. They were written in a flowing script. The prices were in English. That much I could read. It looked like everything was separate, and under entrees nothing was less than $3.75. I felt in my back pocket for my wallet. There was a bar check, too. Even with the fiver I had borrowed, I didn't have nearly enough dough. She had said, "My treat this evening," but Jeez, this was a hell of a place to suggest otherwise. Maybe she could read my expression as I studied the menu, because she said, "Incidentally, the food is out of this world, and so are the prices. But don't worry, we're signing Steven's name."

"That wouldn't be right," I said in mild protest.

"Steven has a charge account here." There was something nasty the way she called him Steven. "It goes on his expense account."

I was sure she wasn't going to let me pay, so I made another attempt. "That's all right for you, but maybe Mr. Powers wouldn't like the idea of your signing for me, too."

"Don't be silly, Tony," she said. "Nobody's paying for it anyway but Uncle Sam." She was carrying one of those painted picnic boxes which served as a pocketbook. She swung it open on its hinges and drew out a gold cigarette case and lighter. "Steven wants me to entertain myself while he's away. He'd be glad to see me out with you. It would amuse him." She opened the case and took out a cigarette. Even though it was one of those tipped kind, she tapped the end from force of habit.

"Then he doesn't know about your going out with me?" There were book matches on the table. I struck a match and held it as she leaned forward for the light. The scarf buckled out and I could see the lacy fringe of her slip.

Vicky thought for a moment. "Not you in particular," she said, resting her cigarette on the ash tray and picking up the menu. Each table had a small lamp, a replica of an old kerosene lamp with a little bulb at the base in place of the wick. Vicky inclined the menu towards the lamp and studied it carefully. Paul came back and stood over us with pencil poised to take the order. *"Avez-vous decidé, Madame?"* he said.

"How's the duck tonight, Paul?" she said.

"Magnifique," he responded. He brought his thumb and middle finger to his lips and blew them away with a kiss.

"I'll try it, Paul," she said, "and bring me a crabmeat cocktail first and a mixed green salad with the entree."

"Very good, *Madame*," he said, scribbling with a flourish. "And you, *Monsieur*," he said, coming around to me.

"I'll try some of that duck, too."

"And something first?"

The crabmeat cocktail was a $1.50. Even the soup was seventy-five cents. I couldn't bring myself to ordering things that expensive, even though I wasn't paying for it. "Nothing first," I said.

"Very good, *Monsieur*," he said, retreating rapidly.

"What's the matter with that guy?" I said. "Is he a fruit or something?"

Vicky laughed. "Just French," she said.

The dining room was small. It held perhaps twenty tables. They all were occupied. It was dark except for the glow of the lamps. It was hard to distinguish anyone. There was a feeling of privacy. A waiter wheeled in a serving table to take care of a foursome at an adjoining table. He lit burners and warmed everything in gleaming copper pans. He deftly manipulated fork and spoon with one hand as he portioned the food. A boy came by with a metal bread basket hung around his neck. He slid back the door, displaying an assortment of hot rolls. Another boy placed butter balls on the bread plate.

"Jeez, this is some swanky joint," I said, taking a roll and breaking it.

"I guess that's what you would call it at that," said Vicky, crushing out her cigarette and finishing her drink.

The waiter brought the crabmeat in a glass dish inside a larger metal dish packed with ice. It looked like lumps of fish, and I didn't see how it could possibly have been worth $1.50. You could get a whole meal for that at a lot of good restaurants. The waiter stood off to the side with his arms folded, waiting patiently. As soon as Vicky put down the fork he swooped over and removed the dish. I had polished off a couple of rolls meantime, with several replacements of butter.

"Do you go to places like this often?" I asked her.

"There are no places like this," she said. "Wait till you taste the food. There's nothing like it."

Before too long the waiter jockeyed the service wagon into position beside our table. He went through the same ritual of lighting the burners before serving the duck. Two slices of orange decorated the plate. Then he came around with the wild rice and the succotash.

It was all solid meat, no bones, and covered with a brownish sauce. The rice was hard and grainy. "Do you like this rice as well as the regular kind?" I said. A few kernels fell off my fork on to my lap. I quickly brushed them to the floor, hoping Vicky hadn't noticed.

"It's supposed to be a real delicacy. Don't you like it?"

"I do. It's wonderful, but it's different." It was really sort of disappointing.

After we finished, and the plates were removed, Paul returned with the menu.

"Bring us some coffee ice cream with the Creme de Cocoa sauce. I'm ordering it for you too, Tony. You'll like it," Vicky said.

"Very good, *Madame*. And demi-tasse?"

"Yes, demi." Paul backed away. "That saved you the trouble of making up your mind, Tony."

As we were sipping our coffee, a tall, dark girl came over to give Vicky a big hello.

"Why, Cynthy, darling," Vicky said, flashing that radiant smile. "Miss Brooks, Mr. Bianchi."

"Don't get up," Miss Brooks said as I jumped to my feet.

She put her hand on Vicky's shoulder. "It's wonderful seeing you."

"You, too, dear."

"How's Steve?" the other girl said.

"Simply marvelous. He's in Washington during the week, you know."

"Yes, I know." Then she leaned over Vicky and said in sort of a whisper which I couldn't help but hear, "Aren't you robbing the cradle, dear?"

Vicky flushed. "Don't be so envious, darling," she said.

"Well, I've got to run. My friends are waiting. Call me, Vicky. We must get together soon." She looked in my direction. "Nice to meet you, Mr. Bianchi."

I started to say glad to meet you, but she tore off before I could get it out. I eased myself back in my chair.

"You didn't have to stand up for that bitch," Vicky said, taking out another cigarette.

"Isn't she a friend of yours?" I said, getting ready with a match, but she had already flicked her lighter.

"I suppose so." She sat, silent, puffing at her cigarette. I put a lump of sugar in my coffee. There was no cream, but I didn't want to ask for it. Vicky drank hers black. Then she took out her lipstick. She applied the color skillfully and smoothed it with her lips. Next she powdered her nose and inspected her face from all angles in the little round mirror of her compact. Paul came over with the check. Vicky signed it without so much as glancing at it.

"Was everything all right, *Madame?*" Paul said.

"Wonderful as usual, Paul."

"Wonderful," I echoed. I was still a little hungry.

After Paul left, Vicky dug into her basket and fumbled with her wallet. She withdrew some bills and slid a dollar over towards me, covering it with the palm of her hand. "Give this to Paul on the way out," she said. I waved it away and started to reach in my inner breast pocket for my wallet. "Tony, please put your money away," she said sharply. "This is my treat. I told you."

"Okay," I said with resignation. She left four dollars on the table for the waiter. Four bucks, I thought to myself, for bringing a few dishes and clearing them off again. What a racket. Paul was standing benignly at the entrance, menus in hand. I slipped him the dollar. He bowed his head and said *bon soir.*

"Do you want to wait and I'll bring the car?" I said to Vicky outside.

"No," she said. We walked across the parking area, our feet crunching on the gravel. It was a beautiful night. The stars were distinct. I recognized the Big Dipper and Cassiopeia's Chair. I thought about pointing them out to Vicky, but she was striding rapidly towards the car several steps ahead of me. She seemed out of sorts. I didn't figure she'd have been interested anyway.

As we drove home, Vicky sat up straight, on the far side of the front seat. The radio was going, and she smoked incessantly. I guessed maybe I had acted like a dope in the restaurant. I felt sort of ashamed at having her treat me. The least I could have done was pay the tip. I should have insisted. The whole thing had made me feel like a little boy out with his mother. In fact, that was just what my old lady used to do—give me the money so I could pay and seem like a man. "Are you mad at me?" I said as we pulled up in front of the door.

"No," she said thoughtfully. "I guess everything has its limitations. I'm just tired."

She softly turned the latch. "Hadn't I better go?" I said, standing outside.

"I should say not," she responded. The downstairs and upstairs hall lights were burning. "Come up," she said, "I want to take off these clothes and relax." I followed up to her bedroom. It was a huge room with twin beds and a chaise longue in one corner. It was decorated in pale blue, even the radio on one bed table and the telephone on the other. Vicky excused herself as she disappeared into another room which led off the bedroom. I wandered over to the dressing table. On top was a tray with almost two dozen different kinds of perfume, almost as much as Mr. Sullivan carried in his entire stock. There were several atomizers and boxes of powder. A twin leather frame showed the faces of an elderly couple. They probably were Vicky's parents. On the other side was a large picture of her husband. It had been taken some time ago, when he had a full head of hair. Several snapshots were stuck in the side of the mirror showing people in bathing suits and on a boat. Vicky returned dressed in sort of a negligee made of smooth, shiny pink material. She went over and draped herself gracefully on the chaise longue. She took a cigarette from a box on a nearby table and eyed me as I looked around for a place to sit.

"For God's sake," she said, "sit down."

I started for a chair across the room. "Not so far away," she said. "Come over here." She moved her legs to make room for me at the foot of her couch. I sat there stiffly. The butterflies moved around inside me. She blew out a wreath of smoke. "You're a funny one."

"What do you mean, funny?"

She crushed her cigarette into the ashtray. "I don't know. Don't worry about it." She held out her arms and pulled me towards her.

17

I slept overnight in the same room I had the time before. The bed had been turned down and the pajamas laid out. She must have planned all along the evening would end the way it did.

I was lying half awake, half asleep in the wonderfully comfortable bed with the sensationally cool, smooth sheets when there was a faint rap on the door. I didn't answer, but then the knock was louder.

"Yes?" I called.

Then that clipped, expressionless voice of the houseman, "It's seven-thirty, sir. Madame asked me to call you."

"Okay." I bathed in the glass enclosed shower and was almost dressed when there was another knock.

"Your breakfast, sir." Jeez, this was really living. I opened the door and Herman came in carrying a tray with folding legs. He was wearing the same black coat and trousers. He lowered the legs and set up the tray close to the window. He brought over a chair. There was orange juice, a coffee pot, a regular cup, an egg cup, napkin, silver and several covered plates. A newspaper was folded at the side of the tray. He lifted the lids, revealing toast under one and a couple of boiled eggs under the other. "Will that be all right, sir?" he said, holding the covers for my inspection.

"Looks great, Herman. Thanks a lot." He replaced the covers, looking at me peculiarly, and left with swift, silent steps. Then I gulped the orange juice and sat down to open the eggs. The table was knee level. I pulled the napkin from under the silver and spread it over my lap. Unfolding the newspaper, I glanced at the headlines as I ate. After I was finished, I went downstairs. Herman had evidently heard me and was waiting at the foot of the stairs. "Did you find everything you wanted, sir?" He made me uncomfortable. He was solicitous, but I had the feeling all the time that he was keeping tabs on me like a private dick. Everything about him was so formal. "Madame said to take the car and to tell you dinner will be served at eight tonight."

"Who said I was coming back for dinner?" I said.

"Those were my instructions," he said, without batting an eye.

I got in the car and drove off, thinking all the time about what to tell my family. I could say I had to stay over at the club to help out, but suppose they telephoned and found I wasn't there. Jeez, were they ever a pain in the neck. A couple of caddies and a fellow who worked behind the desk saw me as I drove in. I wondered what they thought. They probably could figure out the deal. Everybody'd be getting wise soon. If Vicky had asked me to dinner again herself, I'd probably have accepted all right, but it was sort of a nerve to have that creep tell me. But just thinking about Vicky made me suck in and feel tight all over. Anyway, I had to stop worrying about it. Did everybody else always have something on their mind all the time? Maybe I was going nuts.

I phoned my old lady first thing. She told me she hadn't slept a wink, wondering what had happened to me. She sounded all upset. I told her I was at a friend's house, and the car busted down, and I didn't want to phone late at night and disturb her. I said I had to stick around the club tonight, but didn't have the guts to mention staying overnight. The way she said goodbye made me feel like hell. It preyed on my mind all day, and the time seemed to drag. Jeez, if I were to tell Vicky my old lady said I had to go home, that might be the last straw.

As I pulled up in front of Vicky's house after work, another car was parked in the driveway. It was a Packard sedan with a low license plate, just two letters and a single number, the kind you got by being someone special. I walked in the house. There were voices in the living room.

"Is that you, Tony?" Vicky called.

"Yes."

"Come on in."

She was sitting at a card table with another woman. "Tony," she said, "this is Mrs. MacKnight. Sit down, Tony. Help yourself to a drink if you want one." Each of the women had a drink in hand, and there were two other empty glasses. Ash trays were in each corner of the table, and they were filled with butts, red from lipstick. "I just can't play with Jane," Mrs. MacKnight was saying. "It drives me crazy. She sits there touching one card after the other, hesitating, and the longer she thinks, the surer I am she's going to pull the wrong card."

"I know just what you mean," Vicky said.

"You remember the hand she left me in, six no trump. Imagine. She was blank in my suit, and besides I was just Blackwooding, showing her my kings. I knew it had to play in hearts. I just wasn't sure if it was six or seven." The other woman looked older than Vicky. She had short fading hair and wore glasses. The skin on her face was dry and blotchy. She was doodling on the score pad with a stubby wooden pencil, the kind they give away at golf clubs with the score sheets. The other woman must have been wondering who I was and what I was doing, or maybe she knew. Did women discuss those things the way guys did? They didn't seem to be paying any attention to me.

"I know," Vicky went on. "Jane made a terrible overcall with me. Nothing but the ace, queen, ten of spades five times, not an outside trick. And then she went down two more than she had to." Mrs. MacKnight finished her drink. "Let me make you one more for the road," Vicky said.

"No thanks, dear. I must dash. We're going to the Comforts for dinner." She folded her glasses and slid them in a case which she packed into her bag.

"I'll see you to the door," Vicky said.

"Don't bother, dear. Please. I'll find my way." She stalked out as though I wasn't there.

Vicky watched at the window until we heard the motor start and the car move off. It was the first time I had been in this room. It had a huge fireplace at one end with two big chairs at either side. There was a couch and several other easy chairs in rich-looking red or flowered material. A grand piano stood in the corner. Vicky came over, drink in hand and sat on my lap. She bent down and kissed me on the cheek. "How are you this evening, my little man?" she said. She was in excellent spirits. I could smell the whiskey on her breath.

"Fine," I said.

"Did you have a hard day at the office, dear?" she said with a half smile. She shifted on my lap and then got up. "God, you've got an uncomfortable lap." She slid off and sat down on the couch, resting her drink on top of a silver cigarette box on a low mahogany table in front of her. She was wearing a pink, man's button down shirt and a skirt. Lots of the girls at school wore men's shirts with blue jeans, the shirt tails hanging out. It was usually their boy friend's shirt if they had a guy. I had given Betty a couple of my old shirts. I wondered whose Vicky was wearing. She cocked her head on the side and rested it on her right hand. "Well," she said, "what have you got to say for yourself?"

"Not much," I said.

"Well, you're interesting, I must say."

I thought about my old lady and decided to get it straight right off the bat. "Listen, Vicky," I said. "I can't stay overnight like last night."

"Don't flatter yourself," she said, looking faintly amused.

"I didn't mean it that way," I said. "I just meant I have to go home to sleep."

"That's all right," she said. "Are you sure you don't want a drink?"

"I don't think so."

She rose to her feet. "I'm going upstairs to take a bath. Can you entertain yourself for a while?"

"Sure."

"Go in the library," she said, standing at the door. "It's straight across the way. The light switch is on the left."

After she left, I got up to look around. There was an additional room beside the library which I imagined was the dining room. It was closed off with heavy oak doors. The library had drawn curtains so it was fairly dark. I switched on the light. It was a small room with a desk on one side, a fireplace at the end, a bar, and a leather couch and chair. I looked over the titles on the book shelves. There were a lot of legal books, an encyclopedia and lots of sets in matched bindings. I could hear the water running upstairs. I picked up a copy of *Life* from a rack. I went through it, looking at the pictures. The water had stopped. I visualized Vicky undressed, stepping into the tub. I leafed through some back numbers of *National Geographic*. It was like one of those lousy Travelogs. Now the water was draining. She had been gone for over a half hour. It was after eight. I went back to the living room. I fooled around with the cards. Finally I heard her footsteps on the stairs. I sat down on one of the comfortable chairs to appear relaxed. The butterflies started up as she entered the room. She really looked terrific. She wore a white sort of sweater top with an embroidered crest, dark velvet slacks and crocheted-like gold shoes. Her hair hung loose and soft. "I hope I wasn't too long," she said.

"No," I answered, staring at the way her sweater molded her breasts.

"That's good," she said. "Dinner's ready, I believe."

The dining room doors were open. Herman in that same funeral outfit with a little black bowtie was waiting, holding Vicky's chair. I sat down at her right.

The meal was sensational, roast beef, real rare just the way I liked it, roast potatoes, string beans, salad, and a fancy strawberry pudding for dessert. Herman served each dish, holding the platter in one hand and the other hand behind his back. Vicky was sort of strange. The easy conversation we had had the first time I was here was lost. I couldn't think of much to say, and her answers were curt. Maybe she was insulted at my telling her I couldn't stay overnight. If she was, it was my stinking family's fault. Jeez.

After dinner we went back to the living room. She started to put the cards away. "You don't play gin or anything?" she said.

"Casino," I said.

She continued to put the cards away. Then she took a silver pan and dumped all the ashes in it. She walked around the room adjusting pictures and sort of straightening up. After a while she came over and sat on my lap. She put her hand on the back of my neck and pressed her lips heavily to mine. I put my arms around her feeling where her brassiere was joined. Then I slid my hand around until it was just under her breast which— overhung, hard and firm. She put her hand on my knee. My blood was racing. As my hand moved upwards, she grabbed it and pulled it away. Then she stood up.

"What's the matter?" I said.

"Nothing particular." She pulled her sweater down tight. I felt cheated. "I'm tired, Tony. You'd better go home now."

"You're not sore at anything I said, are you?"

"No, dear," she smiled at me. "Take my car and leave it as usual."

I sort of sat there on the couch in a daze. She held out her hand to help me up. "Come on, Tony. Be a good boy."

She waited in the door as I got in the car. The light coming from within shone through the thin dark material of her slacks, revealing her long graceful legs and thighs.

I wanted to go back and take her in my arms and finish what she had started, but I was afraid she'd only turn me away. I'd only be making a worse fool of myself than I already had. I turned the switch and the engine came alive. As I started down the long driveway I had the terrible thought it might be for the last time. I couldn't just pinpoint the trouble, but somehow I knew that I hadn't played it cozy. I was out of my class. It was funny how you could hit it off with someone sometimes, whereas other times there seemed nothing to say. It had been better with Betty. I guess that's because we had more in common, like school and stuff. Even with Betty though, if I saw her too often, it was sort of dull. There were evenings when I was real entertaining, no kidding, particularly after going to see some movie with a guy like Cary Grant who always had a good line of chatter. It wasn't that you repeated any of the same things, but it was sort of contagious to listen to his line of poop. I had to recharge myself— that was all. It couldn't be the end of Vicky. Maybe she was just tired, like she said. It was just as well because I had to get home early.

18

I was walking along the street looking for the blue De Soto. I could see it parked a few blocks ahead, the familiar tail lights, the silver frames setting off the license plate, the big rear window of the black top, but when I had walked a couple of blocks, the car seemed no closer. The road seemed to get narrower. The sidewalks disappeared. The cement gave way to dirt. The houses were left behind. A man seemed to be following me. The car was still the same distance away, parked at the side of the road. It couldn't be moving. Nobody was at the wheel, but I was no nearer. The man behind was gaining on me. I quickened my steps. I turned around and could see the man behind, the slender, sharp features, the thin determined mouth, the sparse hair. It was Vicky's husband. The road had narrowed into a path hardly wide enough for a car. The forest was thick on either side. The car was always just out of reach, like the electric rabbit at the dog races. Steven Powers was only ten yards behind now. I started to run. He just continued to walk at a usual pace, but he was always closing the distance between us. Then he grabbed me by the arm. I tried to shake him loose. He tightened his grip.

"What's the matter?" I said. "Let me go."

He didn't say anything, but his eyes narrowed ominously. His grip was like a vice. "Let go of me," I screamed.

Then I opened my eyes and looked up. Mother was shaking me. "Tony, it's only me. It's time to get up."

I sank back on the mattress, never so relieved to see her sad eyes peering down at me. "What's up?" I said.

"There's a letter downstairs for you from Lincoln Academy. Your father wanted to open it, but I wouldn't let him. He'd like to see it before he leaves. It's time for you to get up, anyway."

I swung my legs to the floor. I padded downstairs in my pajamas and bare feet. My old man was waiting in the hallway. He pointed to the letter on the table. I ripped it open. It started in with, "We are pleased to inform you . . ."

"What's it say?" they chorused, my old man peering over my shoulder.

"Congratulations, my boy," he said, throwing his arms around me and kissing me. "I knew it would come, I knew it would come. You'll be a great man some day, Tony. I always knew it. Thank God. Thank God!" After he had released me my mother kissed me, too. The letter had fallen to the floor. She picked it up and read it.

"That's just the tuition, isn't it, Tony?" she said. "That doesn't cover your room and meals." Then reading aloud, "'Opportunities are provided for scholarship boys to earn their board by registering with the Student Employment.'"

"I'll work, Mom. Don't worry about that part."

"Sure he'll work," my old man said, beaming, "and, Mom, you just lost yourself an oil burner. You can order coal for next winter. I always did like taking care of that furnace. Lincoln Academy and then college!" My father slapped me on the back. "Attaboy, Tony!" There was a lilt to his walk as he walked down the front steps and cut across the lawn to the garage. Mother folded up the letter, replaced it in the envelope and handed it to me.

"You don't know what this means to your father," she said. "And, Tony, don't stand around in your bare feet. You know how easily you catch cold."

"Not in the summer time, Mom."

"Summer colds are the worst of all. Go ahead now."

I went upstairs. Mike was still asleep, of course, one arm under the pillow, the top sheet half off. I shook him. "Hey, Mike, I'm going to Lincoln next year for sure," I shouted enthusiastically.

He opened his eyes and rolled on his back. "Who said?"

"I just got a letter." I waved it in front of his face.

"Let's see." I opened it for him and he sat up to read. Then he put it down.

"So what," he mumbled.

"Go back to sleep, willya."

I dressed rapidly and bolted my breakfast. My old lady came in to sit with me just as I was wiping the egg from the plate with a piece of bread.

"How many times have I told you not to do that, Tony? If you eat that way at Lincoln, they'll wonder where you've been brought up."

"Okay, Mom." I was in too good spirits to answer back. But I knew I was going to hear that argument for anything I wasn't supposed to do the rest of the summer. I walked the few blocks and around the corner to where I had left Vicky's car. It sparkled in the bright sunlight. A particular beam of light reflecting from the bright chrome of the tail light hit my eye, causing me to squint. Some kids were riding along on their bikes. I knew they would be watching me step into the car, and they would be wishing, like I always did, that the car was theirs, and that they were in my shoes. I could feel just for the moment a pride of possession. Some of the fellows at Lincoln might have cars. Lucky little bastards.

Maybe I'd be lonesome. Maybe everybody would have a lot of pocket money like some of those little wise guys at the club and wouldn't have anything to do with me. Well, it didn't matter anyway, because I was going to Lincoln to learn something so I'd have a chance to be a big shot lawyer like Steven Powers, or maybe a banker or something. Then I'd buy myself a big slick convertible like this, or one of those two-seater foreign jobs like a Jaguar. I'd join the Highridge Country Club, too, if I felt like it, unless I wanted to belong to some swankier joint. Then I could take Vicky to Le Canard and sign my own name, and Paul would say, "Good evening, Mr. Bianchi," scraping low as I dangled a five-dollar bill under his nose. In fact, I wouldn't take Vicky. I'd be taking some other queen because by that time Vicky would be an old bag, and when she came over to talk to me I'd give her the brush.

I was thinking so darn hard, I almost didn't see the red light. I jammed on the brakes, and the tires squealed. I was a little way into the cross lane. A police car was parked on the opposite corner. I threw the car into reverse and backed up level with the intersecting sidewalk. I glanced over at the patrol car. The door away from the driver swung open, and a policeman stepped out. Jeez, just my crappy luck. Those little butterflies inside me started to jump around. The light turned and I started ahead. The policeman was motioning me to the side with a quiet movement of his right hand. For an instant, the idea of stamping down hard on the accelerator occurred to me, but I dropped it just as fast. I pulled over and waited as the policeman strutted over leisurely. He stuck his face in the window.

"Where do you think you're going, son?"

"To work, at the Highridge Country Club, sir," I said meekly.

"What do you work at—your golf game?" he said.

"No, sir. I'm a swimming instructor." I was gripping the wheel with both hands.

"You must have a damn good job to afford a boat like this," he said.

"It's not mine, sir."

"Let's see your license."

I reached in my pocket for my wallet and handed it over with the license visible through the celluloid window. He stared at it and then shoved his cap back from his forehead. "Anthony Bianchi, huh? Do you know you could have killed someone, Bianchi? Supposing a car had been coming." He refolded the wallet and returned it to me. "Let's see the registration."

"I'm afraid I don't have it," I said, quaking.

"You don't have it, huh? Where'd you get hold of this ear anyway?" His eyes narrowed.

I looked down. "It belongs to a lady friend of mine," I stammered. "Vicky . . . I mean, Mrs. Steven Powers." He looked at me as if I was trying to pull a fast one. "Please, mister, I'm telling you the truth. Please let me off this once. I don't want to get in dutch."

He shook his head gravely. "We'll find out all about it. You can drive me to the station house." He motioned to his companion in the police car to follow, and he walked around and got in the other side.

"Come on, mister," I pleaded. "Give me a break."

"Drive straight ahead and turn right at the first light," he said.

I hugged the right side of the road. I was sticky under the armpits. I didn't want him to call Vicky and have her get into trouble, too. That would finish me with her. She'd be asleep at this hour anyway, and she wouldn't want to be disturbed. Maybe if there was any trouble, her husband would get involved, and then he'd want to know what I was doing with the car. My folks would find out, too, and besides it would cost money, just when I needed to save for fall. It was all my own fault. If I hadn't ever got mixed up with Vicky, I wouldn't have her car, and this could never have happened. Jeez.

"C'mon, sonny," the cop said. "Step on it a little, willya. I can't spend all morning on this job." I turned the corner at the light, and a few blocks farther on we drew up in front of a neat brick building which was the police station. "Just pull into the parking lot behind." I drew up next to an old Ford sedan, turned off the ignition and drew up the emergency brake. "Now let's have the keys," he said.

He followed a foot behind as we walked up to the huge desk perched on a dais. The police sergeant manning it looked down at me. He was wearing a pair of silver framed glasses. "Driving like crazy, went through a red light, no registration," said the cop who brought me in, counting the charges off on his fingers. "Claims the car belongs to some dame or something."

The sergeant behind the desk clasped his hand under his nose. He looked me up and down from head to foot. I was standing at attention. My hands were clammy. "Who did you say owned the car, son?"

I gave him Vicky's name. He just sat there for a few minutes as though it hadn't registered. He didn't say anything. He removed his glasses carefully and stuck the ends of the ear pieces in his mouth. I shifted my weight uncomfortably from foot to foot. Then he asked me my name, my address, my occupation, my story. He wrote the information on a card, forming each letter like he was a first grader just learning to write. The policeman who had hauled me in stood beside me rigidly, his hands behind his back, watching me as though I might be thinking of making a break.

The sergeant studied what he had written carefully. "Who did you say owned the car?" he asked me again.

I wet my lips and gulped. "Mrs. Steven Powers." My voice broke into a higher octave. The sergeant thought that one over as he drummed on the desk. Finally he said to the other officer, "Go in the back and see if she's got a phone." The other officer looked at me uncertainly and then disappeared through a door to the right. The sergeant turned his attention to some papers on his desk. It was about ten minutes before the other officer returned. "Yeah," he said. "There's a Steven Powers on Overland Road in Elmsford."

The sergeant picked up the receiver and then changed his mind. He motioned to the policeman who was standing aside. "Go in and give this dame a ring."

"Do you have to?" I blurted out.

The sergeant looked down at me over his glasses. "What do you mean, do we have to?"

"I'd rather you wouldn't," I said.

"Would you rather go to jail?" I didn't answer, only looked at him. "Well, would you?" he barked at me.

"No, sir."

The other policeman banged out through the door and was back in a couple of minutes. "I talked to the dame. She says it's okay."

"Well," the sergeant said, "We'll give him a ticket for reckless driving and passing a red light and let it go at that." I swallowed hard. "Is that right?" the sergeant said to the officer.

He thought for a moment wrinkling his forehead and pursing his Ups. Then he nodded vigorously. He handed the car keys over to the sergeant and left. The sergeant wrote out the ticket. He looked it over admiringly, like he was studying a dirty picture, before he handed it down to me. "That's all, sonny," he said, turning back to his desk.

I folded the summons and put it in my wallet. "How about the car keys?" I said.

"I'll take care of them," he answered.

"But I've got to bring the car back."

"You can't drive a car without a registration," he said in a bored voice. "You'll either have to get the registration and come back, or the dame'll have to come down and get the car herself." He didn't look at me. The subject was closed. I turned around and walked out. I had completely forgotten the letter from Lincoln Academy in my pocket. I pushed out the door and stood on the walk. Two red globes were attached to either side of the door with p-o-l-i-c-e in yellow lettering. I spat on the steps.

When I finally got to the club I tried to reach Vicky on the phone. The butler told be Mrs. Powers had gone out, but she had told him to pick up the car. "I'm sorry to trouble you," I said.

"No trouble, sir." He hung up.

I had to tell Jim why I was late. He shrugged. "What are you worrying about?" he said. "It's only money." Jim figured I'd get off for around twenty-five bucks. He made it sound like peanuts. I guess it wasn't much so long as it wasn't his dough. "Why didn't you talk your way out of it?" he said. "I never got a ticket in my life." So I had to listen for a half hour while he told me ten different stories how he had wormed his way out of tickets.

Towards the end of the afternoon, the phone rang and Pete called out, "Hey, Tony, phone for you."

I figured it must be Vicky, and I was scared, but then I heard Betty's voice. "I hope you don't mind my bothering you at work. You're not busy or anything?"

"No, it's swell hearing from you." I really was glad.

"Where you been keeping yourself?" she said.

I told her I sort of hadn't been doing much, and she said she hadn't been doing much. I told her about Lincoln Academy, and she practically lost her teeth. "Gosh," she said, "why didn't you tell me? That's the most wonderful news I ever heard." Betty was a good kid all right. So finally I said, "Listen, Betty, I'd like to see you sometime."

"That's why I'm calling you, Tony. A cousin of mine's coming to visit me, and a bunch of us are going to Rye Beach Saturday night."

"Sure, I'd love to," but then I remembered about the ticket and told Betty why I just couldn't afford to go out this week.

"Listen," she said. "Uncle Ben knows all the police in that town. They always stop in at the store for coffee. I might know him myself." I described the cop to her.

"If I can get that ticket fixed, is it a date?"

"And how!"

"Let me work on it," she said. That Betty was really a peach. You couldn't beat her.

Betty phoned the next night to tell me to mail the ticket to her uncle and that I owed her a date. When I hung up, I was on top of the world. My mother was out in the kitchen finishing up the dishes. I felt so good, I threw my arms around her and kissed her. "I love you, Mom," I said.

She laughed, and then she pushed me away. "What's the matter, Tony? Have you lost your mind?"

"Can I help you, Mom?" I said.

She looked around until her eyes lighted on the silver drying in the rack. "You can put those away," she said.

19

When Saturday night rolled around, I borrowed my old man's car like I always used to before the summer. He and my mother were going out to visit friends, but he said I should drop them off where they were going and they'd walk back. My old man was a pretty good guy about the car. Pop rode in back and my mother sat beside me. I drove very slowly and looked carefully at every crossing, because that was the way Mom liked it. She was always very nervous in a car. When my old man drove, she watched the road more carefully than he did. She never failed to remind him of a red light. It would have driven me nuts, but Pop didn't say much. He only got sore once in a while. After I left them off, I headed straight for Sully's Drug Store.

My old man's car was a 1947 Plymouth, two door sedan. It was the standard model and didn't even have a radio. It was about as dull as they come. It even had a lousy pickup, but I guess when you get older you don't care so much about that sort of thing. I found a parking space right out front and entered the store. Betty's face lit up when she saw me. "Hi, Tony," she said from behind the counter by the cash register. The store was empty.

"Hi, Betty." She looked pretty cute in a short sleeved red sweater which hugged her small, upright breasts.

"Long time no see," she said.

"You said it. Where's your uncle? I want to thank him."

"He went upstairs. He'll be down in a sec." A couple of girls came in and looked over the candy counter. They picked up several different kinds of candy before settling on a Bungalow Bar. "How much is it?" one said, opening a little purse.

"Six cents," Betty answered.

The girl put it back and settled for a package of gum. Mr. Sullivan came downstairs. "Gee, Mr. Sullivan, I can't thank you enough," I said.

He waved his hand casually. "Think nothing of it, my boy." Betty kissed him good-night on his bald dome. "Have a good time, kiddies," he said. I brushed by one of the stools at the fountain, and it teetered. I grabbed and righted it before it went over.

"Clumsy ox," Betty said taking my arm. It felt sort of good to be with Betty again. We drove first to Betty's house to pick up her cousin, and then we picked up John and Dick Sable, a couple of guys I knew from school, and another girl who went to high school in Rye.

Betty's cousin was sort of a fat, little sad sack. She wore glasses. John Sable played center on the basketball team. He stuttered. Dick Sable had been in my French class, and he was one of those wise guys who never did his homework and always wanted to copy yours during class to turn in at the end of the hour. Betty's cousin, Virginia, rode in front with us, and the Sable brothers rode in back until we picked up Joyce, the other girl, a blind date. Dick Sable scrambled out to get her. I guess he figured she couldn't be any worse than Betty's cousin. She wasn't too bad. She had blonde hair, but it was wiry looking. She wore blue jeans rolled up to the knees and a man's white shirt. It was too big all over, and since she wore it with the top three buttons open, you could see down to her brassiere when she bent over to get in back of the car. There was a big space between her front teeth, but she was well built and sort of pert. Betty and her cousin squeezed over against me as Dick pulled the front seat forward to permit them to get in.

"G-g-gl-gl-" John Sable was probably trying to get out a Glad-to-meet-you, but compromised by saying, "Nice knowing you." It was sort of embarrassing, waiting for him to get out sentences. We drove through the gates at Rye Beach and left the car in a parking lot. Dick Sable immediately took Joyce's arm.

As we sauntered into the park, we stopped at a booth where I bought a couple of bucks worth of scrip and so did the other guys. We started off with the scooters. Dick went around banging into all the girls head on. "Zowie," he cried as he threw his weight forward to accentuate the impact. Then he smashed into some other babe who didn't think he was so funny. Her date drove up as they were disentangling and waved his fist in Dick Sable's face. "Listen, jockey," he hollered, "if you got all that extra energy, come on outside and I'll take it out of you." He was a big-boned, square-shouldered guy with curly hair. Dick's enthusiasm was suddenly dampened.

Outside there were crowds of people sporting colored canes and carrying plastic dolls and stuffed animals which they had won at the various booths. The roar of the roller coasters reverberated through the park. Then we were standing in front of the larger of the giant wooden structures with its maze of tracks. Dick and his date were already in line.

We all tagged along. An open wooden car pulled up to the station. We rushed for the three rear seats.

The car gave a jerk as it labored up the first hill. You could see the glow of lights from all over the park. Then we started down. I pushed hard on the steel bar in front of us as my weight was lifted off the seat. Up another hill, and then we banked violently to the right as the train spiraled around a descending series of turns. Betty was on the outside of the turn, and I was thrown over against her. Squeals echoed all around. The roar of noise and wind contributed to the sensation of speed. I put my arm around Betty's shoulder, and she buried her head against my chest. Then there were a short series of dips, and the car slowed as it slid towards the exit.

We threw the supporting rail forward and climbed out. Betty's hair was streaming every which way like a haystack. She took a comb from her pocket and stood before a mirror on a penny scale. I watched her as she combed her hair forward and parted it. Her little, firm breasts pointed downward as she bent over, and then I started to think about Vicky. Betty was cute, but she didn't send me. We walked along, holding hands. But it wasn't like Vicky. When Vicky put her hand on you it was light and caressing. Somehow you wanted her to leave it there. But Vicky could turn it off, too. Then she'd become Mrs. Powers, and I couldn't quite believe how it had been between us.

"A penny for your thoughts," Betty said.

I grew red. "They're not worth it."

A crowd was gathered in front of The Crazy House, a dilapidated wooden house with moving cardboard skeletons lining the entrance. There was a balcony on the second story. Three girls and a fellow came along. There was a blast of air and one girl's skirt flew over her head revealing her pants. The crowd outside roared with laughter.

It was the sort of a place you went because it was dark enough to cop a feel. It wouldn't have been right for me to start in with Betty, thinking about Vicky all the time, and besides maybe she wouldn't have wanted to in front of her cousin.

We all headed up to the box office, tearing off our tickets. The house was a honeycomb of dark passageways with mirrors so placed that you banged against them when you thought the path continued straight ahead. The floor was a series of bumps and mounds. Lighted skeletons and strange-looking beasts darted from the walls giving forth horrible noises. In the darkness Dick Sable must have tried something because Joyce shrieked, "Dick Sable, don't you ever do that again." The floor was sliding back and forth under foot. Betty lost her balance and fell back against me. I held her up and one of my hands was over her breast. My entire hand could cup it. So different from Vicky. She inclined her head back and her soft hair brushed against my cheek. It didn't mean anything though, because as soon as she righted herself, she took my hand away and straightened up. I wondered if Vicky would ever come to a place like this. I guess she would have thought it kid stuff. As we came out of the dark to cross the balcony, I saw the crowd looking up lecherously for a cheap thrill. Air blasted out with a tremendous hissing, but you could see the holes in the floor plainly. The girls who provided the show must have done it intentionally.

We moved on. There was the Whip and the Bug. I was almost out of tickets, and it began to seem sort of foolish to pay two bits just to sit in something that went around for a few minutes.

Instead, we bought frozen custards. "Get 'em while they're hot," the ice cream hawker kept calling. We watched the creamy custard churn around inside the glass-covered machine. We also got some cotton candy.

Betty's cousin had to go to the ladies' room and asked Betty and Joyce to join her. That was something about girls. They never seemed to be able to go alone. John and Dick and I stood together looking up at the rocket ride.

"Some fun," I said.

"Yeah, the h-h-hell with that stuff," John replied.

Dick stuck his hands in his pants pocket and turned them inside out. "Listen, fellows," he said, "let's scram. I haven't any more dough."

I looked at my watch. It was only 10:30. "Okay" I said.

The girls showed up and we walked to the parking lot. The four of them rode in back. Betty's cousin sat in the middle between Dick and John. Joyce rode on Dick's lap. Betty sat up close to me. I could see what was going on in back through the rear-view mirror. Dick and Joyce were talking in quiet tones, and she was giggling occasionally. He tried to feel her up a bit, but every time she took his hand away and said. "Don't be naughty, mama spank." John and Betty's cousin were really going to town. They were folded in each other's arms, their bodies turned together, their feet extended. I couldn't see too well, but not a sound came from their corner, except as they stirred occasionally, shifting position. I was practically floored at Betty's cousin, but then you never know when it comes to girls.

We pulled up in front of Joyce's house. We left John and Betty's cousin alone in the car. "That's some session," I said to Betty, going up the walk.

"Kind of disgusting," she said.

"Maybe they like each other," I said. I guess I was just looking for an argument.

"Don't be silly. John hardly looked at her all evening."

Betty and I were alone on the front stoop. Joyce had forgotten her key, and she had gone with Dick to find an open window in back where they could climb in. "Supposing two people like each other. What's okay then?" I said.

Maybe Betty thought I was trying to proposition her. She thought that one over carefully. "It depends on how long you've known each other. I guess you never go backwards."

I supposed that was the real truth of the matter. Where did Vicky and I go from here? We started where most kids left off. We telescoped years of going together into an evening. Maybe that's what you did when you were older and didn't have so much time to waste. And now perhaps, we were finished. Maybe she was starting with someone else. Jeez, please not.

A series of lights flashed on from within, and the front door swung out. We went out in the kitchen and drank Cokes. After a while Betty suggested we go. Dick said goodnight to Joyce.

I drove the Sables home first. John said to Betty's cousin, "G-g-g-gl-gl-glad to m-m-meetcha." The two boys went in.

When we stopped in front of Betty's house, the girls got out. We walked between the neat rows of umbrella trees. On either side of the front step, rambler roses, now faded, climbed up white trellises. The house was like Betty herself. It was neat and sweet and fresh looking. Betty's cousin went in ahead discreetly.

"Thanks for coming along tonight," Betty said. "I hope you didn't mind too much."

"It was fun," I said. I knew I had to kiss her goodnight. She put her arms around my neck. The sweater was high necked. If I had wanted to get anywhere I would have had to pull it up from the bottom and undo the brassiere in back. It was funny how I always thought of those things. She kissed me lingeringly with slightly parted lips. I thought of Vicky's voluptuous, aggressive mouth which opened almost immediately. Betty was okay though. I didn't want to press anything as long as there was still a chance with Vicky, but I didn't want to throw Betty over either. I guessed she really went for me.

"I've missed you, Tony," she said.

"Me too."

"You'll be going away soon."

"Not so soon. Not till September."

"I hope we can see more of each other before you go." Her eyes were soft and misty. We were standing on the top step, holding hands.

"We will, Betty," I said.

"Next Saturday?"

I hated to commit myself. If I could see Vicky during the week, maybe I would not feel like it. "I guess so," I said. "I'll call you."

"I'll bet you don't like me any more because you think I'm a prude."

"Don't be dopey, Betty. I'll call you. Honest." As I walked down the steps and out to the car, I knew she was looking at me. Poor Betty. She knew there was somebody else.

I put the car in gear and started home.

20

I didn't talk to Vicky all week, but I nearly went nuts thinking about her. I called several times but hung up without leaving my name. Somehow that stupid butler always answered the phone, and Vicky was never in. I was sure he was lying, and I wanted to tell him so. I tried to figure out why she might have been sore at me. Maybe because of the car, but hell, that wasn't my fault. I couldn't even sit through a movie thinking about it. I was hoping she might show up at the club. I had to see her, and, if it was all over, let her tell me herself. Anything was better than just wondering all the time. I'd go over and see her Thursday, if I couldn't get in touch with her any other way. Nothing had happened by Thursday so I lined up Jim's car.

"Who you romancing tonight?" Jim asked as he brought the keys over to my locker.

I was standing in front of the mirror trying to decide if I needed a shave. "I'm going over to see Mrs. Powers," I said. There was no point in trying to kid him.

Jim was wearing golf spikes. Sometimes he went out and played a few holes in the evening with some of the fellows who worked at the golf shop. "Are you still in that league?" he said sarcastically.

"Why do you ask that way?"

"I didn't think it would last long. She's nothing for you, kid." He put his hand on my shoulder.

"I know that," I said defiantly. "She's married."

"I didn't mean that," he said. "A dame like that is no good for anybody, not even her husband." Jim got a club from his locker and putted a box of paper matches on the floor.

I didn't answer him. I fastened the top button of my shirt and pulled up the tie. I guessed I'd have to dress like this all the time next year at Lincoln. Guys there probably didn't wear open shirts and sweaters the way they did at high school. That was another thing that would be expensive. I'd need lots of new clothes. Now that I had been accepted, it didn't mean so much. I was already taking it for granted and wasn't even a hundred percent sure I wanted to go. That's the way it was with me. Everybody else seemed to know what they wanted, but I only seemed to want what I couldn't have. Jim left, swinging his club as he went.

I didn't really want to see Vicky either. It was just something I felt I had to get settled. It annoyed the hell out of me to be put off. Maybe she wouldn't even be home, and then I would have rented Jim's car and got all dressed up for nothing. I felt I had to have a drink. Jim kept a bottle of whiskey in his locker. He wouldn't mind if I took a swallow. I located the bottle behind some dirty laundry on top. I wrapped the bottle up in a towel and went into one of those stalls in the men's room. There I sat down, uncorked the bottle and took a long swig. It burned terribly. I went out and stuck my head under the faucet and drank some water. I rewrapped the bottle and returned it to Jim's locker, hiding it under some dirty clothes the way I had found it. I felt better.

Jim's car was sandwiched between a Chrysler station wagon and a big Olds. As I opened the door, it banged against the side of the Olds, leaving a mark. I licked my finger and rubbed it. Some paint was definitely chipped, but the guy that owned it would probably never notice. The door could be opened about a foot or so. I tried to squeeze in. As I did, my pocket caught on the handle and it ripped. I cursed under my breath. I looked at my pocket ruefully. It was only torn along the seams. I guessed it could be fixed, but it was my best jacket. The battery kicked over feebly, but the car started.

The sun was still well above the horizon. I drove slowly, not to get there too soon. I wanted to arrive around six so if Vicky had been out for the afternoon she'd be home, and if she were going out for dinner, she would not have left. As I turned up the shadowy driveway, a squirrel started across the road. It got half way across, lifted his tail and wheeled around. I swerved as the squirrel bounded back and with a flying leap scrambled up a tree.

Both the convertible and the station wagon were drawn up in front of the entrance. Vicky must have been home. I was starting to get cold feet, but there was no way of turning around without circling the driveway and really making a fool of myself. I pulled up behind the station wagon and got out. I looked at my pocket again. To hell with it, I thought. I went up to the front door and pushed the bell.

The houseman answered, staring at me with his glum, non-committal face. "Madame is upstairs taking a bath," he said. "Would you care to wait?"

A man's voice came from the patio. "Who's that, Herman?"

"It's a friend of Mrs. Powers, sir."

"Send him in. I want company." Mr. Powers appeared at the glass double doors leading out to the patio. Then he saw me. "Come on out, fellow."

I crossed the hallway and stood hesitantly on the steps of the familiar vista. "I'm Steve Powers, Vicky's husband. Haven't I seen you before?" He reached out and extended his hand. I put out mine, and he shook it heartily.

"Yes, sir," I said.

"For Christ's sake, knock off that sir crap and have a drink." His glass was sitting on the floor beside one of the lounge chairs. The newspaper was scattered on the floor on the other side.

"Okay, Mr. Powers."

"And knock off that Mr. Powers stuff, too. Call me, Steve." He had a wide, boyish grin. He was better looking than I remembered him. He had a slender, straight nose, and if it weren't for his balding head, he might have been quite handsome. You could see his scalp plainly through the slick-backed strands of dark hair. "Scotch all right for you?" he asked.

"Anything," I said.

He reached under the bar and got out an old-fashioned glass. He took a piece of ice from a wooden ice bucket. The first piece jumped out of his hand and slid along the floor. I started to pick it up. "Leave it," he said, giving it a kick so it skittered off the patio onto the lawn. "That's the one thing we've got plenty of around here. The water flows like ice is what we always say. What do you always say?"

He talked like a screwball. "That's right," he continued. "You don't say anything. That's much smarter. Most people say too much. You know, I like you." He handed me the drink and motioned me to the other lounging chair. He leaned over and picked his glass off the ground. "I think I'll freshen mine up a little." He added more whiskey and another piece of ice to his glass, and then he came over and lay back on an adjacent couch, one leg up, one leg on the floor. "Now then, tell me about yourself, old man. I gather you're a friend of my wife."

I took a gulp of whiskey and tried to figure him out. Maybe he suspected what was going on and was just toying with me like a cat with a mouse. I sized him up physically. He was a little taller than me, and lean. He was probably in pretty good shape. I watched him suspiciously.

"My wife's a gregarious person," he said. "She's always making new acquaintances. I'm glad, you know. I'm away quite a bit. It's a comfort for me to know that she's being properly entertained." He finished the drink in one swallow.

I guessed he was pretty high. "It would worry me," he continued, "if Vicky were alone all the time. Man's a social animal, and that's why darkies were born." He scratched the back of the head. "Now, let's get you straight. You got a name?"

"Tony. Tony Bianchi." I wasn't going to tell him that I worked at the club. Maybe he'd try and get me fired.

"Bianchi. That's Italian. I've met a Frenchman here, a little Irish fellow, a full blooded Indian, a Jew . . . you're the first Italian. God damned if that Vicky's not the only real internationalist in the country. I run into all these damn politicians in Washington, and they all claim to be in favor of international relations but, by God, my wife's the only one that really practices it."

I wanted to change the subject. "Mrs. Powers loaned me her car the other night, and I got a ticket and they took the car away because I didn't have the registration. I just dropped by to see if Mrs. Powers got it back okay."

He listened attentively, nodding his head. "Darn nice of you to come." He got up. "Can I fix you another drink?"

I held up my glass to show it was still half full. He poured another for himself. "Listen," he said, "if you ever get any other tickets, let me know. I know every judge in the county. Just mail them into me. I'll take care of them." He brought his drink and stood over me. "I guess you've been sleeping with my wife," he said.

Jeez, this was it. The butterflies were stampeding. This is what he had been leading up to. I had to deny it, but maybe he knew. Maybe Vicky had spilled it all. Maybe that's why I couldn't reach her. He wouldn't let her talk to me. Or maybe she was locked in her room, or maybe he had done away with her. I almost felt good about it all, because it wasn't simply that she had been avoiding me.

"N-n-no, sir," I stammered weakly.

"Don't lie to me, boy," he said, swirling the ice around in his glass. I cowered back in the couch and shook my head. "Well, you're a damn fool then," he continued. "She's the best lay in Westchester."

He settled back again in his couch. I bolted the rest of my drink and stared at him in amazement. "Don't take my word for it, Tony. Try it." Maybe I would have preferred it if he had hauled off and taken a sock at me. At least I would have known how to react. "You look like you need another drink," he said. "Go over and fix it yourself the way you like it." I was glad of an opportunity to get up. My face was hot and flushed. I was shaking as I refilled the glass. Everything sort of rocked.

"Known millions of girls," he continued. "Still do. Nothing like my wife though. It's an art, you know. It's not just practice. Some people are born naturals."

Then Vicky appeared, and Jeez, she looked beautiful in a white dress with large red dots and red shoes. The dress had a low, square neck and whatever the material, it draped softly following the contours of her voluptuous body. If she was surprised to see me, she didn't show it. I stood up.

"Why, Tony," she said, giving me her stock smile. "I thought someone must be here. I didn't think Steven had taken to talking to himself yet. You've met, I presume."

"Yes, my pet," Steve said. "Tony, fix Vicky a drink. Much scotch and a dash of water. The water's for her conscience. A lady doesn't drink her whiskey straight."

Vicky took my couch, draping the bottom of her skirt gracefully. I brought her drink and pulled up a chair. I couldn't take my eyes off Vicky. The front of the dress dipped at the crevice of her bosom. Her blonde hair fell into soft waves framing her lovely face. I shouldn't have been too surprised to learn about Vicky. I couldn't have thought I was that special. But I was shocked at her husband. I couldn't stand thinking about her with other guys, but to her husband it didn't matter. He even boasted about her—her—

"Steven, I'm just famished," Vicky said, setting her glass on the tile floor. The sun had already ducked behind the shaggy heads of the trees.

"I'd better go," I announced.

"Go?" Steve said, his voice a mixture of hurt and amazement. "I wouldn't hear of it. You're having dinner with us."

"I can't," I said getting up.

"Never say can't. I like you, Tony. You're a fine fellow. We've just met, like two ships passing in the night. We may never meet again." I wondered what he meant by that. He held up his hand. "Just give me your glass. I don't want to hear any more about it."

"Maybe he's got other plans, Steven," Vicky said.

"That's not the way I would size it up, my pet." He winked at me. "Tony, you're my guest." He dragged himself over to the bar for a refill. I looked at Vicky for guidance, but I couldn't catch her eye.

"Come on then, Steven," Vicky said. "If I don't eat now, I won't be hungry, and if you don't eat now, you won't eat at all." A robin was hopping along the lawn, occasionally ducking his head into the short grass. Vicky was standing up impatiently.

"Anything you say, my pet," he replied. "How about you, Tony?"

"Come on, Tony," Vicky said. I supposed she was just being polite. I should have left before, but I was hypnotized like a bird by a snake.

"I'm all set."

Steve brought his hands together with a resounding clap. "Then we're off." He held out his hand for me to pull him to his feet. He lurched towards the bar.

"Steven, don't you think you've had enough?" Vicky said.

"Just one for the road," he said, filling his glass half full. "It's okay with you, isn't it, Tony?"

"Sure," I said.

He threw his head back and downed the contents of the glass. "Tony, you're a great fellow, do you know it?" He clapped me on the shoulder.

I smiled uncomfortably. We walked outside. Steve got in the back seat of the convertible, and Vicky got in front. "You don't mind driving, do you?" she said.

"I like to." It would give me something to do. Her skirt was caught in the door. I opened it so that she could smooth it out of the way and then slammed it. I got in the driver's side.

"Where do you want to go?" she said, turning to her husband in back.

"*Elsie's Beau,* of course," he said, leaning his arms on the back of the front seat. "And you two be good, because I've got my eye on both of you."

"Steven, be serious a minute," Vicky said. "Aren't you tired of that place?"

"Tired," he yelled in a shocked tone. "Tired of the only place in the country where you can get a good steak? They give you food instead of atmosphere, Tony. You don't give a damn about atmosphere, do you, Tony? All women want is atmosphere."

"All right, Steven," Vicky said quietly.

I started up the car and moved slowly down the drive. "Direct him, Vicky, will you?" Steve said.

Vicky reached in her purse for a cigarette. I pushed the lighter on the dashboard and when it popped out, I held it as she leaned over. She put her hand on mine to steady the lighter. There was something about her touch and the way she smelled which went right through me. As we drove along she called the turns, and finally we pulled up in front of a tawdry little bar with a large wooden cow hanging down from a faded sign. It was crowded, though, and I had to drive on a couple of blocks before locating a parking space. A waiter found us a booth and started to hand us menus.

"Never mind these," Steve said, sticking them back under the waiter's arm. "We can't read anyway. Just bring us a nice thick, sirloin steak for three, rare." He turned to me. "You don't mind my ordering for you?"

"You're doing fine," I said.

He grabbed the waiter's arm to make sure he had his attention. "Baked potatoes, and a tossed salad and three Scotch old-fashioneds."

Steve and Vicky sat on one side, and I sat opposite. Vicky didn't say much and smoked constantly. The waiter brought the drinks. Steve held up his glass. "I propose a toast," he said, and then deliberated. "Oh, the hell with it." He drank up.

He disregarded Vicky completely in the conversation. I told him how I assisted the swimming instructor and taught diving at the club. He thought that was great. "Why don't you give Vicky lessons?" Vicky gave him a dirty look. "You wouldn't have to go to the club, dear. I'll bet Tony could come over to our pool. Tony, do you think Vicky could learn a jackknife with a half twist?"

"She could if she wanted to, I guess."

He was certainly wound up. "Christ, how I'd love a girl who could do a jackknife with a half twist," he continued. "I'm not thinking of you for the moment, my pet. It's a question of my own pride. It isn't every guy whose wife can do a jackknife."

"He'll run down after a while," Vicky said, with a pained expression.

"Tony, my wife never finds my conversation scintillating, but that's the way it is, Tony. A man's never a hero to his wife. Tuck that away in the inner recesses of your brain, my boy. Never forget it, and some day you'll thank me." He was talking loudly. I was glad we were secluded in a booth.

"Ask the man who owns a wife," Vicky said.

Steve plucked Vicky under the chin. "Isn't she lovely, Tony. I could really go for a girl like this myself."

"Steven, please." Vicky took his hand and replaced it on the table.

"Forgive me for mentioning it, Tony. Forgive me."

The steak was a huge piece of meat served on a plank. Steve passed his nose over it, his eyes half closed, savoring the odor. "Succulent," he said. "No sweeter smell in the world. If they'd only bottle it. A few dabs of *Eau de Boeuf* placed subtly under the ears would drive men mad. But women don't understand these things, Tony."

The waiter rubbed his hands on his dirty white apron because a little of the grease had rolled off the platter. Then he took up the knife and fork and started to carve. My mouth was watering. He served a piece on Vicky's plate and then mine, and I started in immediately. Then came the baked potatoes and French fried onions and the salad in a small, wooden bowl. Vicky had also started, but Steve let the food sit and continued to work on his drink. The waiter brought another round, but I had reached the stage where I knew I had had enough.

"Steven, cut it out and eat your dinner," Vicky said.

I had already finished and was dying for some more. It looked like Steve's dinner was going to waste. He reached over for Vicky's glass. "You're not going to drink yours," he said.

"Neither are you," she said, grabbing it back from him. A lot of it spilled on the table.

Steve wiped it up with his napkin. "See what you did."

"Your dinner is getting cold," she snapped.

"Ever since I was a little boy, littler than Tony here, my mother told me to eat or I'd never grow. Well, I never ate, and now I'm big enough, for all practical purposes anyway, so I don't fall for that line any more."

"Steven, stop acting like an idiot. Either eat, or we might as well leave." I hoped they wouldn't start to fight.

I guessed I must have been staring longingly at Steve's plate because he understood and said, "C'mon, Tony, help me out," and he put a couple of pieces of steak on my plate. Steve ate a few bites of steak himself and kind of messed up the potato, and that was all. Then he reached again for the remains of Vicky's drink. "Now may I?" he said. She didn't stop him.

The waiter cleared off the plates. "Dessert and coffee?"

"Just the check, please," Vicky said.

"Nice blueberry, homemade apple pie?" the waiter suggested hopefully.

Vicky turned to me politely. I could see she wanted to go so I shook my head. Steve reached in his pocket and pulled out a wad of bills. Jeez, what a wad. They were put together sloppily. I could see the corners of twenties and fifties all packed together about a quarter of the thickness of a deck of cards. He peeled off a twenty and told the waiter to keep the change. He was feeling pretty good all right. On the way out he put his arm around my shoulder in a fatherly fashion.

When we got to the car, he opened the door and pulled the front seat forward for me to get in back. "Let's you and me just sit back and relax. Let Vicky drive. She's a wonderful chauffeur. Did she tell you she was in the Motor Corps during the war?"

"No," I said.

Vicky got in behind the wheel and Steve said, "Home, James." He relaxed beside me in the back seat. Light flashed into the back as we passed other cars going in the opposite direction. "Great little driver, isn't she?" Steve said, his head bobbing around. As we rounded a curve he started to fall toward me but I propped him up. His eyes opened and then closed.

We finally started up the long driveway to the house. Vicky slammed on the brakes hard, as though she was sore or something, and the car skidded to a stop over the loose gravel. Steve was half awake, and we all went into the living room. There were only a couple of lamps glowing. Vicky selected a cigarette from a silver box and lit it from a table lighter. She stood up. She seemed nervous. In the dim light Steve's beard gave his face a darkened cast, and the rings under his eyes were a deep purple. He yawned.

"Well," he said. "You two have a good time. If you'll excuse me I'm going to bed."

"Can't you wait a few minutes, Steven?" Vicky said. "Tony's leaving right away."

"Stick around, Tony. Vicky'll entertain you. You don't need me. Three's a crowd as they say." He turned around and dragged himself off.

Vicky looked at me and shrugged her shoulders. He was a peculiar guy all right. "I hope my coming over isn't going to make any trouble."

"That didn't matter," Vicky said.

"Does he know about us?" I asked.

"Don't be so naive," she said bitterly. "He wouldn't give a damn anyway."

As Vicky stood there she looked kind of sad. "Be a good boy and go home," she said, turning out one of the lamps. In the semi-darkness, a sudden impulse came over me. I grabbed hold of her and held her tight. She yielded momentarily. Her head was buried, but I planted kisses tenderly on her hair and forehead. Then she pushed me away.

"What's the matter?" I said in a hushed voice.

She moved one shoulder. "I don't know," she said. "I guess you bore me." My face must have drooped to the floor. "Don't look at me like that, Tony. I'm too old for you. Whatever happened to that sweet little girl I saw you with that first night?" I didn't answer. We just looked at each other under the funny, diffused light that reflected from the ceiling. Then her face softened. "Bring her over some night, will you, Tony? Bring her over for dinner next Monday. Steven will be gone. Will you do that, Tony?"

I was breathing hard. "Why would you want us? We'd only bore you." I wanted to smash her.

Her face lit up. "Oh, it'll be fun, Tony. I like company. She seemed like such a sweet kid." She took my chin in the palm of her hand and kissed me lightly on the mouth. She knew she had me. She knew I couldn't say no. She walked me slowly toward the door. "I'll leave the car in the parking space for you, honey." And then she added, "I'll see you Monday around seven."

As I drove home, I got to thinking what an ass I was, the way I let myself get pushed around. I started to seethe. Who the hell was she to tell me I bored her. She didn't have much between the ears herself. She never had anything to say. She was nothing but a damn whore anyway, and her husband knew it too. He hated her, I guessed, and I didn't blame him. The more I thought of it the madder I got at myself. I didn't have to take that sort of crap from her. Why didn't I ever think of the right answers until it was too late? She was only an old bag anyway. You could see the lines around her eyes and on her forehead which she tried to hide with powder. She was getting older every damn day and pretty soon she'd be forty. Betty was a darn sight prettier and she knew it. As I idled along, a car whipped by me blasting an air horn. It was an open job with two guys in it. The guy next to the driver turned around to stare, probably thinking I must have a girl maybe lying on my lap to be driving so slowly. I got all funny inside. I sighed involuntarily. It was like seeing Marilyn Monroe or one of those *Esquire* calendars. Vicky never let you forget. The way she moved, that feathery touch, the way she looked at you sometimes. Yes, I'd bring Betty for dinner, and I'd make a big play for her all evening and Vicky would be damn sorry. I'd show her she couldn't get away with that stuff. Jeez.

21

It was sort of hard to persuade Betty to come. During the week she didn't like to ask her uncle to let her off, particularly before dinner because he needed Betty on the floor when he went upstairs to eat. Anyway, Betty couldn't get all hopped up about going to someone's house for dinner whom she didn't know, even though there was a big house with a swimming pool.

"Can't you pick me up around 9:30?" she said.

"Oh come on, Betty. You can make it."

"Why specially for dinner?"

"Because," I guessed that was silly, but it was the best reason I could think of.

"Can't we make it some week-end?"

Maybe Vicky would never ask us again. "If you can't make it Monday, I can't make it any other time."

There was a long hesitation. "If it's that important to you, Tony."

"If it wasn't that important, I wouldn't ask you."

"All right, Tony. I guess I can arrange it."

I heard a click just before I hung up and guessed it must have been my kid brother listening on the other end. Jeez, did that ever make me sore. I tore upstairs, but by the time I had arrived he was sitting on my father's bed innocently glancing at a magazine.

"Mike. I told you a million times not to do that," I yelled at him.

He was sprawled in the chair with one foot over the arm. His faded brown slacks were rolled at the bottom, and his scuffed brown shoes had a hole in the sole. Jeez, what a slob. He acted very innocent. "What are you talking about?"

"You know darn well what I'm talking about."

"Aw, blow it out your stacks." He put down the magazine and walked toward the door. I stuck out my foot. He wasn't expecting it and went sprawling on his face. "Darn you," he cried. He came over and put a headlock on me. I grabbed him by the waist and twisted him over my leg, and he fell against the small end table. It crashed to the ground. Cigarettes were strewn all over the floor. Mother came tearing up the stairs. I was trying to stand the table up and Mike was gathering up the cigarettes. A china ash tray was broken, and one of the table legs was bent.

"Boys!" she screamed, picking up the ash tray and fitting the broken parts together. "Aren't you ashamed of yourself?" Her hair was pulled back tight, but some straggly, stray wisps were falling in front of her face.

"I'm sorry," I murmured, and Mike said so, too. She stood there with her hands on her hips. Mike was crawling under the chair, picking up a few stray butts, and I was fooling with the table leg.

"At your age, fighting!" she said scornfully. She took the table from me. "Just leave it, Tony. You'll only make it worse. You'll hear from your father when he gets home, both of you. Now get out of here." She looked like she might cry. I wanted to comfort her, put my arm around her and tell it can't be that bad, or something, but I couldn't bring myself to it. Everything around our house was a crisis. Jeez, it was only a table. Mike and I left sort of sheepishly. Would I be glad to get away from here next year! Between that stupid brother of mine, and my old lady treating me like I was five years old.

I wandered into the back yard. The tomatoes were pretty good size, and a few of them were starting to redden. The corn was coming up, too. The ears were showing on the stalks, small and green. The stalks were taller than I was. But I was thinking all the time, too. I hoped that the table wasn't busted. From my old lady's point of view it was a question of money. The table represented twenty bucks to her. She tried so hard to save pennies; any loss was a setback. Not that Pop would say anything, and he could probably fix it, too, because there was nothing my old man couldn't repair. Mother had always threatened all our lives with "You'll hear from your father," and we never did. Still, it made me nervous.

I watched a bee hover around a flower. He stuck his nose in first, his back legs working all the time, and then it disappeared inside. I stretched out on the grass, my hands under my head. White clouds lazed along. The leading edge looked like a steam engine and then like a woman in silhouette, a woman like Vicky with lovely breasts. I wondered if I ought to go in and see if I could give my old lady a hand with something. I should, I supposed, but she was always so fussy. She seemed so harried all the time, but she preferred to do everything herself. Once when she was sick we had a girl in, but mother couldn't stand it. She was continually upset about glasses being chipped and that the girl was using too much butter. I guessed I'd have to make good at school next year, then go on to college and make a lot of money so none of these things like broken tables or ash trays or chipped glasses would matter. Jeez, what a life. There must be an easier way, like Powers had it. He was a lawyer. I rolled over on my side and thumbed through a patch of grass looking for a four-leaf clover. Then I heard my old man's car in the driveway. It bumped as it went over the ledge at the entrance to the garage. Now Pop was rolling down the door, and then Mother was waiting for him on the porch. He kissed her from long habit. I knew we'd be eating in a little while.

22

As I breezed along in the DeSoto, I flipped the steering wheel with one finger like it showed in the ads. Betty would go crazy seeing this car, but I wondered what she'd think of the whole set-up. Maybe it was dumb of me to have agreed to invite her. If Vicky was really jealous, she might treat Betty nastily or let the cat out of the bag about what we'd been doing, and Betty would spread the word all around just to get even. It might even get back to my old man and old lady.

Betty reacted to the car just like I suspected she would. "It's positively the most gorgeous thing I've ever seen," she said, walking all around it. "Where'd you steal it?"

"It belongs to this Mrs. Powers," I said.

"Who is this woman anyway?" she asked suspiciously.

"Oh, just some woman I met over at the club," I said casually. "I guess she's sort of taken a liking to me." And then I remembered that Betty had seen her at Mack's Cabin, so I had to explain to Betty that she had met her before.

"Uh, huh," Betty said with a knowing inflection in her voice. "Well, she's got some car." She looked pretty cute, as usual. Her hair was pulled back behind her ears and held with a silver berette. It made her seem different, older. I guessed you'd call it chic. She wore a plaid dress, bare in back. I was sure she couldn't have worn a bra or a slip or anything underneath, because the straps or something would have showed. I guessed Betty didn't have to wear a brassiere if she didn't feel like it, but I always wondered about things like that. I was never quite sure anyway whether girls wore bras for support, sort of like guys wore a jock, or whether it was to keep their breasts from showing too much. It was really just curiosity, but I always used to look in the shop windows at women's underwear. It was embarrassing to be caught, because a man wasn't supposed to be interested in brassieres and girdles.

At a light I drew up besides a kid in a stripped down Ford. He was rocking backward and forward, letting his clutch in and out, prepared to make a fast getaway. His unmuffled engine roared. The kid probably thought he'd have a cinch breaking out in front, because usually the guys in big jobs weren't trying. When the light changed, I rode even with him for a half a block, and then slowly I fed more gas as the speedometer needle moved rapidly over the dial. The little Ford fell behind.

"You'd better take it easy. You don't want another ticket, do you?" Betty said. It sounded like she was trying to rub it in that she had done me a favor. Betty was sure acting funny tonight. Something was eating her all right. I had turned on the radio, but the street we were traveling was covered with those overhead trackless trolley wires, and the static was terrific. Betty snapped it off. Then we swung off the main street into a curvy black tar road. Pretty soon we reached the imposing stone pillars which marked the entrance to the Powers' estate. The driveway, with the well-ordered row of trees, had become a familiar sight.

"Some place," Betty said.

"You haven't seen anything yet," I said proudly, almost as if I had proprietary interest.

We rang the bell and Vicky greeted us at the door. She was exceedingly cordial. She patted Betty's hand, "So glad you could make it, my dear." Then Vicky said, "You're so pretty. I didn't remember how pretty you really are." I guessed that went over big with Betty because a smile replaced the grumpy expression she had been wearing.

"You're lovely yourself," Betty replied. She could hold her own with anyone, that Betty. She always seemed to know just what to say. Vicky was wearing a simple, high-necked pink dress with a round collar. It made her look younger.

We sat out on the patio. Vicky suggested martinis. I didn't think Betty would want anything. She said she'd love one. "They're awful strong," I warned her. I sort of felt responsible for Betty.

"I've been drinking them for years and none the worse for it," Vicky said.

Betty was standing up. "You know, I'd like to look around. It's so gorgeous here."

"We will later," Vicky said. The martinis were all made. Vicky poured the drinks. "Here's to you both. You're sweet kids." I bolted mine because I knew from before that drinking martinis was like swimming in cold water. It was murder to wade in slowly, but if you plunged in quickly, everything felt fine afterwards. I watched Betty to see if she could get hers down, but she managed a swallow without flinching. Vicky was charming as all hell. She asked Betty all sorts of questions about herself and thought everything Betty was doing, like working in the summer, was simply wonderful. The two of them chatted away. They were putting away the martinis, too. Even Betty finished her second before I did.

Maybe martinis just affected me peculiarly, because I was already beginning to feel kind of free and easy, and my head sort of flopped around, but it didn't seem to bother Betty or Vicky. I stared at the two of them over the top of my glass. The butler came out with a plate of hot canapes, tiny hot dogs in a roll and little melted cheese affairs. Vicky said we should eat plenty, because this was really our first course and maybe there wouldn't be much else. It broke into my train of thought, but not for long because drinks seemed to make me think about women and sex stuff most of the time. The little cocktail napkin fell from Betty's lap, and when she bent forward to pick it up, I decided for sure she wasn't wearing a brassiere. Vicky poured another round, and then dinner was announced. We carried the drinks in with us.

Vicky hadn't told the truth when she said that the hors d'oeuvres might be all we'd get to eat, because we started in with cold soup followed by a tremendous roast turkey. Vicky asked me if I wanted to carve, but only as a matter of courtesy because Herman was standing over the meat with a knife and fork in hand looking damn well like he intended to do it himself. He cut thin, even slices. I only would have hacked it up. Vicky sat at the end of the table with Betty and me on either side. There was a big silver piece in the center of the table with all sorts of fruit, and side dishes of celery and nuts and candy. It reminded me of Thanksgiving or Christmas.

The corn was passed wrapped up in a white napkin with little silver knobs stuck in the end of the cob so you could grab it easy. There was some kind of red champagne also served in a bottle swathed in a white napkin. Betty seemed to take it all in her stride. I was glad she didn't act like everything was out of this world, because when you go with swells you should act like it was sort of what you were accustomed to. I took seconds of everything and four ears of corn, though I really would have held back if Vicky hadn't said she'd be insulted if I didn't. I guessed I was really beginning to feel at home. The corn tasted like sugar, and Vicky told us that was because it had just been picked a few hours ago. The wine was terrific too. It tasted like grape soda, and I had several glasses. So did Betty, and I was wondering if she was feeling woozy. Jeez, if there weren't even finger bowls. I dipped my hands in the water and washed off my face, too. I dried myself with the napkin. For dessert there was a chocolate pudding and a big bowl of whipped cream. The Powers sure had good chow.

After dinner, Vicky and Betty excused themselves and went upstairs together. They were getting along like old friends. I went into the living room to wait for them. They seemed to be gone a long time. I was hoping Vicky and Betty weren't getting too confidential, the way women did when they got together in the John. I wandered around the room impatiently. There was a grand piano in the corner. I lifted up the lid covering the keys and picked out a tune with one finger. Hearing the girls returning, I closed the piano quickly.

"Don't stop," Vicky said.

"I really don't play," I said, getting up from the stool.

"He's not kidding, either," Betty added.

Vicky went over and pressed a bell behind the door. Herman appeared with a tray of bottles. "How about a cordial?" Vicky said, reeling off some fancy names. Betty and I just looked at each other. "All right," Vicky continued, "just leave it to me. I'll fix you something good." She poured a heavy brown liquid from a round, squat bottle into tiny glasses. I brought one to Betty and took one for myself, knowing I shouldn't because my head was spinning. I plopped down besides Betty on the couch. Vicky was sitting curled up in a chair opposite.

Betty picked up a picture of Steve Powers in a Navy officer's uniform from the table beside her. "Is this your husband?"

"That's him," Vicky said dryly.

"He's handsome," Betty said.

"That was taken quite some time ago, when we were first married."

She paused, and for a moment there was a faraway look in her eyes. "I was a pretty dumb kid at the time. I was just about your age, Betty, but you seem older. I guess girls know more today than I did."

Betty said, "What do you mean?"

"Oh, about life and sex. You don't fall for the first guy that gets to you."

I was shocked at her frankness and looked to see how Betty would respond. Vicky must have been feeling pretty good, too, or she wouldn't have spoken that way. She had always put things delicately. Vicky took a sip and looked from Betty to me. "I suppose they still do," Betty said.

I was beginning to wish that Betty wasn't here. My eyelids were getting heavy. Though half-closed eyes, Vicky's chair appeared to retreat across the room and then move forward as if it were on rollers. Maybe I missed something, because the conversation didn't seem to follow from where it had left off.

Vicky was saying that a girl should never let herself get trapped by a man. She should do the picking. A girl can hook any guy who's interested enough to ask her out. Betty was sitting up straight, playing with the empty cordial glass. I shook my head. Vicky's skirts were up above her knees with her legs crossed. She wore no stockings. I looked at Betty with her streamlined chest. If I could have put my hand down her dress where it was loose in front, it would have felt soft and warm, too.

"It's all in the technique," Vicky was saying, seeming to have drifted back across the room. "It's not a question of looks. Some girls just know how to touch a man so it gives him goose flesh and starts a chain reaction all over." I remember that's what Steve had said about Vicky. Vicky hoisted herself out of a chair and walked uncertainly to the bar. She brought over a bottle, and Betty extended her glass. She didn't ask me. It was just as well because I might have said yes. Vicky lit a cigarette and blew out a great cloud of smoke.

"Where do you get this technique? Do you have it or do you get it through practice?" Her voice was thick and sounded unfamiliar. I had to look at Betty to make sure.

Vicky was standing in front of the couch. "I'll prove it to you. Let's experiment." She took the handkerchief from my breast pocket. "We'll blindfold our little friend here and just touch him on the back of the hand and see if he can tell the difference."

Vicky folded the handkerchief and tied it around the back of my head. I knew she'd make her point. It felt good, merely adjusting the cloth over my eyes. "You can't see now, can you?" she said. I shook my head. "Now move over." I wormed over to the center of the couch, and she sat down beside me. Pretty soon I felt the light caress of fingers over the back of my hand, then a similar stroke but with a heavier hand. "Which was the more soothing, Tony?" Vicky said.

I knew the first touch was Vicky's, but then the way I was feeling it didn't make much difference. I just wanted to be touched all over. "Better do it again," I said. They repeated in different order. I liked this game.

"All right," Vicky's voice fading in, "we'll try something else. We'll each give you a kiss. You don't mind, do you, Tony?" Mind? I should say I didn't. I felt Vicky's hands on my shoulders. Her breath was hot and reeked of liquor. Then her full moistened lips pressed against mine, and her body came forward. I started to slip my arms around her, but she pushed me away. She must have changed positions with Betty to fool me. Jeez, did she think I was dumb or something? My feelings were on fire.

Then Betty kissed me. Her lips were hard and tight shut, but after a while they softened and relaxed. She wasn't wearing a bra. I had been right. And she didn't pull away, either. Through my blindfold, I could see that a light was being quenched and then another. If Betty didn't care, neither did I. I couldn't stand this much longer. The bandage slipped from my eyes and was hanging around my neck. Vicky was gone, and the living room door was closed. It was dark except for a heavily shaded light in the corner. I ran my hands all over as she planted kisses on my face wildly. I slid my hands under her dress. She didn't resist. We fell back lengthwise on the couch. . .

After a while we just lay in each other's arms.

23

When I opened my eyes again, I was lying on the floor, next to the couch in Vicky's living room. My shirt was open and hung damply away from my body.

My mouth was parched. I rubbed the back of my hand against it, and I felt the carpet hair on my lips. And then I remembered.

I don't know how it came out of me, but it was like a moan, I guess. At first I didn't know I was making the noise, except I could keep hearing it and when I looked around, there was nobody there, except me.

And that was it. Nobody there. Except me.

Betty wasn't there. Vicky wasn't there. They had played a game on me. That much I remembered. It was a funny game. I hated them for it.

I rolled over and sat up, and in my hand was the silver berette. My hand moved, once, with a jerk, almost as though it wanted to move and I didn't know it, and I could see the name etched in script on the other side of the berette.

I slapped at my face to clear my head, only I forgot what I was holding, and batted myself with the berette. I threw it across the room, and then I ran and kicked at it and the sound that kept coming out of me was hoarser now, less of a moan, more like a terrible panting and I told myself to stop.

I had to think.

I looked at my watch. It was half past six. I opened the living room door. There was nobody there. I tiptoed out. I had something I had to do, but I couldn't remember what it was. It was something important.

Outside, the air felt good. I walked in the gutter, next to the road.

And they all were walking with me.

That was funny, I thought. Nobody was there, yet they all kept walking, right along side. Vicky and Steve and Herman. Steve was immaculately dressed in a dark, double breasted suit and Vicky in a flowing white bridal gown. Pretty soon we came to a clearing in an open field with an altar set in the middle. Steve took his place behind the pulpit. From somewhere in the distance came the strains of the wedding march. Herman and I marched slowly down the green carpeted isle. As we approached the pulpit, Vicky came over and stood beside me. She took the huge glittering diamond ring from her finger and handed it to me.

"We are gathered together in the presence of this assembly to join you, Vicky and Tony ..." Steve's voice was deep and sonorous. I raised my hand and waved it frantically like you did at school when you wanted to ask a question. Steve recognized me with a nod.

"But she's *your* wife, Steve," I said excitedly.

He pondered tugging at his chin. "That's right," he said at length. "I had forgotten. But the hell with that. I don't want her anymore anyway. I give her to you, Tony."

"I hate her," I said.

"She's the best lay in Westchester," Steve said leaning over his desk. Then he straightened up and said in a quiet voice. "Shall we go on?" Herman was looking at me menacingly. I nodded my head.

And now the sun was blazing like a great ball of fire. Steve was droning on. "Do you Tony take Vicky ... ?" When all of a sudden there was shouting in back. Betty's father was racing across the field dragging Betty by the hand. He was carrying a club. "Stop," he was shouting. "Stop, you've got to marry Betty. You took her virginity. She told me all about it."

"Don't be silly, father. It was only a game." Betty pleaded. "We were only having a little fun."

He drew back his club, and I broke into a run. They all followed close on my heels. And then somehow they were gone, and I was running along the side of the road. I was out of breath and slowed down to walk. Behind me I heard the footsteps and the mingled sounds of their voices so I started up again. My lungs were bursting. At the turn of the road I could see a long way behind me, and no one was in sight. It was amazing how clearly their voices carried. Now Steve and Betty's father were arguing. He's got to marry Vicky, got to marry Betty, Vicky, Betty, Vicky, Betty . . .

"Leave me alone," I shouted back. "I hate all of you. Lousy bitches, whores. I hate you, hate you . . ."

A car came by blasting its horn and swerved around me and then I realized I was standing in the middle of the road. I moved over to the side and now the voices were getting closer. Vicky. Betty. Vicky. Betty.

Where was I going? If I could only remember. It was so hot. That was it. I was going to the club. I had to set up the umbrellas and the Beach chairs. Vicky, Betty, Vicky. I looked around furtively and quickened my pace.

24

I climbed over the wire fencing which surrounded the club property. That would fool them. I'd like to see them try and get over those wire barbs. It would stick them right where they deserved it most. The grass was sopping wet, and the water began to seep through the thin soles of my moccasins. The sun was climbing fast. Nobody was around. I went in through the locker room and up the back stairs. It was almost eight by the wall clock. I paused outside Jim's door. Maybe he'd be sore if I woke him. But then I could hear those voices again. Vicky, Betty, he's got to marry Vicky, Betty, Vicky. I burst in.

Jim was lying in bed. He sat up with a start. "My God, what's the matter?" he said.

"I had to talk to you, Jim."

"Talk to me. Look at yourself in the mirror."

I glanced at myself in the glass over the bureau. My hair was matted, and my eyes were sunken. I took Jim's comb and pulled it through the snarls. I could hear those voices again outside. I rushed to the window. The empty fairways stretched in all directions. But they were getting more distinct. Vicky, Betty, Vicky. I threw myself at Jim. "Save me, Jim."

"What the hell's the matter with you?"

"They're after me. I don't have to marry anybody, do I?" I was clawing at him.

Then he was shaking me by the shoulders until my head was beginning to rattle. "You're nuts, do you know it?"

"But what'll I do about everything, Jim?" I said, sitting on the foot of his bed. I tried to hold it back, but I couldn't. The sound kept coming out of me.

Jim grabbed me roughly, propping me up and slapped me hard. The stinging on my cheek felt good. "Take hold of yourself. You're screwed up too tight. Just relax." He was looking at me, his mouth set firm, the muscles in his jaw working back and forth like the main spring in a watch.

Then he got up and took a washcloth from the rack, wet it in the sink and wrung it out. "Here wipe your face," he said, tossing it to me.

I passed it over my burning face. "But what'll I do, Jim?" I moaned.

"Nothing. Just take it easy. You're all through with that babe now. Forget it. It was only a question of time anyway."

"Shouldn't I call Vicky and tell her off?" I had to see her just once more. I couldn't exactly figure why.

"You should like hell. Go downstairs and take a cold shower, and maybe you'll feel better." Jim stood up. "I'll see you later."

The butterflies in my stomach were in an uproar. It felt like I had to go to the bathroom. I entered the lavatory. The bowl was splotched yellow from people with bad aim. The lockerman hadn't been around to clean up yet. I lowered the seat and sat down, but nothing happened. I was too impatient to wait. I looked at myself in the mirror. My eyes were puffy and red, and there were still marks on my cheek from where the tears had streaked down. I ran cold water into my palms and doused my face. Then I stuck my hair under the faucet. I combed it forward to make the part and slicked it back. Jeez, I looked lousy. Suddenly I felt tired and sat down in a leather club chair.

I wanted to sleep, but I just slouched back staring ahead. Relax, take it easy. If was easy enough for Jim to have said just forget it but when I had something on my mind I had to get it settled. I was all through with Vicky, with Betty, with all women, but I had to tell them so. Then they'd really know, and I could forget all about them in peace.

25

I must have dozed off because the next thing I knew it was ten o'clock. I struggled out of the chair and walked outside. I blinked in the brilliance of the sunlight. I had to hurry now. I wasn't sure why but somehow I had the feeling if I didn't do it soon and get it over with it would be too late. I could hear the sound of tennis balls being batted back and forth. Maybe Jim needed me at the pool, but he'd have to wait until I got back because this thing was more important.

A fellow can really get a lift when he has to. Somehow a motorist seemed to know when a guy really needed a ride. The first car that came along outside the club gates stopped to pick me up. He took me all the way to the estate.

On bright, sunny mornings, I knew Vicky often went down to the pool to maintain her tan. It would be better if I could sneak around and catch her alone. If I just went up to the front door and rang the bell, the butler would lead me to her and maybe he'd hang around so I wouldn't get a chance to say what I had rehearsed in my mind.

I walked through the woods paralleling the driveway. The grass was almost knee high. There were great patches of daisies and black eyed susans. Prickly weeds snatched at my trouser legs. When I got within sight of the main house, I noticed both cars parked in front. Vicky was probably home. My watch said half past ten. She must be up, but if not, I'd go down to the pool and wait.

I gave the house a wide berth, sneaking behind the trees and around the garden. Finally I came to the bathhouses and slipped around the side. I peeked out front, and there she was lying on a mat by the water's edge on her stomach. She wore trunks but no bra. Her breasts were crushed flat against a white towel covering the mat. I didn't want to just walk up because with her being half nude. She might have been embarrassed. I just stayed there pressed flat against the side of the bathhouse. Then I think I moved.

"Who's there?" Vicky called sharply.

I had to make up my mind quick. I had to beat it or reveal myself now. I stepped into view. "It's me, Vicky."

She was sitting up with the towel wrapped around her chest, holding it there tight with the hand behind her back. "What the hell are you doing, prowling around here?" she said angrily. "Are you a Peeping Tom?"

"I'm sorry. I didn't mean to frighten you."

Her legs were curled under, and she wasn't really facing me. Mostly her back was turned toward me, and she was looking over her shoulder. "I drove your little friend home this morning," she said. I walked around so she didn't have to strain her neck. Her gaze followed me. "What do you want anyway?"

It wasn't like I had planned. I had to get it out fast or I wouldn't say it all. "I-I-I can't see you anymore," I blurted out. "That's what I've come to talk to you about."

She looked at me coldly and then a smile crossed her face. "I hope you didn't come far out of your way to tell me that." The towel had slipped a little in front revealing the soft whiteness just at the beginning of the rise. She hiked the towel higher with her free hand and tightened up her grip behind.

"I'm sorry," I said becoming aware of the heat of the sun overhead.

"What are you sorry about?" she said. "You're a kid. I'm the one that's sorry. Sorry I ever started with you."

The color was mounting in my face. "Why did you, then?"

"For kicks. Now that's over, and you bore me. I was fed up with you long ago."

"Didn't what we did mean anything to you?"

"I want a man. Do you think you could satisfy me?" She laughed a hard short sound.

I was sweating like a bull. I raised my arms because I was soaking wet underneath. I clenched and unclenched my fists. Relax, take it easy. Let her insult me. That wasn't the point. I only came to get things settled. "Why did you ask me to bring Betty last night, then?" I whimpered. "I wouldn't have except you insisted. Remember."

Her face was relentless. "Because I wanted to," she said. "I watched. I like to watch. You wouldn't know about those things. You're still a baby. Maybe you'll never know." And then, "If you think I was jealous, you're crazy. It was a whim. I was amusing myself so if you've got any wrong ideas, just get them out of your head." Then she threw back and laughed. "And you—you came over to tell me you weren't going to see me anymore."

I just looked at her in horror. She had used me to satisfy her peculiar quirks and now was throwing me out. And she was laughing, *laughing*. "You bitch," I said, not recognizing my voice. I thought she'd get sore, but it only made her laugh some more.

And Betty too. It never occurred to Vicky what she might have done to somebody else. What about Betty? I waited for Vicky to stop. The heat of the sun was unbearable. There was something I *had* to do.

Finally she said. "Get out, and don't ever set foot on this property again." But it didn't register right away, because that thing I was trying to remember before was right on the tip of my tongue. If only it weren't so hot, it would come to me.

"Get out," she was saying, and still I didn't move, and then she started to scream. I rushed over and took the towel and stuffed it in her mouth. It wasn't out of rage. I just didn't want Herman to come rushing down. She grabbed me and sank her nails in my face. I kept the towel in her mouth with one hand forcing her head back against the stone. She had wormed towards the edge of the pool, and now water was splashing over my hands. She drew back her foot and let go at my groin. A terrible pain shot through me, and I gripped hard to keep from yelling aloud.

After a while, when the pain had subsided, I released my hold. I was breathing hard. My hands were shaking, and my fingers were stiff. She seemed to have relaxed. I raised her head out of the water and flexed my fingers, still holding the gag over her mouth. Her hair was plastered to her head and the water rolled off and dripped back into the pool. The towel was bunched around her neck exposing her breasts in their ghastly whiteness, and I covered them with part of the towel.

Still she didn't stir. Maybe she had fainted. She didn't seem to be breathing. Her bathing cap was lying beside her. I filled it with water from the pool and sprinkled it on her face. She didn't react. I raised her eyelids like I had seen a guy do in the movies, but they fell back. The sun was a flaming red ball. I passed the back of my hand over my forehead.

She might have got some water in her lungs. I tried to roll her on her stomach, but my foot slipped on the wet stone. The limp form fell with a great splash into the pool. I stood over the edge and watched as it sank slowly until it rested on the bottom.

26

The body seemed blurred and fuzzy as though I were viewing it through a distorted television screen. And it was fiercely hot, and I had to take it easy. I took off my shoes and socks and dangled my feet in the pool just above her. The water felt sensationally cool. Someone would come along pretty soon. Maybe Herman would be bringing her some lunch. There were no more butterflies. I looked up at the sun and waited.

THE END

THE DEVIL'S DAUGHTER
by Peter Marsh

CHAPTER ONE

The woman who chose to be known only as Laura, appeared at the *Ecuador* with a paid escort, who wore white tie and tails and the ribbon of the Legion of Honor in his buttonhole. But he was a paid escort, the *Ecuador* was crowded, the few empty tables having "Reserved" cards on them, and the captain, talking to Laura and the paid escort, was immune to feminine charms from seven P.M. until four A.M.

If Madame had only telephoned—

"Mademoiselle," she corrected.

Mademoiselle, hell, he thought, with that shape and those eyes. No virgin ever spoke with such rich full-bodied tones. Yeah, and no dame with such a come-on as this one had ever escaped being dragged to the altar by someone, no matter what her inclinations and habits might be. Mademoiselle, hell.

If *Mademoiselle* had only telephoned—

"But I only arrived in the city tonight," she said as if that were a complete and final explanation of why she must be given one of the tables with a "Reserved" placard.

Then the hotel must have furnished the paid escort with the ribbon of the Legion of Honor. Anyway, women with paid escorts usually bought one drink and stayed for hours. She had just the trace of an accent, too. She said *ceety* instead of city. That didn't mean anything, of course, except that the one drink would probably be a cheap *one*. Women with paid escorts figured on so much for the escort, so much for the taxicab, so much for the cover charge, and that left little for food and drink—but then food and drink didn't count with these female tourists. Only this dame (mademoiselle, hell) looked as if she knew the difference between *vichysoisse* and a *suisesse*. She certainly knew the difference made by cutting two inches more from the front of a dress. But it did nothing to him. Maybe, he'd been a bottle baby.

"There are plenty of other places," the paid escort said, thinking it time to put the captain *in* his place.

"But, no," the woman said. "There is only one *Ecuador*. In all the world, there is only one *Ecuador*."

And, she might have added, only one Michel Perry, owner of the *Ecuador,* arbiter supreme of night life in New York, a gutter Ward McAllister, a gangster Delmonico. He appeared at that moment, and the captain knew he had lost the battle. He might as well lead the way and snatch the "Reserved" placard from one of the choice tables. But he was Grik, by God, and he could take it.

"What is it, Andy?" Michel asked crisply. "Surely you can take care of Madame—"

"Mademoiselle," she corrected.

Mademoiselle, hell. Three things happen to a dame. She becomes a woman, she has her first affair, and she becomes a mother. The first two had happened to this one, all right, but Andy wasn't sure about the third. Those firm breasts, the flat hips. If she'd turn around, he'd be sure. She wasn't a filly but she hadn't foaled often. That was a cinch.

"Of course," Michel said with the smile that always slayed them. "Andy, surely there is a table for our old friends?"

Old friends, hell. This dame had never been in the place before. The paid escort wasn't a regular either because they wouldn't give him a commission. The boss knew that. What the hell was all this palaver about?

"Whatever you say, Mr. Perry. But I have four tables left, and here's the list of reservations we've taken—"

Michel Perry disregarded the list. "Show the folks to a table," he directed, "and we'll worry about the others when they get here."

It ain't enough that he's half-dead with ulcers. He wants me to get them, too.

But Andy took his defeat gallantly. He seated them with a flourish and waited to take their order while a waiter and a bar-boy fluttered around. The paid escort wanted Scotch-and-soda, Mademoiselle would have the most expensive Port on the card, sweet Port, and beescuits. Crackers, you bitch, and so he gave the order to the waiter.

Back at the entrance another captain had moved in to insult the best people but Michel was still there.

"Who is she?"

"I don't know," Andy answered indignantly. "She's your old friend. I never saw her before."

"I know her. She's been in here."

"Not in my time, she ain't."

"Maybe you're right, but I know her. It goes way back."

"He's—"

"Yeah, I know who he is."

"Then you know what to expect. We'll get a case note from a table that's budgeted for a century."

"You never can tell."

"Maybe you can't, but I can. She's drinking sweet Port."

"Good. I admire a woman who has courage enough to order a sweet wine. I'd like to gargle it with her."

"You will. Only she'll get crumbs in your bed. Crackers! What the hell does she think she is? A goddamn parrot."

"Find out who she is," Michel ordered. "I don't want anybody around here unless we know them."

He moved away, limping slightly from arthritic pains.

Andy turned to the other captain. "What the hell are we? Captains or coppers or pimps?"

"You know what we are," his confrère replied. "And you'd better have your jacket let out. Your gat shows when you bend over."

"I'll stop bending over. It never did me no good, anyhow. Keep the door for a bit. I'm going to do a little Nerowolfing."

He went into the bar and pulled a woman columnist from one of the high stools.

"You don't have to be so rough," she complained.

"Why don't I? If I wasn't rough, you might think I like you."

"Wrong again."

"All right. So I like you well enough to pull you off a stool but not enough to sock you in the jaw. That's settled. There's a dame in there the boss wants identified."

"You mean you let somebody in you didn't know? That's almost front page news."

"This ain't news at all. The boss knew her once and now he don't know her."

"You can't expect him to remember every woman he's bedded."

"I'm not expecting nothing. He wants to know who she is."

"Well, point her out to me."

"Can't see her from here. Eight Vanderbilts in the way. Sitting down, you'd think she's nekkid but she ain't. She's got plenty of jaw and mouth, not much nose, the blackest eyes you ever saw, and red-gold hair, this week."

"Andy, you surprise me. You've got a photographic eye."

"Sure, I got a grand last year for spotting a guy. If I don't know 'em, I look at 'em plenty careful."

"All right, buy me a drink and I'll see if I know her."

"Don't you ever do anything for love?"

"You know damn' well I do; that's why I have to cadge drinks."

Andy motioned to a bartender. "Anything she wants—not over six-bits."

The lady reporter had her gin and bitters, went to the powder room where she applied a few brush strokes to her lips and received a tearful confidence, which she promised she wouldn't use but didn't say anything about selling, trading or giving to another columnist. Then she went into the main room where she had no difficulty in locating Andy's mysterious customer. But she was completely unknown to the lady reporter, who, after looking over the field, decided that two FBI boys sitting with two pets from Powers might be a possible source of information.

They greeted her cordially enough, but could give out with very little information. One of the boys, who never forgot a face, said he had seen her about six months before in Izzy Gomez's joint in San Francisco. The lady reporter passed that information on to Andy and there the matter ended for that night so far as she was concerned. Later, she might expand the incident into a two-column spread.

Michel Perry received the same information not from Andy but direct from the FBI boys when he sat down to buy them a drink a little later. One of them asked Perry if he knew the glamorous stranger.

Perry looked. "No," he said. "I was wondering myself. Why are you asking?"

That showed the condition he was in. Couldn't keep a wonderful dish like that on his mind for an hour. Time was when he wouldn't think of another thing until he had her all wrapped up in silk. Now it was different. The only thought that stayed with him was extermination, the end of it all. He remembered his father, when dying, had said he felt Satan's hot breath. But Mike Perry couldn't feel that. He had advanced beyond Satan. He could only feel damp earth or the licking flames of cremation.

"No reason," the FBI boy said, "except that dame from one of the papers was asking about her."

The other FBI boy told about having seen her in San Francisco at Izzy Gomez's *bistro*.

"You ought to see that joint sometime," he said to Perry, trying to drag his host out of the depths into which he seemed to have sunk.

"If I get away from here," Perry said, "a saloon is the last thing I want to see."

He bought them a bottle of champagne but ordered milk for himself. "The old ulcers," he explained.

"My mother says," one of the lovelys told him, "that ulcers come from worrying. Why don't you stop worrying, Perry?"

"Yeah, why don't I?" he agreed and then excused himself.

"What's the matter with Perry?" one of the boys asked after he had gone. "Business certainly seems good."

"He'd never worry about business," the other said. "He's made money too many ways."

"I bet it's love—a woman," one of the girls suggested. She was a deep thinker and read one book a month except when the Club sent two. Then she read two.

"What I said about business goes for love—he's had too many women to worry about one. No, he's plenty scared about something."

"Well, why doesn't he spill it? Maybe we could help him."

His companion shook his head. "He's a Sicilian and Sicilians don't run to the law when they get in trouble."

The youngest model sighed heavily. "I think he's terribly attractive."

The object of their regard was very busy the next two hours. It was a big night at the *Ecuador,* a cross-section of the world spending its money. Four tables were filled with South Americans who have a way of making other spenders seem amateurish. Perry, who spoke fluent Spanish, circulated freely and did much to promote Pan-American amity.

They liked him, these swarthy spend-thrifts, and for a little while he forgot his worries and his ulcers. With complete recklessness, he finally joined them in a magnum.

Then they were gone and he was left alone with his worries, his ulcers and the ordinary run of Vanderbilts, Astors and Roosevelts. He suddenly remembered the lovely mademoiselle.

But she was gone and no one, not even the hat-check girl, could remember her departure. Apparently she had slipped out when the crush was the heaviest. The waiter was sure it must have been fairly early in the night because he'd been serving another party at that table for hours.

Perry stormed and raved. His employees were a bunch of dopes and double-crossers. The first, new attractive woman who had come into the place in a year, and what did they do? They let her go without buying her a drink, without finding out whether she was from Persia or Peoria.

He turned his full fury on Andy. "You probably fixed it up for yourself; that's what happened."

"Sure that's what happened. She'll be waiting when my old woman calls for me at four o'clock. Then we'll all go home and sleep together, three in a bed, cozy-like."

Andy's fidelity was well known and he didn't see why he should be the goat for Perry's temper.

Perry apologized with a laugh and a slap on the shoulder.

"All right," he said, "but what the hell did you think I gave her a table for?"

"I knew what you gave her a table for," Andy said, "but I thought you'd go on from there. I didn't know I was supposed to p. i. for you. Excuse it, please, but I thought we was running the swellest night spot in the country, not a waterfront dive."

"You got no instinct about women," Perry said, suddenly taking a parental attitude. "That's why you're still a lousy captain."

"I'd rather be a lousy captain than an ulcerated chippy-chaser," Andy retorted but his heart really wasn't in it. He knew Perry was just demanding an argument so he had to let him have something.

"I ought to fire you," Perry said, "but it'll be more kick knocking you down."

"Why didn't you do it in the first place? It'd saved us both a lot of time. And I don't know why you're taking all my skin off. She'll come back. They all do."

They were calling for Perry in the bar and he stalked off.

Andy turned to the hat-check girl, who had been a not-disinterested bystander.

"Can you imagine that guy getting that hysterical over any one dame?"

"He's a sick man," the girl said. "You don't understand a man like Michel Perry, Andy. He hasn't slept alone for ten years and it's gotten so it's got to be something special. This dame looked like something special, I guess. At least, she must have, to him."

"Well, then, why didn't he take care of it. I'm not getting women for him or nobody else. Anyway, I don't believe this dame was a pushover."

"They're all a pushover for Michel," she said with a deep sigh.

Andy looked at her and shrugged his shoulders. "All right, have it your way."

CHAPTER TWO

Andy was right in his prognostication. She was back a few nights later on the arm of a well-known movie producer. This time there was no argument. Andy would have led them to a "Reserved" table, even if Hollywood hadn't slipped him the V.

So that's what she was, the *mademoiselle*—Hollywood flesh. She didn't run true to form. Most of them were strictly chicken and done to a golden brown. This one would never see twenty-five again and looked as if she'd been rolled in snow. But Andy, he liked them that way, white and soft. He was Grik.

Perry hadn't come down from his apartment. He was arriving later and later every night, and when he did finally appear, he usually looked as if he'd been pressed between the leaves of an old book since they last saw him.

Finally, Andy called him on the house phone. Wouldn't do to let her get away again.

Perry answered immediately but his voice was flat and frightened.

"She's in again," Andy said.

"I'm not here," Perry replied, and then inevitably: "Who?"

"The *mademoiselle* you got so hot and bothered about the other night. Wearing the same dress, too, only she's hiding some of the body tonight with orchids."

There was a long pause.

"Did you hear?" Any demanded. This guy certainly burned him up these days.

"Orchids, huh," Perry said. "Is she with the same messenger boy?"

"Hell, no. She's with a Hollywood fat boy tonight."

"Well find out who she is and don't let her get away until I get down. I'm getting a massage now."

Massage! It would take a bone-setter to massage that guy these days. He's got no flesh to massage.

Andy hung up without further comment.

"'Find out who she is!'" he echoed to the hat-check girl. "'And don't let her out until I get down!' He is certainly one to give the orders."

"She left a wine-colored cape lined with sable," the girl said. "I can lose that for ten minutes or so. That'll detain them while you phone again."

"He'll be down," Andy prophesied. "He was putting on an act. And I'm not blaming him. I took a good gander when I pulled the chair out for her tonight."

"And what'd you see? Hope of Heaven?"

"Nothin' nicer ever sat on that chair and they've all been here. And she's never had no kids either; I'd bet on it. You can say what you please, but once it's been spread—"

"You foreigners make me sick. You can take one look at a girl, fore and aft, and think you know her life history. And anyhow I wouldn't give up my two angels for all the flat bottoms in Brooklyn."

A collegiate crowd, the bane of Andy's existence, appeared, and the anatomical matter was dropped.

A minute later, the automatic elevator opened and Perry stepped out. Half-dead, he looked better to the hat-check girl than all the corn-fed athletes from west of the Rockies.

"Hello, sugar," he said, pinching her.

She greeted him gruffly. "Have you eaten?" she demanded.

"What a gal!" he mocked. "One pinch and she wants to know if I've eaten."

"You louse! Starve and see if I care. Only if you think it's doing business any good to go in there looking like a scarecrow dressed by Brooks and Sulka, you're nuts."

"I've eaten. Milk toast, and for supper I'm to have noodles, unsalted, with sweet butter. What am I living for?"

"I can guess and she's in there with Hollywood."

"Who else is in there?"

"The usual mob."

"No strangers?"

"I didn't see any."

"I told Andy not to let any strangers in even if it meant keeping the place half empty."

"I haven't seen any strangers and they're sitting on each others' laps it's so crowded."

"Good. How're the kids?"

"Fine." Suddenly she whirled around. "Can you tell by looking at my frances that I've produced a brace?"

When he spoke, his voice had a far-away and long-ago echo to it.

"When I was a boy in the old country," he said, "we had a big barn that was painted yellow—"

"You louse! So I'm the side of a barn, am I?"

"That's for calling me a scarecrow!" He lifted her skirt with easy familiarity and slipped a bill under her stocking. "For the kids," he said airily and walked away.

God, how she loved that son of a bitch, she thought as she transferred the twenty from the nylon to her purse. Putting money in her stocking was an old Latin custom at the *Ecuador* and it was bad business to have one bill crackle against another.

Perry walked through the bar into the main room, smiling at all, personally greeting a few, mostly men, but he had a way of brushing ever so lightly against a woman that was a mating call in itself. Or so they regarded it.

Out of the corner of his eye he saw that she was there, the voluptuous, mysterious *mademoiselle,* and with the fat boy from Hollywood, as had been reported to him. Then he stopped to talk to a group of sub-debs because it gave them goose pimples. Or so they said.

The *Ecuador* was the most popular night spot in America for this reason. When he left the table five minutes later, every little girl felt that she had been spiritually raped. Maybe one of the four would have surrendered with plenty of qualms, maybe one he would not have considered, maybe one would not have considered him, and maybe one would have been a pushover for anybody.

But that wasn't what counted. The important thing was that he could convey to all four of them a passionate intention, and that without a word or a gesture that wouldn't have had the full approval of their mothers. It was art, great art, and like all great art, it was half-genius and half-technique.

He progressed through half a dozen different tables, never sitting unless his back could be to the wall, while he surveyed the entire room, until he finally reached his goal.

"Hello, Jules," he greeted the fat boy from Hollywood.

"Hello, Michel! I was just asking for you. Can't you sit down and have a drink?"

"Yes, if you'll change places, I have to watch the room."

"Sure. Laura, this is the boss, Michel Perry."

Michel bowed low from the waist.

"Charmed, Madame—"

"Mademoiselle," she corrected.

"Laura is all she'll give out with," the fat boy said. "So I guess we'll have to make it do."

The men sat down, Perry on the wall divan next to Mademoiselle Laura, and the fat boy on a chair to her left. He was drinking champagne; she was having sweet Port.

"Another glass," the fat boy said to the hovering waiter. "Or would you rather have something else, Michel?"

Perry smiled at the waiter. "The usual," he said, and the waiter smiled back and hurried away.

"The usual is milk," Perry explained to the fat boy.

"No foolin'! You're not looking well, that's a fact. I don't know how anybody lives in this town. I caught a cold before I got from the airport to the Plaza."

"This overcrowded smoke-hole won't do you any good," Perry said gloomily. But enough of the fat boy. He turned to the woman. "Mademoiselle Laura is in pictures or going in perhaps?"

"I've been trying to sell her the idea," the fat boy said, "but she seems to think it's funny."

"You have no idea how funny it is," she said without smiling.

"Your voice is certainly a natural," Perry said. He knew what went with that kind of voice. Of course there might be an exception, but he'd never met one yet.

"It's a little low-pitched," the fat boy said critically, "but we could fix that."

"But I can't act," she protested. "And I don't need money, and I hate the idea of everybody all over the world looking at something that is me, but it is not me."

"That seems to cover it," Perry said. "I have known Mademoiselle before, haven't I?"

It was maddening to him because be prided himself on not forgetting people.

"I was here a few nights ago."

"No, I don't mean that. I think it was quite some time ago. Not here in this place."

"It is possible," she said, without interest. "I have been in many places."

"I haven't," Perry said. "I was born on the other side and came to New York when I was very little. I've never been anywhere else. One trip to Miami. I stayed a week. For ten years I haven't been south of Forty-second Street or north of Fifty-ninth."

The glass of milk arrived and Perry sipped it eagerly. It was rich with cream, although that wasn't allowed. They were all trying to fatten him up. They all loved him, the sonofabitch.

The rhumba quintette was playing now, beautiful, rhythmic tunes and the lights toned down to a pinkish glow. The woman turned to the fat boy.

"Don't you dance, Meester Jules?"

"Not this new stuff," the fat boy apologized. "Better try Michel. He invented this rhumba."

She turned to Perry.

"I'd fall apart if I tried to dance," he said with an apologetic smile.

Get up on that floor and dance! The thought was terrifying. To be jostled by those people. A quick stab in the back or one shot through the temple. Of course, theoretically, they knew everyone in the place, but there was always some stranger. It was impossible to keep them out. Particularly women. Some of his best clients would have a new dame every night. And women can shoot as well as men.

"However," he said, "I would be delighted to present a few of the most expert dancers in the city. They would be more than charmed, I'm sure—"

"Thank you," she said, "but I'm very happy as we are. I wouldn't be nearly expert enough for your dancing men."

She said it with complete sincerity, not as if she were disappointed. She knew her stuff, she knew how to please, Perry decided and let his knee slide against hers. But there was a quick withdrawal.

On the other hand, the fat boy had lost interest. If the dame wasn't excited about a picture test, she wouldn't be putting out anything for him. The fat boy had no confidence whatsoever in his own attractions. However, he had no complaint. She was a good companion for the *Ecuador* and undoubtedly was the magnet that had drawn Michel Perry to his table. Perry had never sat with him before, although several times they had drunk together at the bar.

He excused himself. He wanted to talk to someone across the room. He would only be gone a minute, if Laura didn't mind?

Laura smiled her consent. Perry stood up until the fat boy had joined the party across the room. He had to greet a number of customers and then he ordered one of the waiters to remove the surplus chairs from the table where he sat with Laura. People loved to sit and talk with the boss, camera men made it a focal point, and more than one pair of lecherous eyes was absorbed in Laura.

He turned to her, giving out with the full force of the Michel Perry smile and trying to keep the fear out of his eyes.

"Now tell me," he said, "where we have known each other before?"

She laughed, a soothing, rippling laugh. "We haven't," she said. "You haven't known me before, that is, not this me."

"What does that mean?"

"You may have known some other me—in some other existence, some other life, some other plane—"

"I don't believe in that kind of stuff," he said harshly. "This is our life and our only life."

"Is that why you are so terrified?" she asked gently. "You are afraid of death?"

"I don't want to die now," he admitted, his suddenly trembling fingers just able to light a cigarette. "I don't want to die while I'm still full of youth and vigor. I don't want to die while I still can enjoy a woman."

"And when you are through with women, you will be through with life?"

"Gladly!"

"It's a strange idea," she said, as if lost in thought, "I've never heard anyone express it before."

"What is our life but the expression of sex—the life force. There are a few necessary years of preparation, and for some people a few more years of contemplation when it is over. I do not wish them. When the times comes, I may want them but that would be a weakness."

"And you live only for women?"

"Of course ... what else is there to live for? I mean for men. Of course, women have children and must be mothers."

"And what is this fear that is destroying you? What is this disease that is killing you? I can see that you are a sick man."

"Only because I am afraid. These ulcers are nothing except fear."

"Men have had ulcers and lived for many years—eighty, ninety."

"I know that. They would go away—"

"Then what is it you fear? Tell me."

"No," he said. "I will not tell you because you are a stranger and I am in mortal terror of strangers. I can only tell you that I am marked for death."

"And so you never expose your back and sit always with your fingers gripped around a small automatic?"

He blushed. "I didn't know I was that obvious."

"You're not. It is only that I, too, have known such a fear."

"If you will let me hold you in my arms," he said in a matter-of-fact tone, "I will forget the fear for a while."

"No," she said, "but I will hold you in my arms until the fear is driven away . . . gone . . . exorcised . . ."

"Then you must start tonight," he said, "for the fear within me was never greater. But why should you do this for me? I cannot believe you are interested in money."

"No," she agreed.

"I am only the wreck of a man. There are many younger and stronger men much more worthy of your body."

"You are the first man I have ever known to admit there is nothing in life for him beyond a woman. Don't you think that is an unanswerable argument?"

"It hasn't always been," he said. "Many have complained because I haven't admired their beauty, their clothes, their brains."

"I'm not seeking flattery," she said, and then almost in a whisper: "Only gratification."

She stood up quickly.

"Let us go then," she said, "before that ape returns."

But Michel Perry was still the business man, the most successful night club entrepreneur in New York.

"No, we can't do that. Your little ape is an important beast in the Hollywood zoo. Ditch him and come back. The private entrance to my apartment is just next door to the right. I'll be waiting for you."

The fat boy returned and announced that a party of friends was going to the airport to speed a departing celebrity. Wouldn't Laura, and Michel, too, for that matter, join them?

Michel smiled and declined. He hadn't been outside the building in more than six months.

Laura also declined. She was no good at meeting large crowds of people. She just couldn't do it. But of course he, Jules, the fat boy, the ape, the important beast, must go. She had promised to be back at her hotel before midnight to receive an important telephone call.

"You're sure you won't mind?" the fat boy asked, hastily pouring a full glass of champagne which he noticed was left in the bottle.

"But of course not. You can either drop me or if that is not convenient I do not mind in the least taking a taxicab alone."

"No," the fat boy said, gulping and sputtering over the champagne. "No trouble at all to drop you. Then I'll meet the others at the airport."

He yelled across the room that he would meet the others at the airport.

A waiter, unobtrusively signaled by Perry, appeared with the check. The fat boy seemed a little surprised, but paid it.

"Sorry you can't stay and have one with me," Perry said politely.

He went along to the door with them so that the hat-check girl would not hold up Laura's sable-lined cloak.

Then he went into the bar. He was sure she would return, but that did not allay his fears. She might easily be the harbinger of death. He had often wondered, if he could choose a woman for a last virile day on earth, which of his many loves he would select.

Now it became crystal clear to him that, of course, it would be none of the old loves. It would be a new one, a beautiful one, a voluptuous one. Such a one was Laura and if death were her price, he'd meet the challenge.

CHAPTER THREE

Laura changed her dress before returning to Michel Perry's private apartment in the *Ecuador*. She selected a juvenile black dress, with starched collars and cuffs, low-heeled patent leather pumps, and a black hat that was almost a poke-bonnet without strings. She might have been a convent girl, except that no convent girl could have worn the clothes the way she did.

From a secret compartment of her trunk she took a bottle labeled "Vermouth" but without the name of the maker or the bottler. It was a strange appearing receptacle, reminiscent of the days of prohibition. She did not take a drink from the bottle; in fact, for the moment she did not uncork it. From the same secret compartment of her trunk she next extracted an empty one-ounce bottle and a tiny funnel.

Then she hesitated. He was a man of a thousand fears. There was no good reason to suppose he would not fear her. He might search her—in fact, it was quite probable. She had purses with a secret compartment, but he was probably a thoroughly systematic man with a great deal of experience, and if he decided on a search he would tear the lining from her purse.

On the other hand, he was a jittery neurotic. He could easily be the type of man who would only want a woman once. Her vanity came to her aid there. She had known many men who boasted they only wanted a woman once, but they had always wanted her again. Still, there was something about this Michel Perry different from any man she had ever known.

But if he did make a complete search and found the Vermouth on her first visit, then everything would be spoiled. Finally, after considerable wavering, unusual for her, she returned the bottle, unopened, to the secret compartment of the trunk and with it the one-ounce phial.

Over her school-girl outfit, she put on a plain, double-breasted blue-coat. The obvious astonishment of the elevator man reassured her that she had completely changed her personality. The starter, outside the hotel, also did a double-take when he opened the taxi door for her.

The private entrance to Michel Perry's apartment over the *Ecuador* was almost concealed by tall, potted plants. Laura found a button and pressed it, and, although she could not hear any bell or buzzer, the door was opened almost immediately by a Filipino boy.

"I think Mr. Perry is expecting me," she began, but any explanation was unnecessary.

The boy grinned at her. "Won't you come in, please?" he invited. He spoke without any accent or special inflection.

He took her up, it seemed several floors, in a carpeted, mirrored elevator. It worked automatically and when it stopped there was no door visible, only a heavy, velvet curtain.

Laura gasped. "This seems very dangerous," she said.

The Filipino grinned. "Yes, it is," he agreed. "Very dangerous."

The room into which she stepped was enormous—hexagonal or octagonal in shape, she was not sure which. The heavy velvet curtains through which she stepped enclosed the entire room. It was impossible to tell which were breaks and which merely folds in the drapery.

There was very little light and the room seemed almost bare. There was one floor lamp, brightly illumining a deep, modern chair and a small table beside it. The rest of the room was in deep shadow. A large object in one corner was, apparently, a huge studio couch without foot- or head-board.

"Will you take off your coat?" the boy invited. "I will tell Mr. Perry you are here."

She took off her coat and hat and handed them to him.

"Thank you," he said, indicating the chair in the light. "Won't you sit down?"

She moved over to the large, modern chair. The boy disappeared through another opening in the heavy curtains. She quickly returned to what she thought must be the elevator, but when she pulled aside the curtain, she was confronted by a huge mirror extending the full distance from floor to ceiling. She went to the big chair and picked up a South American magazine from the table.

The boy returned almost immediately. "Mr. Perry will be up in a very little while. He asked if you will have something to eat or drink while you are waiting."

"Nothing, thank you," Laura said, remembering her own "Vermouth."

"Thank you," he said. "The cigarettes in the silver box have nothing in them except tobacco."

"What do the others have in them?"

"I do not know. I have only been told to say that those in the silver box have nothing in them except tobacco."

"It's probably all a little game of suggestion." Laura said, opening the wooden box which was next to the silver one. The cigarettes in it were wrapped in brightly colored papers, and had gold, silver, black and red tips. Presumably, here was a code: gold, marijuana; silver, hashish; black, powdered opium. She couldn't guess what the red might mean, not being sure what other narcotics could be blended with tobacco.

"Would you care for a fire?" the boy asked.

"What'll you do? Build it in the middle of the floor?"

The boy grinned and drew aside the velvet curtains at one end of the room. A fireplace was built flush into a mirrored wall. He applied a match and almost immediately there were flames with flickering vari-colored sparks in them.

"Lovely," Laura said, clapping her hands.

"Would you like the room scented?" the boy next asked.

Laura had been entertained before by men with Oriental ideas of sensuality but she found this a most amusing combination of luxury and nonsense. She was only surprised that the Filipino boy addressed her directly instead of using the third person. Perhaps it was Perry's idea of the brotherhood of man.

"I think not," she said. "I think the smell of the burning wood will do nicely. That is real wood isn't it?"

"Oh, yes, Miss; pine or birch, I think. There will be nothing else then?"

"Nothing else, thank you."

The boy bowed and vanished through the opening in the curtains, by which they had entered the room. Immediately, Laura heard the elevator descending. She hurried across the room and raised the curtain. Again, only the blank, voiceless, mirrored wall confronted her.

She returned to the chair, opened the wooden box of cigarettes, selected all the gold-tipped ones (there were seven), broke them just above the tips, tossed the upper sections into the blazing fire, then lighted each tip, and ground them out in the ashtray on the table. Then she settled down to the South American magazine.

In about a half-hour, she heard a light footfall just behind the chair but she did not turn. She would pretend to doze. Long fingers that seemed all bone closed over her eyes. She was conscious of a masculine perfume and lips pressed against the top of her head.

She put her hands up against the fingers that seemed like iron.

"Men have been killed," she said, "because they came up behind me."

"I've no doubt," Michel Perry said, releasing his fingers, and coming around to the side of the chair.

He was wearing a white, woolly robe and black leather slippers. The robe was drawn tight, accentuating his broad shoulders and small waist, but it could not hide his dreadful emaciation.

He sat at the foot of her chair but she made room for him in it, alongside of her.

"See," she said, "there's plenty of room."

With quick grace, he slid into the space she had made.

"I'm sorry to have kept you waiting," he said. "It was unavoidable."

"It's all right," she said. "It's very peaceful and restful here."

"My little convent virgin," he said, looking at her outfit.

He held his lips to hers and moved his head from side to side, in a regular rhythmic beat. She felt it becoming mesmeric and released herself.

"Can you remember," she asked, "now that you see me dressed differently, if you knew me before?"

"I know I have," he said, "but I don't know where or when it was. Do you?"

She laughed but did not answer his question. "Apparently you're not going back to the club tonight."

"I should say not," he said. "They can get along all right."

Suddenly he reached over and opened the wooden box.

"Did you smoke *all* the gold-tipped cigarettes?" he asked, astonishment in his voice.

"Yes, shouldn't I have?" she answered very innocently.

"How do you feel?"

"Fine. How should I feel?"

He laughed heartily. "Like diving into bed immediately."

"But I don't. I don't feel in the least sleepy. I never felt more wide-awake."

He laughed again. "I don't mean for sleep, you baby."

"On the contrary," she said sliding out of the chair and his tightening embrace, "I never felt less like diving into bed for sleep or any other purpose. In fact, I think I'll go home."

"Home!" He sprang out of the chair and gathered her into his arms. "But you can't go home. You promised me you'd stay. You promised you'd drive away all my fears."

She drew her head back but did not attempt to break away from his embrace.

"You'll find plenty of women downstairs perfectly willing to accommodate you," she said, a little disdainful.

"But I don't want them," he said, almost in tears. "I want you. You promised."

"What are you so dreadfully afraid of?" she said. "But no matter," she went on before he could answer. "I'll stay with you and I will drive your fears away—if you'll let me."

She kissed the tears from his eyes, comforting them with her lips. She was conscious of his strength under his robe and he realized she had little, if anything in the way of lingerie, under her convent-like dress.

He disappeared into the shadows and returned with what appeared to be a large chiffon handkerchief. But when he handed it to her, it proved to be the sheerest possible nightdress, flamelike in texture and color, varying from the deepest red to the palest shell-pink.

"To match the fire," he said. "You will seem like a fire-sprite in it," he continued, as she made no movement.

He drew back all the velvet drapes. The mirrors were solid on all the walls. The fire was reflected in all of them as she stood up beside him, they seemed to be surrounded by a million tongues of leaping flames.

"Is this preparation for a floor show?" she asked, flippantly.

"No," he replied, "I always try to dramatize the personality of anyone kind enough to visit me here."

"And you think I am a lady from hell in spite of my convent dress?"

"In spite of your convent dress," he agreed.

He tugged at the cord holding his robe together but she caught his hand.

"Don't please. I want to know your strength without seeing what fear has done to you."

"All right," he agreed, and the light faded as he touched a switch somewhere. Only the reflections of the flames remained.

"My strength is greater than ever," he promised, catching her in his arms and leading her to the massed shadow in one of the corners.

CHAPTER FOUR

The fire in the grate and in the reflected mirrored walls waned and finally died. But not so the fires in the hearts and bodies of the two—Michel Perry and the mysterious Laura.

For this she had waited ten long years, and now, at last, she knew she had not been deluding herself. No man in those ten years had been like him, and no man, she was sure, would ever be like him. At least, for her. She could not think or speak for other women.

As for Perry, in the dark, with this woman in his arms, he was not so sure that he had known her before. She was a gift from the gods and goddesses of love, and if such a gift had come his way, he was sure he would have remembered.

"Asleep?" he finally whispered. She had lain quiet for some minutes.

"Oh, no," she said, "but this is the most wonderful rest in all the world, the rest of complete relaxation."

She kissed him, a kiss without passion but still a passionate kiss, because it breathed the passion that was spent and the passion that was to come.

"Look," he said, "the monkeys are still capering playfully."

At one side of the huge couch, long cylindrical tubes reached up from the floor, looking not unlike the carriers for money and sales-checks in a department store. There were snap tops to them and he held one of them open for her.

She looked into it, and through an ingenious periscope device, she could see the scene in the cafe below. The crowd had thinned out (it must have been later than the regulation closing hour) but those who remained were dancing, drinking, and, in what they thought were dark corners, embracing. They had only one thing in common: most of them were in a state of intoxication, varying only in degree. Without being able to hear a strain of the music, the dancing seemed particularly strange—orgiastic, obscene.

It was aphrodisiac and when his arms tightened around her, she let the top of the periscope tube drop and turned to him. He twisted a knob somewhere and then the music came to them from the cafe below. Under it, but quite faint, was the noise of the dancers, the shuffling of their feet, the murmur of their voices.

"Turn it off," she said. "It gives me a strange feeling that they are watching and listening to us."

"Wouldn't they like to," he said, twisting the knob again.

There was silence in the room again.

Later, considerably later, he asked if she wouldn't like the fire built up again. Not, she said, if it meant having the Filipino boy come into the room.

Perry laughed. "What do you care about him? He's as uninterested as a cat."

"I don't care to have cats watching me."

He sprang lightly from her side and across the room. One of the mirrors revolved at his touch and he disappeared for a minute, returning with his arms filled with wood.

Crouching in front of the fireplace, he looked for all the world like an Indian. Naturally dark, he was tanned, probably by a sun lamp and not the sun itself, to a brown, almost black. The sparks burst into flames, illumining his sensitive face, lined and haggard with fear.

She slipped quietly from the couch and across the room to him at the fire. She put her arms around him, reaching from behind.

A half-suppressed scream came from him as he swung quickly around, hitting her with his open palm.

She fell back on the carpet, almost stunned, not by the force of the blow but the shock and surprise of it.

"Don't ever do that again," Perry said, his voice shaking with emotion. "Don't ever come up on me from behind."

Then he dropped to the floor next to her, kissing her, asking if he had hurt her, begging her forgiveness.

"It's nothing," she insisted. "I should have had better sense. It's lucky for me that you didn't have a log in your hand."

He stretched out on the thick carpet next to her. Against its dark surface they looked like statuary—she, marble; he, bronze. The fire illumined the rose tints of her body, outlined its perfections as she turned to him.

"Tell me," she said, "what you fear, so that I can really help you. To share your fears is to half-lose them, you know—"

"Why should I give half of them to you?"

"Because I want to share all of you. Not just your lust—"

"My love."

"Perhaps—but I want to help you. My body can only help you to forget for a few, brief moments. I want to do much more than that. Tell me—who is it that threatens you?"

"No one is threatening me. I wish they were. I would know better how to act. Maybe I will tell you later . . . not now . . . I don't want to think about it."

The fire warmed them, toasting the soles of their feet. It flamed up and in all its mirrored reflections, catching with it the marble and bronze on the floor, blending all into one fiery whole.

Finally, it became too hot, and he carried her back to the cool, silken couch.

"Let us see if there are still people down there," she said.

"There'll be some, maybe more than before," he said. "The dawn patrol drifts in from other places."

She opened the top of one of the tubes, but to her surprise she was not looking into the main room of the *Ecuador*. A woman sat in front of a mirror, carefully powdering. Another in the background was adjusting a stocking. A Negro girl was making change.

"Why, you wretch!" Laura whispered for although she knew she could not be heard, watching these others gave an illusion of being overheard. "It's the ladies' room."

"Sure," Perry said, laughing. "The men's is right next."

"Thank you, no," Laura said, blushing in the dark.

"I can do more than that," Perry boasted. "Some of the tables have concealed mikes."

He turned them on, one by one. Most of them revealed only banal, drunk talk. One lady, in sailor's language, was telling the boy friend she had observed his dancing with one of the season's debutantes and if she hadn't been a lady she would have drenched them with ice-water, pitcher and all.

Perry switched to another table. They heard the crisp, biting tones of Andy, the headwaiter.

"No," he said. "Michel won't be back tonight."

"He wasn't feeling well?" a woman's solicitous voice asked.

"He was feeling all right when he left here," Andy said. "I don't know how or what he's feeling now."

"The bastard," Perry said.

"Doesn't he know about the mikes?" she asked.

"Sure he knows about them. He was speaking for our benefit, not for those dopes he was talking to. He does it all the time, figuring I'll be listening at least for some of it."

"I'm never, never again coming into your place. It's like the eye and ear of God—or the devil."

"It's just a gag," Perry insisted. "I've never let any customer know, or given out a single thing I've learned this way. Anyway, mostly it's dumb stuff like this."

"Where do I go," she asked, sitting on the edge of the couch, "to brush my teeth?"

He revolved another mirror for her, switched on a light, and a perfectly appointed dressing room, with connecting bath, was revealed.

"You'll find," he said, "cellophane-wrapped tooth brushes in the cabinet. Or anything you need."

When she came back to the couch, having spent some time in the luxurious dressing-room and bath, she thought he was asleep and sat down quietly beside him. But instantly his arms were around her.

"I was afraid," he whispered, "that you had gone."

"How?" she asked. "Down the drain?"

"I cannot believe you are real," he explained. "You are like a dream and I'm afraid you'll vanish."

Again she kissed the tears from his eyes and let her lips remain, cool and comforting, on his.

"But this is real," she said.

All was real, but it was a feverish sort of reality and as the night progressed she did not feel that he was losing himself in her embraces. If anything, his tenseness increased and there was a diabolical quality in his fervor that frightened her. She felt exhausted, completely enervated, and, as if reading her mind, he asked her if she wouldn't like a snack.

She said she thought she would. He explained the Filipino boy would have to serve them.

"All right," she agreed. "But let me get a robe. I saw some in the dressing-room."

He had to find the right mirror for her. To her, the place was a hopeless maze.

When she returned wearing a mandarin coat she found in the dressing-room, the Filipino boy was putting a table-cloth on a card table in front of the fire. He served them cold chicken, toast and milk. She discovered that she was very hungry and ate a great deal. Perry only nibbled at the chicken and toast but drank large quantities of milk.

When they had finished, the boy reappeared and deftly cleared away.

"Shall we take a pill and try to get some sleep?" Perry suggested.

"I won't need a sedative," Laura said with a great yawn.

The Filipino boy brought Perry a tiny sealed envelope and a glass of water. Perry broke the seal, took a pill from the envelope, and then swallowed the pill, following it with only a sip of water.

The Filipino boy said "Goodnight" and disappeared. Laura went back to the couch which the boy had completely remade with fresh silken sheets and pillow-slips.

She was just drifting away into sleep when she was conscious of hands on her shoulders. Instinctively, sleepily, she drew away.

To her amazement, then, the bony fingers gripped her painfully and she was thrown from the couch to the floor. The couch was a very low one and the floor was completely covered with the very thick carpet. She was not hurt, but she was shocked into full sensibility. She lay there quietly, waiting.

"Goddamn you!" he swore hysterically. "There never was a woman yet who could take care of me."

She looked up, disdain in her eyes. "You're mistaken," she said. "I'm a woman and I can make you beg for mercy. I was sleepy for a moment but now I'm wide awake."

She tried to get back on to the couch but he pushed her away with his foot.

"Get the hell out of here," he said.

She went over to the chair where she had left her clothes and picked them up.

Instantly he leaped from the bed and with his powerful fingers tore the clothes from her hand. He turned on the floor lamp by the side of the chair. Then, as she had foreseen, he dumped the contents of her purse on to the table. He ripped out the lining and tore the purse apart. Then with powerful blows on the end of the table, he knocked the heels from her slippers.

There was nothing more to tear apart and he sank, exhausted, into the chair.

She laughed at him. "Does it make you feel any better to beat me, to kick me, and to tear my belongings to shreds?"

Now, very gently, he pulled her down beside him. She felt his scalding tears against her cheek.

"Tell me," she whispered.

"All right," he said, "I will."

Then, seated on the floor, her arms ground him, she heard his quick confession of fear.

"There were eight of us," he said. "For five years we ran the liquor racket in this town. Then it got too hot. We were all rich men, we saw repeal coming and we quit. Now I am the only one of the eight who is left."

He was talking to her, not looking at her, and he did not see the exulting look which came into her eyes.

"What happened to them?" she asked.

"Dead," he whispered. "All dead. The last one just a few weeks ago. One has disappeared completely—but I am sure he is dead, too."

"How did they die?"

"Some were murdered, though their murderer was never caught; some died accidentally; some naturally—but they all are dead. And my turn is next—it must be next!"

"You have been warned—threatened?"

"No, and I don't think any of the others were. Death just struck them down."

"If it is fate, if it is the will of the Lord, there is nothing to do but eat, drink and be merry."

"If I thought that was it, I would do nothing. But I do not believe in the will of the Lord, and I cannot believe it is just an accident. Several of them may have died naturally or accidentally, but this is just a break for the murderer, and I believe there is a murderer killing us off, one by one, and I am the youngest."

"Do you know who this enemy can be?"

"No, but men who controlled the liquor racket for five years made many enemies."

"These men—your partners, their deaths have been connected?"

"No," he said, "I found it out only by accident. They were scattered all over the country. Accidentally, I heard of the death of one of them—a mysterious death. So I thought I would find out what happened to the others. It cost me a great deal of money to learn that they had all prospered—and then died, one by one . . ."

"As all men do."

"But not so quickly. Not one of them was really old, and I am the youngest."

He sighed heavily and kissed her gently.

"Now I have told you and I feel better. I am getting sleepy. Will you forgive me and stay with me. I cannot bear to wake up alone."

It was only a short time later that his heavy breathing told her he was asleep, or almost so.

She raised her head and murmured into his ear: "You have nothing to be afraid of, Mike Peruzzi; nothing to fear, Mike Peruzzi."

He stirred, trying to shake off the effect of the enveloping narcotic.

"Mike Peruzzi . . . that's right . . . you know me . . ."

"Yes, and you have nothing to fear."

But he was completely gone now.

She felt wide awake, as if sleep were hours away. She opened the top of one of the periscope tubes. All the customers were gone now from the *Ecuador*. The busboys and the scrubwomen were cleaning the place. Some of the waiters were having a crap game on one of the tables.

She watched for a little while and then realized that she was drowsy. She lay back, and slept.

Suddenly, she awakened and realized that the room was flooded with light, not daylight, but light from dozens of fluorescent tubes in the ceiling. The effect in the mirrors was startling.

Michel Perry was standing over her, wild-eyed and trembling. For an instant she thought her end had come. But he was not murderously inclined.

"It can't be," he said, "it's impossible!"

"What's impossible?" she asked.

"I woke up," he explained, "and suddenly I thought I remembered who you were. I remembered who you were like, but I see now it is impossible."

She smiled. "Come, sit down here," she said.

"Did you," he asked, "or did you not, call me by name, the name I used to have?"

"I did," she admitted.

"But it is impossible, impossible . . ." he repeated.

"Tell me," she said. "Who is it, I cannot possibly be?"

"She would be older, her hair was different, her eyes were different, her nose was different, her chin was different, everything about her was different."

"What was her name?"

"Her name was Maria Buonarotti."

"Maria Buonarotti," she repeated.

"Maria Buonarotti," he said again and then switched out the fluorescent lights.

CHAPTER FIVE

Maria Buonarotti. Incredible to believe that this red-gold, white-skinned, exotic Laura could be the chunky, pimply child born and brought to maturity on the thickly populated island in the Mediterranean.

Brought up to fear God, the priest, and man in general; to venerate the Virgin, and love only her mother. Her virtue assumed an importance that made even death seem unimportant, and it was years before she was released from the firm conviction that an unchaste woman was not eternally damned.

It was the priest who warned, questioned and frightened the child before she had any idea what he was talking about. But the priest had noticed that the child was becoming a woman and while she was not pretty, they were not fussy on the island. It was enough that she was young and uncaught.

But no one had spoken "wrong" to her, she insisted, and no one had attempted to touch her. That is no one except her step-father. Under artful prodding by the priest, she said that sometimes at night her step-father came to the bed where she slept with her two little step-sisters to see that they were properly covered. And several times, of late, she would awaken when she felt his hand lightly touching her. When he saw that she was awake, he put his hand quickly over her mouth so she would not awaken the little ones. He told her she would soon be a woman and squeezed her developing breasts.

"And your mother," the priest questioned, "she is awake when your step-father comes to cover you?"

"Oh no, holy father," the child explained. "My mother works very hard and sleeps the minute she lies down and makes a great deal of noise until the sun rises. Then she jumps right out of the bed. Sometimes when my step-father kisses and hugs her she goes right to sleep while he is doing it."

"And you like it," the priest suggested, "when your stepfather puts his hand on you?"

No, the child said, she did not like it because her stepfather's hands were rough and he smelt bad, and his body was not like her mother's and sisters' but like the beasts in the fields and that frightened her. So when he came in the night, she would roll over against her little sister who would usually awaken and cry out. Then he would leave her and go back to his bed.

"You must never let him touch you in the night," the priest admonished. "If he does, you should awaken your mother."

"But he would beat me if I did that," the child said. "He used to slap me sometimes and that was all, but now he says I am older and should know better, and when I do anything wrong, he really whips me with his hard hands on my bare skin."

She offered to show the priest the marks of a very recent whipping but the priest said that was not necessary, he was sure she was telling the truth. He cautiously told her that, of course, she owed obedience to her mother and step-father and they had the right to punish her, but that it was sinful for her to allow any man to put his hands upon her body.

Then the priest sent for Maria's mother and warned her that her oldest child had reached the age where she should sleep alone and not be accessible to any man.

The woman understood and wept. She had seen her husband look upon her daughter with lustful eyes, but what could she do? Her husband was strong, and when he had wine he always wanted women, and she no longer was pleasing to him.

"You must fix a sleeping place for your daughter," the priest said, "where your husband will not be tempted, and as soon as she is old enough, you must find a husband for her."

But he knew as he said it, that was easier to say than to do. There were not enough men on the island any more, and a girl, as plain as Maria, entirely without a dowry, would not find a husband so easily.

The mother prepared a mattress on the kitchen floor for her budding daughter and put a bolt upon the door. The step-father, when he saw what was in the wind, surprised them by not being angry but only highly amused. He laughed and laughed. He would not harm the child. He, too, had an immortal soul to save.

But that was when he was sober. When he was drunk, it was another matter, and several times the mother had to bring him away from the kitchen door or he would have battered it down. On those occasions he would beat her, but she would take those beatings philosophically to a point. When he went beyond that point, she would throw water over him.

Against this danger at home, the pitfalls and temptations of the island were minor things. Maria was not attractive enough to arouse the men to mental or physical rapine, and short of that, there would be no way of having her. The priest, her mother, and her step-father had done their work well. Men, except in matrimony, led only to damnation. That the bestial body of man could in some way complement her own and bring great joy, was something entirely outside her realm of knowledge or imagination. It was long years before she learned the truth.

Matrimony did not teach it to her.

Just as she was about to decide that maybe if no man wanted her, God might take her, the letter came from America. It was just as well for the priest, either in infinite wisdom or understandable greed, doubted if she had a vocation. The island convents did not want heavenly brides without a dowry any more than the mercenary males did.

Then as a reward from the Blessed Virgin, herself, they were sure, came the letter from America, from her uncle, her mother's brother. He wrote that Maria must be of an age now to marry and he realized, since there could not be any dowry for her, she must be still unwed. In America, he wrote, in those prosperous post-war days, men were willing not only to marry dowerless maidens but would pay their passage from the old country, provided, of course, they were pure in body as well as spirit.

If the reply was favorable, he wrote, he would advance the money for Maria's passage and collect it later from the bridegroom. The priest answered the letter, dwelling upon Maria's virtue and domestic accomplishments, and not saying much about her beauty or lack of it. However, it was apparently a good sales talk, as a letter with full instructions and the necessary money for a third-class passage was received by return steamer.

The dangers of life in America as related on shipboard and at Ellis Island confirmed in her mind the high price set upon a woman's purity not only in heaven but on earth. There were many more men on the ship than women, and most of them would not have been averse to teaching the facts of life to the bewildered young immigrant.

She became friendly only with Giuseppe Buonarotti, who proudly announced that he was known in America as Joe Brown. He made no actual nor tentative assaults upon her person but was content to sit and talk about America. He was a bootlegger and had prospered. He had returned to Italy to claim a bride but had discovered that his betrothed had not waited for him. If he had not been delayed in leaving America by a thirty-day jail sentence, he might have been deceived, but as it was, her condition was all too apparent.

Other girls, whose purity had been guaranteed, had been offered but for the time being he was soured on matrimony. He was not a passionate man, being more interested in eating, drinking, gambling and making money than in making love, either for diversion or propagation. He could have well afforded to have travelled in first class, he assured Maria, but he felt more comfortable in the third.

He was a naturalized citizen and did not have to go to Ellis Island. On the last day, he was so carried away by sympathy for the frightened, praying girl that he made a tentative offer of marriage. He did not know how he would find business; he might have to go away on a long trip and in that case it would be foolish to marry. However, a man should marry and he was convinced, from all he had seen and from all he heard from his fellow travelers, that Maria was a good girl, worthy to be the bride of a prosperous bootlegger.

But Maria was sure she was betrothed. Somebody, other than her uncle, had paid for her ticket. As a naturalized American, Joe Brown said that was old-fashioned and she shouldn't allow herself to be forced into a marriage with a man she did not like. That was a meaningless argument, as Maria had never liked one man better than another. There was nothing in the pock-marked, roly-poly Brown-Buonarotti to arouse her libido, although she was grateful for his disinterested comradeship.

In the end, he gave her two dollars (he said the food on Ellis Island was very unpalatable) and a slip of paper with his address, in case her uncle's deal fell through. Of course, understand, he was not promising her anything definite—he would have to see how business was—but perhaps. He shouted most of this as Maria was climbing, with the other third class immigrants, into the barge that was taking them to Ellis Island.

A woman friend told her she was being very foolish. She should accept Buonarotti's offer and let him call for her with a priest at Ellis Island. Undoubtedly her uncle was a *padrone* who would sell her into white slavery. But Maria was sure her uncle was a good man. The priest had sent her to him.

The United States Government apparently shared her opinion and released her almost immediately to her uncle's custody. The uncle did not seem to find her appearance disappointing and said she would soon be a good wife and a good American. Joe Brown had already taught her a few words: *whiskey, wine, breakfast, dinner, church.*

Her fiancé was Henry Amblate, who worked as a wholesale grocery salesman. He was not a rich man, but he seemed to be doing very well. Maria's uncle suspected that Amblate was gradually getting into the liquor business. In the old country, Maria had heard that her countrymen in America were either in the fruit or restaurant business. Now it appeared most of them were engaged in bootlegging, that strange business, which apparently was forbidden to Americans but was all right for foreigners.

Henry Amblate was a morose, dark young man who had sent to the old country for a bride, her uncle explained, because the Americanized girls made fun of him. He had a long, red scar on his throat and it must have been a very neat job of surgical sewing that saved his life.

Maria's aunt, by marriage, shook her head over the prospective bridegroom but Maria made no objection until one Sunday when her uncle announced that Henry Amblate would take her away that night.

"And," her uncle concluded, "tomorrow he will take you to the priest's house and be married."

But the one thing Maria did know from the old country was that marriage should come first, not tomorrow.

"But tonight," she protested; "where will I be tonight?" Her aunt said something in English which Maria, of course could not understand.

"You will sleep with Henry," her uncle said, blushing. "It is the custom when brides come from the old country. Otherwise he could not be sure that you are a good girl. Tomorrow he will marry you—that is, if no man has touched you."

"No man has," Maria insisted, beginning to sob, "and no man will until the priest has married us or says it is all right."

Her uncle explained, at first patiently and then with growing anger, that it was all right. If she was a virgin, she had nothing to fear. But Maria was stubborn. It was the one thing the priest had instilled in her from her first confession—purity. She was not going to surrender it.

Her aunt continued to talk in English and her uncle was becoming purple. And who was going to give them the money for her ticket and other expenses? Perhaps she would like to walk the streets to earn that money.

Then suddenly Maria remembered Joe Buonarotti (she never liked the name Brown) and produced the bit of paper with his address. She was sure he would give her uncle the money for her ticket, without demanding any pre-nuptial trial.

There were more conferences between uncle and aunt in English, with an occasional involuntary lapse into their native tongue. The gist of it, Maria gathered, was that perhaps this Buonarotti, an established bootlegger, had more money than Amblate, the salesman, and they were under no obligations to Amblate since in the first agreement he had not specified this pre-nuptial flight.

Amblate was stalled and became suspicious. If they would refund him the amount of the ticket, he'd be delighted to call the entire thing off. If, at that point, Maria had compromised with her conscience, the hideous course of her life would have been changed. He would have taught her the real art of love, which she was not to know except, in anguish and guilt, many years later. Joe Brown, whom she married, was no more adept at love-making than she was.

Amblate would have insisted upon a family and she would have led the good life. Joe Brown, she fooled with her first American acquisition, birth control, taught her by her American aunt. So completely new was this to Maria, that she had no idea it was forbidden by the priest. When she discovered the interdiction, her faith had already begun to weaken. There were things which were the priest's business and things which were not.

Joe Brown was delighted to take over Henry Amblate's contract. He was going to a mid-West city where there was an excellent opportunity for a bootlegger with a little capital. He wanted a wife to accompany him. Otherwise, he would look foolish because it was well known that he had gone to the old country to be married. He was convinced that Maria was a good girl, but even if she were not, who would know the difference in the mid-West city. The girl in the old country had been a swollen scandal.

At the time, Henry Amblate made no complaint, but five years later, he decided he had been badly treated—not by Maria or by her uncle, but by Buonarotti-Brown. He was not then, or ever, interested in the woman he knew as Maria, but he was looking for a grievance against Joe Brown.

Their union blessed by the priest, and Maria's uncle and aunt, Maria and Joe Brown consummated their marriage on the back-end of a beer truck. Joe Brown was combining business and pleasure, honeymooning while he conveyed the beer to the mid-West, where he was to make his fortune and lose his life. And Maria saw the sun rise that morning over the Pennsylvania hills, more than ever convinced, after a night on the truck, fore and aft, interspersed with coffee and doughnuts, that man is a necessary evil in the life of woman.

CHAPTER SIX

Five years did nothing to change her opinion, although she learned to speak English, fluently and almost without accent; learned to waste her time in picture houses and with other frivolities; learned, as Joe Brown made money in great quantities, to hire servants to do the things she had done all her life.

Joe was the leader of a bootlegging and slot-machine gang that operated first in the mid-West city but expanded until it controlled the underworld in three states. His lieutenants were Ralph Bandinelli, Peter Tribolo, Frank Connors, Bennel Stein, Jack Sandro, Mike Peruzzi, the youngest, the baby of the outfit—and finally Henry Amblate.

Maria warned against the inclusion of Henry Amblate but Joe laughed at her fears.

"Women never forget," he said, patronizingly; "men don't think about things like that."

"I know the men from my island," she said, "they never forget. They may wait one, two, or ten years, but someday they strike. They never forget."

"But you, yourself, have said," Joe pointed out, "that he was not too eager to marry you, that he was glad to get the money back he had advanced for the ticket."

"I am not sure that he wanted to marry me," Maria agreed. "But he wanted to be the first to possess me. He will never forgive you for that."

"I think he has forgotten. He said he would like to meet my wife, just as if he did not know who she was."

Maria smiled grimly. "He has not forgotten. He has never married. I know—my aunt wrote it to me."

"He has had hundreds of women. He has a beautiful blonde American girl with him now."

"That is not the same. You married me, took me away from him. His revenge will never be satisfied while you are alive."

For a while she was lulled into a false security. She met Henry Amblate and he treated her strictly as the boss's wife, friendly and respectfully. He congratulated her on doing so well. Now, he was a no-good and she was lucky to have passed him up. The only thing that bothered him was how a green girl from the old country had been so perspicacious.

Only Mike Peruzzi, the kid, forgot that she was the boss's wife and behaved as if she were any other woman. And all women were for the young Mike, as they were for the older Michel, strictly objects of passion, to be used for his bodily needs just as he used the apparatus in the bathroom and about as often. At thirty he was to cry that no one woman had ever been able to meet his need; at twenty he had still been hopeful.

The boss's wife was to him just another woman, made a little more interesting by the fact that her pursuit was supposedly dangerous. The other boys said the boss never looked at a dame when he was away from home and, therefore, must be inordinately fond of his wife. But the young Mike, wise beyond his years, had observed that when men aren't interested in many women, they are seldom greatly interested in one. He suspected that the boss's wife had never known what real love could be, and he was the boy who could show her. He was right on the first count but she wouldn't give him a chance to prove the second.

She was Americanized enough by then to enjoy flirting with him, but she did not, for a second, contemplate infidelity. She still went to confession once a week, but stronger than any religious motive, was a conviction that she couldn't possibly enjoy giving herself to any man. She was willing to concede that some women did, but she was convinced that most women were like herself—submitting to their husbands because it was their duty.

She was very grateful that Joe Buonarotti's need had degenerated into a once-a-week habit, usually on a Sunday afternoon before he took his bath. He was seldom home at night but his absence, as she knew, was due to business and not infidelity. She wished he had a mistress so that she might even be relieved of her Sunday afternoon stint.

Left alone, night after night, she had every opportunity to be unfaithful and Joe probably would not have minded if she were discreet about it. But of course that did not include one of his own men. That would have been fatal to discipline.

He did not reproach her because she did not bear him children. In his innocence, he thought she was sterile. It was just as well, he said. The business he was in could mean death or imprisonment any day, and that was no background for children. At the beginning, he had spoken about making their pile and going back to the old country to raise, or even adopt, a family. But he did not mention that any more. The excitement of the racket had him. He was becoming an "American," superficially sophisticated and drunk with money and underworld power. He had only contempt for the law and boasted that he could take care of himself against musclers, chiselers, and hijackers.

But better men than Giuseppe Buonarotti have said that and become worm food in their prime.

One Sunday, the day he could always be counted on, Joe did not show up. Maria waited until it was time for the last Mass and then hurried to church. It was the first time since they had married, that he had not attended church with her on Sunday. When she returned to their modest suburban home, he still had not appeared.

She began telephoning his lieutenants. They said "no" too promptly; they did not offer to try to locate him. She became suspicious. Henry Amblate, alone, was friendly and talkative. He would get in his car and make the rounds. Joe probably had taken one too many and had fallen asleep somewhere. Maria did not believe that, and she did not believe anything Henry Amblate said. If there was any trouble, Amblate was at the bottom of it.

Finally, it was Mike Peruzzi's attitude which convinced her that something was really wrong. For once he did not try to make a date with her. His manner was tender and kind, rather than harsh and seductive. He had never been that way before and it frightened her.

In her way, which was a way completely without sex, she was fond of her husband. He had released her from slavery and had given her every comfort. She could have had luxuries except that she didn't care for them. There were fabulous sums of money in the banks, the checks for which she could sign as well as Joe, but never did.

She ate a lonely dinner at two o'clock, dismissed the servants for the rest of the day (she could fix the spaghetti for Joe if he came in) and then lay down for a nap. A thumping noise awakened her. She decided the dog was either trying to get in or out, and, although the noise was not repeated, she slipped into a dress and slippers and went downstairs.

Joe had come home, she saw as she opened the front door. He lay there all trussed up and, she knew immediately, dead for hours. She went primitive, dropped on her knees beside the body, screaming so that she could be heard three blocks away.

The neighbors came, the police came, the priest came, and all Joe's lieutenants. They swore vengeance on the hijacker who had killed their leader and Henry Amblate's oaths were loudest of all. She was sure Amblate was responsible for Joe's death but she could not yet prove it.

Joe's way of killing (he was not sadistic and killed sparingly) was to have the victim take a cocktail. Maria had a bottle of the instantaneously deadly Vermouth which Joe had given her to hold as a reserve. But Joe had been shot to death. That did not mean anything. If he had been killed by his own men, led by Amblate, they would not use his own method, even if they had some of the poisoned Vermouth, which seemed unlikely. Joe was cagey.

She was sure she could get the information from only one source—Mike Peruzzi. She whispered to him to come back when the others would be gone. He nodded understandingly. Probably he was a little revolted by the idea that she would want to see him alone the very first night her husband was dead. But he returned. A woman was a woman and Mike was willing to substitute for any husband, alive or dead. Nevertheless, he was glad when he had passed the open door of the room where Joe lay beneath a sheet, waiting for the undertaker to call for him in the morning.

Mike soon learned that the only thing she wanted from him was information. He insisted that he had none to give. So far as he knew, Henry Amblate was telling the truth. Hijackers must have removed Joe. He was lying and she knew it.

He put his strong arms around her (he was young then and without fears; flesh covered his muscles and there were no deep lines to distort his ever-ready smile) and instead of feeling revulsion, nature asserted itself and she knew that she had been living a lie.

Men were not necessarily like beasts. They could be like Gods and archangels. He felt her strange tumult and misinterpreted it. He thought it was a sense of guilt because her man had not been dead a complete day.

"It is all right," he whispered, getting up to extinguish the lights. "You can't harm him now. Anyway he was too old and fat for you. You should have a young man."

He drew back the curtains and the street lights threw a dim illumination into the room. Cars were passing in almost a steady procession, slowing down to see the home of the murdered gangster. He drew the curtains again to shut out the glare of the headlights.

He stumbled as he sought the couch. She pushed him away.

"Don't touch me," she said, "unless you tell me the truth."

She was getting hysterical and he wondered if he ought to get the hell out of there, but something about having an affair with a woman on the first night of her widowhood appealed to him and besides she was young and tender, and, stranger still, there was almost a virginal appeal about her.

He suggested she needed a drink. She agreed with him and told him where the real bonded, uncut stuff was kept. They had a drink, several drinks. Apparently she was more accustomed to this genuine, heady stuff than he was. She responded to his kisses, at first innocently, then savagely, but there was none of that sophisticated passion, the dispensation of which came so naturally from the women on whom he was accustomed to spend his gangster wealth.

He couldn't figure her out. Here was a woman who had been married for more than five years and yet she was behaving like a school-girl. He never had looked upon Buonarotti as a great lover, but at some time in her life, she must have at least been kissed by some other man.

No use wasting time. But she beat his arms down with peasant strength.

"No," she said, "not until you tell me the truth."

"It is the truth," he said. Then he weakened a little. "Amblate may be lying. I don't trust him myself, but he didn't tell me a thing."

She saw that he was breaking down so she let him kiss her again. The difficulty was to keep from responding. She suddenly wanted to drink to the dregs and she had never had a sip before. But when his teeth cut into the soft flesh of her neck, she slapped him hard, an instinctive slap of self-protection.

Then she brought him more liquor and it was the one drink too many. He drained it, and was in no mood for mere kissing.

"Do we or don't we?" he demanded.

"Not until you tell me the truth," she replied monotonously.

He turned out the light again and went for her. In the dark he heard her moving around the room. He stumbled after her, swearing as a chair impeded him and crashed to the floor.

"I don't believe you've ever had a real man in your life," he said as he caught her. "Have you?"

"Only Joe," she whispered.

"You didn't like him, did you? You didn't like him to touch you?"

"No," she admitted.

"But you don't mind me touching you, do you? It's pretty good isn't it, even if it is wrong?"

"Yes . . . but . . ."

"Then what the hell are we waiting for?"

He tugged at her but she scratched like a wildcat.

"You bitch!" he swore at her. "All right, you asked for it."

They fought all over the room. He, starting half in jest, soon found that it would take all his strength to subdue her. She bit, scratched and kicked. Her muscles were hard and her flesh was firm from years of domestic labor. His open-hand blows did not really hurt her.

Then suddenly as he pushed her down on the couch and believed that she was about to yield, he felt a pistol pushed against him.

"Don't move," she cautioned.

"Put that thing away," he said. "Accidents can happen."

"This wouldn't be an accident," she said. "And I will say that you tried to rape me on the night my husband died and I killed you. And any judge will release me. Is that not so?"

"Is that what you brought me here for?" he asked. "To kill me?"

"No," she said. "I brought you here to have you tell me the truth. Tell me that and I won't fight. You shall have everything you wish. I don't know much but you shall teach me."

Her hand gripped the revolver firmly. He dared not grab for it. Otherwise, she was soft and yielding against him. Her clothes had been torn in the struggle.

"All right," he said. "You guessed right. Amblate let him have it. He called us all together this morning and said Joe was holding out on us. He had some statements and figures to prove it—"

"It's a lie! Joe was honest with his men."

"I think so, but the take has been much less this year than last. Anyway, when Joe came in, Amblate let him have it. Maybe a couple other guys pumped lead too, just to get in right with the new boss. I swear to God I didn't."

"That's all I want to know," she whispered.

In the dark, he heard her revolver drop to the floor. He picked it up and fingered it expertly. It was not loaded.

"Just for that," he said, "I'll have to tear your heart out before I leave here tonight."

She did not say anything. She knew he would not harm her. She had the truth now. If she really wanted to evade him, all she had to do was to run to her room and bolt the door. But her mortal sin was that she didn't want to evade him.

"I suppose you know what will happen," he said, "if you do go to the police."

"I won't go to the police," she said scornfully.

"What will you do?"

"I don't know. But you need have no fear—"

"I've never been afraid of anything," he swaggered. "But why think about it? We've done you a favor. You didn't care anything about him."

"He was a good man."

"Good for what?" he jeered. "He wasn't any good to you this way, was he?"

"No," she admitted, "he wasn't any good this way."

"Then what are you kicking about? You've got me and you've got plenty of money, haven't you?"

"Yes," she said, "plenty."

"Then what are you beefing about? You ought to thank Henry Amblate."

"I'll thank him with a knife through the heart," she said without heat.

"Have it your way," he said and that ended the argument.

Death had come to her that day, and yet she knew, when Mike Peruzzi finally slept and she lay by his side, she had never tasted life before. She had to revise all her ideas of man and God. Now she understood the temptation of the devil and she wondered how any one ever resisted.

This man by her side was surely, if not the devil, a demon of the first order. She should plunge the bread-knife into him as he slept. But she only kissed him very gently. He awakened instantly and his demonology began all over again.

When she awakened next, the room was filled with sunshine, the telephone was ringing, people were hammering on the door, and he was gone.

That night at the rosary, she wore mourning crepe from head to toe. All the members of the gang were there in black ties, with mourning bands on their sleeves. Henry Amblate had sent a blanket of orchids.

She was flanked by women friends who spent the night with her. . . .

The day after the funeral when Mike Peruzzi tried to get in touch with her, he was told she had gone to New York and from there would sail to the old country.

He did not regret the loss of her body, which was all right but unexceptional. He could have used her dollars, which he was sure ran into the hundreds of thousands.

He soon forgot about her, Maria Buonarotti, but his memory became only more vivid to her as time went on. Other men, she met and knew, were mere mortals. He remained a demon.

CHAPTER SEVEN

"Turn off those lights," she requested. "I feel as if I were nude on Broadway."

Michel Perry obeyed and sat down on the broad couch.

"You're going to tell me who you are," he said, "if you want to get out of here alive."

She laughed at him.

"It isn't important whether I get out of here alive or not," she said. "I really don't care. But you are afraid that you won't get out of here alive."

That was true. Death was in the air for him and he was mad to have brought this woman into his apartment.

"But you must take my word," she said, "that you are in no danger. How can you think that I would harm you?"

"You probably wouldn't do it yourself," he conceded, "but you're the finger for whoever is rubbing out the old Amblate mob. You won't try to deny that, will you?"

"It wasn't really the Amblate mob," she corrected, "and I'm the finger for no one. I am alone."

"Who are you?"

It was his final question, the one to which he always retreated.

"You guessed it," she said. "You called my name. I was Maria Buonarotti."

"But that is impossible."

"Nothing is impossible," she contradicted, "with time, money and will."

"I could believe it possible that you are Maria Buonarotti's daughter but not Maria Buonarotti."

"Thank you, Mike," she said, "you are flattering."

He winced. He did not like to be called Mike any more and she understood.

"You are not Mike now," she said, "any more than I am Maria. I am Laura, although I have been many women and had many names."

"Why Laura?"

"In Florence, a man told me I was a woman of mystery like Laura, to whom the great Petrarch wrote his love poems. So I took the picture of Laura and had the beautifiers and the plastic surgeons use it as a model."

"Why did you do this?"

"So that the murderers of my husband would not know me."

"And you succeeded?"

"You are the first who had any idea of having seen me before."

"I am the only one who ever really knew you," he said, bitterness in his voice.

"I am a Sicani," she said. "My mother said there is not a drop of Italian blood in our veins. It is the pure blood of the Sicani tribes."

"Killers—murderers—your Sicani."

"Yes," she admitted. "Those whom we hate. But the devoted slaves of those we love. No conquerors ever really subdued us, but we always followed the leaders we loved to the death."

"How have you done it?"

She yawned heavily.

"It is a long story, my Michel. It will take many nights to tell it?"

"I tell you I will never let you out of this room alive!"

"Then," she said placidly, "you will never know the story."

"I cannot believe that you alone can have killed six men and not have been suspected."

"I was a very rich woman," she answered indirectly. "The money was all in my name; most of it in cash in my possession. I was the only person in the world Joe Brown trusted and I betrayed him before he was buried."

"And that is why you killed all the partners?"

"Perhaps," she admitted. "He had no sons—and that was my fault. The first law of the Sicani is the blood law—murder must be revenged."

"And what about the law of the church—thou shalt not kill."

The words came reluctant and absurd from his lips.

"The laws of the Sicani come first," she explained; "then the church and even the church says an eye for an eye."

"And I am next and last?"

She pulled him over against her.

"I am powerless against you," she pointed. "You can choke me with your bare hands, suffocate me with a pillow. I have no power against you, would not use it if I had."

"Why? I was also one of those responsible for the death of Joe Brown."

"Until you held me in your arms, the night that Joe Brown was still unburied, I thought that all men were vile."

"You only did it to get the truth out of me."

"So I thought. I thought you were the Devil, himself, sent to tempt me and I ran away."

"And you found there were many other devils just as tempting?"

"No. After a while—it was many years—I thought that and yielded to many men in curiosity, in frustration, and in order to kill them. But not until tonight again have I found what frightened me so that other night."

"I am the finger," he cried out in agony. "I really killed Henry Amblate and all the others."

"They deserved to die," she said contemptuously. "Even if they had not murdered Joe Brown, they deserved to die. They misused life—all of them."

"And I?" he asked, equally contemptuous. "What have I done with my life? I run the most popular night spot in New York at the present moment."

"You have made many women happy," she suggested.

"So has a bottle of perfume or a new hat," he said cynically.

"Twenty years ago," she reminded him, "you were a boot-black and a petty thief. Then in five years you were a bootlegger and a cut-throat. Today you are a gentleman and all the great names of the country are flattered when you sit with them."

"Now you are making fun of me," he said, "because you know that under the fine clothes of Michel Perry, there is still the bootblack, the bootlegger."

"I would have liked to have known you when you were fifteen," she said. "I want to know you when you are seventy. I wish you might have been the only man in my life as really you are—"

"I cannot believe that you killed six men without help, without being caught," he said, always returning to his great fear. "If I could believe that I might trust you."

"It is true," she insisted, "and I will tell you about them—but it is a long story and now I am too tired. I want you to make love to me until I fall asleep in your arms."

"No," he said harshly, "I never want to touch you again. Or see you. God, I can only taste blood on your lips."

"Then," she said, "you will always be afraid of me unless you kill me now. Why don't you?"

"I don't know why I don't," he agreed. "You'd better get the hell out of here before I do."

She moved out of the bed.

"You forget," she pointed out, "that you haven't left me any clothes to wear."

He jumped up and turned one of the revolving mirrors. He brought her some clothes that would do well enough to get her back to her hotel. He drew on his robe and smoked cigarettes, watching her but not saying a word.

When she was ready for the street, she faced him, an enigmatic smile on her lips.

"I shall come to dinner every night," she said, "and when you become frightened again, you will bring me up here and I will tell you why you have nothing to fear."

He jumped up and then dropped down again without saying a word.

The Filipino boy, looking as if he had an excellent night's sleep, showed her out.

She judged from the appearance of the crowded street that it was around noon. Otherwise, she would not have had any idea.

"I don't like it," Andy the Grik said to the hat-check girl. "A woman eating alone every night never done no place no good."

Andy could speak better than that but he was class-conscious and indulged in Third Avenue idiom as a relaxation. And, anyway, wasn't the *Ecuador* near Third Avenue?

"Dinner business is up fifty percent since the columnists started noticing her and quoting *Sonnets to Laura,*" the hatcheck girl reminded him.

"That's because the chef's putting out better food."

"And he's putting out better food because it was appreciated. The night the golden one asked to be presented to him, meant a lot after the way you guys had been kicking him around."

"Well, what does all the business mean with the boss getting grouchier and grouchier every night? I'm getting fed up, I am."

"What's the matter with him? Think this dame has something to do with it?"

"No, it started a month before she showed up. Something's got him jittery and it seems like business, dames, or nothing can bring him out of it. Here's M'Lady now."

This was her third week as a dinner patron and she had not yet repeated a frock or a wrap. Fashion scouts accounted for a portion of the increased business at dinner. Tonight she was a medieval madonna with nothing missing except the babe. She wore a brocaded coat matching her frock but, incongruously, also carried, over her arm, a fox cape.

This she handed to the girl who came hurrying to meet her. "I'll keep my coat on," she said. "And the cape is for you."

"For me!"

"Yes, you said the ether day you thought it was the prettiest one you ever saw, so it's yours—"

"But Miss Laura—" The girl was really speechless, not merely putting on an act.

"Why, I'm delighted for you to have it, child. My fur box really looks like a zoo. It's quite disgusting."

"But it's finer than Rita Hayworth's."

"That was probably the idea. It's from Hollywood."

"Were you in pictures, Miss Laura?"

"No, but quite a few of my clothes have been. You must wear it to my hotel some afternoon and let me see how *chic* you are. And you must bring the babies, and we will find some Hollywood clothes for them."

"We'd love to and I—I just don't know how to thank you."

Laura patted the girl's hand. "Don't," she said and regally moved on to her corner table, where the captain, the waiter and bus boy awaited her.

Behind the candles on her table, her madonna-like appearance of the evening was accentuated, and for the next week the fashion designers scurried around for reproductions of fourteenth and fifteenth century paintings.

Her face was placid and untroubled as the face of a madonna should be. It was in complete contrast to the twitching features of Michel Perry when he finally dropped into the chair opposite hers.

"Will you have a little dinner?" she invited.

He declined. He had just had breakfast.

"What are you trying to do?" he asked. "Demoralize my help? The kid says you gave her a fox cape and Andy says it's worth five grand if it's worth a nickel."

"I have a hundred fur capes. It makes her very happy. I am glad that some good can come out of it. A very bad man gave it to me. You knew him."

"Who was he?"

"In Hollywood he was known as Ralph Jamison. You knew him as Ralph Bandinelli. He was smarter than most of the other men. He didn't change his first name so when he accidentally met old acquaintances they could call him Ralph and it wouldn't arouse suspicion."

"And you had him bumped off?"

"I've had no one bumped off," she denied. "Everything that was necessary, I did myself."

He leaned toward her, his bloodshot eyes peering deep into hers, as if her serenity infuriated him.

"Listen, it isn't that I am afraid. It isn't that I want to hear your stories of murders. It's only you I want—"

She let her cool hand drop on his feverish one.

"Why haven't you said so then? Haven't I been here every night?"

"Yes, but no woman has ever had the drop on me. I've had a different woman every night trying to get you out of my system."

Her eyes filled with tears as she turned away. "Why do we human beings fight so hard to keep from being happy?"

"You can't be happy with a trigger at your heart!"

"Why not? The whole world has a trigger at its heart; bombs bursting over them; mines exploding beneath them. All I ask is to live long enough to have you hold me in your arms just once more."

"Is that what you told all of them before you gave them the *coup de grace?*"

"I didn't tell any of them that I loved them, and not one of them meant anything to me alive. You are the only man with whom I would want life to last forever."

"All right," he said. "Right now I want you more than I ever wanted any woman, but don't get me wrong. I'm promising nothing—"

"I'm asking nothing."

"Fair enough," he said. Then he sighed: "I suppose it's because I know you're dynamite."

Andy sauntered over.

"Some of the defense boys are beginning to go to war in the bar," he said to Michel. "Maybe you'd better go in and play General."

"All right," Michel agreed. "I'll be right in."

Andy moved away. Michel stood up.

"You don't have to go back to your hotel first, do you?"

"Yes," she said, "I think I'd better. I really don't want to have this dress torn to shreds."

He laughed. "That's out. No rough stuff. I promise."

"Perhaps I like rough stuff. Perhaps I made you get rough. Perhaps I'll do it again."

"All right, keed," he said, grinning. "But it takes two to get rough."

"Not the way I play," she said.

He left her and she went on leisurely finishing her dinner which, as always, was superlative.

Andy sauntered back in a minute or two.

"Everything all right?"

"Everything is fine," she said.

He made a gesture indicating the filled tables. "You ought to get a commission on this," he said.

"What have I got to do with it?"

"We never used to get this crowd at dinner. The columnists had a lot of dope about the lady who dines alone."

"Oh. Well, maybe you can do something for me, Andy."

"Anything at all."

"Point out some of the women Michel has been sleeping with the past three weeks."

Andy betrayed no surprise. "I wouldn't know," he said. "Them tubes only work one way. Anyway they wouldn't be around here this time of day. Late at night when the crowd thins out he looks around and taps somebody on the shoulder. That means she's elected to Pillow and Sheet. If there's no Grade-A available there's always his little red book and there are plenty of numbers in that little red book."

"Don't you ever call them for him?" she persisted.

"Listen, lady. I only pimp for the customers; not for the boss."

"I only want to know what his type is. What he really goes for when left to do his own selecting."

"Why don't you look in your mirror?"

"He didn't really select me. I made the play for him."

"That doesn't mean a thing. Plenty make the play every night but only a few land the puck in the goal. I've been watching him for quite a few years, lady, and I'm telling you, you've got him plenty bothered. Take that for Christmas and goodbye now."

"Thanks, Andy, that's a wonderful Christmas present."

He moved away. She finished her coffee, initialed the check, left a folding money tip for the waiter, and went back to her hotel. More attention was then given to their food by the other diners.

At peace with nature and the fanaticism which had molded her life, she rested her head against his arm and wondered how she could bring him to faith in her and some assurance of the continuance of his life.

"Now tell me about Ralph—Bandinelli."

"I was just about to," she said. "What did you know about him in the old days?"

"Not much. I was only a kid then. I didn't know what the guys were up to. But I was a dead shot and afraid of nothing. That's what I was there for. Bandinelli had been an actor, I believe, before he got in the bootlegging racket. Now, that I come to think of it, some of the boys said he was a hophead."

"He was, though he always had it under control. But before I tell you about Ralph Jamison, as I knew him, I must tell you a little about myself."

CHAPTER EIGHT

My problem was to kill without being caught. I had sworn vengeance on six men. I knew I would never do anything to you. I have tried to convince myself that it is not only because of what you had been to me. You were younger than the others; Joe Brown hadn't meant to you what he did to the others. And then in giving me the information I needed to make sure, I felt you had earned the right to live. But all the time I knew I was being untrue to my Sicani blood. Your body alive meant more to me than your immortal soul, dead. Time for that together, perhaps.

It took five years for the doctors and the beauty experts to make me over and it took five more years for me to make myself over. I had always thought I would start with Henry Amblate so that if I were caught, then or later, at least the man chiefly responsible would be dead. But as it happened Ralph Jamison was the first, and by that time I had read so much and studied so much that I was sure I would not fail.

In Paris I met a beautiful woman who had once been a great Hollywood star. She belonged to the era when narcotics were as much a part of the picture as benzedrine and Vitamin B are today. She was a popular hostess in Paris where her addiction was well known. It did not make any difference to us, of course, and we did not try to cure or reform her, though we were not in sympathy because we were not addicts. She was a little strange in that she did not care for the company of other addicts.

In her apartment I saw a picture of the man she called Ralph Jamison and whom I recognized immediately as Ralph Bandinelli. She said he was an actor who had become quite a successful director. But actually, she said, this was all a great surprise to him because his real business was selling drugs. He had been an actor merely to make connections, and yet, through some fluke, he had so impressed his superiors that he had been made a director.

I asked her what he was to her because I had become very fond of her, and since this Ralph Jamison was one of the men I had determined to kill, I did not want her to be hurt any more than possible. The sex life of Ritha Sloane was a matter of considerable speculation in Paris. Because she was beautiful and had no lover, it was said that she was a lover of women. But I was vain enough to believe that was not so. Later I learned that sex was not a part of her life at all. She lived in a strange aura of mysticism, and drugs were a necessary part of it. But she used them judiciously and only died a few years ago.

"He is my very good friend," she said, answering my question. "At least that is what I would like him to be. But he is too much in love with me and I cannot make him happy."

But since she was in Paris and he was in Hollywood what difference did it make?

"That is why I have stayed in Paris," she explained, "but now I must go back to Hollywood. I have to make money and I am unhappy about Ralph."

I suggested that it would probably be kinder if she didn't see him at all since she could not return his love.

"But that is impossible," she explained. "He is my only source of supply. I would not dare trust anybody else."

A plan was beginning to form in my mind.

"Maybe," I said, "I will go to Hollywood with you. I have always wanted to see it. Maybe I will be able to win him away from you."

She jumped at the idea. She would play all my expenses! She would need a companion in Hollywood. But I was cautious about that. I did not want my identity too well established. I said that I would not think of letting her pay my expenses and that I was sure I would be a complete failure as a companion, but it would be nice to know some one important in Hollywood and I would live very close to her. I wanted her to know immediately that I did not wish to live in the same house with her.

I did not go to Hollywood with her but followed two boats later. I did not want to be identified with her or anyone in particular and I was completely successful. In all the publicity that followed the death of Ralph Jamison, my name was never once mentioned.

I was careful that his interest in me was well aroused before he met me. Ritha Sloane told him about my Parisian life, and I'm sure she made it strange and romantic. He invited me to the large cocktail party he gave to welcome Ritha back to Hollywood but, of course, I didn't go, although I would have loved to have seen all the celebrities gathered together.

Then Ritha gave a party to bring together her old friends. I promised faithfully I would go to that, but I didn't. I developed one of those sudden Hollywood colds. Then one day, Ritha insisted I must drop in for tea. She was having just a few of her oldest and dearest friends, all women. I suspected it was a trap to have me meet Ralph Jamison, but I was ready to fall into the trap.

My finesse and strategy were wasted. Or maybe they weren't. I don't know. Jamison was intensely interested in me as a person and possibly as a potential drug-buyer, but, physically, I meant nothing to him and I soon saw that I would have to work along different lines than I had planned.

He had aged a great deal since he had posed for the photograph which I had seen on Ritha's table in Paris. His hair was white, his face was deeply-lined, there were heavy pouches under his eyes. I don't think I would have recognized this tired, aging man as Ralph Bandinelli, and he did not have the faintest idea he had ever seen me before. Perhaps he never had except at Joe Brown's funeral, and then I had worn a heavy veil. Except for you and Henry Amblate, none of Joe's men ever gave me a second look.

He was the only man present and Ritha said he hadn't been invited. He had just dropped in and insisted upon staying. The women there were old California friends of Ritha's. If they had been in pictures, they were now married and domestic. I had never had tea and rum with a more respectable, conservative crew, and yet the hostess was a drug addict, while the one male guest was a drug-seller, a killer, a former gangster and racketeer.

The women talked old times with Ritha, which threw Ralph and me on our own resources. He was terribly disappointed that I hadn't been to his cocktail party. He would have to give another especially for me. I told him that I never went to large parties but I would be very glad to come to a small one. He said he would speak to Ritha and make a definite date with dinner.

He offered me a cigarette from a two-way case; on one side there was a brand with a popular label, plainly visible. I declined. Then he reversed the case and offered me one from the other side. These were unlabeled but I still declined.

He said he was delighted to see how well Ritha was looking. He had been worried about her return to Hollywood, but apparently it was all right. He did not sound to me like a man who was hopelessly in love, but I knew from personal experience how expert we become at hiding our true feelings.

Then suddenly he showed his hand. At least to me, although I don't believe any of the other women at the party realized what was happening.

Ritha's maid announced that a car was calling for Mrs. Goldman, one of the guests.

"That'll be Janey," Mrs. Goldman said. "I told them to pick her up first at school and then stop for me."

"Why don't you have her come up for a minute," Ritha said. "I promise not to remind her that I used to change her diapers."

"It will give her a terrific thrill," Mrs. Goldman said, and then to the rest of us: "She's just at the age you know."

Just at the age seemed to be about fourteen when the child appeared. She was dressed younger than that, as is the Hollywood custom, but all the convent styles of Wilshire Boulevard couldn't conceal the budding body of a woman. Mary Jane pumps only accentuated the trimmest of trim ankles. She made a modest curtsy, but there was a world of knowing in her eyes.

Ritha gave her a recent photograph, specially autographed, of course, and all would have been well if the fond mother, anxious to make a hit with her spoiled child, had not called attention to the merchant of death, Bandinelli-Jamison.

"Why don't you ask Mr. Jamison for his autograph, darling?" she suggested. "He's a very famous director."

"Mater, darling," the brat said. "Of course I know who Mr. Jamison is. His *Perennial Honeymoon* was voted our favorite in school last year. Would you sign my book, Mr. Jamison?"

Her voice was neither a child's nor a woman's, but it was chuck full of character. I saw our Ralphie's hand shake as he drew out his gold fountain-pen to sign her book.

His voice was very bland when he handed back her book and asked: "Have you ever seen a picture made, Jane?"

"Oh no," she said. "Not a real important picture on a sound stage. They never let us in to them—"

"Then you must have your mother bring you around someday to my stage and I'll be delighted to let you stay as long as you like."

I was probably the only nasty-minded female there who realized what the old lech was doing and how well he was doing it.

"Oh mother would be bored," the brat said. "Couldn't I come with some of the kids from school; I mean just one other kid—"

"And a teacher," her mother interrupted.

"Oh, of course, a teacher," the brat agreed, and, as she took the book from the director and coke merchant, I saw her deliberately cross two fingers holding the book so that he alone could see the gesture. Or at least so she thought. I was so completely dead-pan that apparently she hadn't given me a second thought.

Ritha hadn't noticed a thing, yet, when I called it to her attention later, she sat perfectly still for a moment and then said that probably I was right.

"Ralph has changed greatly," she said. "I noticed it immediately. At first I was glad. I thought it meant he had found someone else—but then I realized if he had, it certainly wasn't good for him. He looks so very badly."

"Yes, he does," I agreed and almost made a slip. "I wouldn't have known him as—the same man whose photograph I saw in Paris."

"He told me," Ritha went on, "that because he realized I would never marry him, he had taken to very unworthy substitutes. I thought he meant drugs—"

"Children are more dangerous," I said. "Drugs only kill you."

"He's having trouble with the Smith family; they're the parents of the kid he was grooming to be another starlet, but something happened and she didn't twinkle. I thought it was just because she didn't develop the talent, but it could be the other thing—"

"It could be," I agreed.

"And he's having trouble with a pay-off man in the police department. I thought it was for protection on the narcotics but I realize he's been paying off on that for years. There are some things that even pay-off men don't like, and maybe this one has a young daughter of his own. What can we do about it, Laura?"

"Nothing, I'm afraid." I reminded her that the Greeks had a monster they used to feed fifty girls and boys a year. The Greeks just thought of everything.

"We'll have to stand by him," Ritha said.

I didn't say anything, but I had no intention of standing by him, in front of him, or behind him when the shooting started. Think of a guy like Ralph Bandinelli starting as an errand boy for some Bleecker Street Black Handers becoming a snowbird and actor, developing into bootlegging and murder, and winding up directing motion pictures, selling narcotics, and now this.

"He'll probably wind up in politics," I said but Ritha thought I was kidding.

I let my friendship with Ralph Jamison develop very quickly. Ritha and I had dinner alone with him a few nights later. He had a bungalow on the grounds of one of the swank hotels in Los Angeles. I couldn't understand why he would pick such a conspicuous spot but he seemed to think it gave him some sort of protection. Apparently he was sure of his technique and knew there would never be any screaming.

His butler, valet, chauffeur, and bodyguard was a flat-nosed thug with a cockney accent.

"Hi 'aven't seen you since the Savoy," he said when he took my sables.

"You're mistaken," I said. "I've never been in the Savoy." That was a lie, of course, but I knew he had never been in the Savoy unless with a mask over his face.

"Garn," he said.

A few afternoons later I had Ralphie over to my apartment and showed him my collection of French prints, bought hastily in a Cahuenga Avenue bookshop that afternoon. There were still-life studies of flowers and fruit, and nudes. He feasted on the not-quite ripe.

"The neuroticism of modern life," he said, putting away his glasses, "is due to the delay in sex fulfillment. In countries and at times in history when sex fulfillment was simultaneous with sex development there was no neuroticism."

Can you imagine Ralph Bandinelli talking like that? That was what Hollywood had done to him. Well, I had ten years on the continent and I could translate.

"I don't know," I said. "I had spaniels once. They had sex fulfillment and sex development at the same time and they were plenty neurotic."

"Spaniels are an artificial breed," he argued.

"And what about Hollywood adolescents?" I asked him.

Keeping my apartment in Hollywood, I rented a room overlooking his bungalow. Under a different name, of course, and unknown to him. I sat there with a fine pair of German field glasses for hours on end and I saw plenty. But nothing that wasn't de luxe. Vice drove up to the Jamison bungalow in limousines or Lincoln coupes or it didn't get in.

One night, after about two months of not-too-patient waiting on my part, there was just the set-up I had hoped for, but was beginning to think I would not be lucky enough to get.

It was the thug's night off. Jamison said he spent it on Main Street, rolling drunks to keep in practice, but I think that was just a story. I have no idea what a thug valet to a narcotic salesman does on a night off, but it's probably something very special. Anyway it was his night off, and I judge that Ralphie had had his dinner in the hotel as I saw him crossing the grounds without his hat.

In just a little while Ritha appeared driving her own car. She was very simply dressed with a hat pulled down over her face. They didn't bother to let down the Venetian blinds or draw the curtains. They had a drink, brandy judging from the balloon glasses, considerable conversations about books, I think, as he kept pulling them from the shelves. Several times she stood up as if about to leave but each time he persuaded her to sit down again.

Finally, he went out of the room, returning almost immediately with a gift-wrapped package which might have been perfume or a bracelet but was probably heroin. But before she could get away a coupe (Cadillac) had driven up and three very snappy, but very slightly built, boys were leaning on the bell.

My God, I thought, not that, too. Not Ralphie. Then I realized I did have a Parisian mind. These lads were jockeys from Santa Anita and their quest was snow not sex. Ritha hurried out without waiting to be introduced, taking two or three books with her. I noticed she put her glass on the table and I was sure it was covered with fingerprints.

The boys also had drinks but they had theirs in tall glasses. Some crisp bills were brought out of their wallets and they received their gift packages in a briefcase. They were barely out of the bungalow when Papa Smith, father of the child star who hadn't twinkled so well, appeared. He was flanked on either side by gentlemen who brought their briefcases with them. Undoubtedly lawyers.

This time the curtains were carefully drawn and I couldn't see into the room. But about fifteen minutes later, another car drove up and two muscular gentlemen emerged. Politicians, probably, but I was sure that at one time they had been just plain coppers. They were admitted but Papa Smith and his attorneys did not emerge. I began to feel almost sorry for Ralphie with such an assorted lot of guests.

In a very little while another visitor appeared, this one on foot, either from the hotel, from a car parked outside, or from a taxi. It was a slight, feminine figure which I did not at first recognize but when she stood under the fan-light over the doorway I saw it was the Goldman child, wearing a long close-fitted coat undoubtedly belonging to her mother.

Her hand did not touch the bell. Apparently she heard some masculine voices. She went to the window and tried to peer in between the drawn curtains. I don't think she had any luck as I could not see even a flicker of light through my field glasses. She waited there for almost an hour in the shadow of a hibiscus bush, smoking a cigarette, while I was doing the same thing in the dark hotel room.

And then after about an hour, the two parties of men came out together, noisy and affable. Apparently some excellent liquor was served and everything was outwardly *gemutlich* no matter what threats may have been made to their host privately. And several of the bastards, gentlemen to the home folks, were carrying books. To this day Ralph Jamison's library must be scattered all over Hollywood and Los Angeles.

Their tail lights had not disappeared when Janey was pressing the bell button. But Ralph apparently had entertained enough for one evening. Or more likely, he had been thoroughly frightened and nature was having her way. At any rate, Janey had to ring three times before he opened the grill to see who was so persistent.

Of course, he opened the door immediately, and I saw both of his hands go out to draw her into what must have been by then a smoky and alcohol-drenched living room.

She ran her lips along his arm, which must be numb. Her head had been resting on it while she told her story.

"How am I doing?" she asked. "As Scheherazade?"

"Great," Michel said. "It all comes back to me now. I remember all those people were mentioned, but I thought they finally pinned it on the valet."

Laura laughed. "That was what you call the police saving their faces. But I'll tell you all about it tomorrow night."

"Tell me now. I'm not at all sleepy. You didn't let him have that little kid, did you?"

"I'm not sleepy either. But I don't feel like talking any more."

He understood.

CHAPTER NINE

"I think," Michel said the next night, "that you are deliberately torturing me instead of reassuring me."

"You can always refuse to see me," she said.

"You're showing me all your cards, but you'll still take the last trick. You'll kill me—"

"Unless you kill me first?" she suggested.

"It's in my mind," he admitted. "But go on, you didn't let Ralph have that kid, did you?"

"He wasn't such a rat. She came to his house of her own free will. I'm not at all sure that she had ever seen him or talked to him since that day her mother introduced them at Ritha's. I really felt badly that I spoilt the party. She probably had a much crueler initiation a little later."

"But you did go over and break it up!"

She smiled. "If I had done that, my sweet, it isn't likely I'd be here with you now."

I was afraid to call Mrs. Goldman. She might recognize my voice. Yet, I must do something quickly, although I doubted if Ralph would rush into action. After all, he was a man of some finesse.

I finally decided that it was unlikely Mrs. Goldman would be at home. Otherwise, the child would not have been able to slip away.

I went down into the hotel lobby and used one of the booth telephones. A man answered. Whether it was a butler or Mr. Goldman, I did not know. Without waiting for anything except the "Mr. Goldman's residence" I spoke my little piece saying that Mrs. Goldman should be notified at once that her daughter was in Mr. Jamison's bungalow, and located the bungalow for them.

I hung up just as the man at the other end began to sputter something completely unintelligible. I went back to my seat in the window.

Whoever I had spoken to got very quick action. It couldn't have been twenty minutes before a taxi drove up to the bungalow. Mrs. Goldman stepped out. Someone else was in the cab. I couldn't tell for sure whether it was a man or a woman, but I think it was another woman, possibly Ritha although she never admitted it to me.

Mrs. Goldman just leaned against the bell. I'm sure if Ralph hadn't opened almost immediately, she would have broken a window. When he did appear, she made no effort to brush past him or do any of the things they always do in movies. I think she merely called into the bungalow for her Janey.

The child appeared fully clothed, and carrying her coat. Apparently her mother realized, as I did, that nothing had happened and her fright turned to anger. She slapped the child once and Ralph twice. Apparently she was wearing a heavy band of diamonds or other sharp stones since a clotted spot of blood on Ralph's cheek occasioned a great deal of discussion later.

Then she literally threw her child into the taxi and they drove away. Ralph, representing Hollywood male glamour, in a velvet coat and a batik scarf, rubbed his face for a minute or so and then went back into the bungalow.

I waited twenty minutes and since no one appeared, I went over to the bungalow. I was surprised when Ralph answered immediately. I would have supposed that he had entertained enough for one evening.

"I was in the hotel," I said truthfully enough, "for dinner so I thought I'd dash over and say hello."

He laughed. "Everybody seemed to have that idea tonight," he said.

"If you have company," I said quickly, "I won't come in."

"No," he said, "the company is all gone and I'm delighted to see you."

"I can only stay a minute," I said as he took my things.

"We'll have a drink, anyway," he said. "God knows I need one."

"Why, what's been happening?" I asked, only polite interest in my voice.

"Oh, nothing," he answered rather bitterly. "It is nothing that a hundred grand wouldn't take care of nicely."

"Don't tell me," I said, "that a great Hollywood director hasn't that much money."

He just snorted. "What'll it be to drink?"

"I don't know," I said, "I feel like some sort of liqueur. Let me mess around your bar and whip up my own, may I?"

"Sure," he said. "I think you'll find all the makings."

He opened a door into a windowless bar, a converted closet, I imagine.

I began picking out bottles. "I think," I said, "I'll have some white mint, with a little Vermouth and curacao."

"That doesn't sound too bad," he said. "Make it two."

He roamed around the room gathering up glasses. I didn't want him to do that. I wanted him to leave them where they were with their fingerprints.

"Come on talk to me," I said, having already put his bye-bye drops in a glass. "I'm blue, too."

He immediately came over to me. "What have you got to be blue about?" he asked. "Also something a hundred grand will cure?"

"Oh, no," I said, gently stirring the drinks. "I haven't any money troubles."

He put his arm around me and kissed me but nothing was there.

I laughed at him. "I didn't come for that," I said. "What ails me can't be cured that way."

"I know what you mean," he said, taking the drink I held out for him.

We went back into the main room and sat in front of the fire which was dying out.

"You should have known me ten years ago," he said.

"I did," I said, but only to myself. To him I said: "You mean you wish you had known me fifteen years ago?"

He almost groaned. "You've got me," he said. "I suppose everyone has. I can't hide it any more. You remember that kid we met at Ritha's?"

"The Janey one?"

"That's the one. She was here tonight."

I pretended to be awfully upset and remonstrated with him but he reassured me.

"Her mother appeared almost immediately," he explained.

"I don't understand," I said, playing dumb.

Neither did he. He thought the kid, in a spirit of bravado, had started an adventure and then had either telephoned her mother or had left a note.

"It's going to take a lot of joy to make me forget tonight," he said. "I wonder why I don't take just a pinch too much."

"You won't," I prophesied.

"No, I won't," he agreed. "Although I have no idea why I keep on clinging to such a life."

"We do," I said, "but we'll laugh at our troubles in a month—a week—"

"Maybe," he agreed.

"There must be someone who can let you have the money you need," I suggested. "They make that in a month."

"There are plenty who could," he said, bitterly, "but they won't. I can't borrow it here—I'd be all washed up. I tried to get it from an old friend—he's a millionaire now, controlling a chain of department stores. He said he could have let me have it a month ago but now he's having labor trouble and needs every penny he's got."

I made a note of that. An old friend probably meant one of Joe Brown's mob, one of the eight.

I raised my glass. "Better luck next time," I said and drank the sweet, minty mixture.

He drank also. "It isn't really the money I worry about," he said. "It's the kids . . . I know where they'll land me . . ."

"Not necessarily," I said.

A spasm of pain crossed his face. "My God!" he cried. "What did you put in this drink?"

"It won't bother you for long," I assured him.

He collapsed. But he was still twitching and I made up my mind I would never take that chance again. He could have gotten to a telephone or screamed my name out the window.

I had tried the deadly Vermouth on dogs and cats and even a horse in France, but, of course, human beings react differently. But now the twitching was over. I forced myself to feel for his heart although it was unpleasant. There was nothing. What a weak flame is the fire of life.

The telephone began to ring and that brought me out of my reverie. I hurried back to my room at the hotel. Again I sat at the window. I wanted to know exactly what went on in the bungalow before the body was discovered.

In about an hour the thug valet returned. He was only in the bungalow about twenty minutes. Then he came out carrying two suitcases. I'm sure he wasn't afraid of being accused of having killed his employer, but there were probably all sorts of things hanging over him that would develop if he were picked up and fingerprinted.

They didn't ever find him because they didn't want to find him. You remember the hue-and-cry that followed Ralph's death. It kept up for weeks. All the visitors were identified but the Goldman name was never mentioned. It ruined Ritha Sloane's comeback; it ruined the starlet and her family; it ruined several local police officers and politicians.

Before I left town I went to see Mr. Goldman, the banker. I carefully explained to him that I was not blackmailing him but I knew that his daughter and his wife had been in the murder bungalow that night. I said that I wasn't in a position to say anything even if he didn't give me any money, but I thought he might want to show his appreciation. He gave me ten thousand dollars and that was the money that took care of Ritha Sloane until she died.

My name was never mentioned in connection with the case in any way.

CHAPTER TEN

Michel looked at the beautiful creature lying in his arms. She told her story as she would tell something which she had heard and which interested her, but only impersonally. And yet she had admitted a cold-blooded murder, carefully planned and brilliantly executed.

"You're not human," he cried out accusingly.

"If I were," she replied, "you wouldn't interest me!"

"Who was next?" he asked her.

"Frank Connors," she said. "He didn't hold on to either name but kept the initials—"

"Yeah, I remember," Michel said. "He had 'em on everything—hats, shirts, and shorts—"

"He still did," she admitted.

Ralph had given me a clue, and when I read in the newspapers that the department store clerks in San Francisco were on strike, I went there. A visit to the public library and I soon learned that Frank Connors had become Frederick Cole, the department store king of the Pacific Coast. He hadn't changed much although his flaming red hair was now white. But it was still a fighting face and he was still a fighter. At the time I located him he was fighting organized labor.

I didn't try to rush anything. I just drifted along. It was my first time in San Francisco and I liked it. I was sure it would be a bad time to try to establish any intimacy with Mr. Frederick Cole but, on the other hand, during a big strike anything could happen—including the violent death of Mr. Cole.

I watched the picket line in front of his big San Francisco store. The papers said that he occasionally came out and talked to the clerks and would even take two or three of them to lunch. It was almost a week before I saw him.

That particular day, I noticed one frail girl walking in the picket line and although the signs, made of crating wood, were very light, it seemed to me she was about to drop from exhaustion. I went over to her and said I would be glad to take her place in the line for a while. She accepted gratefully and as she handed me the sign, I managed to slip a dollar bill into her hand and told her to go and get something to eat.

I was wearing my plainest clothes and, as all the women took great pride in their appearance on the picket line, there was nothing to distinguish me from the rest of them. Suddenly, I looked up and there he was standing in the doorway of his store—Mr. Frederick Cole, Frank Connors, "Red", to you and me. Next to him was a husky young man—secretary, bodyguard, and male nurse, I later found out.

Red stood there in the doorway, a model for *Esquire,* the smile of a killer on his face. He looked over the picket line calmly though intently. Suddenly he caught my eye and his expression changed. He asked his companion something and then the young man stared at me. I was a little uneasy. It didn't seem possible that he could have recognized me.

But I didn't have to worry long. Red came over to me.

"You didn't work in the store, did you?" he asked.

"No," I said, "I'm just a volunteer picket."

He turned to the young man who had followed him over to where I was walking.

"See," Mr. Cole said to his stooge, "I told you I knew every girl in the place."

I kept on moving. So, in order to talk to me, they had to tag along with me. That struck the other pickets and the crowd of sightseers as funny. They began to laugh and guy the two men walking in step with me.

"Let's get out of here," Red said, putting his hand under my arm. "Come on have lunch with us."

"I can't," I said. "I'm on duty. I wouldn't doublecross the union."

Red wanted to know how long I was going to be on duty. I said I didn't know but if his stooge would carry the picket sign I could go with him. Red seemed to think that was a mighty funny idea.

"Yeah, Stanley," he said to the young man, "you carry the banner for a while."

Stanley took it good-naturedly. "All right," he said, taking the sign from me, "you're the boss."

The crowd watching us was getting bigger all the time. Somebody yelled an obscene insult at Mr. Frederick Cole. Stanley, the stooge, swung around. A man standing near said something about "white slaver". Stanley brought the sign down squarely on the man's head. Immediately there was a free-for-all, with the girl pickets squealing like geese on my native island.

Red was striking out right and left, having a wonderful time. Then suddenly he went white and staggered back. If I hadn't caught him, he would have fallen.

My first thought was that somebody must have knifed him. But there wasn't any blood.

The stooge rushed over. "He's had an attack," he said. "Help me get him into the store."

Somebody blew a police whistle and the fight stopped as quickly as it had commenced. The picket line started moving slowly again just as if nothing had happened except that the sign I had been carrying was smashed to kindling wood. A man had rushed out of the store and was supporting Mr. Cole.

I was watching Stanley. He pulled two bottles and a folding cup out of his pocket. He handed the cup to me.

"Hold it," he said and, of course, I obeyed. From one bottle he poured a few drops of a darkish liquid; the other bottle contained water, distilled water, I found out later.

I wondered if Red Connors would die then and there if I dropped the cup. Probably not and besides it would be publicity that might spoil the other things I had to do. I handed Stanley the cup and as he bent over to give it to the gasping man, I disappeared into the crowd.

I lay low for a week. That is I lived in an inconspicuous apartment-hotel and took my meals in nearby restaurants. I was sure that Red Connors-Cole would be trying to locate me and I wanted to see how effective his espionage system was. Apparently it wasn't any too good.

Then one afternoon I put on my best bib-and-tucker, seasoned it with a few diamonds and sables, and started out on a round of the best bars. In the long corridor between the lobby and the Circus Room in the Fairmont,

I met Stanley, the stooge. I recognized him immediately, but not until he had passed me, did he remember where he had seen me before.

I heard him turn, felt a hand of iron on my elbow, and then I was spun completely around.

"My God, woman," he cried. "Where've you been keeping yourself? We've been combing the town for you for a week."

I could see and smell that he was a little drunk, but I didn't think that it went beyond that. He was one of those brutes that have a completely false good-nature about them. He was my first experience along that line.

"You haven't been using a very good comb," I said. Then I told a whopper. "I've been on the picket line all week."

"The hell you have," he said, not believing me for a second. "I've made all the picket lines myself at one time or another. Anyway," he went on before I could say anything more, "I've found you now. What say, we have a little talk."

"All right," I agreed. "What about?"

"The boss took a fancy to you. He liked the way you carried the banner. He said you walked that street like an old-timer. The boss has got you in his head and when he gets a dame in his head, he isn't any good until he gets her somewhere else."

"I'm not interested in your boss's fancies," I said, "or what he's got in his head or anywhere else. There's only one thing about him that I am interested in."

"Which is?"

"The strike of his employees."

Stanley, the stooge, tugged away at his chin, studying me very carefully, not missing the sables or the diamonds.

"Well, maybe we could talk that over," he said. "How about coming over to my apartment for a quick one and then you can decide just how much you will do labor."

"All right," I agreed.

He had an apartment on Russian Hill, not very far from the Fairmont. It was such a swanky apartment. I decided it must be one of Red's hideaways.

I hadn't been in the apartment many minutes before I figured that maybe I had made a mistake. I prided myself on being able to take care of myself under any circumstances, but I had been in a few nasty spots with drunks and this looked as if it might turn out to be another one. Still, there was a phone handy and a snap-lock on the door.

I was pouring my own drinks so I knew no Mickey Finns were going into them. Stanley was handing me a great sales talk—for himself and Red Connors. There wasn't anything Cole wouldn't do for me, if Stanley was on my side.

"What do you mean, on my side?" I asked him.

He laughed. "You get me," he said. "You see whenever he makes a gal, I have to be in the next room with the medicine, in case he passes out. Can you imagine what that does to me when he's with a swell dish like you, frinstance?"

"What's he doing this afternoon without you?" I asked. "What's to stop him from dropping dead?"

He explained there was always someone around the boss with the restorative—a nurse at home—a stenographer at the office. That particular afternoon, the boss was at the doctor's so he probably was safe until Stanley picked him up.

I told Stanley his situation was certainly a pathetic one. The best I could do was to promise him that he would never have to wait in the next room with restoratives while the boss was with me. But that didn't cheer Stanley at all.

"You don't know the boss," he said. "When he wants something he gets it. And he's wanted you plenty since that day of the fight."

"Well, I'm not interested," I said. "I'm not interested in a man who expects women to live on ten dollars a week."

"Ten dollars a week! What the hell are you talking about?"

"I'm talking about the women who slave for him so he can hire other women at a thousand dollars a night. Tell your boss I'm not interested in making any living at the expense of slaves."

"You're a hell of a labor agitator," Stanley said. "I guess you wear your rocks and sables on the picket line."

"No," I said standing up. "I just wear them on the bread line."

"Sit down, jerk," Stanley said, pushing me back into the chair. "The boss is on his way up here now."

"Well, he won't find me here," I said, standing up again.

And that was the last thing I did say. The big bruiser tapped me very gently twice on the jaw and I was out like a light. That kind of knockout doesn't last very long, though, and I think he must have followed it with ether or chloroform. I was vaguely conscious of something sweetish, but I may have been mistaken because when I came to, my head seemed clear enough.

I was in a big, comfortable bed in a dimly lighted room. I was covered with clean, sweet smelling linens and a silk quilt. At the foot of the bed, fully clothed and grinning at me, sat Red Connors-Cole.

"How are you feeling, baby?" he said. "It happens to the best of us."

"It happens to those who go up against Joe Louis," I said. "I didn't sign up to fight."

"Those cocktails Stanley hands out are dynamite," Red said. "I've warned him often that some girls can't take it."

I didn't say anything. It was not the time for me to be making threats.

"When you passed out," Red smoothly went on, "Stanley was plenty scared and telephoned to me right away. I came right over with my doctor and we managed to get you into bed; he gave you a mild shot and said he was sure you'd be all right."

I heard what he said but I knew what he meant. They had a doctor ready to swear that I had passed out from liquor. I saw I'd have to change my tune.

"Listen, Mr. Cole," I said, meek as one of his bundle girls before they went out on strike. "I don't know what that heavyweight stooge of yours told you but here's what happened. I came over here this afternoon like I've been doing every other afternoon—"

"That's a lie right off," Red Connors said, but I could already hear the uncertainty in his voice.

"Who says it's a lie? Your Stanley. Why don't you have some of your other stooges ask them downstairs if he hasn't already paid them off what to say. Anyway, while we were having our fun, the telephone rang. I don't know what went on but Stanny-boy tells me you're coming over and wasn't I going to be nice to you?"

It wasn't reasonable and I knew it, but I also knew that the hot-tempered Irishman wouldn't be sure whether it was all lie or fifty-fifty. That's what I wanted him to think.

"And you said you weren't going to be nice, I suppose?" Red asked, with plenty of sarcasm.

"I asked him if that was what he'd been leading up to all week and told him I didn't need anybody to do pimping for me. Then's when he landed the two haymakers and you'd better have your doctor look at my jaw. I bet it's broken."

Red rubbed his thick hand over my face as gently as he could. "I'm sure there's nothing broken," he said.

He let his hand start wandering down my throat but before he had gotten very far my teeth were deep into his thumb and the blood flowed.

He yelled so loudly that it brought Stanley on the run.

Here I go again, I thought, but to my surprise Stanley didn't hit me. He started to laugh.

"What the hell are you laughing at?" Red barked at him.

"I thought you were being murdered," Stanley explained, "and she's only petting you."

"How'd you like to be petted with tiger teeth?" Red said, sucking his thumb.

"I'd love it," Stanley said.

"He's got my teeth marks all over him," I said brazenly. "Make him pull his shirt off."

"What the hell are you talking about?" Stanley demanded, suddenly serious.

"She claims she's been here every day for a week," Red explained.

Stanley turned on me furiously. "Tell him you're lying."

"I'll tell it to the judge," I said.

Red prevented Stanley from hitting me and, seeing that his thumb wasn't going to drop off, suggested we all have a drink.

We had the drink and they brought me my clothes.

"Before you leave," Red said, smooth as silk, "it's just as well you realize exactly what happened. You came here and after a few drinks became very noisy and abusive. Stanley had to slap you gently to quiet you. Then my doctor, a very reputable doctor, I might add, was called, observed your condition thoroughly, and gave you a sedative. I don't know, of course, what your reputation is in this city or elsewhere—"

He looked at me inquiringly.

"Go on," I said.

"Except for a few labor agitators who undoubtedly would like to frame me," he went on, "my reputation in the city is excellent. I'm sure my word would be accepted under most circumstances. Needless to say the newspapers would not be too anxious to print unverified scandal against their largest advertiser—"

"That'll do, boss," Stanley interrupted. "She's going to be O. K. We're all going to be the best of friends."

I grinned as I brushed my hair at the dressing-table.

"You bastards!" I said. "I'm going to kill you both!"

They thought I was kidding.

"You mean," Michel said, when she had paused so long it was evident she was not going to continue, "that you let the stooge have it as well as Red Connors?"

"The state attended to that for me," she said.

"How come?"

"I'll tell you tomorrow," she said.

"I don't like that," he objected. "The other day when you pulled that, I couldn't think of anything else all day."

"That's exactly the idea," she said. "You don't have time then to think of yourself."

"No, I don't," he admitted. "But you don't really think I believe these yarns you're telling me, do you?"

She turned out the light and snuggled against him. "You know those men are dead, don't you?"

"Yes," he admitted, "I know that."

"Then," she suggested, "don't you think it's a good idea for us to live while we're alive?"

But apparently he didn't find the idea of violent death as stimulating to the passions as she did.

CHAPTER ELEVEN

"If it isn't love," the hat-check girl said, "what is it?"

"I don't know," Andy admitted. "Maybe she brings him home-made candy."

"If he's looked at his watch once, he's looked at it a dozen times and she keeps dancing with those college kids."

"They'd have twice as much fun if they knew it was the boss's woman."

The college boys, who weren't college boys at all but a mission from Great Britain, disposed of, Laura rather reluctantly left the club and joined Michel in his apartment. He had gone up at least an hour earlier and pretended to be asleep. She slipped in very quietly next to him. If he were asleep, she decided he was having a very pleasant dream and she saw no reason why she shouldn't merge into it . . .

"How did you frame the stooge?" he abruptly asked her an hour later.

"I've never framed anybody," she insisted. "What stooge are you talking about?"

"Red Connors' stooge."

"Oh him—you know I've thought of the nicest name for our little game."

"Spill it."

"*Ecuador Nights*—not so very original, of course, but still I think it's nice."

"Fine—we'll have 'em copyrighted. But what did you do to the guy if you didn't frame him?"

Stanley? I pretended to be crazy about him and, of course, it had him spinning. Nothing like it had ever occurred to him before. I had no idea when I started in what was going to happen. All I wanted was easy access to that medicine which revived Red Connors when he had his heart attacks.

He was still "Fighting Red" Connors even if he was Frederick Cole, the merchant prince. He was terrifically proud of his success and bragged to me that he had once been a "money" gangster and, of all the mob, he was the only one who had made a success of a legitimate business. I found out later that wasn't entirely true, but through Red's talk, I managed to locate the rest of Joe Brown's mob.

Now Red's great desire was to beat the labor unions and he didn't care how he did it. His interest in me was not due to the fact that I was a woman and he a man, but because he had discovered me on the picket line and that I had been properly beaten up.

Every time he was with me, he picked a fight and shoved me around a little. After a day when business at the store had been particularly bad because of the picketing, he would call in Stanley to really mess me up. He didn't dare do it himself; he was afraid of his heart. But he seemed to get almost as much enjoyment out of watching Stanley toss me around.

I submitted and they finally decided I enjoyed it. What I enjoyed with each blow of the clenched fist was my inner knowledge that it was another shovelful of earth from their own graves, another coal in their crematory extinction, another whiff of lethal gas in the death chamber.

Stanley didn't get any thrill from using me as a punching bag. He was merely earning his salary. Alone with me, he was very gentle and, also, very ineffectual. I hated him more than Red since Red really enjoyed my welts and bruises, my bleeding nose and blackened eyes, my squeals of pain and cries for mercy. But Stanley was doing it for his lousy hundred-a-week or whatever Red was paying him. Stanley began to pull his punches and it was because of that, I think, Red learned we were deceiving him. Stanley said he was bound to find it out, sooner or later, but it was worth it.

I couldn't understand how he could possibly figure it was worth it, but since then I have learned that the ineffectual man seems to enjoy himself just as much as the great lover. He does not realize his own impotence and ineffectuality, and doesn't believe it when a woman tells him. I'm sure that Stanley's gratification came entirely from the fact that he was having an affair with his boss's woman and not from anything directly connected with me.

Riding up Howard Street one day, Stanley was forced over to the curb by four thugs in another car. They made him get in the car with them. He thought, of course, he was being taken for a ride but Red Connors knew a good stooge when he had one. The thugs took Stanley to a room in the Mission district and beat him until his entire body was raw meat. Stanley was sure that Mr. Frederick Cole was watching through a peep-hole.

Then Stanley was photographed and the whole thing appeared in the newspapers under the headline: FREDERICK COLE'S SECRETARY BEATEN BY STRIKERS!

Stanley spoiled the effect, however, by getting roaring drunk while he was still bandaged to the eyes and going from saloon to saloon, swearing he'd kill the son-of-a-bitch, and he didn't leave any doubt as to which son-of-a-bitch he meant.

But Frederick Cole was very much a business man those next few days and didn't have much time to bother about his stooge, Stanley, or his woman, me. Single-handed, he was fighting the unions to the death—and that is exactly what he did, but it was his death, not the unions. The other stores and the Chamber of Commerce wanted to settle, but not Mr. Frederick Cole. He was financing the battle. He seemed to be thriving on it. He had not had a heart attack since the day he had taken me out of the picket line.

I decided that I had taken about all the punishment I cared for, and while Stanley was convalescing from his beating and the terrible drunk, I substituted my Vermouth for the restorative drug in the little phial. But, perhaps foolishly and certainly dangerously, I decided that since there can be so many slips between the cup and the lip, I'd better stick around and make sure that my plan worked.

On the night before Frederick Cole was to address a mass meeting of citizens (Housewives Protective Association or some such phoney organization), he decided we needed a little relaxation, so we made the round of the so-called International Settlement. Izzy Gomez's upstairs saloons, Pinocchio's, with its decadent floor show, Mona's with its

Lesbians, the Black Cat with its artists, the Bal Tabarin with its jitterbugs, La Tosca, with its coffee royals and its domestic atmosphere, and finally Joe's with its sandwiches.

We arrived (Red, Stanley and I) in Red's apartment along about three o'clock. Red's hands were clammy, his face was beet-red, and every now and then he would twitch from nervousness or pain, I didn't know which. I went to his apartment in the same spirit that allows a condemned man his choice of food for the last meal.

I was sure Red would never get through the night, and certainly not the mass meeting the next day, without a heart attack. But whether my plan worked or not, I felt that the time had come for me to clear out and, if necessary, reach Mr. Frederick Cole later.

The minute we stepped into his apartment we heard a woman shrieking. Hard-boiled as Red and Stan were, this startled them. Then we realized the woman was shrieking as monotonously as a phonograph record: "Slave Driver!" "Slave Driver!" "Slave Driver!"

She was handcuffed to a bedpost in his room, a beautiful, early American four-poster mahogany bed with a canopy.

"By God!" Red cursed. "They've scratched my bed and I just paid three hundred dollars to have it refinished."

"And you pay three dollars a week to your bundle girls!" the woman shrieked.

She was unprepossessing, this creature who had been selected or selected herself for an unusual job of picketing. Red looked at her with great distaste.

"Quiet her down," Red said to Stanley.

Stanley gave her his well-known one, two, one to the jaw but she was of tougher fibre than I had been. She continued to scream at the top of her lungs that she would have us all in jail. Naturally, Red's apartment was completely soundproof.

"You'll have us in jail!" Red said quietly. "You break into my apartment, ruin one of the finest beds in America, and you'll have me arrested!"

Nevertheless he stopped Stan from further assault.

"Gag her," he instructed. "I don't want to deprive her of the pleasure of knowing what's going on."

Stan selected a pair of shorts from the soiled clothes basket and gagged the shrieking martyr.

"Get the Japs on the telephone," he instructed.

When the connection was made, Red explained to the Jap or whoever was on the other end of the telephone, that he had a bundle to be dropped into the Bay.

"Come around in about an hour," he said. "I'll have to find somebody with a blow-torch to take her off my bedpost."

He turned away from the telephone.

"Tie her feet," he instructed. "She's kicking my bed."

Stan tied her feet with a Sulka necktie.

"Who do we know with a blow-torch?" Red asked Stan.

"We don't know anyone, and we're not going to get anybody else into this," Stan said belligerently. "You're going to have to lose a bedpost."

"Are you crazy?" Red shrieked. "That bed happens to be worth five thousand dollars."

With a jerk of his head, Red indicated that I was to follow him out of the room.

"Stan will entertain the lady," Red said.

Stan grinned and I heard a ripping sound as we went out of the room.

"She's got a key hidden somewhere," Red said when we were on the other side of the door. "They wouldn't leave her here without a key. Give her ten minutes with Stanny and she'll be only too glad to tell where the key is."

"Are you really going to kill that girl in cold blood and dump her body into the Bay?" I asked.

Red looked surprised. "What else is there to do?"

"Somebody knows she was chained to your bed," I pointed out. "There's bound to be an investigation."

"Sure," he agreed, "and they won't find out a thing. But if we turn her loose, she and her pals will raise such a stink that something will have to be done."

"They're bound to find out something," I argued. "They always do."

"You've been reading detective stories," he said. "When I get through they don't find out anything. Don't you see the point? All right—they, the labor union, say she was handcuffed to my bed. I say I never saw her, wasn't there when I came home. Suppose they do find something in the room to indicate she had been there—what does that prove? If they got her into the room, what was to prevent somebody else from getting in? All I know is when I got home she wasn't there, and I don't give a damn what they find in the room. I never saw her, and I'll bet you a grand to a buck they won't ask me more'n a couple of questions."

He, I realized, then and there, next to Henry Amblate, had enjoyed himself the most when they killed my husband, Giuseppe Buonarotti. I also knew that I had better watch my step or he would decide I knew too much and have me dropped into the Bay, too.

When I returned to the bedroom all the girl's clothes had been torn off. She looked for all the world like one of the martyred saints about to be burned at the stake. Her body was much better than her face.

Stan was sitting on the bed breathing heavily.

"Not bad, huh?" he said.

"The boss wants you for a minute," I said and he went out.

At first I thought the girl was unconscious, but now she raised her head and looked at me. There were no tears but I had never seen such terror in a human being's eyes.

"If I let you talk," I said to her, "will you behave yourself?"

She nodded vigorously. I removed the soiled shorts from her mouth.

"If you have a key hidden somewhere," I said, "you'd better tell me and I'll see what I can do."

"It's under the rug," she said. "They're not serious about putting me into the Bay are they?"

I turned up the rug and there was the tiny handcuff key.

"I'm afraid they're entirely serious," I said. "Who put you up to this little stunt?"

"Nobody put me up to it," she said. "I just read about something like this and thought it would be a good stunt. I didn't think there were such monsters in the world."

"I'm afraid you don't read the newspapers," I said.

"Why should they kill me? I'm of no importance in the organization."

"You know too much," I explained, "and you spoiled his bed."

"If I swear that I won't say a word, don't you think they might let me go?"

"An oath under such circumstances wouldn't mean anything to you, a loyal worker, the minute you were free."

"If I swear to you, woman to woman, by the mothers who bore us, that I'll never say a word, won't you release me and let me go?"

"And have the Japs put me in the Bay instead of you?"

"They wouldn't do that to you!" I think she was genuinely astonished at the idea.

I laughed. "You misjudge my boyfriends. If they thought I had double-crossed them, they'd do it cheerfully. They might do it anyway if I'm not smarter than they are."

"You are smarter than they are," she flattered me. "Let's get out of here together. The unions will protect you."

I was spared answering that one by the appearance of Red and Stan.

"Here's your key," I said tossing it to Red.

"Good girl," he said. "I was telling Stan you don't think we ought to give her to the hungry little fishes in the Bay."

"I swear I won't say a word if you'll turn me loose," the girl said. .

They were both surprised, not having noticed that I had taken the soiled shorts away from her mouth.

"What's the idea?" Red asked.

"How do you think she told me where the key was?"

"I'll swear on the cross, on the Bible, on anything, that I won't say a word," the girl pleaded. "Please let me go!"

"Shut up," Stan said, letting his ham of a fist slam against her mouth.

She spat out blood and teeth but she was still conscious and continued to plead with them.

"You see," Red said apologetically to me. "Now we have to do it."

Suddenly he saw some of her blood spattering on his bed. "For Chrissake," he yelled, "that's a fifteent' century brocade!"

He hurriedly unlocked the handcuffs. The woman crumpled to the floor unable to stand on her feet.

"For Chrissake get some newspapers," Red yelled. "Look at my Aubusson carpet. You certainly are messy. Finish this up, quick."

Stan looked ruefully at his bleeding knuckles and then picked up an iron poker from an andiron set by the early American fireplace.

I forced myself to keep watching. I was a Sicani and no Sicani had ever been afraid of the sight of blood. I might have to draw much of it before I had avenged the murder of Giuseppe Buonarotti.

The woman was no longer pleading with them. She was praying. Apparently she had believed in God before she believed in Stalin and John L. Lewis.

I realized only one thing could save her—if Red Connors would have a heart attack at that moment, but it was not to be. The poker descended first on her ankles and knees to break her legs, then on the throat so there would be no more sounds, then point down into her breasts and finally the *coup de grace* on her head.

"My carpet! My carpet!" Red moaned.

Michel leaped from the bed.
"My God!" he cried. "I'm sick to my stomach."
"Sissy!" Laura called after him, lighting a cigarette, making certain first that it was just a common garden variety.

He returned in about ten minutes, pop-eyed and pale.
"You!" she mocked him. "One of Joe Brown's men."
"I've gone soft," he admitted, lying down next to her.

She kissed him. He had taken a strong antiseptic to cover the smell of the vomit.

"When did Red Connors have his heart attack?" he asked.
"I'll tell you tomorrow," she promised.
"My little Sicani," he whispered, relaxing in her arms with a sound of contentment.

CHAPTER TWELVE

"Another *Ecuador* night," she said almost twenty-four hours later. "And how are you feeling?"

"It wasn't your pretty little story that made me sick," he insisted. "It was just that I hadn't been feeling too good all day—"

"Something you ate, I suppose?" she asked without obvious sarcasm.
"It must have been," he agreed.
"You ought to be more careful what you eat," she said as he nibbled at her throat.

"I don't usually like the neck," he said, "but this is a very pretty neck."

"Several States would like to stretch a rope around it," she said. "Where were we—you wanted to know when Red Connors had his next heart attack?"

"Yes, I did," he agreed, "but that'll keep a few minutes."

"Oh, certainly," she said, and added: "in fact an hour or two."

"You flatter me."

Red Connors, alias Frederick Cole, had his heart attack the next evening, just about the time I stepped from a plane at Newark. I had had enough. The rest of it—I only know what I read in the papers.

It was at the mass meeting of citizens where he was going to make a final, master effort to break the strike. He had prepared a good speech (he had read it to me several times) but he never had a chance to deliver it. Somebody threw a pop bottle as he started to speak and he collapsed, although the bottle missed him.

Stan, a little drowsy after his blood orgy of the night before, I imagine, came forward with the heart medicine. Red Connors managed to swallow it, and five minutes later he was dead. No one was surprised. Heart attacks of that sort always end fatally at some time.

The strike was settled the next day. Frederick Cole was the heart and soul of the opposition. Without him, the other merchants were glad to settle. I never saw one word in the paper about the girl who was handcuffed to his bed. Where she came from, nobody seemed to know, and where she went, nobody seemed to care. Or perhaps Red had arranged to have it all forgotten before he went on the platform.

Nothing happened for a few days but when it was discovered that Frederick Cole had left half his fortune to his stooge-secretary, there began to be a lot of talk. The other half went to his children by his divorced wife. She had received her share in a lump sum at the time, but now she was yelling because the children didn't get all that was left.

The body was dug up, an autopsy performed and the poison discovered. Then it was remembered that Cole and his secretary had been quarreling and Cole had told several people he was going to change his will. Stan had access to poisons in the drug and camera department of Cole's big store. In fact, he had the run of the store at all times.

His record made the newspapers bitter about the parole system in the United States. Stanny had been in reformatories, penitentiaries, chain gangs, and insane asylums in a dozen different states.

However, he refused to plead insanity and the experts testified that he was legally sane at the time of the crime and afterwards. He told a fantastic story (not admitted at his trial) about a woman who had been his mistress and also Mr. Cole's but he couldn't identify her by name or locate her and no one could confirm his story. The newspaper reporters freely admitted they didn't believe any such person existed.

He didn't have a chance and, finally, before he was executed, he sold his confession to a magazine syndicate for five thousand dollars. I have no idea what he wanted with the five thousand dollars, but maybe he had a dependent hidden away somewhere or maybe he just got a lot of satisfaction from gypping the magazine out of five grand, since the confession was a phony.

That was the longest rest I took. I didn't do a thing until Stan was executed. I was afraid that if, through some fluke, my picture would get into a newspaper or magazine, he might see it and have me dragged back to San Francisco. I spent almost a year in small resort hotels, never more than a month at any one place, reading, studying, and playing bridge, and noticing now and again in the New York papers items about the exploits of Irving St. Leger, who I happened to know from my deceased friend, Mr. Cole, was none other than Bennel Stein, the smartest man in the Joe Brown Mob.

And so when the State of California finally eliminated Stanny as a possible annoyance, I moved into New York to consider the case of Mr. St. Leger. I soon discovered that he was not going to be an easy nut to crack. He absolutely refused to have anything to do with any women except his wife and his sweetie. He wouldn't meet them, he wouldn't tolerate them anywhere, and if a woman came into a room where he was gambling, he would get up and leave immediately.

I rather liked that, but it did make it tough. He was a man who was everywhere—at baseball games, at the hockey matches, at the six-day bicycle races, at every race track, and at all other times playing poker in a midtown hotel, but it was impossible to get near him. Sometimes he had hired guards, sometimes he was just surrounded by friends. But for my purpose, it was all the same.

He was afraid of something—everything, perhaps. I am sure his fear had nothing to do with old days in the Joe Brown gang. He probably never thought of them. But he had been in a dozen, a hundred, dirty deals since then, and never knew when one of them would kick back.

I decided I would have to get a job as waitress in one of the restaurants where he ate, and then I found out that he never ate in restaurants. He had breakfast at home with his wife and kids, and dinner in his sweetie's apartment. He never ate in the middle of the day as he was always fighting overweight. If he didn't want to go to his sweetie's for dinner, he would have his dinner served in the rooms he used for gambling in that midtown hotel. There, dinner would be sent up from the hotel dining-room and served by a man waiter.

He took every possible precaution against attack but no man can protect himself forever against a determined killer. At least no man has been able to protect himself against me. I finally got to him through that midtown hotel where he and his pals rented the entire second floor for their games, for their lodgings when they didn't want to go home, and for their love affairs, although I don't think many of them used the rooms for that purpose since there was very little privacy. But, of course, privacy didn't mean anything to some of that gang.

There was only one thing always to be kept in mind. The dames weren't to get in Irving St. Leger's way. If one of them dared go into a room when he was sitting in a game (poker and crap-shooting were the only things in which he participated), it was just too bad. Not only for the dame but for the boy friend.

So it wasn't a bit of use for me to give free samples to his sucker list. That would get me just nowhere, and I had been spoiled for a year. I found sleeping alone too comfortable. But I had to get to him and that second floor was where he spent most of his time.

I went on a spree of heavy eating with plenty of desserts and put on ten pounds. Then I bought some nifty clothes from the Goodwill Industries and applied for a job as a chambermaid at the midtown hotel. When the personnel man asked me for references, I said I didn't have any, but that it was worth fifty dollars to me to get into the hotel and if he didn't think I could make a bed, he ought to come up and see me sometime.

He wasn't interested and, to my surprise, he wasn't interested in my reason for being willing to give fifty dollars for a job in the hotel—and I had such a nice reason all ready for him. He was German, and when he discovered that I spoke his language fluently, he decided I wasn't a spotter and he could trust me.

He told me that he couldn't give me a job for fifty dollars but he would sell me some excellent references. Then I could apply for a job in the regular way and he would see that I was recommended. That would cover his records.

I went to work the next week, but it took me almost six months to make the second floor. I did it by splitting tips with housekeepers, buying drinks for porters and waiters, and just plain bribery. It didn't excite suspicion because all the maids wanted to make the second floor. Tips were good, there was inside dope on horses, and two of the girls had found husbands and an uncomputed number, boy friends.

On the day I finally was told to report to the second floor, Irving St. Leger left for Miami, supposedly to spend the winter. And yet I knew I must hold on to that job or I'd be another year making the second floor again. But I want to tell you I got plenty tired of beds all around.

But the time wasn't wasted. One of the occasional patrons of the crap game was Henry Arnold Peters, the bridge expert—and Henry Arnold Peters was none other than our old friend, Peter Tribolo. Think of "Dummy" Pete turning into a bridge expert! He told me later that at one time he had been a waiter in a bridge club and that was how it happened.

I first spoke to him one day when he said he had a very bad headache and wanted to know if I could give him some aspirin. I prepared it for him and spoke to him in Italian. I wasn't sure how he would take it, but he was very pleased and began pinching my thighs immediately just to prove that he was Italian.

He was hot after me from then on, but I stalled. I didn't want to start anything with him until I had finished off Bennel Stein-St. Leger, and to get him, I knew I had to stick to the second floor. So I told Mr. Peters that I had to be very careful because many of my husband's friends worked in the building.

I promised him, however, that sometime I would try and visit him, and he gave me his residence address and telephone number. Just to keep him interested, once or twice a week I would let him pinch me. It always seemed worth a dollar to him and one day when he had made six straight passes at the crap table he gave me five dollars and didn't make any pass at all.

My luck was with me and Bennel's wasn't. There was a reform wave at Miami Beach and gambling was stopped so, of course, Mr. St. Leger returned to New York and to the second floor of my hotel. I began to make my plans.

His daytime bodyguard was a dumb cluck of an Irishman, Paddy something-or-other. Paddy was usually propped up against the wall outside the room where Bennel was playing. The nervous Mr. St. Leger didn't seem to think he needed protection right in the room, but he wanted it within call and as escort when he left the game. I decided to cultivate Paddy and Paddy was all ready for fertilizing or what have you. He had five kids at home and he was sick of corned beef and cabbage and the priest. At least, that's what he told me after I had brought him a few tired highballs, strengthened with a shot from a private bottle (not the Vermouth) and a little fresh ice.

I had also been lucky enough to acquire two automatics in very good condition with plenty of ammunition. They had been in the baggage of one of the gamblers who had gone for a one-way ride. I had received the news ahead of the hotel detective. It seemed to me that it would be easier and excite much less suspicion to shoot Bennel than to poison him. The other gun I could keep for an emergency—Mr. Peters, the bridge expert, perhaps.

One hot, spring day I saw Bennel come in and I noticed there was a very slim crowd on hand. With any kind of luck, I might catch him alone. I went to work on Paddy and it was too easy. Spring was in his blood. In no time at all I had him in a vacant room, his shoes off, and a drink in his hand. A Mickey Finn in the second drink, and he was lying back on the bed, snoring with his mouth open.

Then I stationed myself with my automatic in another vacant room further down the hall. When Bennel came out of the room where he was playing poker, he would have to walk the full length of the hall to reach the stairs. He always used the stairs, never the elevator.

I waited more than two hours. There were only thirty minutes left. Then one of the other girls would come on and my opportunity would be gone. And I might never have such a good chance again.

She yawned daintily.

"I know you didn't get him that time," Michel said, "because I remember that St. Leger was shot on the street in front of the hotel."

She caressed him as if he were a child or a puppy.

"You're so sweet," she said, "you believe everything you read in the papers."

She yawned again. "I'll tell you tomorrow," she promised.

"If you think you're going to sleep you're crazy," he said.

"I admit the potency of your argument," she agreed.

CHAPTER THIRTEEN

It was late, almost dawn the following night, when she went on with her tale. Andy had insisted that the crowd began to thin the minute Michel and Laura disappeared, so they stayed on, and sure enough, Andy was right. Business kept up until the scrubwomen arrived.

Standing in that vacant room, I almost hoped that Bennel would not come along. I really had done Ralph Jamison a favor in putting him out of the way. Frederick Cole and his stooge Stanley deserved what they got, although they got it too easy. But with St. Leger it was different. I had to keep reminding myself that I was avenging the death of the man who had been my husband. There was no pleasure in it, only a duty.

Afterward, the papers said he was killed because he had welched on his gambling debts, but I didn't know anything about that. So far as I knew, he was leading a good, moral life with one wife and one mistress. He was hard-working, devoting at least twelve to sixteen hours a day to gambling.

But when I saw the door of the gambling room open and St. Leger come out alone, I knew that God had decided for me. Bennel looked around for Paddy, his guard; did some swearing when it was apparent that Paddy wasn't there, and then came slowly down the hall.

Giuseppe had taught me to use a revolver, but I hadn't had very much practice. Still I had confidence and now that the moment was there, I wasn't nervous. If he had come down the other side of the hall, I'm sure I would have missed him, but luck was against him and he came very close to the open door where I was waiting.

I let him have it and then slammed the door turning the catch. But he didn't try to get into the room. Apparently, he kept on going, went down the steps, and out on to the street, where, as you remember, he dropped dead. Either his bleeding was all internal or somebody in the hotel mopped up the blood very quickly. Several of the detectives thought the shooting took place inside the hotel but that was not proved.

I wiped the gun and holding it with a towel threw it out of the window. My luck held, and it landed close to the spot where Bennel died. But even with this, the cops who claimed he was shot inside the hotel, insisted he couldn't have been killed on the sidewalk without anyone seeing it. I hurried through the rooms, hitting Paddy with a wet towel to awaken him.

They kept Paddy locked up over-night but couldn't shake his story that he had just gone to the men's room for a minute. He had no idea he had been given a Mickey; he thought the drinks and the heat had made him pass out and he didn't mention my name.

A couple of detectives asked me some questions but I wasn't taken to headquarters. I said I had been working on the other side of the floor and hadn't heard a thing. A few people had heard the shots but thought them backfire. The gun, pawnshop records showed, had at one time belonged to some gangsters and so it was decided that it was a gangland murder because St. Leger had welched on some gambling debts.

I stayed on at the hotel and then quit, saying there was too much notoriety. The man who had sold me the job thought I was leaving because the hotel had to shut down the gambling temporarily, and the easy-money boys weren't around any more.

While I was in New York, I wanted to finish off Mr. Henry Arnold Peters, our old friend Tribolo, but I knew I must be careful going from one to another so quickly. If anyone recognized me as the former maid at the hotel, and remembered it when Peters died, I could easily be on the spot. I realized it was more than likely that some of the gamblers who played poker with St. Leger were patrons of Peters' bridge club.

However, I decided that probably by the time I had taken off the weight I had put on for my job as chambermaid and had my hair well bleached, he wouldn't recognize me. But I never had a chance to see whether I was right or not, as I read in the paper that Mr. Henry Arnold Peters was closing his bridge club and going to South America for the summer.

I couldn't let him do that. Once he went to South America, I might never be able to catch up with him again. So I decided to try another stunt. I had my hair cut like a boy's, bought a straight up-and-down girdle that flattened me out, and had a theatrical tailor make and deliver a collegiate suit in twenty-four hours. It wasn't too bad, but it wasn't too good either. My face was rounder then than it is now, but, even so, if I were a boy, I was certainly a swishy one.

I took a cab to the Peters Bridge Club, and, when I reached it, I found I didn't have the courage to ring the bell. The taxi driver had looked at me too peculiarly. I had just about decided that the whole idea was whacky, when the door opened and out stepped Peter Tribolo, in person.

He noticed me but didn't really look at me.

"Anybody taking care of you?" he asked. "Did you ring the bell?"

"Not yet," I answered trying desperately to make my voice deep, but bringing out something that sounded like a croaking frog.

Then he did look at me. "Well, if you want something," he said, "ring the bell."

"I wanted to see you," I managed to get out.

"What about?" he asked.

"I thought maybe you could give me a job as page-boy."

"You did, huh?" He started to laugh and began to pinch me.

Good Lord, I wondered, does Peter Tribolo pinch young boys as well as women?

Then he looked at me carefully, still laughing, and I realized I hadn't fooled him.

"I never forget a face," he said, almost to himself.

I began to go cold. Surely he couldn't be recognizing Maria Buonarotti. Then suddenly I realized what he meant.

"You were a maid at the hotel weren't you?" he asked.

"Yes," I said, greatly relieved. "I quit after Mr. St. Leger was killed. It's no good any more."

"What's the idea of the get up?"

He had taken a key from his pocket and opened the front door again. He motioned me to follow him into the house.

"I noticed at the hotel that the bell-boys make a lot more than the maids, so I thought I'd try and see if I could get by as a boy. Then I remembered one boy had said page boys in card clubs made a lot of money and I thought maybe you'd give me a job. But I guess I won't get by as a boy, will I?"

"I'm afraid you won't," he said, "but then I never forget a face—or a body." And he began pinching me again.

We were in the foyer just inside the doorway. There was no sound of anyone in the house; it was completely quiet.

"I'm not supposed to be in town," he explained. "I was down at my country place and not due back in town until tomorrow. I guess that all the servants are out."

"Your club is closed?" I asked.

"Yes, it's closed for the summer," he said. "I'm going to South America in a few days."

"I wonder if you have any idea where I could get a job," I said.

He was holding on to me and giving me further going over.

"Doing what?" he asked.

"Anything that I can do," I answered.

"How'd you like to go to South America?"

"With you?"

"Not exactly. But I have a friend who could get you work there paying plenty of money."

I suddenly realized that he probably meant our old friend, Jack Sandro. Red Connors had told me that Sandro was engaged in some sort of smuggling enterprise out of New Orleans. His name? It came to me immediately.

"Sam Jackson?" I asked and then immediately realized I had made one of my greatest mistakes.

An expression of surprise came into Peter's eyes followed immediately by fear or, perhaps, caution would be better since it wasn't exactly fear. But it was only a second. Then the old poker-bridge expression came back.

"What the hell do you know about Sam Jackson?"

"Nothing very much," I said. "One of the fellows at the hotel told me if I ever wanted a job in South America, Sam Jackson in New Orleans was the man to see."

It sounded reasonable and he accepted it. The men who hung around the hotel might easily have known about Sam Jackson and his South American activities.

He led me into the long, narrow club room. It was very impressive with crystal chandeliers and lots of red plush. If he could handle cards as deftly and quickly as he handled me, I'm glad I never played bridge with him.

"Let's get out of that armor," he said. My boyish-form girdle was blocking him on every move.

He led me through the club room into a tiny bedroom which was just behind it.

"The first emergency ward," he explained as he opened the door.

I hung back coyly. "Mr. Peters," I said, "I really came here for a job."

"That's what you're going to get," he said, propelling me into the room and closing the door behind him.

If only I had brought my revolver with me, I thought. I might never have another opportunity like this one. No one in the house. And the next day he was leaving for South America.

"Maybe," he said, "if you're as chummy as I think you can be, you'll make as much in the next hour as you did in a week at the hotel."

"Mr. Peters," I said, with dignity, "if I wanted to make money that way, do you think I'd take a job as chambermaid?"

"I know, I know," he said impatiently, at the same time starting to work on my expensively tailored clothes. Then he threw back his head and laughed heartily.

"Somebody ought to be here with a candid camera," he said, "that's all some of my dear friends would need. Henry Arnold Peters undressing a boy!"

I know I must have looked silly standing there in boy's oxfords and socks, and shorts over that absurd strait-jacket girdle.

The telephone rang, somewhere; not in the room where we were.

"To hell with it!" Peter said.

I made the usual play for time—the bathroom. He pointed to a door—the only other door in the room besides the one which led in from the club room.

I closed the door, though there was no lock or catch, so he could have barged in at any moment. I didn't think he would, but just to make sure, I braced a chair under the doorknob.

There was a window, with a frosted pane. Letting the water run to deaden the noise, I turned the catch which locked the window and raised it. It was only a few feet from the ground, opening on a tiny, paved backyard. I quickly closed the window but did not lock it. With luck, I had found my back way into the house.

When I returned to the bedroom, draped, not unbecomingly I thought, in a Turkish towel, instead of finding him ready for what is quaintly called love, he wasn't there at all. I stretched out on the bed. A mirror, expertly hung, reflected all of me. There was certainly no trace of boyishness left.

And then Peter hurried in, looking at his watch. Apparently, he had been answering the telephone. Anyway, he had other things on his mind and the dish on the bed didn't tempt him at all.

"I'm sorry," he said, "but I have to leave immediately." He pulled his wallet out of his pocket and looked into it. There was a little pause and, finally, he took out a crisp twenty and tossed it on the bed.

"Step on it," he said, "I've got to be on my way."

I threw the twenty dollar-bill on the floor and rubbed my bare foot over it.

"What the hell are you doing?" he asked.

"You told me to step on it," I said.

He flared up. "I think that's pretty good pay for taking off your clothes and putting them on again!"

"I'm a working woman," I said. "I don't take money that I don't earn."

"All right," he said. "Give it to the Community Chest."

"Not your dirty money," I cried, picking up the bill and running into the bathroom with it. I left the door open and he watched while I threw the bill into the toilet and pressed the flush button.

But he was only interested in one thing—getting me out of the house.

"Get your clothes on," he said, harshly. "I'm in a hurry."

I saw there was no use arguing or playing for time. Something had blocked desire out of his mind, or, quite possibly, something had made him suspicious of me again. At any rate, it was apparent that no matter how much of a hurry he was in, he had no intention of leaving me alone in the house.

He had to help me with that ridiculous girdle, but even then there was not a pinch. No, he was through with me. At least so he thought. He led me to the front door when he had finally hustled me into my boy's outfit, but he did not go out with me.

"If I give you taxi-fare," he said as he opened the door, "what will you do with it?"

"*About* what I did with the twenty," I said.

"Then," he said, "I won't give it to you," and slammed the door with me on the outside.

A little after dark, still in the boy's clothes, I returned to the house. The revolver, which was a mate to the one I had used on St. Leger, was too large to carry in any one of my pockets and, of course, I couldn't carry a handbag. I held it in my hand wrapped in a piece of brown paper.

I had noticed, that afternoon, there was an areaway running alongside the house, but there was an iron gate into this areaway and the chances were that this gate would be locked. It wasn't, however, and the areaway did lead into the backyard.

There were no lights visible in the house, from the front or the back, but there were lights in both next-door houses and I was afraid to climb in through the bathroom window, if it were still unlocked, as some one might easily be looking from one of the adjoining houses.

I decided that the areaway would be the safest place in which to hide, and there I stayed for three or four hours until all the lights in the neighboring houses had been extinguished. Then I climbed through the bathroom window, though I had to take off that absurd girdle before I could jump from the ground to the window sill. I put it on again immediately, however, as that would have been wonderful evidence to have left behind.

I didn't hear a sound in the house. I turned on the bedroom light. It was exactly as we had left it, even to the hollow made in the bed by my bottom.

Just then I heard the sound of a car driving up and stopping in front of the house. I looked quickly around the little bedroom but there was no place to hide. There was no closet. The bathroom was no good. Anyone coming into the bedroom would certainly go into the bath.

I turned out the light and just as I opened the door leading into the club room, I heard a key in the lock. I was too late. I ducked back into the bedroom and slid under the bed. There was no other possible hiding place. I made myself as small as I could against the wall so that even if a person, coming into the room, could see under the foot of the bed, they might miss me, flat against the wall at the head.

The walls were thick. I could hardly hear a thing. Then in about five minutes (it seemed an hour) a beautifully dressed woman, no longer young, came into the bedroom, pushed on the light, and went right on through to the bath. She had left the bedroom door open so I could hear Peter mixing drinks in the club room.

She was only in the bathroom a few minutes. Then she went back into the club room, apparently not quite closing the door, as I could hear the murmur of voices but not what they were saying. The telephone rang several times and I think Peter answered it. The door bell rang, and then again before he answered it. Then I heard two more voices, a man's and a woman's, and also the sounds of more drinks being prepared.

They went on talking interminably as paralysis crept over me. Fortunately it wasn't dusty under the bed, or sneezing would have betrayed me. Then the voices in the club room were raised and it seemed to me there was a quarrel which became more and more violent. Finally, a woman was sobbing hysterically.

After that there was considerable moving around and some door slamming. Then complete silence. I thought maybe everyone had gone out, but when I ventured a peep I saw that all the lights were still on in the club room. Then the telephone rang and Peter answered it. He talked on and on and I couldn't hear what he was saying until he began to shout. He was shouting that she on the other end ("Darling") must not come over, but apparently it was useless. He broke off in the middle of a sentence and hung up.

That was my chance, but I was not quick enough. It was going to be awkward to crawl out from under the bed with the revolver in my hand. I could not be sure just how much the door was ajar. Then while I was trying to make up my mind the doorbell rang again.

He answered it and I could hear a woman's voice in the foyer. It did not sound like either of the women who had been there before but I could not be sure. They didn't come into the club room. At least the woman didn't apparently.

I suppose Peter did, as the lights were turned out. Then I heard them going upstairs. Peter apparently had been defeated in his attempt to remain chaste on the night before he left on his trip.

Now I was in a pickle. I certainly wasn't going to remain all night under that bed. I couldn't go upstairs and let him have it without the woman seeing me, and I didn't want to kill the woman. It's one thing to let a sadistic stooge like Stanley have it, but I wasn't going to kill a woman just because she was foolish enough to love Peter Tribolo.

The place was pitch-dark and, knowing nothing at all about the house, I didn't dare turn on any lights. Moving an inch at a time I worked my way into the club room. There, a street lamp threw enough light for me to see what I was doing. There was no closet in there, no possible place to hide, but moving into the foyer, I noticed an inconspicuous door under the broad stairway.

I opened that door and a light came on, startling me for a second, but, fortunately, I made no sound—or if I did, it wasn't heard. Nor was there any sound from upstairs. If they were still engaged in the sweet exercise of love, they were very quiet about it. More likely, though, they were working behind closed doors. I say working because with Peter Tribolo, it certainly would have been work for me.

The closet under the stairs was very spacious and almost filled with folding bridge tables and chairs. Nevertheless, there was a cleared spot on the floor large enough for me. I sat down and was very comfortable with my back against the tables. I closed the door and waited in the dark. I may have even dozed a little, although I was plenty nervous, not knowing whether I would have an opportunity or not.

However, I was wide awake the minute I heard steps moving around. Lord knows how I managed to get even five minutes sleep in that girdle. The steps were very busy. They were the quick, short steps of a woman. I heard the rushing flow of water. My closet must have been directly under a bathroom. Maybe I wouldn't have liked to have stepped out of those absurd Mickey Rooney clothes and gone under a shower!

The steps, the click of a woman's high heels and the padded tread of a man's bedroom slippers, came down the stairs. They spoke in low tones; I could not hear what was said. I dared not open the door the least crack or the light would pop on. Then the front door was opened, and immediately closed. The padded, slippered steps went through the foyer and down the hallway, passing the door behind which I waited.

He had probably gone to the kitchen, I decided, and I was right. Five, ten minutes passed and just as I was about to emerge, the steps came back and with them the smell of hot coffee. I heard the front door open but not close.

What was happening? He couldn't be going out in his bedroom slippers. Apparently, he was standing there waiting for someone or looking at someone. Suddenly my heart missed a beat. Had I left some trace of my presence out there? Had he telephoned for the police and was standing there in the open doorway waiting for them. If so, I'd better have it over with.

My hand was on the knob of the door when I heard him talking to someone and a masculine voice answered. Then steps died away and the door was closed. Probably a delivery man or, even more likely, the postman. Mr. Peters had been standing there waiting for the last mail that would be delivered to him; the last before he left for South America, he thought. The last ever, I had decided.

I was right. When I opened the door, as noiselessly as possible, I could see him sitting in the club room, reading his mail. He was in pyjamas, slippers, and a robe.

When he looked up, I was standing in the archway leading from the foyer, my hands behind me. Of course he must have been amazed, but the expression on his poker face didn't change and he didn't move.

"Where did you come from?" he asked, and then answered his own question: "I suppose I left the door open."

I let it go at that.

"Well, what do you want?" he asked irritably. "More money to flush down the toilet?"

Then he noticed that my hands were behind me and a little alarm crept into his voice. "Who are you, anyway?" he asked. "What's the game? You were no more a chambermaid than you are a boy."

"What do you think I am?"

He put down the coffee cup and I could see that his hand was trembling.

"I think you were the finger for the rat who shot St. Leger," he said.

"Bennel Stein," I corrected.

That did scare him. Every particle of color left his face. It probably was the first time he had heard that name for years.

"Now you're fingering me," he said. "For who? Why? I don't owe a red cent. How much do you want? I can't raise much cash today, but when I get back from South America, it will be different."

He kept talking on, desperately, never taking his eyes away from me. I did not say anything.

"There must be some way of settling this," he said. "Were some of the wrong girls sent to South America? That can be taken care of."

"Sure," I said, "if anybody cares!"

"Who are you?" he repeated. "I'd swear I never saw you before I met you in the hotel."

"You'd swear wrong," I said and let him have it.

It seemed to me that the shots echoed and re-echoed through the empty house. He slumped forward without a sound. The police didn't give him enough credit. They decided he couldn't have known he was in any danger. He was relaxed and smiling.

I took a few gulps of coffee, wiped the revolver with a handkerchief and put it on the table. Then I left by way of the front door and walked several blocks before getting into a taxi. I had the taxi drop me at a hotel a block from where I lived. That was where the police lost the trail.

Peter's housekeeper on her way to work saw me going down the street and gave the police a pretty good description, although from where she was, she didn't suspect I was not what I seemed to be—a well-dressed young man. She thought I had come from her employer's house but she wasn't sure of it. At any rate, she hadn't thought it unusual. All sorts of people came and went into and from the club.

The police rounded up everyone who had been with Peters the day before and there was plenty of grief, but they finally decided, after tracing the revolver to the same source as the one which had ended St. Leger, that this was another gambling murder and the well-dressed young man was the hatchet man. For once they weren't too far off.

"It was after you got Tribolo," Michel said, "that I decided some one was out gunning for the old Joe Brown mob, although I told myself it still could be a coincidence. Plenty of people had it in for St. Leger and Peters."

"But you didn't warn Jack Sandro or Henry Amblate?"

"No, I didn't know where they were then and I doubt if I would have warned them anyway. I wasn't sure of anything."

"And you aren't sure of anything now?"

"Not a thing," he agreed. "Are you?"

Her eyelids dropped. "You haven't failed me yet," she said.

CHAPTER FOURTEEN

"This comes nearest to being a true *Ecuador* night," she said to him almost twenty-four hours later. "Jack Sandro's agents were all over South America while he lived a quiet life as Sam Jackson in New Orleans."

I went to New Orleans while the heat was still on over the Peters case, but I lived very quietly in a cheap hotel in the French quarter. I spoke French and Spanish and pretended I knew very little English. That was one way to find out plenty. I had myself done over almost platinum, and that made me specially good for the export trade.

I found out that Sam Jackson was a good Huey Long man with plenty of political drag and so long as he stayed in New Orleans, his business of exporting feminine live-stock to South America was as safe as road-building, or any of the other rackets.

But Sandro was hard to contact. He was married to the daughter of one of the old Creole families and had a flock of children. He gave orders, furnished protection, and took the money but he seldom appeared in the quarter.

But I was in no hurry. I found New Orleans very congenial. I was glad to be talking French and Spanish again. I said my husband was a sailor and everybody took my word for it. In one of the freest spots in the country, I was bothered much less than I had been in pure Los Angeles, cynical San Francisco, and sophisticated New York.

I found out that the headquarters for the Jackson outfit was a night club on Bourbon Street, and the chief pimp, or procurer, rather, since he was more of a procurer than a pimp, was the piano player, the regulation "professor" except that this one drank absinthe instead of smoking marijuana.

He took an interest in me immediately, of course, but I think the very first night he decided that I couldn't be shanghaied, and if I were, I'd turn out to be more trouble than I was worth. Business suddenly went sour—a cold spell after Mardi Gras—and there wasn't anybody around. The "professor" didn't have money enough for his absinthe and he was plenty jittery. I staked him to a couple of quarts and he was my friend.

Then he told me, friend to friend, that I could undoubtedly clean up in Quito, Rio, or B. A. "If we sent you down," he explained, "you have to work out five hundred dollars before you'd make a dime, but if you go down on your own, no reason why you shouldn't be in the big money right away."

I told him I wasn't interested and he said no, that was the way it usually was, women didn't really get interested until their best days were over. That was the reason why Jackson had to shanghai them for the business.

I said I was curious about this Jackson guy. Wasn't there ever any chance of seeing him. The professor said sure, Jackson was in early every afternoon just before he went home to dinner, but not even all the bartenders knew him. He just came in for an hour or two, to give orders, collect and have several brandy sours, his favorite drink.

"Then he goes home, every night," the professor said, "and has dinner with his wife and family."

Of course I was in the place late the next afternoon. And sure enough, there was our old friend, Jack Sandro, now Sam Jackson, although I had to look the crowd over twice before I was sure. He certainly had changed. With his white hair, and silky white mustache, he looked like all the Southern colonels in the whiskey ads.

He spotted me before I was sure about him and immediately told the bartender to serve me a drink. But I said I was just "looking for a friend" and couldn't stay. I had located Sandro and he had spotted me. That was enough for a beginning.

That night the professor told me I was elected. Sam Jackson had left word that a date was to be made for me to meet him at *my* convenience. But I laughed it off. I said I didn't know how long I'd be in town and there was no reason why I should meet Sam Jackson. I knew what his business was and I wasn't interested.

Of course it worked. I didn't go to the place any more in the afternoon, but I was there every night, and in less than a week Sandro appeared. I was sitting at a table with a Greek wrestler who was buying me drinks and making indecent proposals—and you have no idea what an indecent proposal can be until it's been made by a wrestler in a Bourbon Street joint. But he made a good background and Sam Jackson was impressed. At least, I was reasonably sure I wouldn't be knocked down and dragged out that night.

Sam Jackson just moved in and said he'd like to buy a drink.

"She no spik muck Eengleesh," the Greek wrestler said.

It gave me a bang to have this ball of Athenian fat interpreting for me.

Sandro looked skeptical.

"Swede? German?" he suggested.

"She spik all language more better Eengleesh," the wrestler explained.

Sam Jackson said that his wife and all her folks spoke only French but he, himself, hated the goddamn' frog language.

I decided it was time to take part in the argument, so in my best Spanish, I suggested that maybe that was the language he preferred to talk in—next to English, of course.

He beamed all over. Sure, Spanish was his language. He thought in New Orleans there'd be a lot of Spanish spoken but not at all. They all spouted that goddamn' frog croaking. And even in Brazil where most of his investments were, they spoke Portygee instead of white man's Spanish.

He sat down and ordered brandy sours for everybody. It was a little peculiarity of his. He was very generous about buying drinks, but it had to be his drink—brandy sour.

He asked me, in Spanish, of course, why I was wasting my time in New Orleans. "You and your boy friend," he said, indicating the wrestler, "could clean up in South America."

I asked him why he thought that mess of fertilizer was my boy friend and explained I had never seen him before until that night. The wrestler, who didn't understand a word of Spanish, beamed and flexed his muscles.

Sandro said that made it all the better. I could clean up alone. I told him I was living the kind of life I liked to live and had no desire to clean up in South America.

He said I misunderstood him. "Anybody can tell to look at you," he explained, "even if you do hang out in a joint like this, that you're no common prostitute."

I told him in no uncertain Spanish that I wasn't a prostitute, common or otherwise, and where I hung out was my business.

"No," he answered with a courtly smile, under his mint-julep mustache, "what anyone does in New Orleans is Huey Long's business."

I shrugged my shoulders in French and answered in Spanish: "There are plenty of other towns."

But friend Sandro had South America on his mind. "A fine blonde like you who speaks Spanish—there is no limit to what you could make in B. A. You could have a fine apartment with a telephone, a few girls, and you, yourself, of course, would only answer hundred-dollar-calls."

I told him I still wasn't interested. A woman could only wear one dress at a time, eat three meals a day, and sleep with one man.

"Sometimes one is too many," Sandro suggested, indicating the wrestler, who again grinned and flexed his muscles.

He said if I really didn't want to make money the easiest and oldest way, I could probably get a very good job as hostess in a night club. I told him I wasn't interested in going to South America in any capacity, and if they tried to make me go against my will, they'd find they had caged a wildcat.

"I not only speak Spanish," I told him, "but I can stab Spanish, and I will, Huey Long or not!"

He insisted that nobody was going to make me go to South America or anywhere else against my will, but I was being very foolish. Then before the evening was over, he decided he didn't want me to leave town at all. It was talking to me in Spanish that he enjoyed so much. English, of course, was now easier for him than Spanish, but he liked the old language—it brought back his boyhood days.

He apologized for not making any effort to seduce me but explained that he had a devoted wife and two mistresses, and also—*pobrecito*—he wore a truss. But he would like to drive me home. We left the Greek wrestler asleep at the table.

Sandro was shocked when he discovered I was living in a third-class hotel in the French Quarter, and insisted that the next day he would find me an apartment with a gallery, the ideal of comfort in old New Orleans.

"For conversation?" I reminded him.

"For conversation, only," he said.

And so help me, that was all he ever required. The next day he found me a wonderful old apartment, with a gallery and high ceilings and a view of the river, through a vista of streets. There he came and brought his brandy (I furnished the lemons) and sat, and told me his troubles.

Business was terrible. The demand was there, but his procurers were either inefficient or double-crossers. They claimed they could make more taking their girls to Hollywood than by sending them to South America.

And then his private life was difficult. His wife was very jealous; his daughter was too wild; his son, too tame. His mistresses were very exacting, but he couldn't shake them because they had important connections in the Huey Long machine. He ought to be operated on so he wouldn't have to wear the truss any more, but he had a peasant's fear of operations. His only pleasure, he said, was to sit and talk Spanish to me.

I found life very pleasant. New Orleans in many ways reminded me of my native land. There was sun and flowers and delicious tropical fruits. I didn't go to the Bourbon Street saloon any more, but quite often Sandro brought his friends to the apartment and we had little parties. He liked to show me off to them and so great was their fear of him, and of Huey Long above him, that no one ever made the slightest pass at me. I felt like St. Anne, living in a brothel and remaining a virgin. The great man himself never appeared. He was assassinated just after I left New Orleans, completely obliterating the little tragedy which ended Sam Jackson.

One day, to my great astonishment, my part-time Negro maid announced, with bated breath and great rolling of the eyes, that Mrs. Jackson and her daughter were calling to see me. I sent word that I would be right in and told the maid to prepare chocolate, sandwiches and cookies.

They were a lovely sight on the Victorian sofa in my "parlor". It was parlor or drawing room in New Orleans—never living room. Mrs. Jackson was a tiny, dark woman who would have been considered a light Negro in any part of the country except New Orleans, where the dusky creoles are not *cafe au lait* but *creme de la creme*. She wore black moire and jet jewelry, with tiny red slippers and red gloves. Her daughter was a radiantly beautiful girl of about seventeen. When I last heard about her, she was in a convent and, I'm sure, more beautiful than ever.

"I hardly know how to apologize for this intrusion," Mrs. Jackson said in beautifully, soft-spoken English, unaccented but with a slight inflection due to careful spacing between every word.

"Apologize?" I answered, glad that my rusty French was not going to be put on trial. "But I thought it was a beautiful Southern custom to call upon the newcomer."

"You are trying to make it easy for me," Mrs. Jackson said. "But I prefer to be frank. I do not interfere with my husband's friends but I like to know them. I knew there was going to be a new friend this year—"

"How did you know that?" I interrupted.

"By the stars, the leaves, and Emzy—"

"Emzy is mother's voodoo woman," the girl explained, her eyes conveying the fact that, between herself and me, her mother was a fool.

"Then, since we are being frank," I said, "and although you probably will not believe it, I am not your husband's mistress. I am his friend, but his real interest in me is the fact that I speak his native tongue to him."

"That doesn't matter," the woman said. "Whatever your relationship is, he is away from home more and more. He is not a young man, not a well man. I worry so about what he eats and drinks, and he is careless about his truss—"

"He should have a valet or a male nurse," I suggested.

"Of course he should," she agreed, "but he won't. I wonder if you would mind very much if I gave you his diet list and implored you not to let him drink too much brandy. The doctor has said it will kill him."

The Negro girl appeared with the refreshments. I told her I would serve and she went out. I think Mrs. and Miss Jackson were surprised that I didn't serve them pretzels and beer. Probably some one had told them about the Bourbon Street saloon. The girl in particular was eyeing me very intently.

"You know, mamma," she finally said, "I think this lady is telling the truth. I don't believe she is Papa's sweetheart."

The mother fluttered and her jet tinkled.

"That does not matter," she said. "I'm sure she is telling the truth but I almost wish she were his sweetheart—then I might believe that those other bad women were losing their hold on him."

"If I were mamma," the girl said to me, "I would have thrown the old son-of-a-bitch out years ago."

"But you are not me," the mother said, apparently not in the least disturbed by her daughter's language. "And I am worried about your papa's immortal soul." She sighed. "If it were only for this earth, it would be easy. I would have had him castrated years ago."

They were going pretty fast even for me. "Do you think he'll need them in the next world?" I asked.

"There's a difference of opinion," Mrs. Jackson told me. "The holy men are not agreed. I do not dare take the chance. But it would certainly make things much easier in this world."

They smoked tiny, thin black cigars and gave me one. I found them very pleasant and smoked them the rest of the time I was in New Orleans. Having eaten daintily, they waited around the polite time and then left, after giving me the diet list, although I assured them that "papa" seldom had a meal with me.

I thought that the girl wanted to talk to me alone but her mother would not give her the opportunity. When the girl expressed a wish to "wash her hands" after the chocolate, mamma trotted right along with us.

My guess was correct. A few days later the girl called me on the telephone and, without any apologies, asked me if she could use my apartment for a few hours that afternoon.

"With a man?" I asked.

"Sure. Do you think I want to play with my dolls?"

"You'll be playing with live dolls if you don't watch out," I said and told her I could not possibly let her use my apartment for such a purpose. I was afraid of her father.

"Papa won't know a thing about it unless you tell him," she argued. "And if you don't let us use your place, we'll just go to some awful road camp—"

"Go where you like," I told her, "but you can't use my apartment."

But apparently her boy friend had no intention of taking jail bait to any public place. They showed up at my place twenty minutes later and he was as handsome a young devil as I had seen since the days of Mike Peruzzi. Annette, the kid, put him down in a chair and said she wanted to talk to me alone. I took her into the bedroom.

"He doesn't know who I am," she explained. "No man in this town will touch me. They're scared to death of my father. This is my man and I'm going to have him. You know damn' well it's ridiculous for me to still be a virgin."

Looking at her eager, ripe beauty, I agreed with her, but I merely pointed out that some girls kept their virginity until they were eighteen or nineteen.

"How old were you?" she demanded.

I said that had nothing to do with it. I was a foreigner.

"I'm a foreigner," she said passionately. "There isn't a drop of cold Anglo-Saxon blood in me. I'm wop, spik, frog and a little nigger, probably. I should have had a man two years ago; I'm going to have this one today."

I told her it was a great gift she was handing out; was she sure this was the right man?

She answered with a question. "Who is the right man?"

I thought of Henry Amblate and Giuseppe Buonarotti and Mike Peruzzi.

"The one who's the best lover," I answered.

"Don't you think this man will be a good lover?"

"Perhaps," I admitted, realizing that the creature gave out sex from every pore, "but you can't tell a book by its cover."

"Every time he touches me, I feel it in every part of my body. It's the most exquisite, undescribable sensation I've ever had. I stay awake at nights thinking about him, I dream bad dreams about him, I wake up thinking about him—"

"He's your man," I agreed, surrendering without further argument.

I gave them the bedroom, but I would not leave the apartment. I trusted her Pepe, as she called him, as I would trust a rattlesnake. But there was no sound from behind the closed door and when they emerged after a few hours, the girl was starry-eyed.

She threw her arms around me and whispered, "We made no mistake." I wasn't sure whether *we* were the girl and myself or the girl and the man. The man was dead-pan, going in and coming out, but it was the dead pan of a panther.

My telephone was privately listed, but apparently both of them had made note of the number.

The girl called first. "I know he's a rat," she said, "but I'm mad about him. I'd rather die tonight than to live on and not have had this afternoon with him."

"That's the spirit," I agreed.

"But I don't want him to find out who I am," she said. "Papa would kill me."

"He'll find out if he wants to," I said. "But he won't find out from me."

"I know he's following me," the girl said, "but I fooled him by going into a Girl's Hotel. He thinks I live there."

"Your papa isn't going to hand me any flowers for helping you," I reminded her.

"He won't blame you," she said. "He knows when I make up my mind, nothing can be done about it."

I told her, yes, they could have the bedroom any afternoon they wanted, but wouldn't it be a good idea to find out something about the man?

"I don't want to know anything about him beyond the body he's enclosed in," she said. "I know he's bad, completely bad. But that doesn't matter."

And I, remembering Mike Peruzzi, who had helped kill my husband and then had made me know what love could be, said nothing.

The man telephoned. He wanted to know if I were for him or against him. I told him I was for him as long as he played square with the girl and not a minute longer.

"Want to make some easy money?" he asked.

"No," I said and hung up. But that night I made the "professor" get a revolver for me.

So it went on for a few weeks. They were in the apartment almost every afternoon. Then one day, the girl came first and told me the man was trying to get her to go away with him.

"Where to?" I asked.

"New York, he says, by way of Cuba."

"You're not thinking of going with him?"

"No, of course not, but I don't know how I'm going to live without him."

Remembering Mike Peruzzi, I couldn't tell her there were other men in the world. Maybe there weren't any others for her, just as there had been no other for me since Mike Peruzzi.

"You mustn't go with him," I said firmly. "He will sell you or degrade you."

"I know," she agreed. "I don't mean a thing to him. I was something young and exciting the first few times, but I'm beginning to bore him already."

So it stood that day, and after they had been in the room about an hour, the man came out and asked me for a couple of glasses and a little ice.

I called the maid, and then asked him why he didn't cut me in if he had something special. He said I'd get mine later and I had a pretty good idea what he meant. He would have liked to have kicked my teeth in but he was afraid of me. I knew he wasn't serving a drink just for the sake of being sociable. I decided it was time to take action.

I got Sandro on the telephone and told him to come over immediately and be prepared, maybe, for a little trouble. He had confidence in me. He didn't ask any questions but said he would be there immediately.

I had just hung up, when the bedroom door opened and the rat came out, dragging the girl with him. She wasn't completely out, but she was in a fog, her eyes glazed and her feet just dragging over the floor.

The rat was annoyed that I was sitting there watching him but he tried to brazen it out.

"The drink was too much for the kid," he said. "I'm going to ride her around a little while in the air."

"Not in the condition she's in," I said, "you're not going to take her out of this house."

"I wouldn't advise you to interfere in this," the rat said, putting all the menace he could into his voice.

But I wasn't in the least scared. I was holding the revolver under the afternoon newspaper on my lap and he had his hands full with the drugged girl.

"And I wouldn't accept your advice on any subject," I said very sweetly.

He turned to Annette and tried to prop her up.

"Tell her," he said, "that it's all right. You want to go with me."

"Sure," the girl said, articulating very thickly. "Sure I want to go with Pepe."

I didn't answer. I called the Negro girl and she came hurrying into the room.

"Take Miss Annette back into the bedroom," I said.

The Negro girl stepped forward to obey me. The rat was livid with fury.

"Nobody's touching this girl," he snarled.

The Negro girl looked to me for orders. Oddly enough, she showed no signs of fright either.

"Let her go, louse," I said lifting the newspaper and showing the leveled gun.

He released the girl immediately and the maid half carried her back into the bedroom. The rat was completely caught by surprise. I don't think he was armed. His revolver was probably in his car.

He looked at me but now he didn't look so evil—just yellow and scared. "So you're a stool, are you?" he said.

"A stool?" I said. "I thought a stool had to work with the crooks. I haven't been in your game."

"You rented us a room."

"I *rented* you a room? Have you paid me rent for a room?"

"The dame said she attended to it."

"She told you she paid me for the room?"

"She said you lent it to us."

The door opened behind him and Sandro stood there. He saw the revolver first and then he saw the rat.

"Pepe!" he said. "What the hell are you doing here?"

Pepe swung around. "The boss!" he shouted and then began to laugh. He turned to me, still laughing heartily. "Why didn't you tell me you was the boss's girl. It's all in the family."

"Yes," I said. "I believe it is."

In Spanish, I told Sandro to go into the bedroom and see who his henchman was trying to shanghai on a South American boat. Sandro immediately went into the bedroom.

"Who's that dame?" the rat shrieked at me. "What is she to the boss? Is she one of his women, too? What goes on here?"

"Spik no Eenglish," I said to him.

He turned to flee, but Sandro caught him in the hallway. I heard the rat falling down the long flight of iron steps. The professor told me later when they picked him up there was a knife through one eye, six inches into the brain. There wasn't one word about any of it in the newspapers, but I knew that I was a marked woman and would certainly have to watch my step.

I wondered why I had done it. What the devil difference did it make to me what happened to Jack Sandro's daughter? But on the other hand I didn't hate Sandro; I had to kill him because I was a Sicani but there was no reason why I shouldn't do him a good turn before I removed him.

"It must be very late," Laura said, reaching for a cigarette. "I've talked and talked and talked."

"What happened to the girl?" Michel Perry asked. "Did she find another man as good as the one her papa killed?"

"Wouldn't you like to know?" Laura teased him. "Wouldn't you like to show her that her Pepe wasn't so much of a muchness?"

"I wasn't thinking of that at all," Michel said, gathering her to him. "I've got all the woman I need—or want."

"You're sure not more than you need or want?"

"I'm not complaining."

"If you want the lovely Annette, you'll have to go to a convent. Aaron Burr is supposed to have had an affair with a nun in a convent in New Orleans. What one man has done, another can do."

"She really went into a convent? She was that heartbroken?"

"She wasn't heart-broken at all. She had always been religious. I think she tried two or three other lovers but she said they were all as nothing compared to Pepe. She knew she'd never find another man like him. It was absurd to keep on trying. She decided to give herself to God."

"And Sandro?"

"I'll tell you tomorrow."

CHAPTER FIFTEEN

"Sometimes," Laura said the next night, "I wish we could go to New Orleans together. It is so beautiful. You would like it there. The coffee in the market at five cents a cup is better than yours at fifty."

"You wouldn't be afraid to go back to New Orleans?" Michel suggested.

"Oh no, not at all. I have some very nice friends there."

I realized I should do my job and be on my way. Mrs. Jackson was becoming increasingly troublesome. She blamed me completely for her daughter's downfall. The fact that I had finally saved her from a South American brothel did not mitigate her hatred. She said I had her husband and her daughter bewitched and strange chalk marks began to appear on the stairs and the door of my apartment, put there, my Negro maid assured me, by the voodoos. She said it was no use my trying to catch them because they were always invisible when they worked. I had an idea that if I kept an all-night vigil I might catch some of the invisible voodoos, but I was not that much interested.

Sandro's one passion in life was brandy and so when I read that some fine old Napoleon private stock was going to be sold at auction, I bought it in, paying around two hundred dollars for six bottles. Then I began doling it out to Sandro, one drink at a time.

He offered me a hundred, and then a thousand dollars a bottle for it, but, of course, there was no sale. Then he said the brandy he enjoyed and needed most was the pony he took after his dinner, and since he always dined with his family, he couldn't have any Napoleon brandy.

He begged for a half-pint at a time, but I wouldn't give it to him, because of doctors' orders, I said. Finally, I agreed to let him have a one-ounce dram every day to drink after his dinner, and, do you know, I let him enjoy almost all six bottles of brandy before I put my dose of deadly Vermouth into the dram.

I was taking more of a chance than usual. I was known to his family and probably they knew where he got the dram of brandy every day, but I'm sure that greedy as he was for brandy, he would pour every drop out of the bottle, so there would be no more reason to suspect the brandy than anything else he had eaten or drunk.

Of course, an analysis of the brandy I had left would not show anything, and the remaining Vermouth I had shipped out of town. But I was afraid to skip out of town myself until I knew that my plan had worked. Anything might happen to that dram of brandy although I realized that Sandro guarded it as if it were gold.

I did not think there would be an autopsy. Sam Jackson was known to be a sick man, and even if there were any hint of scandal in connection with his death, it was certain that the organization would not want it made public. It wasn't fear of the police that kept me from leaving town as soon as I read that he was dead. It was fear of the Huey Long organization. If they suspected me, I was sure they would find me.

I was wrong about the autopsy. Mrs. Jackson demanded one and the poison was discovered. It was the fifth member of the Buonarotti gang I had killed, but, for the first time I was nervous. It seemed to me that the investigation must involve me, although I kept telling myself they couldn't prove anything, and, above all, there was no motive. No possible motive the police could discover.

I called the professor and asked him if he thought it would be necessary to go to the funeral.

"Haven't you heard the latest news?" he asked. "It's funerals, not funeral."

"Who else?" I asked breathlessly. He had split the ounce of brandy and there was enough of my Vermouth to kill two! But who? And why hadn't he or she died at the same time?

"Mrs. Jackson," he answered.

"Heart attack?" Poor little creole.

"No, she killed herself, and left a letter admitting that she had murdered her husband!"

I began to laugh hysterically. So, she was jealous of his murder as well as of his trussed-up body when it breathed.

"If you feel hysterical," the professor said, "how do you think I feel? I haven't had a drop to drink today."

I promised him a bottle of absinthe and he went on with his story.

Mrs. Jackson had left a note saying she had unwittingly killed her husband and the only atonement she could make would be to kill herself. She had been feeding him, it seemed, love philtres, sold her by a voodoo doctor and apparently through some terrible mistake one of them had been a deadly poison!

Now, the police had something they could really go to town on. Every cultist, fortune teller, astrologist, and half the druggists in town were thrown into jail, but nothing happened. No one could say from whom Mrs. Jackson had bought the love philtres, and she had carefully not given the names, apparently convinced that an honest mistake had been made. There were two or three confessions, apparently from publicity motives, but they were repudiated and nothing could be proved, but I don't believe the Negro fortune tellers have even yet become re-established in New Orleans.

I had a touching farewell with Annette in the convent where she was serving her novitiate. She said she thought my relationship with her father was really a beautiful thing. I was sorry to leave the lovely city but I had a mission in the Blue Ridge Mountains of North Carolina. . . .

Henry Amblate, as Henry Alexander, was a tobacco baron, real estate operator and banker in a beautiful Carolina mountain town. It happened this way: just before the end of prohibition and the breaking up of the old Buonarotti outfit, the heat was really on Amblate and, to save his neck, he had himself cooled off in one of the Federal Pens for a year.

There he met this millionaire big-shot from Carolina who was in for income-tax fraud. They became pals; the bigshot was released first, but as soon as Henry was free, he joined his friend and was taken right into the business. He made good, I believe, right away, and for once in his life he didn't outsmart himself. He finally cinched the whole thing by marrying the big-shot's daughter, an only child.

His sponsor had died just a few months before I appeared on the scene and everything belonged to Henry, his wife, and their two kids. Henry was ripe for something to happen. He had been a good boy too long. The older man apparently had known exactly how to handle him and Henry had not only taken it but liked it. Henry didn't love his wife and he said the children weren't really his; they were hers. He had respected and liked the older man, but now, suddenly, he felt alone—and at that logical moment I appeared.

"But come to think of it," Laura said, suddenly slipping out from under Michel's arm, "I don't think I'll tell you about Henry and me."

"Why not?" Michel demanded, something almost like alarm in his voice.

"It's told better than I can tell it," Laura explained, "in his own letters to a doctor friend living in Florida. These letters were later introduced in court by Mrs. Alexander when she applied for a divorce sometime later."

"How did you get them?" Michel asked.

"The newspapers printed them in full. I have the papers and I'll bring them along tomorrow night."

"And this is the last story?" Michel sighed heavily as he said it.

"The very last, I promise you," Laura answered, kissing him with just the tip of her tongue. "What happened to Scheherazade when she finished her thousand and one nights?"

"I don't know," Michel said. "It seems to me there were some supplemental nights."

"I'm sure the Sultan didn't kill her—"

"But then he wasn't afraid that she'd kill him!"

Laura raised herself on her elbow and looked down at him.

"You don't really believe that, my darling. You can't."

"You killed all the others. It was probably your vow made on the Blood and Body of Christ. You are a Sicani."

"Yes, I am a Sicani but I am also a woman, and the Sicani in me will have to be satisfied that I killed six men for the death of one man I did not love. That is enough. Even my Sicani blood does not tell me to kill the only man who has ever meant anything to me."

"Some day when you are tired of me," Michel said, great melancholy in his voice, "you will remember that I was one of those responsible for the death of Giuseppe Buonarotti."

"If I ever tire of you," she said, "it will be your fault not mine. The Blood and Body of Christ are nothing to me compared to your blood and body."

"Don't say that," Michel cried, moving away from her. "It's sacrilegious."

"But it's true," she said, and then added: "Oh, I could hate you perhaps as madly as I love you, but it would have to be for something you did to me, and not because you helped murder Joe Brown."

"What could I do to you?" he cried out, fright still in his tone, his body drenched with perspiration.

"Nothing," she said tersely. "Let us talk of life not death. It is only life I want from you—life . . . life . . . life . . ."

CHAPTER SIXTEEN

The next night she brought the newspapers that told the strange story of the love of Henry Alexander for the woman he knew as Mrs. Laura Forsythe. It began in the first letter he wrote after meeting her to his doctor friend whom he had known while he was serving his prison term. The young man, just from his internship, had been one of the prison doctors, and later Henry had established him in private practice.

A strange thing has happened, Henry Alexander wrote to the young doctor; a woman, a stranger, made a deposit of more than ten thousand dollars about ten days ago and also rented a large safety deposit box. Of course, I am notified of all transactions of this magnitude, and I wrote her a personal letter thanking her for the deposit and offering my personal services as well as those of the bank if she were going to become a resident of our community. It was more or less routine, as we are accustomed to wealthy people coming here for a vacation or for their health. When I wrote to her, I had no idea that she was alone.

She came in a few days ago, about a week after I had written. She is a lovely creature closer to thirty than twenty, I imagine, but with something youthful and yet ageless about her. And it is that way about everything. She is an extraordinary mass of contradictions. She is beautiful but with not one really good feature. She gives an exotic effect and yet her clothes are expensively conventional. Her English is perfect, without accent, and yet I am sure it is no more her native tongue than it is mine. All in all, I have the feeling that like myself and so many foreigners, who accumulate money, she was made over completely sometime during her life just as I was made over in prison.

And that is the extraordinary thing about her. I am sure I have known her before and yet she says I must be mistaken as she has always lived on the West Coast and in the Orient. It is probably because ridiculously, and in some way I can't define, she reminds me of a woman I once intended to marry. I told you about her. I paid her passage to this country and then she married someone else. You may have an explanation of this strange mental twist whereby I feel I must have met her because she is, in some intangible way, like a woman I once knew, although she couldn't possibly be she, since that woman would now be ten to twenty years older than this one.

All this after just one visit, you will say. That is all and a very short visit it was. I don't know when anyone ever had such an immediate effect upon me. I have never been a chaser. I have always been shy with women. That is why I had to send to the old country for one. I have always been suspicious of them, and that is why I lost the woman I sent for. I have never been in love. I was never in love with my wife but I have been faithful to her. She suspects this, I know, and so gives all her love to our children, who are really her children.

So I cannot be in love or infatuated with this woman I've only seen once—but I must confess I can think of nothing else, and so am writing to you. If it continues, maybe you can help me. She only stayed a very little while. She thanked me for my letter and said she might have me find a house for her, but she hadn't quite made up her mind.

I asked her what kind of house she would want. She said she was afraid that would be the trouble. She would want a large house, not too close to other houses, but not an estate. She would want to be right in the mountains or as close to them as she could get. It must be high and have a view. I told her she had come to exactly the right place as our town was really built on a small plateau surrounded by mountains and it was rapidly building right into them.

I suggested that I get a guest card at the country club and I was sure my wife would want to call upon her. She thanked me and begged me not to think her unfriendly but for the time being she did not want any social life whatsoever. Of course, if she stayed, she would consider it a great privilege to meet Mrs. Alexander and *her* friends. Although she looked perfectly healthy and untroubled, something, again entirely intangible, gave me the impression that she was recovering from either an illness or an emotional entanglement.

That is how it stands now. I haven't seen her again but I'm gathering a list of houses and in a few days, I will write to her if she doesn't come in. And there aren't many houses, I'm afraid, that will meet her requirements.

I told my wife all about her but she wasn't interested. She doesn't flatter me by being jealous. She said she would call, of course, if I wanted her to, but she hoped the necessity wouldn't arise.

Henry Alexander's second letter about the wealthy stranger was written about a week later.

A doctor, he wrote, I am told receives more confessions these days than a priest. Thus you will have to serve as my father confessor, because I am bursting with what has happened to me. I am afraid if I don't tell you, I will unburden myself to my stenographer or barber or caddy, and anyone of them, I'm sure would call the police immediately, convinced that I was crazy.

And, of course, I am. Crazy with the love of one woman, crazy at the realization that only now, at well over forty, I have learned the meaning of life. You know pretty well what my life has been—poverty, war, lawlessness, murder, lust, prison, and, on the upgrade, friendship, comfort, domesticity, and the stewardship if not the possession of wealth. But never before love.

What is your definition of love? Never having known it before, always having been completely skeptical of it, I have had to make my own definition. Well here it is: Love is when another person means more to you than yourself. That is what has happened to me. Never before has anyone else come first. Now I feel that Laura Forsythe is much more important to me than I am to myself.

It just happened yesterday. I've called her every day suggesting this house or that one, but always she'd pick a flaw from my description and wouldn't look at them. It was probably a mad idea, she said, to think of taking a house. I told her I thought it was a beautiful idea and I was determined to find a house for her.

Then yesterday I had an inspiration. I don't know if you ever heard of Baron's Folly or not. It's a house that he literally had carved out of rock on the side of the mountain. He finished and furnished three or four rooms for himself, and the rest of the place was never completed, is still unroofed and open to all the elements. From the living room and bedroom windows there is a sheer drop of hundreds of feet, down a rock canyon. Baron said it solved the problem of bottle tops, razor blades, and articles of hygiene.

After he died, the bank had tried to sell or rent it but nobody would touch it in its incomplete condition. To finish the place would have bankrupted the estate. And there it stood, waiting for the State to take it over eventually for taxes.

I called Laura Forsythe and, half apologetically, told her about it. She was immediately enthusiastic about the idea. Was it furnished? I said I wasn't sure but I thought it was furnished to the extent that Baron had thought necessary for living. She said she was sure that would do. She could live as primitive as anyone.

Almost as an afterthought I told her we would have to walk the last half mile as Baron had never finished the road, which was another reason why the place was unsalable and unrentable. But she said that only made it more interesting to her. I arranged to take her right after the bank closed.

Some wish, some hope which I had dared not put into words to myself led me to telephone my wife that I might not be home for dinner: I was showing important real estate to some buyers. I wondered if I dared take Mrs. Forsythe to dinner anywhere. Ours was a small city and there would inevitably be gossip. Some fellows get away with it, but I had been the model husband. There were, I remembered, some places away out on the State Highway where I might not be recognized, but, of course, I couldn't ask her to go any place that wasn't dignified.

We had no dinner and I don't think either of us missed it. I know I didn't. The god of love or passion, or some god, anyway, was with me. When we got out of the car at the foot of the winding path that led to the crazy house toppling toward the brink, I noticed that thick clouds were forming. You know how suddenly storms come up in our mountains.

I said perhaps we had better not try to make it, but she insisted she did not mind a little wetting; it would not hurt her summer cotton dress. We had gone about two-thirds of the way when the storm broke over us. The thunder and lightning were continuous; we dared not seek the shelter of a tree as we could see them being struck to the right and to the left of us.

She did not show the slightest fear. In fact above the noise of the storm, she yelled that it was wonderful. I was beginning to be alarmed. The storm was cutting into the path and rolling boulders around us. But I didn't care. I had my arm around her, helping her up the path and the pounding of my heart was not caused by fear.

We made the house just as the storm increased in intensity and violence. It seemed to me just about the worst I had ever known in these mountains. But inside the house it was magnificent. We took off our drenched clothes—modestly in separate rooms—and draped ourselves in blankets. There was plenty of wood and I soon had a fire roaring in the huge grate. I had a flask I had brought from the car.

My companion was mad about the house and said she never wanted to live anywhere else! She roamed around examining every nook and corner of it. The electricity was on, but suddenly it went out. Undoubtedly the main line had been struck or poles had been blown down. I lighted matches looking for candles and a lamp but didn't find them for the very good reason that I didn't look in the one closet where I knew they were kept. I was blazing like the fire by that time and I thought I might have better success in the dark.

I couldn't figure her out. She was a sphinx. She was friendly—a good sport—as unafraid as anyone I could think of, and yet I had the feeling she wasn't completely there. It seemed to me that more than half the time her thoughts removed her from my presence.

We talked aimlessly, and then when the lights went out and the storm was at its worst, we sat silent and watched the spectacle on the mountain and in the canyon. She sat contented enough with my arm around her, but when I tried to go further, she pulled away gently with a murmured "please." I wanted to talk, to rationalize, but I was tongue-tied and I certainly had no intention of a forcible seduction. The maddening thing was that I was sure she was not really unresponsive. But there was something there I couldn't penetrate either by words or action.

Finally the rain let up, although the storm was not completely over. We put on our clothes which had been drying by the fire. We opened the door and realized immediately it would be impossible to go down the path—it was a rushing torrent of water.

She was only concerned about me and the alarm of my family. I assured her they would not be alarmed. I had said I was showing a house and might not be home for dinner. They would know I had sought shelter somewhere. My wife was not given to undue worry. She was accustomed to rough country and mountain storms.

Would they worry about her at the hotel? I asked. Her voice sounded sad to me when she said there was no one in the world to worry about her. The storm started again with renewed intensity and we hurried back to the fire. I told her we couldn't possibly get out until daylight. She agreed.

I brought blankets and quilts and stretched them out in front of the fire. The bedrooms were bleak and damp. I put my arm around her and drew her close to me.

Then suddenly she yielded. She said nothing, made no move, but I felt her relax in my arms and I knew that the greatest moment in my life had come. It had.

It just happened last night, Doc, but I have no recollection whatsoever of the details. There must have been a period when my desire was so great that it blotted out everything else. I remember a mad exultation before the dying fire in that great room which the lightning illumined every few seconds. But I have no recollection of seeing anything in those seconds of light. Only the great exultation, the sense of power, and the life force she yielded.

Then it was over, Nature's storm and ours, and I realized she was deathly still in my arms. Panic-stricken, it seemed to me I could detect no heart beat, no pulse. I kissed her wildly and shrieked her name.

She moved against me and I burst into tears. She asked me gently what had happened to me and I said I had been terribly frightened: I could not feel her heart beat.

"It often misses a beat or two," she said indifferently.

There is no other person in the world I would write this to, Doc, and even to you I cannot tell the full wonder of last night. I tremble when I think I might have died and not have met this woman. I cannot believe that anywhere in the world there is another one like her.

And yet although she yielded, without reservation, time and time again, there was still a baffling feeling of aloofness as if she were not completely there in spirit. I was sure she was not sharing my feeling of supreme ecstasy; that somewhere, sometime she had known something better—and that realization gave me an inferiority feeling such as I had never known before. But it did not keep me from demanding from her endlessly through the stormy length of the night—and do not misunderstand me. Her response was passionate and full-womaned; the reservation she made was mental not physical. Her lips remained icy even while her body was on fire. Eventually, she fell asleep in my arms, and I lay back with the most wonderful exhaustion I had ever known. But I could not sleep.

The storm abated. There was a fiery, brilliant dawn. Tenderly I put her out of my arms; she muttered something but did not fully awaken. I went over and looked at the dripping, green trees and the cleansed, brilliant mountains. The path would be muddy, of course, but in the daylight with a few logs, I was sure we could make it back to the car.

The room was warm now and my companion, in her sleep, had thrown back the blankets. Her body was beautiful, and it was a young body, younger than her eyes or her cynical mouth. And yet as I looked at the lovely body and felt the blood rushing through my veins, it seemed to me that she was ivory or marble, not flesh and blood. Nothing about her was completely real. She was the work of some master artist.

Gently as I could, curbing the rush of passion, I put my arms around her, but she released herself and slipped away as graceful as a snake.

"No," she cried, almost harshly. "No."

I caught her and held her, feeling ridiculous as I had never been like this in the daylight with any woman except a bad one.

"My darling," I said. "I will never have enough of you."

And I know that I never will.

But she would not let me touch her. She stood before me, deathly pale, her eyes filled with tears.

"Oh, my dear," she said despairingly, "it is a terrible thing that we have done."

I tried to talk her out of that attitude, to tell her that it was absurd but she would not listen to my arguments. What we did was not just our own affair, because I had a wife and children. I told her that my wife had no interest in sex and I was sure that she was completely indifferent as to whether I was true to her or not.

I felt it was foolish to argue then, to make any plans or promises. I was sure then, and I am sure now, that she is the only woman I want for the rest of my life—but at the moment her conscience was stabbing, and anything I might say would only make matters worse.

I found some boots and we had no trouble in going down the path to the car.

I will give her twenty-four hours before I call her. In the meantime, I feel strengthened by having written of my great happiness to you.

In Alexander's next letter, written a week later, he was full of bewilderment and frustration.

I really think I am going nuts, doc, he wrote. This woman who showed me the meaning of life will not let me touch her. At first I thought it was a natural reaction, a sense of shame, that would surely pass when the life force re-asserted itself, but now it is a week and she is still adamant.

But she sees me and is willing to be friendly. That is the maddening thing. I thought when she would not talk to me the day after it happened, that perhaps in her repentance she would leave town. It did not occur to me that she would take the house. And then the next morning when she called and left word with my secretary that she would rent the house on a month to month basis, without a lease, I decided that her spell of conscience was over and that I had a mistress as fine as ever a man possessed.

Of course there would be some scandal; that would be inevitable, but it need not be disastrous. My wife was not jealous; so long as I did nothing to openly humiliate her, I was sure she would not do anything drastic.

That afternoon I sent a staff of cleaners to give the place a thorough going-over. She said she just wanted it cleaned, no painting or re-decorating. The next day she moved with her small amount of hand luggage from the hotel to Baron's Folly. The telephone had been connected and she was very friendly when I called her.

Yes, she would be glad to see me that evening and would I bring out some cooked food as she hadn't put in any supplies yet? I asked her what she had done about servants and to my great surprise and alarm, she said she did not want any living on the place. She would just have them come in several times a week to clean. She liked to cook, she explained.

Our dinner hour at home was quite early on account of the children. I told my wife I had rented Baron's Folly to Mrs. Forsythe and I was driving out that night to take her some food and other supplies. You see I was forestalling gossip and so sure was I of myself and my wife that I dared to ask her if she wouldn't drive out with me.

My wife said she couldn't that evening, but as soon as Mrs. Forsythe was settled she would call upon her and if wished, she would give a tea or a dinner. I said that Mrs. Forsythe was apparently determined not to have any social life but, of course, we would invite her to dinner.

And so with the blood pounding in my veins, like that of a virile boy on his first date, I rode up the mountain. It was not quite dusk and she was waiting for me perilously near the edge of the cliff. I cried out in alarm but she merely smiled and waved her hand.

An hour later I went down the mountain again, cursing the absurdity of women, the cruelty of life, my manhood outraged, my body moist with frustration. She would not let me touch her. That night had been madness. The storm had been the wrath of God; our love had been the wrath of man.

Against her calm obstinacy, I felt that words would be useless and I could not bring myself to use force, particularly since I had the feeling that if I did, she would not hesitate to kill me.

She said, when I cried out that I would never see her again if she would not accept me as a lover, that she valued my friendship. She said we had no right to call our night of passion, love. Love must grow out of friendship and even if we did get to love each other, she said, it must remain a pure love.

I told her that was convent nonsense and she did not reply, but I imagined I saw a strange expression come into her eyes. And it flashed upon me that might be the explanation. She might be a runaway nun. She seemed to have no background, no family, no friends, no past at all.

Then I must be gentle with her. It was easy to see how she would feel that her sin was enormous. I must take my time, above all not to drive her back into the convent.

But it is maddening and exhausting. I have seen her every day and twice she let me kiss her icy lips but she will not let me touch her body, that body so ripe, so beautiful, so incomplete without a man. Something's got to happen soon.

The next letter was dated almost two months later.

We are still not lovers, doc, he wrote, unbelievable as that must seem to you, a normal man who I know believes that love is man's natural state and that the chief crime of prisons is their crime against nature. Convicts, I have heard you say, should be allowed their women as they were in less cruel days.

I am not sure about her. I have a different idea every day. All I am sure of is that she is the most beautiful and desirable of all women, that she must love me, and yet will not let me touch her.

I am not sure about the convent theory. It may be true, but I doubt it. She laughs when I accuse her of it and says that is absurd but she does not completely deny. But then she does not completely deny or affirm anything. There is no background of people or family, but she has been many places and has a knowledge of life which seems unlikely for a nun. But it could be possible.

She is not interested in my money. That is a certainty. She has much more than I have. In fact, her resources seem unlimited. She brings in bond coupons, years old, to be cashed and only laughs when I suggest putting some order into her business affairs. Her jewelry represents a fortune. To keep me from giving her a bracelet for her birthday, she spread out the riches of her jewel box. I had never seen anything like them and I did not try to compete.

She says she does not believe in divorce, particularly when there are children and she will not promise to marry me, or to be my mistress, even if my wife will divorce. But my wife will not divorce me. I have suggested it, but her refusal is tight-lipped and she has no longer mentioned calling upon Mrs. Forsythe.

The town is seething with the scandal, of course, but so far no one has dared say a word to me. I look like hell, and everyone thinks it is what *that* woman has done to me, not dreaming my condition is due to what *that* woman will not do for me.

What should I do? Don't suggest other women. I cannot tell you how revolting the thought is.

Don't tell me she is playing with me as a cat plays with a mouse. I know that. If she really wanted to end all this, she could do it in a minute by going away. She stays on in the house, which she says is the most beautiful home she has ever had, and that she wants to live in it forever—with me, presumably, as landlord and platonic friend. Not advisor, because she needs no advice about anything.

There may have been some intervening letters but if there were, they were not introduced in court or, at last, not published in the newspaper. The final letter, which won an immediate divorce for Mrs. Alexander, was dated almost six months later.

This is the last letter you will have from me, he wrote, and I want you to know how much I have appreciated your sympathy, understanding and sound advice. You have told me that what a woman has done once she will do again and you are right.

Laura is going away with me, but she has made it one of her stipulations that we must start a completely new life, that I must cut away from my past, clean and sharp, as she has cut away from hers. I have done it once before in my life and I know that I can do it again. So you will not be hearing again from me for a long time—perhaps never. But you will understand.

The bank will take care of everything. I am taking less with me than I had when I came here. Everything is left for my wife and children with the bank as administrator or guardian. If she wants a divorce I'm sure she'll be able to get it either here or in Nevada. I doubt if she will bother.

We are taking Laura's car. I have a strange feeling, almost a certainty, that she has had this thing planned from the beginning. Why, I do not know; perhaps will never know. But I do not care. I know that she is the woman of my destiny and, if it were a choice I had to make, I would rather have one more night with her than the rest of my life without her.

I am writing this sitting in the huge window at the Folly. Below me, for hundreds of feet, stretches the canyon, unknown, silent, impenetrable, and so, I feel, stretches my life ahead of me.

We will mail this as we drive through the city for the last time, the city that regenerated me and the city that I am now gladly deserting.

Laura is moving around quietly, putting the last few things in the suitcases. I still don't feel that I know her and wonder if I ever will.

Now she has taken an automatic revolver from a box and is looking at it in that impersonal way of hers. I didn't know she owned one.

She explains that she wouldn't have thought of living in the Folly without one and, of course, she is right. Strange that I who once lived with pistols as the ordinary man lives with a watch or a fountain pen, now find the sight of one rather disquieting.

Whatever happens, doc, in this strange adventure I'm embarking on, I'm glad to have known you during my years of normal and moral living. I'm wondering if great passion and comfort have ever gone together?

CHAPTER SEVENTEEN

That was the end. Laura put down the newspaper and turned to Michel with a quizzical smile.

"What do you think?" she asked.

"How do you mean?" Michel asked, a startled expression on his face. Obviously, he had not heard the last few sentences. His mind was elsewhere, in some fear-laden place.

"Do you think great passion and comfort can go together?" Laura asked, a teasing quality in her voice.

Michel turned out the light by which she had been reading from the newspaper. His lips closed down on hers.

Then he released her and whispered. "No more, tonight; don't tell me any more tonight."

"There is very little more to tell," she said. "I—"

But again his lips silenced her. It was the first time he had ever stopped her.

"Tomorrow ... tomorrow," he whispered. "There'll be another night."

"Just one more," she said, "and then the tale is done."

The next night the *Ecuador* was packed to suffocation, but a corner table was roped off for them in a little island where there were no other tables close enough for anyone to eavesdrop.

Laura was in white, seductive white, cut very low and worn without bra or girdle, making a definite liar out of the Grik. Dripping with pearls, the hat-check girl said, a strand in her hair, an extraordinary flat necklace, and a loose girdle of them over her hips.

Michel, looking as if he hadn't slept for years, dropped into the other chair.

"I've been looking up the news stories on Henry Alexander," he said.

She interrupted and put a finger on his lips.

"That is for later," she said.

"Not tonight it isn't," he contradicted. "I looked up the newspapers. No one knows whether he's dead or alive. His wife got her divorce on the evidence in those letters."

"Sure, I told you that," Laura said. "And she has since married the doctor to whom those letters were written."

"No foolin'?"

"No fooling, and it seems to me I read somewhere they had a child of their own."

"But—Henry—Henry—Amblate—Henry Alexander," Michel demanded breathlessly, "what about him?"

"Why are you spoiling my last *Ecuador* night? Why don't you let me tell it in my own way?"

"Because we're never going into that room again," Michel said violently. "I had the mirrors ripped out today."

She accepted that without surprise.

"I didn't kill him while he sat there writing that last letter," she explained. "I was afraid blood would splash on it. But he saw it coming and if they had found his body at the bottom of the canyon, there would have been a look of complete astonishment on his face.

"But now," she went on, a little regretfully, "if they find him there'll only be a few bones and a handful of dust."

"Don't talk that way," Michel said, imploringly. "I can't take any more of it."

She smiled. "You've had all of it," she said.

"You haven't asked me why I had the mirrors ripped out of the room."

"It's obvious isn't it? It's like the one about why did the fireman wear red suspenders."

"I don't get it."

"You don't want to see yourself any more; you don't want to see me any more; you don't want to see us together any more."

"What's that got to do with a fireman and red suspenders?"

"Suppose we skip the fireman and the red suspenders."

"I had the mirrors pulled out because I don't want to see you slip the knife between my ribs, give me a poisoned drink or shoot my guts out."

She smiled. "You're such a tough baby I might have to do all three. What is all this about, Mike, my darling? You know I'm not going to kill you—never really had any intention of killing you."

"How should I know it? You may have told me all this to prolong the agony. To make it a little more perfect. Each one of your murders has been better than the one before."

She waited more than a little while before she replied.

"If I have not been able to convince you," she finally said, "that I am in love with you, that my life has no meaning without you, then there is nothing I can say and there is only one thing for you—"

His blood-shot eyes asked the question.

"You must put me out of your life completely."

"There is another thing I could do," he said, "that would be more certain because I know I could never trust myself to keep away from you."

She waited.

"I could turn you over to the police," he said, defiance in his voice.

"Would that make you happy?" she asked, completely impersonally.

"It might give me a night of peace," he said.

"You have found no peace with me?"

"No, only happiness, excitement, and a tension that has become unbearable."

"Strange," she said. "Yet you have given me the only real contentment I've ever known."

"And now I'm turning you over to your death."

"You're not really going to do that, Mike. You're just enjoying torturing me. Can't you be sadistic some other way?"

"I've already done it," he said, and then almost screamed it at her. "I've already done it, I tell you!"

She leaned back in her chair. "Order me some more champagne, please," she requested.

"Goddamn it!" he cried. "How do you expect me to believe a word you say when the only emotion you show is when you're being—"

Andy, who had been hovering ever since the boss had raised his voice, decided this had gone far enough.

"Boss," he interrupted, "how long are you going to hog this corner? I've got half a dozen parties waiting."

He held his ground against the fury of Michel's blood-shot eyes.

"Bring me another bottle of champagne," Laura said, "and we'll be on our way very quickly."

"Yes, mademoiselle," Andy said, and, oddly enough, he did not add *bitch,* under his breath, any more.

"I tell you I've already done it, I've already done it," Michel chanted.

"All right, you've already done it. Do we have this last night together?"

"I guess so. I don't know. Of course we do. They have to do a lot of checking, I suppose."

"How much have you told them?"

"I haven't told them a word, not one word."

For the first time a trace of annoyance came into her voice. "Pull yourself together, Mike, and tell me yes or no."

"I haven't told them a thing, but a machine was put in the room the night before you started talking. Every word you've said to me has been recorded."

"I'd like to hear them. I suppose I will."

"You've asked for this, haven't you?"

"Perhaps," she admitted; "it seems to be the only period to the sentence."

"And what am I going to do now?" he demanded, for all the world as if she were the one at fault. "You were just a dame who scared me to death when I called the cops—"

"And now?"

Andy brought the champagne and poured into the two glasses. Michel Perry raised his.

"And now," he said, "you're a woman I can't live with or without. I can't imagine ever touching another woman, and I can't imagine ever overcoming my fear that some day you'll kill me."

"It's like the infinite," she offered. "You can't imagine it and you can't imagine the end."

"The end of what?" he asked stupidly.

"Of everything," she said.

"This isn't going to be the end," Perry said, pouring more champagne into his glass. "We're going to beat them."

"How?"

"I'm going to charter a plane and get a boy I know to pilot it. We'll be in South America in three days. I know a spot where enough money will keep us safe."

She sipped her champagne. "What makes you think you won't be just as afraid of me in South America?"

"I've got to take that chance. I know I can't turn you over to the coppers. How much cash money can you raise tonight?"

"Not much, I'm afraid. About ten or twenty thousand, perhaps."

"I'm sure I can get fifty. That'll be enough."

"My jewelry will probably bring more in South America than it would here."

"That won't be necessary. I'd better get on the 'phone."

"Not from here," she suggested. "The wires just might be tapped."

"Yeah, you're right," he agreed. "Let's get out of here." They stood up and Andy hurried over.

"Thanks, folks," he said. "We sure need the acreage."

"Keep all the cash tonight," Michel ordered, "don't handle any checks."

"Right boss," Andy agreed.

The hat-check girl produced Laura's sable cape, and Michel asked for his hat and topcoat.

"Where you folks a-goin'?" the hat-check girl asked, familiarly.

"God knows," Michel said laconically. Laura merely smiled.

They stood in the doorway. Rain was beginning to come down.

"Have you really destroyed our room?" Laura asked.

"I pulled the wires out with my own hands," Michel said, "and broke the mirrors with a shoe tree. Where'll we go?"

"It doesn't matter. My hotel?"
"Will it be all right?"
"Why, of course. I have a suite."
"All right," he said. "I'll be there in an hour. I've got to see about the plane and find but how much money I can raise."

In separate taxis, they left the *Ecuador*.

CHAPTER EIGHTEEN

Fog. And a driving, cold mist. The mechanics turned up the sheep collars on their leather jackets.

"There won't be a thing leaving the ground until noon," one of them said.

"That dark guy'll bust a couple of blood vessels before then," the other mechanic said. "Wonder what he's running away from?"

"Some husband, I guess. I'd be nervous, too, if I thought I was going to lose that dame!"

"Me—I'd take her home to a nice warm bed instead of hanging around in this dew."

"She doesn't seem excited about it."

"I heard her talking to their pilot—Hansen, I think his name is. He said he wouldn't go up in that crate in this soup for ten grand, and he couldn't get any other ship."

A shrill siren interrupted their speculation. A police car swung into the field, its special yellow lights piercing the fog and mist. The mechanics watched with interest.

"I told you he was running away from something, and it must be something more'n a husband, or there wouldn't be so many coppers out," the one mechanic speculated.

And the other agreed that it must be a husband and a bank. Neither suspected for a minute that the beautiful, calm woman could be running away from anything.

Who had informed the police? Had they become suspicious because they heard no bedtime story from the mirrored room that night? Had they visited the *Ecuador* and discovered the absence of Michel? Andy the Grik and the hatcheck girl said they were not questioned. Had the police then made a routine check of the railroad terminals, steamship piers and air fields?

Or had Laura, herself, telephoned to them? She had gone into the waiting room, saying she had one last call to make. Had she recognized the madness into which Michel was driving himself? Did she believe that he would kill her and himself? And did she therefore take this method of sacrificing herself for him? If so, she had a complete change of heart later. But the questions were never answered.

At least not publicly. The newspapers merely reported their arrest—Laura as a female Bluebeard who had murdered six men, and Michel as a material witness or possibly an accessory. The newspapers at first weren't sure, but the arrest of the prominent and popular nightclub host made more of a sensation than the apprehension of the murderess.

Most people didn't believe the full story anyway, not realizing that only a few of the facts were revealed. Maybe she killed one or two men but the rest was typical tabloid exaggeration. Stories of the Mafia and the Black Hand were revived but the connection was remote. It was smarter to think of the woman as a gold-digging murderess instead of an avenging angel.

She was tried for the murder of Bennel Stein (Irving St. Leger) in New York, while Californian, Louisiana, and North Carolina alertly waited to claim her if she escaped the electric chair. But she didn't escape it. She was convicted by a jury which decided that she was a monster to be exterminated. Her attorneys wanted her to plead insanity, caused by the murder of her husband and her desire for vengeance. But she would not consent.

No, she would not admit the murders. She said she had told her stories to Michel merely to divert him. But with the stories turned into typewritten manuscripts, there was plenty of corroboration. There were undoubtedly six men who had died violent deaths, six men who had been her husband's henchmen. Without her stories, she could not have been convicted. She had done her jobs well.

Her lawyers, trying desperately, pointed out that even if the jury did believe she was a murderess, they must realize that her work was done, that she had completed her duty of vengeance and was no longer a menace. They discreetly did not mention the half-mad hysteric, Michel Perry, a patient in the police ward of one of the city hospitals.

Shortly after her conviction, Michel was released. The charge that he was an accessory to the crimes had never been taken very seriously. It had been placed against him so that he would not be tempted to withdraw his corroboration of the woman's stories. But he had no intention of retracting. He would not feel a moment's safety until she was dead, and he still valued his sex-ridden life.

The Club Ecuador was closed, sold and reopened. But the curiosity seekers and the morbid did not keep it going long. They came once and that was all. The regulars shunned the place and even under different names and with a completely different decor, it was a failure.

Laura wanted no applications for a new trial, no appeals for executive clemency. But a modern State will permit no rushing to the electric chair. The due processes and niceties of law must be observed. It was almost a year before she paid the penalty. She observed bitterly that the press and the people were indignant because she had only one life to give for the six she had taken, not to mention the legal execution of Stanley, the stooge.

She felt she was ready to die. She had done her work. She had had her cake and eaten it, too. Her revenge on Michel, who was to outlive her, was the most subtle of all. She had not wanted to hurt him because she loved him, but a stronger force than her own will had directed her. What more was there to live for? Nothing really.

She had never really given up religion and faith. She made her final confession and was given the Sacrament. But the priest did not understand. He was not a Sicani and he did not understand that God and the Virgin have special laws for Sicani, laws that were made long before the Sicani accepted Christianity.

She had not communicated with Michel. He had looked at her in the courtroom only when he had been compelled to for purposes of identification. Now on her last day on earth, she wrote him a letter; not a long letter, just a note.

He would not leave her body to the quicklime of the State? The Church would bury her and she had left all her money to the Church, because, after all, he did not need money. He must have a great deal.

But she wanted something more personal than just the Church burial. She begged him for one last rendezvous before she was put into the earth. Just one last kiss before the coffin lid closed down forever on the lips he had bruised so often. Surely he would not deny her that?

For a while they had not let her exercise the art of keeping her beauty, or the artificial attractions she had used to stimulate beauty. Her hair had become streaked; her skin, neglected, betrayed her age. Prison pallor completed the work of devastation. Then, as always, money talked and she was able to buy back the appearance of youth and beauty. She died as she had lived those last few years—an exotic, alluring woman.

So Michel need not be afraid to claim the body of the woman he had loved, feared and betrayed. Except for the burn of the electrodes, she would be as he had always known her.

She did not break. She took her last walk with the same nonchalance that she exhibited when she had moved from the entrance of the *Ecuador* to a table in the center of the room. With her were the priest, the doctor, and the matron—she had lived without women, and she would have preferred to have died without them—but the proprieties had to be observed.

She noticed that the arms of the electric chair were covered with dust.

"I guess it hasn't been used lately," she said with a smile.

The matron angrily dusted the chair with her pocket handkerchief.

"Asking a lady like her to sit in a dusty chair," she muttered.

The warden asked Laura if she had any last word. She begged for just a few seconds to fix her make-up. The wish was granted. The matron held the vanity as Laura carefully made her last application of powder and rouge. Then she used the lipstick.

As she carefully drew it over her lips, not looking into the tiny mirror which the matron was holding, the doctor observed that she seemed to shiver and her throat muscles moved. She did not quite finish the job of reddening her lips. Her hand, holding the lipstick, fell to her side. The matron removed the stick from the rigid fingers.

The doctor leaned forward and looked intently at the woman. She was dead; he was sure of it. His first impulse was to tell the warden but just as quickly he decided against it. It would be a minor scandal, perhaps. A woman dying just as she was about to be put to death. No—let them go through with it. And so a woman already dead was electrocuted.

Michel's friend and stooges kept her last letter from him. They arranged for the funeral and sent a blanket of orchids, but they would not let him look at the body or grant her request for a final embrace.

The curse of this fiendish woman, the newspapers reported, extended beyond the grave. An undertaker's assistant preparing her body for burial dropped dead at his work. A heart attack, the medical examiner said. The undertaker couldn't understand it. His assistant had worked on many subjects, horribly mangled in accidents. Laura's body, the undertaker said to reporters, was really a beautiful thing, marred only by the slight burns from the electric chair.

Her death released Michel Perry from his fear but not from his love.

He had aged ten years in ten months. There was no release in drink or drugged sleep.

His friends and stooges decided that only another woman could make him forget the one who was dead. None of the old ones would do. A campaign was planned. She must be young, lovely, naive—completely different in every way from Laura. And she must not be too willing.

That was the difficult part of it. Michel's charms and his wealth, in spite of the loss of the *Ecuador,* were well known. Being the center of a mass murder case, had not made him any the less attractive.

But finally the right girl seemed to be found and for the first time in months, Michel appeared to be returning to normalcy. He had taken a place on Long Island. Sailing, swimming, and fishing were supposed to be the things which would help restore him mentally and physically.

They hadn't done the trick, however, and the wistful young beauty who hated men because of a "terrible, terrible" thing that had happened to her, seemed to be the final hope. Michel was interested and her reluctance was refreshing.

She finally consented to a sailing party. Another couple was to go along but, of course, at the last minute they did not appear.

Champagne seemed to help and the soundproof cabin and the secret doorway through the clothes closet were unnecessary. Michel decided that he had never seen a lovelier sight than the girl lying there illumined by the moonlight streaming in through the portholes. The gentle lapping of the peaceful Long Island Sound added to the peace of it all.

How completely different from the hothouse atmosphere of the mirrored room. Why should he think of it at all? He hated the thought of it. It was treason to this beautiful child to think of another setting, another woman.

Far off across the water, from another boat, came the low, pleasant sound of guitars. Everything was perfect. This was romance—youth.

The girl opened her eyes and smiled at him. He pretended a passion that didn't exist as he took her into his arms.

"It had to happen, didn't it?" she whispered.

"Yes," he agreed, "it had to happen . . ."

But it hadn't happened and it didn't happen. A few minutes later he pushed her away, almost angrily. For the first time in his life he was incapable. Her reluctant, young beauty had only awakened a mental response.

Alone, he strode the deck, cursing the woman who was dead and who in death robbed him of the only life that meant anything to him.

He did not have courage to go over the side into oblivion, and yet he knew that no matter how long he went on living, he would always have a form of death with him.

He sobbed aloud and the master of the boat muttered, "A crying jag, this time," as he steered the boat through the moonlit waters.

THE END

Paul S. Meskil Bibliography
(1923-2005)

Fiction:
Sin Pit (1954)

Non-Fiction:
Hitler's Heirs: Where Are They Now? (1961)
Don Carlo: Boss of Bosses (1973)
Cheesebox (1974; with Gerard M. Callahan)
New Sexual Life Styles of the '70s for Today's Man and Woman (1975)
The Luparelli Tapes (1976)

Paul Meskil was born July 2, 1923. He earned a journalism degree in 1943 from the University of Missouri, and worked at the *New York World-Telegram* and *World Journal Tribune*. He only wrote one novel, *Sin Pit*—published by Lion Books in 1954—but achieved a cult status with this work. Meskil went on to write several non-fiction works during the 1970s, and became a consultant on organized crime for BBC and Thames Television. He died October 11, 2005.

Walter Untermeyer Jr.
(1915-2009)

Dark the Summer Dies (1953)
Evil Roots (1954)

Walter S. Untermeyer Jr. was born September 19, 1915 in New York City. He graduated from Yale in 1941 and then served as a lieutenant in the Naval Reserves during WWII. He only wrote two novels, both published by Lion Books in the early 1950s, spending most of his adult life as a New York lawyer. Untermeyer died on February 14, 2009 at age 93.

Alan Williams
(1890-1945)

Fiction:
Free to Live (1934)
Holiday Madness (1934)
The Night Must End (1935)
Tear Stains (1935; as by Peter Marsh)
Room Service (1936)
The Leaves Unfold (1936; as by Peter Marsh)
The Devil's Daughter (1942; as by Peter Marsh)

Non-Fiction:
American Hurly-Burly (1937; with Ernest Sutherland Bates)

Alan Williams was born Louis William Lowenthal on June 13, 1890, in Washington, DC, of German Jewish immigrants. At age 20 he joined the Immigration Service and was assigned a post in Alaska, where he handled enough high profile cases that he was hired as personal secretary to the governor of Arizona. Leaving the world of politics behind, he moved to New York where redefined himself as Alan Williams. As Williams he wrote over 200 stories, then moved to California in the 1930s to become a novelist. His most critically acclaimed novel was *Room Service*, published in 1936. Williams gave up writing in the 1940s and opened a Los Angeles bookstore. After years of ill-health, he drowned off Long Beach on November 2, 1945, an apparent suicide.

www.ingramcontent.com/pod-product-compliance
Lightning Source LLC
LaVergne TN
LVHW010155070526
838199LV00062B/4375